Downhome

Downhome

AN ANTHOLOGY OF
SOUTHERN WOMEN WRITERS

Edited by Susie Mee

A HARVEST ORIGINAL • HARCOURT, INC.

San Diego   New York   London

Requests for permission to make copies of any part of the work
should be mailed to: Permissions Department, Harcourt, Inc.,
6277 Sea Harbor Drive, Orlando, Florida 32887-6777.

"Isis" by Zora Neal Hurston, reprinted by permission of Lucy Ann Hurston for the estate of Zora Neal Hurston. "Economics" copyright © 1991 by Elizabeth Seydel Morgan, first published in the *Virginia Quarterly Review,* reprinted by permission of the author. "Sarah" from *Baby of the Family,* copyright © 1989 by Tina McElroy Ansa, reprinted by permission of Harcourt, Inc. "The Star in the Valley" from In the *Tennessee Mountains* by Mary Noailles Murfree, published in 1884. "The Ugliest Pilgrim" from *Beasts of the Southern Wild and Other Stories,* copyright © 1973 by Doris Betts, reprinted by permission of Russell & Volkening as agents for the author. "Music" from *Victory over Japan* by Ellen Gilchrist. Copyright © 1983, 1984 by Ellen Gilchrist. by permission of Little, Brown and Company. "The Wide Net" from *The Wide Net and Other Stories,* copyright 1942 and renewed 1970 by Eudora Welty, reprinted by permission of Harcourt, Inc. "After Moore" from And Venus Is Blue by Mary Hood. Copyright © 1986 by Mary Hood. Reprinted by permission of Ticknor & Fields/Houghton Mifflin Co. All rights reserved. "White Rat" from *White Rat: Short Stories* by Gayl Jones. Reprinted by permission of Random House, Inc. "Dare's gift" from *The Shadowy Third and Other Stories* by Ellen Glasgow, copyright 1923 by Doubleday, Page & Company, Inc., and renewed 1951 by First and Merchants National Bank of Richmond, Virginia, reprinted by permission of Harcourt, Inc. "First Dark" copyright © 1959 by Elizabeth Spencer from *The Short Stories of Elizabeth Spencer* by Elizabeth Spencer. Used by permission of Doubleday, a division of Bantam Doubleday Dell Publishing Group, Inc. "Shiloh" from *Shiloh and Other Stories* by Bobbie Ann Mason. Copyright © 1982 by Bobbie Ann Mason. Reprinted by permission of HarperCollins Publishers, Inc. "Good Country People" from *A Good Man is Hard to Find and Other Stories,* copyright © 1955 by Flannery O'Connor and renewed 1983 by Regina O'Connor, reprinted by permission of Harcourt, Inc. "Everyday Use" from *In Love & Trouble: Stories of Black Women,* copyright © 1973 by Alice Walker reprinted by permission of Harcourt, Inc. "Yellow Ribbons" by Susie Mee, reprinted by permission of the author. "Tongues of Fire" reprinted by permission of G. P. Putnam's Sons from *Me and My Baby View the Eclipse* by Lee Smith. Copyright © 1990 by Lee Smith. "Gospel Song" by Dorothy Allison from *Trash,* copyright © 1988 by Dorothy Allison, reprinted by permission of Firebrand Books, Ithaca, New York. "A New Life" by Mary Ward Brown reprinted by permission of International Creative Management, Inc. Copyright 1989 by Mary Ward Brown. First published in the *Atlantic.* "The Grave" from *The Leaning Tower and Other Stories,* copyright 1944 and renewed 1972 by Katherine Anne Porter, reprinted by permission of Harcourt, Inc. "And with a Vengeance" copyright © 1972 by Margaret Gibson. First published in the *Southern Review.* Reprinted by permission of the author. "The Third of July" copyright © 1993 by Elizabeth Cox. Originally appeared in *Story.* Reprinted by permission of the author.

Library of Congress Cataloging-in-Publication Data
Downhome: an anthology of Southern women writers / edited by Susie Mee.
    p.   cm.
"A Harvest original."
ISBN 0-15-600-121-7
1. Short stories, American—Southern States. 2. Women—Southern
States—Social life and customs—Fiction. 3. Southern States—
Social life and customs—Fiction. 4. Short stories, American—
Women authors. 5. Family— Southern States—Fiction.
6. Home— Southern States—Fiction. 7. American fiction—20th century.
I. Mee, Susie, 1938–
PS551.D69   1995
813'.01089287'0975 — dc20   95-18978

The text was set in Perpetua.
Designed by Lisa Peters

Printed in the United States of America
A Harvest Original
First edition
E G I K M L J H F D

To Richard Dillard and Hollins College,

where five of the women writers in this anthology

have either studied or taught

CONTENTS

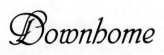

Downhome

INTRODUCTION

THE CIVIL RIGHTS and anti-war movements of the 1960s surged through the South like a shock wave, forcing southerners, along with the rest of the country, to reevaluate traditional standards and mores. Following directly in the wake of civil rights came outcries for the rights of women—which is not altogether surprising since racism and sexism often stem from the same source.

But these were not the only causes of change in the South. A wider economic prosperity and increasing cultural homogeneity signaled the breakdown of the social caste system, which left southerners, especially southern women, freer to be themselves instead of adhering to stereotypes. The diversity that has resulted from such change is reflected in the work of contemporary southern female writers, both black and white.

Yet within this diversity is a shared legacy: the act of speech—of stories handed down in which a distinctive language is honored, a language rich in Biblical and regional contexts; the love of place—where individuals, relationships, and family histories not only matter but buttress everyday life. Both are part of that rarest and most indispensable groundspring of literature, memory. The memory of being "Downhome."

What is that memory?

It's made up of particular smells: honeysuckle and nasturtium, spring arriving early and staying late, wet woods, pine fires, cigar smoke and tobacco juice, the inside of mountain cabins, hot irons on starched dresses, dusty dirt roads, a jarful of lightning bugs, rutting hogs, funeral flowers; and sounds: country music and gospel, fatback frying on the stove, sayings that startle, the wheeze of old pickups, the squeak of porch swings, the whip of weeping willows in a storm, a preacher's ringing tones, long-winded sermons, gossip over bridge; and tastes: spring water, a Dr. Pepper drunk outside a filling station on a summer afternoon, greens, butter beans, pintos, homemade ketchup, biscuits and gravy, hot corn bread, field peas, cabbage, fried okra, fresh coconut cake, fried apple pies, boiled spare ribs, a sweet-gum toothbrush; and touches: a mossy spring, bare feet on damp grass, fingers tamping down clay soil, hugging kinfolk, sweat collecting around the neck, the sting of chiggers, squeezing blackberries, the nuisance of gnats in July and August, the graze of wind while riding a horse bareback through an open field; and the sights . . . well, my favorite is driving north from Atlanta, heading up over Taylor's Ridge before making a sudden turn where I can see the whole of Chattooga County spread out below me. Then I know I'm home. Dorothy Allison, in her novel *Bastard out of Carolina*, put the feeling another way:

> The world that came in over the radio was wide and far away and didn't touch us at all. We lived on one porch or another all summer long, laughing at Little Earle, teasing the boys and picking over beans, listening to stories, or to the crickets beating out their own soft songs. When I think of that summer—sleeping

over at one of my aunts' houses as easily as at home, the smell of Mama's neck as she bent over to hug us in the dark, the sound of Little Earle's giggle or Grannie's spit thudding onto the dry ground, and the country music playing low everywhere, as much a part of the evening as crickets and moonlight—I always feel safe again. No place has ever seemed so sweet and quiet, no place ever felt so much like home.

But Downhome was not always sweet and quiet. It had, and still has, its dark side. Constraints were terrible, and role-playing (servant, lady, belle, good ol' girl) was the norm, causing true thoughts and feelings to be buried under a morass of social niceties. I vividly recall, in the late 1940s, one of my mother's friends showing up at a bridge party with a black eye that she tried to hide with thick makeup. No one asked what had happened—although it was common knowledge that her husband had a drinking problem—and she didn't venture an explanation. Only in times of heightened tragedy—a suicide, a runaway, an accident that was not quite accidental—did the truth come out, and even then, only in bits and pieces.

Also, there was, and is, the problem of racial relationships. The ambivalence, the closeness, the precarious balance of power in intimate, day-to-day interaction has been the subject of dozens of memoirs, stories, and novels. In one of these, Alice Walker raged on behalf of her mother, who worked in the houses of white women for forty years.

> [She] was convinced that she did not exist compared to "them." She subordinated her soul to theirs and became a faithful and timid supporter of the "Beautiful White People." Once she asked me, in a moment of vicarious pride and despair, if I didn't think that "they" were "jest naturally smarter, prettier, better."

The central refuge for both races was church, the one institution that gave southern women a sense of vocation and freedom outside the home. Yet the church was often dead set against those very changes that might promote female emancipation. Thus the emotional tie of southern women to their religion and their rising consciousness of the need to be free of traditional roles produced a philosophical conflict that added one more layer to a history thick with dualities and double binds.

But other kinds of binds or "bonds" worked to the southern female's advantage; in fact, for some women, bonding together was their saving grace—I know it was for my mother during a time of great marital and economic stress. Every morning at ten o'clock, she and her best friend, "Miss Stella," would take off "down the road" to have a Co-Cola and talk. Occasionally I was allowed to go along—at which time, in the words of Eudora Welty, "my ears would open up like morning glories"—but most often I was left behind in the care of Daisy Lee, the "colored" woman who looked after me. There were secrets—things told in whispers—that I was not supposed to hear. Usually these had to do with sex.

Although sex was rarely mentioned, it was implied in every lingering glance and raised church fan. The lush surroundings, the magnolia trees with their huge overhanging branches, the fragrant gardenias, the water oaks dripping with Spanish moss, the coverts of boxwood and shady cypress—all conspired to produce an erotic atmosphere. Yet—in some circles, at least—sexual purity was still considered either a moral issue or a commodity, and though young women could flirt outrageously (and often did), consummation was strictly taboo.

Manners and a certain etiquette were ways of defusing this highly charged ambience. These same young women were expected to "act pretty," which meant being nauseatingly superficial. But acting pretty was also a way of distancing oneself from another person, especially an outsider, who might be forgiven for sometimes confusing genial repartee with the underlying reality. On the other hand, manners did have a positive function. One southern woman has called them, quite aptly, "the oil that makes the wheels go round." From this "doublespeak"—the gap between what's said and what isn't—has evolved the fascinating dialogue that distinguishes much of southern fiction.

The characters in this fiction are as varied as the culture itself: mill girls, housewives, later-day Scarlett O'Haras, male and female rednecks, society matriarchs, professional go-getters, crazy mothers, rebellious daughters, the enlightened and the illiterate, the mean-spirited and the gracious, the weak and the courageous. In the following stories, we see them during childhood, and later, during courtship and marriage; we see the memories that haunt them, the objects and symbols that affect them, the religion that sustains or oppresses them; in the last section, we see their reaction to the final passage: death.

The stories here have been divided into thematic sections, with each section arranged chronologically so that the reader can detect the difference, say, between the way that Ellen Glasgow dealt with a particular theme and the way that Bobbie Ann Mason handles a similar theme over a half century later. It also highlights resonances that otherwise might pass unnoticed.

The central thread of the anthology is that each story is informed and enlarged by the southern home—embodying family, community, history, as well as the physical house itself, whether it be a shack in the hills or an imitation Tara mansion in the suburbs. With the house goes the surrounding landscape: the particular sights, smells, sounds, and touches that make the downhome experience unique.

Growing Up

GROWING UP

AS WE KNOW, childhood is the time when innocence is sloughed off and ambiguities begin to emerge. If one is southern, the problem of race is involved in these ambiguities, thereby doubling or tripling their prismatic surfaces: whites holding up a mirror to blacks; blacks holding up a mirror to whites; both holding up a mirror to themselves, singly and in relation to one another. Each of the stories in this section reflects this kind of mirror holding, which, in the end, in a reversal of position, swings around to face us, the readers. The images that we see in the glass may be unsettling—truths about ourselves, terrible truths both expected and surprising—though never more than we are capable of understanding and accepting.

Zora Neale Hurston was one of the first black writers, male or female, to depict the broad humanity of her people. It is fitting, therefore, that she lead off this anthology with the portrait of a young black girl named Isis, who by the very strength of her vivacity and creativity refuses to allow her spirit to be crushed by the formidably negative forces surrounding her.

> Music to Isis meant motion. In a minute razor and whipping forgotten, she was doing a fair imitation of a Spanish dancer she had seen in a medicine show some time before. Isis' feet were gifted—she could dance most anything she saw.
>
> Up, up, went her spirits, her small feet doing all sorts of intricate things and her body in rhythm, hand curving above her head. But the music was growing faint. Grandma was nowhere in sight. Isis stole out of the gate, running and dancing after the band.

Indeed, on the story's most simplistic level, Isis's bright though fragile figure might serve as the enduring symbol of her race. Hurston knew what she was doing when she gave the child the name of the Egyptian goddess of fertility. Isis's fecundity is artistic and cultural, thereby transcending the boundaries of race, of time, and of place.

But the story is more complicated than mere allegory. Isis is so alive that her energy is contagious, even to the spiritually moribund white people who invite her—in a moment that hints of exploitation—into their sleek automobile. These whites seem related to those who cruised up to Harlem in the twenties to hear jazz and are forebears of the children of rich suburbanites who imitate rap stars.

IN ELIZABETH SEYDEL MORGAN's story, "Economics," the mirror swivels again, not to show truth this time, but to catch us out in our denial of truth and to examine the background of this denial.

> Our mother taught us to substitute the word "tiger" for the word "nigger" when the neighborhood gang chose up teams. Sitting here on my brother's porch, watching my nieces play in the yard with their friends, I think how much has changed since

he and I grew up in Atlanta—for one thing, two of their play-mates are black. Yet children, their summer games, even this ancient choosing rhyme—catch a tiger by the toe—haven't changed at all.

Only by understanding and acknowledging this background, Morgan seems to be saying, can future truth-telling be possible. Inherent in the story is the question of guilt. Is guilt passed on from generation to generation along with certain traditions and conventionalities? Can people erase the prejudice they knew as children? And finally, that age-old dilemma: is change possible? Perhaps guidelines to some of these, if not all, can be found in the story itself.

"SARAH," BY TINA MCELROY ANSA, is a complex rendering of the relationship between two black girls, Sarah and Lena, the former from a poor family, the latter from a wealthy one. Their pretend games, carried on beneath that southern icon—the chinaberry tree—are rich in imagination; but along with imagination comes Eros, the dark side of imagination—that same Eros that whites have often punished blacks for possessing.

> "This what you got to do," Sarah explained as she crumpled a sheet of the newspaper up into a ball, lifted up her skirts, and stuck the paper down into the front of her panties. She leaned back against the stump of the tree and looked down at her crotch, appraising the difference the addition made. Lena sat next to her staring at it, too.

In this story, however, blacks punish themselves. Sarah's mother, discovering the two children pressed together imitating the act of intercourse, is shocked and forbids her daughter ever to see Lena again. The rain of hatred that falls onto the two unsuspecting little girls has everything to do with poverty and grown-ups' loss of innocence, and little to do with the game that Sarah and Lena have been playing between themselves.

As these stories are read and reread, other resonances will arise among them: differences and similarities in home life; the importance of sex in both "Economics" and "Sarah," and the relative lack of it in "Isis"; the shedding of innocence in all three (in "Isis," the reader feels that it will occur soon after the story ends); the implied projections into the future.

Isis

Zora Neale Hurston

"You Isie Watts! Git 'own offen dat gate post an' rake up dis yahd!"

The small brown girl perched upon the gate post looked yearningly up the gleaming shell road that lead to Orlando. After awhile, she shrugged her thin shoulders. This only seemed to heap still more kindling on Grandma Potts' already burning ire.

"Lawd a-mussy!" she screamed, enraged—"Heah Joel, gimme dat wash stick. Ah'll show dat limb of Satan she cain't shake herself at *me*. If she ain't down by the time Ah gets dere, Ah'll break huh down in de lines."

"Aw Gran'ma, Ah see Mist' George and Jim Robinson comin' and Ah wanted to wave at 'em," the child said impatiently.

"You jes' wave dat rake at dis heah yahd, madame, else Ah'll take you down a button hole lower. Youse too 'oomanish jumpin' up in every-body's face dat pass.''

This struck the child sorely for nothing pleased her so much as to sit atop of the gate post and hail the passing vehicles on their way South to Orlando, or North to Sanford. That white shell road was her great attraction. She raced up and down the stretch of it that lay before her gate like a round-eyed puppy hailing gleefully all travelers. Everybody in the country, white and colored, knew little Isis Watts, Isis the Joyful. The Robinson brothers, white cattlemen, were particularly fond of her and always extended a stirrup for her to climb up behind one of them for a short ride, or let her try to crack the long bull whips and *yee whoo* at the cows.

Grandma Potts went inside and Isis literally waved the rake at the ''chaws'' of ribbon cane that lay so bountifully about the yard in company with the knots and peelings, with a thick sprinkling of peanut hulls.

The herd of cattle in their envelope of gray dust came alongside and Isis dashed out to the nearest stirrup and was lifted up.

''Hello theah Snidlits, I was wonderin' wheah you was,'' said Jim Robinson as she snuggled down behind him in the saddle. They were almost out of the danger zone when Grandma emerged. ''You Isie,'' she bawled.

The child slid down on the opposite side of the horse and executed a flank movement through the corn patch that brought her into the yard from behind the privy.

''You li'l hasion you! Wheah you been?''

''Out in de back yahd,'' Isis lied and did a cart wheel and a few fancy steps on her way to the front again.

''If you doan git in dat yahd, Ah make a mommuk of you!'' Isis observed that Grandma was cutting a fancy assortment of switches from peach, guava, and cherry trees.

She finished the yard by raking everything under the edge of the porch and began a romp with the dogs, those lean, floppy-eared hounds that all country folks keep. But Grandma vetoed this also.

"Isie, you set on dat porch! Uh great big 'leben-yeah-ole gal racin' an' rompin' lak dat—set 'own!"

Isis flung herself upon the steps.

"Git up offa dem steps, you aggravatin' limb, 'fore Ah get dem hick'ries tuh you, an' set yo' seff on a cheah."

Isis arose, and then sat down as violently as possible in the chair. She slid down, and down, until she all but sat on her own shoulder blades.

"Now look atcher," Grandma screamed. "Put yo' knees together, an' get up offen yo' backbone! Lawd, you know dis hellion is gwine make me stomp huh insides out."

Isis sat bolt upright as if she wore a ramrod down her back and began to whistle. Now there are certain things that Grandma Potts felt no one of this female persuasion should do—one was to sit with the knees separated, "settin' brazen" she called it; another was whistling, another playing with boys. Finally, a lady must never cross her legs.

Grandma jumped up from her seat to get the switches.

"So youse whistlin' in mah face, huh!" She glared till her eyes were beady and Isis bolted for safety. But the noon hour brought John Watts, the widowed father, and this excused the child from sitting for criticism.

Being the only girl in the family, of course she must wash the dishes, which she did in intervals between frolics with the dogs. She even gave Jake, the puppy, a swim in the dishpan by holding him suspended above the water that reeked of "pot likker"—just high enough so that his feet would be immersed. The deluded puppy swam and swam without ever crossing the pan, much to his annoyance. Hearing Grandma she hurriedly dropped him on the floor, which he tracked-up with feet wet with dishwater.

Grandma took her patching and settled down in the front room to sew. She did this every afternoon, and invariably slept in the big red rocker with her head lolled back over the back, the sewing falling from her hand.

Isis had crawled under the center table with its red plush cover with little round balls for fringe. She was lying on her back imagining herself various personages. She wore trailing robes, golden slippers with blue bottoms. She rode white horses with flaring pink nostrils to the horizon, for she still believed that to be land's end. She was picturing herself gazing over the edge of the world into the abyss when the spool of cotton fell from Grandma's lap and rolled away under the whatnot. Isis drew back from her contemplation of the nothingness at the horizon and glanced up at the sleeping woman. Her head had fallen far back. She breathed with a regular "mark" intake and "poosah" exhaust. But Isis was a visual-minded child. She heard the snores only subconsciously but she saw the straggling beard on Grandma's chin, trembling a little with every "mark" and "poosah." They were long gray hairs curled every here and there against the dark brown skin. Isis was moved with pity for her mother's mother.

"Poah Gran-ma needs a shave," she murmured, and set about it. Just then Joel, next older than Isis, entered with a can of bait.

"Come on Isie, les' we all go fishin'. The Perch is bitin' fine in Blue Sink."

"Sh-sh——" cautioned his sister, "Ah got to shave Gran'ma."

"Who say so?" Joel asked, surprised.

"Nobody doan hafta tell me. Look at her chin. No ladies don't weah whiskers if they kin help it. But Gran-ma gittin ole an' she doan know how to shave lak *me*."

The conference adjourned to the back porch lest Grandma wake.

"Aw, Isie, you doan know nothin' bout shavin' a-tall—but a *man* lak me——"

"Ah do so know."

"You don't not. Ah'm goin' shave her mahseff."

"Naw, you won't neither, Smarty. Ah saw her first an' thought it all up first," Isis declared, and ran to the calico-covered box on the wall above the wash basin and seized her father's razor. Joel was quick and seized the mug and brush.

"Now!" Isis cried defiantly, "Ah got the razor."

"Goody, goody, goody, pussy cat, Ah got th' brush an' you can't shave 'thout lather—see! Ah know mo' than you," Joel retorted.

"Aw, who don't know dat?" Isis pretended to scorn. But seeing her progress blocked from lack of lather she compromised.

"Ah know! Les' we all shave her. You lather an' Ah shave."

This was agreeable to Joel. He made mountains of lather and anointed his own chin, and the chin of Isis and the dogs, splashed the wall and at last was persuaded to lather Grandma's chin. Not that he was loath but he wanted his new plaything to last as long as possible.

Isis stood on one side of the chair with the razor clutched cleaver fashion. The niceties of razor-handling had passed over her head. The thing with her was to *hold* the razor—sufficient in itself.

Joel splashed on the lather in great gobs and Grandma awoke.

For one bewildered moment she stared at the grinning boy with the brush and mug but sensing another presence, she turned to behold the business face of Isis and the razor-clutching hand. Her jaw dropped and Grandma, forgetting years and rheumatism, bolted from the chair and fled the house, screaming.

"She's gone to tell Papa, Isie. You didn't have no business wid his razor and he's gonna lick yo' hide," Joel cried, running to replace mug and brush.

"You too, chuckle-head, you too," retorted Isis. "You was playin' wid his brush and put it all over the dogs—Ah seen you put in on Ned an' Beulah." Isis shaved and replaced it in the box. Joel took his bait and pole and hurried to Blue Sink. Isis crawled under the house to brood over the whipping she knew would come. She had meant well.

But sounding brass and tinkling cymbal drew her forth. The local lodge of the Grand United Order of Odd Fellows, led by a braying, thudding band, was marching in full regalia down the road. She had forgotten the barbecue and log-rolling to be held today for the benefit of the new hall.

Music to Isis meant motion. In a minute razor and whipping

forgotten, she was doing a fair imitation of a Spanish dancer she had seen in a medicine show some time before. Isis' feet were gifted—she could dance most anything she saw.

Up, up, went her spirits, her small feet doing all sorts of intricate things and her body in rhythm, hand curving above her head. But the music was growing faint. Grandma was nowhere in sight. Isis stole out of the gate, running and dancing after the band.

Not far down the road, Isis stopped. She realized she couldn't dance at the carnival. Her dress was torn and dirty. She picked a long-stemmed daisy, and placed it behind her ear, but her dress remained torn and dirty just the same. Then Isis had an idea. Her thoughts returned to the battered, round-topped trunk back in the bedroom. She raced back to the house; then, happier, she raced down the white dusty road to the picnic grove, gorgeously clad. People laughed good-naturedly at her, the band played, and Isis danced because she couldn't help it. A crowd of children gathered admiringly about her as she wheeled lightly about, hand on hip, flower between her teeth with the red and white fringe of the table-cloth—Grandma's new red tablecloth that she wore in lieu of a Spanish shawl—trailing in the dust. It was too ample for her meager form, but she wore it like a gypsy. Her brown feet twinkled in and out of the fringe. Some grown people joined the children about her. The Grand Exalted Ruler rose to speak; the band was hushed, but Isis danced on, the crowd clapping their hands for her. No one listened to the Exalted one, for little by little the multitude had surrounded the small brown dancer.

An automobile drove up to the Crown and halted. Two white men and a lady got out and pushed into the crowd, suppressing mirth discreetly behind gloved hands. Isis looked up and waved them a magnificient hail and went on dancing until—

Grandma had returned to the house, and missed Isis. She straightaway sought her at the festivities, expecting to find her in her soiled dress, shoeless, standing at the far edge of the crowd. What she saw now drove her frantic. Here was her granddaughter dancing before a gaping crowd in her brand new red tablecloth, and reeking of lemon extract.

Isis had added the final touch to her costume. Of course she must also have perfume.''

When Isis saw her grandma, she bolted. She heard her grandma cry—''Mah Gawd, mah brand new tablecloth Ah just bought f'um O'landah!''—as Isis fled through the crowd and on into the woods.

ISIS FOLLOWED THE little creek until she came to the ford in a rutty wagon road that led to Apopka and laid down on the cool grass at the roadside. The April sun was quite warm.

Misery, misery and woe settled down upon her. The child wept. She knew another whipping was in store.

"Oh, Ah wish Ah could die, then Gran'ma an' Papa would be sorry they beat me so much. Ah b'leeve Ah'll run away and never go home no mo'. Ah'm goin' drown mahseff in th' creek!"

Isis got up and waded into the water. She routed out a tiny 'gator and a huge bullfrog. She splashed and sang. Soon she was enjoying herself immensely. The purr of a motor struck her ear and she saw a large, powerful car jolting along the rutty road toward her. It stopped at the water's edge.

"Well, I declare, it's our little gypsy," exclaimed the man at the wheel. "What are you doing here, now?"

"Ah'm killin' mahseff," Isis declared dramatically, "Cause Gran'ma beats me too much."

There was a hearty burst of laughter from the machine.

"You'll last some time the way you are going about it. Is this the way to Maitland? We want to go to the Park Hotel."

Isis saw no longer any reason to die. She came up out of the water, holding up the dripping fringe of the tablecloth.

"Naw, indeedy. You go to Maitlan' by the shell road—it goes by mah house—an' turn off at Lake Sebelia to the clay road that takes you right to the do'."

"Well," went on the driver, smiling furtively, "Could you quit dying long enough to go with us?"

"Yessuh," she said thoughtfully, "Ah wanta go wid you."

The door of the car swung opon. She was invited to a seat beside the driver. She had often dreamed of riding in one of these heavenly chariots but never thought she would, actually.

"Jump in then, Madame Tragedy, and show us. We lost ourselves after we left your barbecue."

During the drive Isis explained to the kind lady who smelt faintly of violets and to the indifferent men that she was really a princess. She told them about her trips to the horizon, about the trailing gowns, the gold shoes with blue bottoms—she insisted on the blue bottoms—the white charger, the time when she was Hercules and had slain numerous dragons and sundry giants. At last the car approached her gate over which stood the umbrella chinaberry tree. The car was abreast of the gate and had all but passed when Grandma spied her glorious tablecloth lying back against the upholstery of the Packard.

"You Isie-e!" she bawled, "You lil' wretch you! Come heah *dis instant.*"

"That's me," the child confessed, mortified, to the lady on the rear seat.

"Oh Sewell, stop the car. This is where the child lives. I hate to give her up though."

"Do you wanta keep me?" Isis brightened.

"Oh, I wish I could. Wait, I'll try to save you a whipping this time."

She dismounted with the gaudy lemon-flavored culprit and advanced to the gate where Grandma stood glowering, switches in hand.

"You're gointuh ketchit f'um yo' haid to yo' heels m'lady. Jes' come in heah."

"Why, good afternoon," she accosted the furious grandparent. "You're not going to whip this poor little thing, are you?" the lady asked in conciliatory tones.

"Yes, Ma'am. She's de wustest li'l limb dat ever drawed bref. Jes' look at mah new tablecloth, dat ain't never been washed. She done traipsed all over de woods, uh dancin' an' uh prancin' in it. She done took a razor to me t'day an' Lawd knows whut mo'."

Isis clung to the stranger's hand fearfully.

"Ah wuzn't gointer hurt Gran'ma, miss—Ah wuz just gointer shave her whiskers fuh huh 'cause she's old an' can't."

The white hand closed tightly over the little brown one that was quite soiled. She could understand a voluntary act of love even though it miscarried.

"Now, Mrs. er-er-I didn't get the name—how much did your table-cloth cost?"

"One whole big silvah dollar down at O'landah—ain't had it a week yet."

"Now here's five dollars to get another one. I want her to go to the hotel and dance for me. I could stand a little light today—"

"Oh, yessum, yessum," Grandma cut in, "Everything's alright, sho' she kin go, yessum."

Feeling that Grandma had been somewhat squelched did not detract from Isis' spirit at all. She pranced over to the waiting motor-car and this time seated herself on the rear seat between the sweet-smiling lady and the rather aloof man in gray.

"Ah'm gointer stay wid you all," she said with a great deal of warmth, and snuggled up to her benefactress. "Want me tuh sing a song fuh you?"

"There, Helen, you've been adopted," said the man with a short, harsh laugh.

"Oh, I hope so, Harry." She put her arm about the red-draped figure at her side and drew it close until she felt the warm puffs of the child's breath against her side. She looked hungrily ahead of her and spoke into space rather than to anyone in the car. "I would like just a little of her sunshine to soak into my soul. I would like that alot."

ECONOMICS

Elizabeth Seydel Morgan

OUR MOTHER taught us to substitute the word "tiger" for the word "nigger" when the neighborhood gang chose up teams. Sitting here on my brother's porch, watching my nieces play in the yard with their friends, I think how much has changed since he and I grew up in Atlanta—for one thing, two of their playmates are black. Yet children, their summer games, even this ancient choosing rhyme—catch a tiger by the toe—haven't changed at all.

Back then my brother and I said "tiger," but we didn't have much influence on our next-door neighbor, Carson Foster. He poked his finger in our chests as he chanted "eenie, meenie, miney, moe" and emphasized the forbidden word even more. "If he hollers, let him go." He also added codas if "moe" brought his finger to one of us girls. "Eu-gene Talmadge told me so," or "My father said. To pick the. Very. Best. Man."

But then my mother said a variation of the word herself. "Can you imagine a nigra named Queen Esther Parris?" I overheard her say to Daddy, who answered, "Is that her name or her title?"

"Name," said Mama. "Wants her checks written out to Queen Esther Parris."

"Checks?" I heard his low voice repeat.

"Queen Esther wants to be paid by check."

"Strange," said my dad.

This fact, which I now understand to have been phenomenal in the forties, was strange to me, too, because I thought I knew what checks were—money that was not real, the pale blue of Great Aunt Tisha's Christmas check for a million dollars that Daddy stuck in his mirror frame, the many-colored money that stuck out from under the Monopoly board at the Foster's next door. When we weren't playing softball or strip poker, we'd gather around the board on the Fosters' screen porch and play Monopoly. Though sometimes he let a boy get to the hotel stage, Carson Foster usually won all the money, his pile of gold thousands as big as our worthless pink fives and white singles.

QUEEN ESTHER, PAID by check (how much, I wonder) on Fridays, worked for us when I was around ten. I remember my age because I can picture and hear the moment in my backyard when Carson laughed at my mother working in her garden and said behind her back, "Your mother's a hoer. Get it?"

I didn't get it, but I was certain he had insulted my mother, and I was sick of him and sick of his games. That day in the garden as my mother hoed the border, I stood, I imagine, with my hands on my hips and told Carson, "Look. I'm almost ten years old and I'm not doin' that strip poker and movie-love stuff with you anymore." I have no memory of exactly what he looked like—except that he was big, and he had long square fingers that he liked to put on me—but today I can hear my own words perfectly: "I'm almost ten years old." And I know I didn't say them until after Queen Esther had been with us awhile.

"Hey Mary Meade . . . your maid's sure some Ubangi," Carson had jeered over the hedge when she first came. Later I saw a movie, *King Solomon's Mines,* I think it was, and there were those six- or seven-foot Negroes—blacks I mean—and true, I guess Queen Esther might have come from such a tall African tribe. She was at least six feet. She towered over me (though now I'm very tall myself); I remember most her pink-palmed hand turned slightly outward at her side, and what would I have been then—maybe four feet tall? We'd walk to Connell's with me skipping at her side to match her long strides, my younger brother and sometimes other children trailing behind, Queen Esther tickling her nose all the while with her triffle.

Queen Esther's triffle was a piece of cotton, frayed into a fringe at the end, that she wound around her forefinger and used to tickle her lips or nose or cheeks. Now I know that it was the same kind of habit as smoking, or fingering a blanket's satin edge, as I do every night to get to sleep; then it was mysterious, like her height and her name.

"Queen Esther, why you have that whatchacallit?" one of us would ask.

"That's my triffle," she'd reply.

"What's a triffle?"

"Your business is to direct us all to this drugstore. My triffle is to help me following you, so we get there."

But she never followed us, and after the first time we walked to Buckhead, she never needed help to get there. I suppose she meant the triffle habit was to help her be where she was.

QUEEN ESTHER IRONED. She did everything else, too: the vacuuming, the laundry, the beds, the scraping scrambled eggs out of the iron skillet left in the mornings before she came, the picking up of toys and children's clothes and grown-up underwear in the sheets when she changed the beds, the tossing of empty bottles, scraps of hardened cheese on Chinese plates left from Sunday on the screen porch, the emptying trash cans of Modess and deposit slips and green Coca-Cola bottles.

When Queen Esther ironed, she put books under the legs of the ironing board. After she'd tried the Atlanta phone books once, she never used them again. She'd go to the bookshelf in the den or the living room and try a different selection every Tuesday. I was pretty much loving books myself then, so I'd notice, sitting on the floor by the ironing board, just what was raising it up to her arms. I think back now to the selection of books available to her for lifting the ironing board: Reader's Digest novels, *Up Front, Gone with the Wind,* volumes of *Collier's Encyclopedia, Clothes Make the Man, Leave Her to Heaven, The Decameron, Southern Textiles,* and *Warp Sizing,* the last two either written or given to us by our uncle.

She came to use only the brown encyclopedias, eight to an ironing, and I think she and I were probably the first in our house to crack every one open and look at it. We'd find a picture or more often a map she'd be interested in, and while she was sprinkling down the sheets, I'd read about it out loud. After a time, we started reading a little together—I'd read some words, then she'd read some words—"while the iron heats up," she said.

One day before she placed **E** on the floor, we discovered Esther, the biblical queen of Xerxes who saved her people from destruction. After we read the short column aloud, her namesake read it over to herself.

"Left out the best part, Mary Meade," she said.

"Tell," I said.

"Esther, she knows her husband kicked out his first wife on account of she didn't come when he called her."

"They got a divorce?"

"No. He the king, she out in the street."

"Oh."

"But even so, when time comes to save her people, Esther said, 'Then I will go to the king though it be against the law and if I perish, I perish.'"

She pronounced the quotation slowly, like a teacher.

"That straight out of the Bible . . . from Esther's own book." Then she said quickly in her getting-down-to-work voice, "Now you read your own story for a while?"

I remember the brown books under the wooden legs, the scratch of the rug through my cotton underpants, the book in my lap—probably one of the Black Stallion novels—as I sat by the ironing board, reading while Queen Esther intoned the throaty songs that repeated every line with just a little change. *When you get up tomorrow I'll be gone, babe, when you wake up tomorrow, I'll be gone.*

After Queen Esther found out I could charge money at Connell's Drug Store, we walked to Buckhead every Friday, just the two of us. Doc Connell, or Miss Presson, would write my father's name on the pad with carbon paper, write "money" on the first line and "$1.00" beside "total." Then he'd hand me the dollar bill. For several weeks, I'm not sure how long, Queen Esther would stand tall and silent behind me as I made my transaction. After the first surprised look from Doc Connell and Miss Presson, they didn't look at her at all. It was clear she was my maid. "Thanks a lot," I'd say politely. "You're welcome, Mary Meade," he or both of them would answer. If it was Doc Connell, he usually added something about how come I never spent my money in his store, and I always said the same thing, that it was for the Saturday double feature and serial.

I'd pocket the dollar and walk past cosmetics with Queen Esther, out the screen door to Peachtree, down to the corner at Paces Ferry Road where we waited for her bus. "Well, bye," I'd say when the Five Points bus to downtown Atlanta came, "see you Monday." She's nod her head to the side with this way she had, and I'd start back to our neighborhood to hand over the money to Carson.

One Friday afternoon, standing at Connell's counter, I was surprised by the long black arm extending from behind me, Queen Esther's boney fingers holding out three beige checks to Miss Presson. Miss Presson looked from my face way up over my head and then down at the checks in the black hand. "We don't cash checks," she said to me.

"Those are Mama-an-Daddy's," I said.

"No, sweetie, those are your maid's. And Doc don't allow cashing except for charge customers."

"Mary Meade a charge customer," said Queen Esther.

"What's cashing?" I suppose I asked, because it was then I got a lesson in finance from Miss Presson, learned the difference between my parents' checks and Aunt Tisha's, and watched Queen Esther's arm retreat. As we walked to the bus stop, I asked her how she was going to get real money in place of those beige checks. She stopped still and swiveled her head around on her long neck, looking up and down Peachtree Street. "Somehow," she answered.

WHO KNOWS WHO called my parents, Doc or Miss Presson. "We have to have a talk," said Daddy in his lowest voice, guiding me with a pinch of the back of my neck into the den. "It looks like, Mary Meade, that we need to talk some economics tonight."

"Yes sir," I said.

"Do you know what I mean?"

"No sir."

"Economics is a big word for, uh, hmmm. Uh, money. Things about money."

I remember his hemming and hawing more than his exact words. But Daddy always kept you standing for a long time, getting to the point, and I remember that word "economics" so well from that evening that even today it gives me a catch in the stomach.

"I've been letting you charge a dollar here and there at Connell's—figured it would teach you something—but it looks like you been at it every week. And I would like to ask just why you need so many dollars. I know about the shows at the Buckhead and all, but you also have your allowance, and your money for sitting with Robert."

"Yes."

"Yes what."

"Yes sir."

"I mean yes, what are you doing with the money, Mary Meade?"

I looked at Daddy and opened my mouth. Probably the only two times I've ever been as terrified as that was the time with Carson and the day before my wedding when I told Clifford Sealew that I could not go through with it. Without planning to, I had lied to Clifford, told him there was someone else.

"Well?" said my father.

From my opened mouth the words slipped easy as a prayer. "I gave the money to Queen Esther."

Unlike Cliff, Daddy didn't explode or break down. He said something along the lines of "I thought so" and went on to question me about Queen Esther going in Connell's with me and trying to cash checks. Then he came back around to my lie. He asked me if she'd forced me to give her money.

"Oh, no, no, no!" I saw immediately what I'd gotten into. I saw his angry look gathering, and I knew it was directed at her. "No, Daddy. I wanted to give it to her. She can't get real money for your checks. She tried, and she can't."

He said something like "So I heard" and changed into being real sweet to me. He praised me that night, which I'll always remember, and my fears subsided. We hugged and kissed and I was sent on somewhere, having learned that lying pays, while Daddy stayed in the den in his leather armshair, smoking a cigarette.

THAT FRIDAY AFTERNOON I ran to catch up with Queen Esther, who'd already started for Buckhead without me. Even after I caught up with her, breathless, she walked faster than I could keep up beside her.

"What you running for?" she called loud enough to keep from turning her head. "You don't need to go to Connell's anymore. Your charging days are over."

I remember the back of her, its motion—slim thighs, boxy rear end, long, long spine showing through something like jersey, wide shoulders. I think of her in something gray or tan, with a shiny red belt—probably patent leather. I think of her moving, her hips moving smoothly, and me running behind her, eye-level to her red belt.

"How do you know?" I yelled at her shoulders, the long loops of earrings touching them.

"Your daddy."

"He wouldn't tell *you*."

"Oh yes he would. He did." She wore a sort of glittery turban that day, and she turned her head in a flash of shine and swinging earrings. Running, looking up, I saw the profile of her moving lips.

"You are a liar," she said.

"You are a hoer," Carson had rasped slowly at the opening we'd made in the ligustrum hedge.

"Un uh," I said, shaking my head and toeing the soft dirt with my bare foot.

"Yes you are."

"Un, UH." I was getting scared. Fear was suffusing my body the way pleasure had when Carson and I had been in the bushes.

"A hoer is a girl who does stuff like you did with me. A bad girl."

"I'm not a bad girl."

"You let me tickle you . . . down there."

"No."

"Come on, you already forgetting movie-love?" He pointed at a bunch of tall azaleas in his backyard. "Under there? Those times you let me tickle you with my finger? A long time. And you said it felt good."

"No."

"Well you can say no all you want to, girl. But I'm telling."

The fear was pushing out at my surfaces. I know my pale white skin was red.

"You liked it," Carson said real low, looking up and down my red skin.

"I said I wasn't . . . I said stop it, you know I did."

"Yeah—later you say, *'I'm ten.'* Big deal. You're still a hoer. You still *liked* it. And I'm telling."

"Ah, Carson. Please don't," I whined. I wonder now why I didn't say "Tell who?" "Tell what?" but to a child "I'm telling" needs no who.

He reached through the opening in the hedge and yanked down the elastic top of my sundress, pulling my bare chest into the pruned branches.

"What'll you pay me?"

"Huh?"

"What'll you pay me to never tell?"

I had no idea what he meant.

"You get an allowance, dontcha?"

I just stood there burning with this new, unbearable feeling.

"Listen!" he spat. "Do you?"

"What?" The backs of my legs prickled like poison ivy.

"Do you get an allowance? Do you get lunch money? Movie money?"

"Movie . . . allowance."

"I want one dollar a week."

"Why?" I'm pretty sure I said. I remember being completely confused.

"Why! To keep me from telling you're a hoer. That's why."

"Okay."

He seemed surprised. "Okay?"

"Okay." It seemed easy that afternoon to stop the burning. Just pay my next-door neighbor one dollar and he would never tell that I let him put his finger between my legs and move it around and make me feel good, and bad.

"WAIT A MINUTE, Queen Esther," I yelled, catching up. "Please wait!"

She didn't exactly wait, but she must have slowed her long-legged stride a little because I came up alongside her, puffing.

"Queen Esther, I really wish I could give my dollars to *you*."

Far above me I saw the whites of her eyes as she rolled them. She just kept walking, getting ahead of me again.

"If you can't get cashed."

She looked over her shoulder. "If you knew somethin' beside nothin', you'd be trouble." And then she raised her arm as if to swat me backward, but she only stroked her upraised chin with her triffle.

That slowed her a little and I caught up. My heart was thudding with running and what I was about to do.

"Queen Esther—I have to give all my dollars to Carson!"

"Say?"

"Carson. The charge money. I give it to him."

She stopped. "Wuf fo?" she said in the language I knew as well as I know French now.

What I told Queen Esther as we stopped on the road to Buckhead was surely not the whole story. I never told anyone about feeling the sweet sensation that had spread over my body and made me bad.

I told her we'd played strip poker and doctor and I had to pay to keep it a secret.

"Blackmail!" sang Queen Esther. "Bluemail, man-mail, exto. Strong-arm, strong, strong."

It sounded like a chant. Whatever she was saying or chanting, her stride had slowed to let me stay beside her.

We walked together, past my school, past the bungalows smaller than my house, to Paces Ferry Road. Her bus stop was ahead, down at Peachtree.

"Don' pay'm mo'." she said, and I heard this clearly as *Don't pay Carson any more dollars.*

"But how?" I looked up and she heard that clearly as *Without his telling Mama and Daddy I'm a hoer.*

"Say: I'm good. And I know it. And I ain't givin' you a cent. Say: You boy, I am a good girl."

I thought about it. "He'll still tell."

"No. He won't." said Queen Esther.

WE'D COME TO Connell's Drug Store and both tried to look the other way.

"I won't be coming back, Mary Meade. I been let go."

"Where you going?"

"Some other house."

"Where you cashing?"

"I knows a man." She looked down at me. "If I perish, I perish . . ."

"Oh. Can I wait with you for Five Points Bus?"

We waited with the group of maids and yardmen at the corner. Queen Esther was taller than all of them, and the men looked embarrassed to have her standing like a giraffe in their midst. The women seemed ashamed to be dressed so ugly. Every one of them looked drab and dusty. Queen Esther, in her shining turban and earrings and glowing skin, was beautiful. I remember understanding that for the first time.

WE WATCHED THE bus make its circle around the Buckhead traffic island to head back downtown. Queen Esther looked down and said, with no smile or sadness, no emotion at all, "Tell the boy no mo' dollars, and tell your daddy they never were for me."

Then she took the steps up the bus with one step, ducked her head, and was gone.

All the black people around me moved toward the bus, and I turned toward Paces Ferry Road.

I went home and lied to Carson that my daddy had found out anyway so I couldn't pay him anymore, and I lied to Daddy by never saying another word about it. I never told anyone, then or now, that I am good.

SARAH

Tina McElroy Ansa

WHEN LENA RAN onto the side screen porch she was too excited about her new friend Sarah to remember not to let the screen door slam. But her grandmother only smiled absentmindedly when she ran into the sewing room chattering away about the little girl across the street.

"Lena, baby, be careful 'round that hot iron," she said as Lena nearly collided with the ironing board that was always set up in the room while her grandmother and mother sewed. Then she made the girl stand straight and still while she held a green-and-red plaid pleated skirt with matching suspenders up to the child's waist. The entire woolen skirt was only about half a foot long.

"Hmmm-huh," the old lady muttered with a few straight pins still in her mouth as Lena wove the story about magic fruit made out of red jewels and a little girl named Puddin'.

Her mother, when Lena found her sitting in the living room in her favorite rose-colored chair reading a thick book without any pictures in it, was no more receptive.

"Lena, baby, sit still for just a minute so Mama can finish this one last page. You've been such a good girl all afternoon. As soon as I finish this one last page, I'll put on some music for you. Some Billie Holiday or some Sarah Vaughan, how about that? Then you can help me bake a cake. What kind do you want? A chocolate or a coconut?"

Nellie's voice was as seductive as the thought of homemade cake.

"Chocolate, chocolate, chocolate," Lena screamed as she jumped down from the arm of her mother's chair and ran over to the sofa to sit quietly until her mother finished her reading. The thought of a moist yellow cake covered with warm smooth brown icing pushed the image of Sarah right out of her head.

But the next morning, with the sun barely breaking through the trees and the boys still stumbling into each other half-asleep in the bathroom as they got ready for school, the household seemed to rock with the sound of banging at the front door.

At first everyone but Nellie, who knew she had left him snoring in the bed next to her, thought it was Jonah again firing off shots from the pistol he always carried with him—*bam, bam, bam, bam, bam*—the way he had done late one night when he came home and found that Nellie had locked and barred all the doors against him. Weary from a long night of poker and carousing, he hadn't yelled and he hadn't cussed. He had just pulled the gun out of his back pocket and fired into the roof of the side porch, and the doors of the house had magically opened to him.

The five small holes that the gunshots made were still in the porch's forest green ceiling. Lena giggled whenever she looked up and saw them. Her father's brashness frightened most people, but it didn't scare her one bit. She knew she was immune.

The gunshots had not only opened the locked door for her father, they also had held in check all the talk Nellie had said she had for him about him staying out as late as he wanted and not expecting anybody to say anything about it. About what did he think she was, anyway? About how sick and tired she was of him and his whores.

Overhearing Nellie's mutterings, Lena, sitting on the toilet, had wondered what a whore was, since it didn't exactly sound like the thing her grandmama used to turn the dirt over in her garden. A simple garden tool couldn't have made her mother as mad as this whore seemed to. And Lena didn't think anything that sounded as bad as her mama made the word sound could be so harmless. The way her mama said it, "whore" sounded like it was covered with spikes and prickly barbs.

So, as she pulled up her panties, she asked her mother for a definition. Nellie just snapped, "Go back to bed, Lena."

The early morning banging at the door was loud and insistent. Lena's grandmother strode down the stairs with Lena beside her. Lena was walking so close to her grandmother that she almost got tangled up in the length of chenille robe flapping between the old lady's legs and tumbled down the steps head over heels. Grandmama scratched the side of her nose again and marched down the downstairs hall on her way to the front door muttering to herself, "Who the hell is this come to our door this time of morning banging like the goddamn police? If it's one of Jonah's half-witted flunkies, they'll be sorry they were ever born. Yes, if it's one of those fanatical fools from The Place come here this time of morning to borrow a couple of dollars to throw away on some foolishness, they'll be sorry they ever learned how to count pennies when I finish with 'em. Knocking on this door like they the damn police or something."

Lena had to walk fast to keep up with her grandmother. Despite the threatening banging at the door, she wasn't a bit afraid. She thought nothing could befall her as long as the older lady stood between her and the world.

Grandmama was out of breath and still cussing out "that fool out there" when they reached the door. She didn't even peep out of one of the panes of glass that edged the big door first. She just flung it open and stood there with her arms folded over her flat breasts as Lena peered around her legs.

At first all Grandmama and Lena could see in the breaking morning light was a wide smile and a pink blouse. Then Lena recognized her friend.

"Sarah!" Lena screamed as she dashed past her grandmother's legs and ran up to the door, pressing her face against the screen.

Grandmama, still annoyed at the early morning visit, looked down at Lena with a confused expression.

"It's Sarah, Grandmama, Puddin' Tame. I told you all 'bout her yesterday. She's my friend. Don't you remember?"

Grandmama was still puzzled. It had never occurred to her that Lena could have anything to do with this early morning commotion at their front door. On top of that she was having a hard time believing that Lena, her baby, had made a friend without her grandmama knowing about it. And what a friend!

The dark little girl who stood on the front porch smiling for all she was worth looked to Grandmama like a little piece of street trash who had tried to doll herself up.

Grandmama was halfway right. Sarah had stayed up nearly all night preparing for her first visit to Lena's big house. It felt like the most important event of her short life, and she knew if she didn't prepare for it, nobody would.

Everyone in Sarah's family was used to her doing things on her own. So the night before, when her mother had heard her bumping around in the nearly darkened house, the woman had just smacked her lips a couple of times sleepily, turned over against the warm body of her husband, and gone back to sleep.

Sarah had stopped rummaging through a cluttered drawer and stood perfectly still when she heard her mother stir. She knew she had her work cut out for her, and she didn't need anybody asking a lot of questions and getting in the way while she tried her best to piece together some kind of outfit.

Sarah wanted so much to look nice when she met Lena's people. But she had so little to work with. When she thought she couldn't find a decent pair of matching socks in the whole house, Sarah sat in the middle of the cold bathroom floor and wept.

The only matching set was the tiny pair of faded lacy pink baby socks she found stuck in the back of a drawer, which her mother had bought for one of the children but had never had a fancy enough occasion to use. Sarah brightened when she found a dark blue sock and a dark brown one that belonged to her younger brother. If she didn't fold down the cuffs of the socks, they almost looked like they were bought for her. And in the light thrown off by the lone lamp with the broken shade in the front room, the brown and blue socks looked like a perfect match. Sarah didn't realize until she was standing in Lena's mama's big bright kitchen that she was wearing mismatched socks. By then she was too happy to care.

There was no shoe polish of any color in the house, so Sarah just took a damp rag and wiped the red dust from her lace-up brown oxfords. They looked fine as long as the leather remained wet, but as soon as the shoes began to dry, they reverted to the smoky hue they had been for months.

At least, Sarah thought, I don't have to worry that much about my underwear. If I keep my dress down and don't flounce around too much, it won't matter if I got holes in my drawers or not. As luck would have it, she found a pair of her own panties that were still white and didn't even have a pinhole in them in a pile of clean laundry someone had taken off the line and left on the swayback chair in the kitchen.

Then her main concern became finding a dress without a hole in it. Because she was usually as raggedy or neat as anyone else in her house, Sarah rarely gave any thought to her attire. She woke in the morning, put on something to cover her body, and went on with her day. But the way Lena had been dressed that day, and the size of the house Lena lived in, had made Sarah look at herself for a long time in the wavy mirror of the old hall dresser and decide she wanted to wear something special to her new friend's house.

With tiny lines of concentration creasing her forehead, she picked up and discarded nearly every piece of clothing she found in two chests of drawers, stuck down between the frayed cushions of the couch, or lying under the cot where she and two of her sisters slept. She had long ago outgrown the only "nice" Easter dress she had ever owned. It had been passed down to her next sister, who despoiled it right away by putting it on and playing in the mud.

The search seemed hopeless. Then she remembered the cardboard box full of old clothes that a white woman her mother had once worked for had dropped off at their house the Christmas before instead of coming up with the five dollars she owed for almost a week's work. Her mother was so disgusted that she had thrown the box into a corner of the porch and dared anybody to go near it.

At the time, Sarah had shared her mother's anger and disappointment and wouldn't touch the box of old clothes for anything in the world. She had even stopped her sisters and brother from messing with it. But that was then. Now Sarah needed something that wasn't ripped and torn and soiled beyond repair, so she broke down and dragged the box into the kitchen from the back porch.

She pulled out dozens of old men's shirts and plaid housedresses and faded pastel dusters before she came to anything that looked like it might fit her. At the bottom of the box, under a piece of a yellowed sheet, she found a layer of children's clothes. She lifted them all out and laid them on the kitchen table. Then she threw everything else back into the box.

The bare lightbulb hanging from the cord in the ceiling was one of the brightest ones in the house, so Sarah stayed in the kitchen to examine her discovery.

"Too little, too little, too big, too little, too big," Sarah muttered to herself as she held up each piece to examine it briefly and then dropped it into one of two piles on the table. When she had gone through all the children's clothes on the table, she realized she hadn't once said, "My size." So she picked up the small pile of "too little" clothes, dropped them back into the cardboard box, and pushed it back onto the porch. Then she returned to the "too big" pile on the table to see what she could use.

First Sarah went through the pile to check for pants and dresses and blouses that had no holes or rips in them. Earlier, while Lena had been engrossed in the piles of rocks and sand they had been building to dam up the flow of the stream cascading beside the street, Sarah had examined her new friend close up. She had been struck with the vivid red of Lena's frock, which was unlike anything she owned.

But later, going over the afternoon meeting in her mind, the thing that stood out about Lena's dress was not only its bright color but also its neatness. No rips or tears at the seams, no threads hanging down—none of the hem of the wide skirt dipping like a shelf below the rest of the dress. Sarah was sharp enough to see that the collar was hand sewn and the sleeves were eased into the armholes so they didn't pucker. And she just somehow felt that the hem of the skirt had been turned under, ironed flat, and stitched before the final edge was expertly measured and hemmed. That's the kind of dress she was looking for in the pile of "too big" items on the kitchen table.

In what was left of her childish hopes, Sarah fully expected to find it there. But there was no handmade red dress to fit her in the pile of children's apparel on the kitchen table. The closest she came to it was a long-sleeved pink blouse with stitching on the cuff and around the buttonholes that was only slightly frayed at the collar, and a navy blue pleated skirt with elastic at the waist that some little girl had worn as part of her school uniform.

The blouse's long sleeves hung below her knuckles and the armholes sagged beneath her shoulders, but when she tucked the hem of the blouse down into the elastic waistband of the blue skirt, it settled into neat little pleats all around her rib cage and looked kind of cute, Sarah thought. The skirt was longer than she would have liked, but it made a pretty umbrella-like display when she twirled around, and since she had a clean white pair of panties to wear that weren't holey, she figured she could twirl around a few times and remind everyone who thought the skirt was a sad little sack that it was really quite attractive on her.

She planned to hit the skirt and blouse a few times with the ancient iron her mama kept on a kitchen shelf under the sink. But when she plugged it in, the iron shot golden sparks from the raw copper coils exposed beneath the ragged black covering on the cord. Sarah jumped back and yanked the plug from the wall socket for fear of going up in flames before she got the chance to see inside Lena's house. She spread the outfit on the kitchen table and tried to press out the wrinkles by running the palm of her hand over and over the material. But she gave up after a few tries.

"I'll just walk fast and whip them wrinkles out, like Mama say to do," Sarah told herself as she went into the bathroom and started running warm water into the sink.

It was much too cold in the small bathroom for Sarah to think about stripping naked and getting into a tub full of tepid water—the only kind that came out of their hot-water faucets. And besides, if she had run water into the tub, everybody in the house would have awakened to find out what was going on that deserved a full bath. Instead, Sarah took the bar of rough gray soap from the wire dish above the sink, held it under the warm running water, and rubbed up enough suds on a rag she took from hanging on the side of the tub to run over the trunk of her body and leave a light trail of suds behind on her skin. It was the type of bath her mother took when she was late running out to work or going down-town to a juke joint. "I don't have time to bathe," she'd mutter to herself as she undressed. "I'll just take a wipe-off."

The toilette was what most women in Pleasant Hill, regardless of where they lived, called a "whore's bath," but Sarah didn't know what a whore was any more than Lena did.

After she rinsed the suds off with the wet rag, she dried off with a stiff towel hanging on a nail behind the door and quickly slipped into the pair of panties and undershirt she had found in the laundry. As she walked around the house in her bare feet turning off lights, she shivered a bit as the air seeping through gaps in the thin walls hit her damp skin. When she finally settled in for the night, she was grateful for the warm spots her sisters, asleep in their narrow cot, made for her to snuggle into.

The walls of her house were so thin and holey that in winter the wind whistled through the small rooms like a prairie storm through a log cabin. The floors, buckled and rough in unexpected places, creaked each time someone in the house shifted, let alone walked across them. And the whole place smelled of dried and fresh urine that seemed to have soaked into the very wood of the structure so long ago that its residents no longer even noticed the scent.

When Sarah awoke the next morning, she didn't feel as if she had slept a bit that night. She had dozed off a little, but the excitement of her visit to her new friend's house woke her before daylight and before anyone else got up. She put on her socks and shoes in the dark room, turned on the light in the bathroom only long enough to find the hairbrush and rake it over her head one time, then switched the light off and headed for the kitchen.

Her new pink blouse and blue skirt were still lying on the table, wrinkled as they had been the night before, but Sarah didn't pay the wrinkles any attention as she quickly buttoned up the blouse and pulled the skirt over her head.

She twirled one time to make sure the skirt still ballooned prettily the way it had the night before and headed out the door to Lena's house without waking anyone—not even her father who woke early to get a spot on the day-worker's truck that drove through the neighborhood. By the time she got halfway down the driveway leading to Lena's house, she couldn't keep from grinning.

Before Sarah knew anything, she and Lena were standing on opposite sides of the screen door beaming at each other in the glow of their new friendship. But Lena soon grew impatient with her grandmama's dazed gaping from one to the other of the two little girls and pulled a handful of chenille robe.

"Grandmama, open the door. Let Sarah in. She came to visit me."

'Okay, baby," her grandmother answered vaguely as she flipped the metal hook from its eye and pushed the door just wide enough for Sarah to squeeze through.

Sarah bounded into the hall and stood beneath the overhead light, excitement and awe written all over her ashy face. It was like a palace to Sarah: the highly polished hardwood floors, the pictures hanging on the wall near the door, the simple chandelier over the dining-room table in the next room, the dining room itself with its big oval table and six high-backed matching chairs pulled up to it, the mouthwatering bowl of fruit sitting in the middle of the table were like something in her dreams.

Grandmama thought just what Lena knew she would when she got a good look at Sarah: I sure would like to scrub that little rusty neck and grease her down with Vaseline. And when the old woman got a whiff of Sarah's mildewed clothes, she thought, I bet she hasn't ever had a real good hot soapy bath in a tub in her life.

"So you're our baby's new friend?" Grandmama said out loud.

"Yeah," Sarah answered, her voice gravelly from getting up so early but so respectful that her short answer didn't imply rudeness, even to Grandmama.

"Say, 'yes, ma'am,'" Grandmama instructed Sarah gently.

"Yes ma'am,'" Sarah said carefully, repeating Grandmama's gentle inflection.

"Well, next time wait till the sun has come up good before you come visiting," Grandmama said pointedly. Then, "I guess ya'll want something to eat. You had breakfast yet, Sarah?"

"Bre'fast?" Sarah was puzzled.

"Have you eaten this morning?" the old lady rephrased her question as she headed for the kitchen.

"Oh, no," Sarah answered with her eyes caressing the fruit on the dining-room table as they passed by.

All three of them had to blink a few times as they entered the black-

and-white kitchen situated at the eastern corner of the house. The early morning sun flooded the spacious room with shafts of startlingly bright light that hadn't reached the other parts of the house yet. Sarah felt as though she were walking out onto a stage: it didn't seem real. She had seen kitchens similar to Lena's when she accompanied her mother to her occasional day-work jobs in the white neighborhood behind their house. But those kitchens didn't smell like Lena's. In fact there had been no smell at all except the ones she and her mother brought there.

But even first thing in the morning, Lena's kitchen smelled wonderful. And it wasn't just the fresh aroma of coffee brewing on the stove and buttery grits and sausage grease and cinnamon and sugar dusted lightly on buttered slices of toast. It was the layers of smells that had settled on the walls and floor and worked their way into the fiber of the room that made Sarah come to a halt near the threshold. Sarah could smell the vegetable soup Nellie had made the week before when the weather first turned chilly. She smelled the fish dinner they had had that Friday. She smelled the chocolate layer cake even before she saw it sitting in a glass-covered cake dish on the top of the refrigerator. She came close to bursting into tears with the yearning that the room called up in her swelling heart.

Lena grabbed her friend's dry hand and pulled her into the kitchen and over to the white enamel table to sit down.

"Nellie," Grandmama said to Lena's mother who stood by the sink looking out the window in the direction of the woods. "Look who was making all that noise at our front door this time of morning."

Nellie turned around with her thin eyebrows raised. They shot up even higher when she saw Sarah.

"Well, I be damned," she said. "Now, who is this?"

Lena giggled and so did Sarah.

"This is a new friend of Lena's," Grandmama said with a strange lilt to her voice on the word "friend" that made both little girls stop laughing and look into the old woman's face.

Lena kicked Sarah under the table to encourage her to speak.

"Girl, what you kicked me for?" Sarah asked in her gruff, raspy voice.

"This my mama, Sarah," Lena said as she reached under the table and patted the spot on Sarah's leg that she had kicked.

"Where do you live?" Grandmama asked Sarah as she placed a small glass decorated with circus animals and filled full with orange juice in front of each girl.

"She lives across the street in those houses next to Mrs. Willback's house. Next to that big tree. What kind of tree is that?" Lena asked Sarah.

Sarah couldn't answer at first because she had picked up her glass of juice and was drinking down the fresh tart drink in small continuous swallows, allowing the citrus tang to coat the inside of her mouth and throat. With one last gulp and a loud smack of her lips, she put the glass back on the table and answered.

"Chinaberry."

"And just how did the two of you get together?" Grandmama asked as she walked over to the table with more orange juice and poured another stream into Sarah's glass that made the child's eyes light up even more.

But before Sarah had a chance to answer, Nellie jumped in and said nervously, "Oh, with our little girl, it's no telling, but I assume that you didn't cross that street out there, Lena."

"No, Mama, Sarah did. You ought to see her dodge those cars," Lena said proudly.

Nellie laughed softly. "I bet she can."

After that, Sarah would show up on their doorstep regularly to join Lena and the boys for breakfast. Some days she had to run home after eating to "do something." Other times she stayed all day until Grandmama made her go home. When anyone asked her why she didn't go to school, she'd say, "We going up there any day now, soon as Mama gets a chance to 'roll me." But for more than a year she never attended any school other than the one she found in her own backyard.

"Lena, what are you and old Rough-and-Ready doing today?" Grandmama would ask as the two girls came into the kitchen and took seats next to where she sat making peach puffs or carefully cutting the seams away from a pile of pole beans covering the table. Lena's father said he had gagged and nearly choked on strings Nellie had left on the beans soon after they got married. From that time on, Grandmama always prepared the pole beans in their house.

"Don't know yet," Sarah would answer for both of them, not minding the old lady's all too appropriate nickname for her. Grandmama made a point of always having something healthful for Sarah whenever she came into the kitchen—a piece of fruit, a sandwich with extra slices of tomato, a pile of raisins—and she always gave the bigger portion to Sarah.

But whatever their plans were, everyone knew that they would involve pretend. It was their favorite game. Everything they played hinged on the basic unit of Let's Pretend. These games sometimes involved props and background and sometimes they didn't, and that was fine, too. At Lena's house, where her attic, filled to bursting, yielded all kinds of costumes and paraphernalia to fill in the chinks of the stories, their games were elaborate and staged. But Grandmama or Nellie or one of the boys always had to go up the steps and drag down boxes or armloads of stuff because Lena still refused to go into the attic as long as she knew the portrait of her dead infant aunt was stored up there.

For the few days each winter when it was too cold to play out-of-doors, Sarah came to Lena's house and they played and danced in the big upstairs hall in front of the wide floor-length mirror so they could see every movement they made. In the daytime, with her friend by her side, Lena was never frightened of the big mirror, as she was during the nights on her bathroom runs.

At Sarah's it was bare-bones pretending under the chinaberry tree, which was the only place they were allowed to play at her house year-round, but that didn't bother the girls. Despite the house's deficiencies—glaringly obvious to the adults in the neighborhood—Sarah had two things in her yard that Lena and every other child in Pleasant Hill envied her for: a mature and flourishing pomegranate tree and the ancient chinaberry whose broad sturdy limbs swooped down to the ground and back to the sky to form natural nooks and dens. Lena and Sarah called it their "house."

The year Sarah and Lena discovered each other, the two of them planned all winter that, when the warm weather came, they would both move into the chinaberry tree by themselves and live off the fruits of the pomegranate.

"You'll have a room, and I'll have a room," Lena assured Sarah. Sarah's two sisters still wet the cot she shared with them in the front room of her house. "We'll make two beds out of pine straw and Grandmama's flowers, and it'll smell so good in our house, we won't never have to clean up." It was hard for Lena to believe, considering the number of babies and toddlers that roamed the house and yard all day long, but Sarah was the eldest child in the Stanley household. She had responsibilities that Lena never knew about.

They were best friends, sharing games and secrets, special words and questions. But the first time Lena remembered seeing Sarah's world clearly, it was winter and raining very hard, too hard for Lena to head out the door into the cold sheets of water. Lena was stuck at Sarah's for dinner, even though her mother had told her not to accept dinner invitations because Sarah's family had enough trouble feeding their own members without having guests' mouths as well.

"Just say, 'No thank you, I already ate' or 'I'm going to eat when I get home,'" Nellie instructed Lena.

By the time Raymond came running up on the porch with her yellow raincoat and an umbrella, Lena had seen Sarah's family at home for dinner. It was a revelation.

Sarah's mother stood in the tiny kitchen, moving quickly from the sink to the tiny white stove, opening cans, stirring, and chopping.

She worked quietly, not saying a word to Lena and the other children assembled on the floor and sitting in the room's one swaybacked chair. When she was finished, Sarah's mother laid down the big metal spoon with holes in it, turned to the children, and announced, "Catch as catch can." Then she walked out onto the lean-to porch to light up a cigarette, blowing long furls of white smoke out into the driving rain.

The other children rose quickly and lined up behind Sarah with small plates and bowls in their hands. Lena could tell what was cooking in the big blue pot even before Sarah lifted the lid off and steam roiled up to the cracking ceiling.

It was neckbones. The distinctive pork scent mixed with tomatoes from the two big yellow-labeled cans sitting on the kitchen table had wrapped itself around the very hairs in Lena's nose. She didn't dare look in the pot for fear of going against her mother's orders and succumbing to the temptation to share the meal, but she guessed that Sarah's mother had put in lots of onions and pungent bell peppers and fistfuls of spaghetti that she broke in half first. Neckbones was one of Lena's favorite dinners. They had them two ways at her house. If her mother cooked, they were made the way Sarah's mother did, with tomatoes and spaghetti. If her grandmother was in charge of cooking the meal, the bony meat was always prepared with potatoes and thick brown gravy.

Although Lena knew both her mother and grandmama wanted her to lean one way or the other in her preference for neckbones, prepared red or brown, she never made a choice. She could never bear the thought of life without neckbones both ways.

When Sarah had filled all the children's bowls and plates, she filled her own plate, broke off a piece of bread from the charred hoecake in the black skillet, and sat on the floor with the others who were already wolfing down their food. Not a word was said until every plate was clean. When Lena asked why everybody was so quiet while they ate, Sarah looked at her as if she had just pointed out the holes in her sisters' drawers, and Lena was sorry she had said anything.

One warm murky day in their second summer, Lena found her friend sitting beneath the protected wings of the chinaberry tree, playing with mounds of dirt between her opened legs. Sarah's house seemed strangely quiet, free of the noises and traffic that usually encircled the house.

The dirt in Sarah's yard was gray and dusty and didn't look as tempting to Lena as the rich brown loam under the pine trees in her own yard. But she had to fight the urge to reach down and put a handful of it into her mouth anyway. Lena understood perfectly why Estelle, who came from time to time to help clean the house, kept chunks of stark white laundry starch in her apron pockets and munched on it throughout the day.

But Lena had promised her mother that she would stop eating dirt. And it seemed no matter how hard she wiped her mouth, Nellie could always tell when she had been eating the stuff. So, instead of picking up a palmful, holding her head back, and letting the grains of dirt trickle into her open mouth from the fist of her hand, she just sat down next to Sarah and started building her own pile of earth into a hill.

"What's your name?" Lena asked playfully, in their customary greeting.

Sarah looked up from the sandhill of earth at her knees and smiled at Lena. "Puddin' Tame," she answered.

"What do you want to play?" she asked Sarah after a while.

"Let's play like we married," Sarah said without hesitation.

"Okay," Lena agreed.

"I'll be the man and you be the woman," Sarah said as she pushed aside the top of the pile of dirt.

"You sit at the table and I'll cook us some breakfast," suggested Lena as she looked around the yard for the few pieces of plastic and china plates and cups they used for serving pieces of sticks for bread; rocks for meat; mounds of dirt for rice, mashed potatoes, and grits; and dark green leaves from the trees around them for collard and turnip greens.

It was a careful game of pretend eating they played. Lena treated it with as much reverence as the real thing was accorded in her own household. She always got a pan of water and washed the rock of "meat" well before putting it in an old dented pot or shoebox "oven" to cook. And she washed and fingered the chinaberry leaves carefully and tenderly, just the way her mother and grandmother did before shredding them and putting them in a pot with a rock for seasoning.

She had been in the kitchen once and seen her grandmother stand at the sink for the longest time examining each leaf in a pile of collards she had just picked from her garden, where they grew year-round. Lena had thought at first that the old lady was looking for worms until she beckoned her over to stand on a chair at the drain beside her.

"Look at this, baby, all these little roads in a single leaf," Grandmama said softly as she traced the separate pale veins in the dark verdant leaf with her wrinkled index finger. "And listen, just listen to this music." Then she had run the soft pad of her thumb over the dark green surface of a leaf, and the thing let out a little baby squeak. They both just smiled in wonder.

Sarah sat near her pile of dirt and thought a while. Then she shook her head as she watched Lena begin to gather the plates. "No, not like that. You want me to show you how to really play house? I know. I seen it plenty of times."

"Okay," Lena agreed easily, even though she knew she had watched her family all her life and knew how to play house just as well as Sarah. But she figured she and her friend enjoyed each other too much to waste time disagreeing over something that didn't matter all that much.

"We just need one thing," Sarah said. "I'll go get it."

And she hurried off to the empty front porch of her house and returned right away with a copy of the *Mulberry Clarion* in her hand. It looked so stiff and clean, Lena knew it had to be that day's copy of the newspaper. Besides, it was Friday and Lena knew that most people in Pleasant Hill, even those who didn't read the newspaper every day, took the *Clarion* on Fridays because that was the day the paper included the page that Rowana Jordan wrote and edited. Stretched across the top of that inside page, just before the want ads, was the standard heading "News of Our Colored Community."

When Mulberry's one colored newspaper had gone out of business at the beginning of the fifties, Miss Rowana, as everyone called her, persuaded the *Clarion* to insert black folks' news once a week by promising to sell ads, take photographs, and write all the stories herself. And she was true to her word, rushing all over town in her too-fancy dresses and outrageous hats collecting news, church notices, wedding and birth announcements, and gossip, along with receipts and ads from funeral homes, barbershops, grocery stores, and the Burghart Theatre. She already had a tiny storefront office on Cherry Street, far enough away from the newspaper's building to please both her and her employers. So she just changed the sign from the *Mulberry Crier* to the *Mulberry Clarion* and continued working.

The newspaper Sarah carried was still rolled up the way it had been thrown. And the little girl held it out in front of her like a magic wand. As soon as she got back to their spot under the tree, she plopped down in the dust and began unrolling the paper.

"Sarah," Lena said, "your daddy read that paper yet?"

"Uh-uh," Sarah answered as she continued to spread the paper out in her hands.

"Then you better leave it alone till they do read it. Nothing makes my daddy madder than for somebody to come and tear up the paper before he gets a chance to read it. He says it shows a goddamn lack of consideration."

Sarah sucked her teeth derisively as she separated one big broadsheet from the others and laid it up on the elbow of a limb of the chinaberry tree they sat under. "Shoot, nobody'll even notice it's gone. If I didn't move it, it woulda sat there forever."

Lena still wasn't convinced, but she was too intrigued with what Sarah was going to do with the paper to press her argument.

When Sarah had all the sheets separated from one another, she divided them evenly, giving Lena four double wide sheets and keeping the others for herself.

"What we gonna do with these?" Lena wanted to know.

Sarah looked around the base of the tree that was their "house" and picked a corner where the limbs touched the ground.

"We need to go over to our bedroom. It's nighttime," Sarah said as she picked up her sheets of newsprint and stepped into another part of the "house."

Lena followed her.

Sarah sat down and pointed to the spot next to her for Lena to join her in the dust. Lena sat down. She was beginning to realize that this was a private, ritualized game they were about to play. And when Sarah said, "Our children 'sleep so we gotta be quiet," Lena knew she had been right, and she was excited. As many times as she had been frightened by some apparition or discovery, she couldn't keep herself from loving a mystery, especially when she was with someone in her family or Sarah and felt safe.

"This what you got to do," Sarah explained as she crumpled a sheet of the newspaper up into a ball, lifted up her skirts, and stuck the paper down into the front of her panties. She leaned back against the stump of the tree and looked down at her crotch, appraising the difference the addition made. Lena sat next to her staring at it, too.

Lena couldn't take her eyes off Sarah's dingy panties, now bulging at the crotch as Sarah added another ball of newspaper, then another. The newspaper balled up like it was and nestled inside Sarah's drawers didn't look like anything other than what it was. But Sarah continued to fool with it, arranging the rounded part against her body and making one end of the clump of paper into a pointed edge, which she aimed at the pad of her panties.

Lena knew she was supposed to keep quiet because the ritual had begun, but she just had to ask. "Sarah," she whispered, "what's that supposed to be?"

"I'm the man," Sarah said authoritatively. "That's my thing, my johnson. I'm supposed to have it."

She patted her newspaper growth one last time, then grabbed one of Lena's sheets of paper and scooted over to her spot in the dust.

"Here," Sarah said as she handed Lena a ball of the newspaper. "You do the same thing. That'll be your thing, you a grown 'oman, so that'll be your pussy."

"I already got one," Lena said as she started to pull down her panties to show Sarah. "We call it a matchbox at our house. It just ain't as big as a grown woman."

"I know you got a thing," Sarah said, with a touch of exasperation creeping into her voice. "All girls do, but you right, it ain't big enough. So, go on, put the paper down in your panties like me."

And Lena complied, shoving the stiff paper into the front of her white panties, now rapidly turning gray in the dust. "Ouch, that's scratchy," she complained as she moved the paper around trying to find a more comfortable place against her skin.

"That's okay," Sarah said as she scooted over to Lena to sit facing her between her opened legs. "I think it's supposed to hurt some. That's what my daddy make it sound like. He say, 'Oooo, baby, yeah, that hurt so good, do it some more, uh, yeah, that hurt just right.'"

Sarah had moved in so close to Lena that their two panty fronts, both bulging out in front of them, were now touching. Without any further explanation, she started moving her body around, rubbing her paper penis against Lena's panties and making short sucking sounds as she pulled air between her clenched teeth. She threw her head back and closed her eyes, imitating her father, the whole time repeating, "Uh, yeah, uh, yeah, right there, un-huh."

Lena watched in fascination as her friend continued to rub up against her in the dust and to suck her teeth as if she were in pain.

Sarah's face was a picture of pleasure glazed over with a thin icing of pain, like the faces of women at The Place who danced and ground their hips to the beat of a saxophone solo played on the jukebox. She seemed to pay Lena no attention, so Lena figured she was supposed to imitate her friend.

She threw her own head back and closed her eyes like Sarah and began rotating the bottom of her body, the part in her panties stuffed with stiff newspaper, up against Sarah. Lena felt a little silly at first and couldn't stop thinking about how dirty the seat of her panties was getting from being ground into the fine gray dust under the big chinaberry tree. But since Sarah, with her eyes still closed and her raspy voice still spitting out the litany of "Yeah, ooh, yeah, ooh, yeah, do it," seemed intent on playing this game, she closed her eyes and gave herself over to the pretending.

"Oh, baby," Lena mimicked her friend in earnest and scooted her bottom a little closer to Sarah's. The movement forward suddenly pressed an edge of the newspaper in her panties into the split of her vagina and across her clitoris. "Uh," she yiped in surprise, and the prick of pleasure shot through her pelvis and slowly melted in her stomach.

Her elbows, resting on the crook of a low limb of the chinaberry behind her to prop her back up off the ground, suddenly lost their gristle and slipped off the edge. Her shoulders landed on the ground with a dull plop, raising a dry dust storm around her ears. But Lena didn't stop to give the fall a thought. She was lost in the exquisite wet feeling that was spreading through her hips and rolling down her thighs. Letting the ball of newspaper lead her, she rose up on her elbows and pushed her bottom back toward Sarah, brushing her stuffed panties back up against her friend in search of more of that quick warm feeling.

She opened her eyes briefly to stare into Sarah's face to see if it mirrored what she imagined her own must look like. Satisfied that it did, she closed her eyes again and continued gyrating her little body against her friend's, sucking air between her teeth the way she had done auto-matically when the quick warm thing inside her had melted before.

Suddenly she felt the large strong grasp of a fist clutch her upper arm just below the sleeve of her dress and pull her roughly away from Sarah. At first Lena thought it was the strong arms of the chinaberry tree come to life to grab her. Her eyes flew open.

Sarah's mama's face was a mask of rage. She had just been weary when she came looking for Sarah, calling her name over and over to ask what had happened to the newspaper, but when she found her with Lena pressed together, rubbing against each other in the dust, their panties protruding with the turgescence of her Friday newspaper, she turned furious.

"What are ya'll doing!" she screamed as she loomed over the two girls. "What are ya'll doing over here?"

But she didn't wait for an answer. She just screamed at Lena, "Don't be trying to hide from me. I see you. I see what you doing. You little nasty girl. I shoulda known better than to let Sarah play with you."

Sarah and Lena didn't know what to say. Sarah's mama still had Lena's arm in her grasp and lifted her away from her daughter like a rag doll. "Think you so damn fine with your little red dresses and your hair ribbons and your big house. Well, you ain't so fine, is you? Just another dirty little girl, trying to do nasty when you think ain't nobody looking."

Sarah, seeing the attack on her friend, tried to jump in with an explanation.

"It was me, Mama, it wasn't Lena. It was my game."

But the woman didn't want to hear any of that. "Shut up, Sarah. I know what I see with my own eyes. You go on up to the house. I'll deal with your butt later. You know better than this." But Sarah didn't move.

Then, turning back to Lena, who was trying to wrench herself away from the woman's grasp, "I got a good mind to go across the street and tell you fine-ass ma just what I caught her precious baby doing. Yeah, I oughta go tell her what her precious daughter was doing with my little girl."

Then she turned on Sarah again. "Sarah, if you don't get your ass in that house, you better, girl."

With her attention wandering from Lena, her grasp on the child loosened, too, and Lena, suddenly free, started to dash away from the screaming woman. But Sarah's mama looked back in time and caught Lena's skirt tail in her fist.

"Yeah, but she probably wouldn't believe me. Yeah, probably put it off on Sarah. That's right, little girl, you better run on home, get on out of my yard. You don't own everything, you know." Sarah's mother was about to release her grip on Lena's skirt. Then she had a thought. She flipped the girl's skirt tail and grabbed the elastic band of Lena's panties and reached inside.

"And gimme back my newspaper," she said with a snarl as she yanked the crumpled paper from Lena's drawers. "I ain't read it yet."

Lena ran all the way home and sat quietly on the side porch steps getting her breath until her mama called her in to dinner.

The last thing Lena thought before she fell into a dreamless sleep that night was that she and Sarah would be friends forever, no matter how her mama had acted earlier that day. Nothing could change that.

SARAH HAD ALWAYS been there when Lena called her. Usually, when Lena's household got busy midmorning, she would just go to the end of her driveway and yell for Sarah, and Sarah would emerge from her house or the chinaberry tree and lead Lena safely across the street or just come over to Lena's house to play. Lena could count on Sarah's consistency. Consistency of any kind pleased and reassured Lena in her world of apparitions and uncertainties.

So she couldn't understand it when, late in the afternoon, three days after Sarah's mother had found them rubbing their bodies together, she went to the end of her driveway as usual and shouted for her friend and no one appeared in the yard across the street. No one. Lena didn't think she had ever seen Sarah's house when there wasn't someone playing in the yard or sitting on the porch or standing in the doorway. Whenever she and her family drove past, she always threw up her hand in greeting before she even looked over that way good, as her grandmother said, because she was so sure there would be someone there to return her greeting.

Lena called for Sarah a couple more times, and when she still didn't get a response, she looked both ways up and down Forest Avenue then dashed across the street by herself. She giggled with pride at having made it safely across the street, but as soon as she stepped into Sarah's yard she felt something was different. It was so quiet and still.

Not only was no member of Sarah's family visible, there was no sign that any of them were even there. The front door, usually standing wide open except on the few bitterly cold winter days, was shut tight. No light burned in the front room or the kitchen window on the side. The radio that was turned on every time Lena had ever been there was gone from its spot on the front-room windowsill and the window itself was tightly shut.

"Sarah! Sarah!" She called as she headed around the side of the house past the low limbs of the chinaberry tree that looked as deserted as the house did. But there was no answer. When Lena got around to the back of the house she saw that even the raggedy curtains that had hung at the kitchen window in back were no longer there.

Maybe they're doing spring cleaning like at my house, Lena said to herself. She headed up the plank steps leading to the back porch with the idea in mind of looking through the low kitchen window and rapping on it to stir someone inside. With each step she took, the tiny porch made a mournful squeak that sent small shivers up her legs. But even before she made it to the window, Lena had a strong feeling that she wouldn't like what she saw. So the kitchen with its dirty linoleum floor bare of its few pieces of furniture and the hall without its old dresser and mirror and what she could see of the empty front room didn't surprise her. It just left her very sad. As if she had lost the delicate pearl necklace her grandmama had given her.

At first Lena tried to tell herself that Sarah would probably show up soon, laughing in her familiar raspy way, her brother and sisters in tow. But even as she thought of her friend, Lena realized with a start that she couldn't even remember what her friend's voice sounded like, and her sadness turned to fear.

A sudden cool breeze raised goose bumps on her arms and she looked up and noticed that dark clouds were gathering in the western sky. When the smell of rain blew in on the next gust of wind, Lena knew it was time to go back home. There didn't seem to be anything else to do. She couldn't wait any longer.

As she hurried back through the empty yard in front of Sarah's house, big drops of rain began hitting the ground, raising tiny clouds of gray dust like puffs of smoke. Suddenly, going through Sarah's yard felt like a walk through a graveyard. As a sense of loss enveloped her, Lena began to feel as if her friend Sarah were dead.

Not bothering to look either way, Lena dashed across the street toward her house as the rain started coming down in pellets. She didn't stop running until she had reached the kitchen, where she found her mama and grandmama cleaning out the pantry.

"Mama, Mama," she cried as she ran into the first pair of arms she came to, knocking her mother to the floor. "Sarah's gone, Sarah's gone!"

"What, baby? What in God's name is wrong?" Nellie asked, becoming frantic at the sight of Lena's tears.

"Sarah, she's gone—nothing there. I think she's dead!" Lena sobbed.

"Oh, sugar," Grandmama said as she stooped beside Lena and Nellie sitting on the floor. "I forgot all about it. I shoulda told you, baby."

"Told her what, Miss Lizzie?" Nellie demanded.

"It's Rough-and-Ready, Lena's little friend Sarah. She and her family moved away. Moved on the other side of town, to East Mulberry. You know, Nellie, Yamacraw, you know that neighborhood. Miss Willback 'cross the street told me. Sarah and her people got put out over there. Miss Willback saw their pitiful little few sticks of furniture out in the yard yesterday."

"Sarah's gone, Sarah's gone," was all Lena could say.

"Oh, don't worry, baby, you and your friend can still visit each other," Grandmama tried to reassure her. She would say anything to make Lena feel better.

"Oh no she won't, not in that neighborhood she won't," Nellie said.

"See, I told you Sarah was gone, she's gone for good," Lena cried, her sobs turning into hiccups.

"Lord," Nellie said to Miss Lizzie as she kissed the top of Lena's head and rocked her in the salty, sweaty valley between her breasts.

"My baby is getting to be so high-strung. Just like I was when I was her age."

Nellie's ministration finally calmed Lena down, but it did nothing to ease the knot of pain Lena felt at the loss of her friend. The following fall when she went to grade school for the first time, she stood around in the yard searching for a little girl who looked like Sarah. There was none. All these girls were shined, polished, and pressed, their hair neatly snatched back into braids and barrettes. None had Sarah's rusty beauty. Then one of her first-grade classmates, a chubby girl who stood alone with her blouse already creeping out of her skirt first thing in the morning, caught Lena's attention. Her eyes didn't sparkle like Sarah's, but they did seem to be full of as much mischief. And when Lena sidled up to her, she smiled and slipped her hand into Lena's.

The gesture reminded Lena of Sarah.

When the first bell clanged, Lena and her new friend Gwen marched bravely into the strange schoolhouse side by side.

Still, on her way home from school that day, Lena felt a tug at her heart when she passed Sarah's house and missed her all over again. From time to time down at The Place, Lena saw Sarah's mother, but when the girl tried to speak and ask about Sarah, the woman pretended she hadn't heard and kept walking from the back door on out the front.

Kinfolk and Courtship

KINFOLK AND COURTSHIP

IT IS NO ACCIDENT that kinfolk and courtship are linked here—in the South, courtship was often performed in the service of kinship—or, in some cases, as a rebellion against it. However, in the first story in this section, it is relegated to a mere symbol: a distant star.

"The Star in the Valley," written by Mary Noailles Murfree, a native of middle Tennessee, and published in 1884 when she was thirty-four, will try the reader's patience by its excessive use of dialect. But by persevering, the rewards are many—among them, the purest notion of what it was like, for women particularly, to dwell among those isolated hills during the last century. At times the story seems to take on an Elizabethan ruggedness and crudity that complements the language and the terrain. Yet, even in the most primitive situations, someone can emerge who, by the sheer force of his or her innate moral sense, is able to rise above the limitations of family, home, background. Such a person is Celia Shaw, the heroine of "The Star in the Valley." Her courtship (by the aristocratic stranger, Reginald Chevis) takes place mostly in the minds of the parties involved—the differences between them being, after all, too vast for true courtship:

> She understood him as little. As she sat in the open door-way, with the flare of the fire behind her, and gazed at the red light shining on the crag, she had no idea of the heights of worldly differences that divided them, more insurmountable than precipices and flying chutes of mountain torrents, and chasms and fissures of the wild ravine: she knew nothing of the life he had left, and of its rigorous artificialities and gradations of wealth and estimation. And with a heart full of pitiable unrealities she looked up at the glittering simulacrum of a star on the crag, while he gazed down on the ideal star in the valley.

Yet she—or his idealization of her—has a profound effect on Chevis. She becomes the lodestar by which he leads his easeful life. The story ends on the same note of wistfulness that informs many nineteenth-century novels, including those of Henry James and Edith Wharton— namely, a nostalgia for "what might have been."

IN CONTRAST, the protagonist of "The Ugliest Pilgrim" is no distant symbol; in spite of the awful scar that distorts her face, she is so *prescient* that men are drawn to her. At first the attraction may be mere curiosity, but the quality of her heart and mind soon transforms it into a real interest—a turn of events that causes the reader to increasingly rejoice, and empathize. Violet's need is so compelling that her flaw becomes our flaw, her longing ours, her forgiveness ours, her triumph ours: the Soul made Flesh, the Flesh made Soul, the genius of resonant storytelling.

Maybe the Preacher will claim he can't heal ugliness. And I'm going to spread my palms by my ears and show him—this is a crippled face! An infirmity! Would he do for a kidney or liver what he withholds from a face? The Preacher once stuttered, I read someplace, and God bothered with that. Why not me? When the Preacher labors to heal the sick in his Tulsa auditorium, he asks us at home to lay our fingers on the television screen and pray for God's healing. He puts forth his own ten fingers and we match them, pad to pad, on that glass. I have tried that, Lord, and the Power was too filtered and thinned down for me.

As obsessive as Captain Ahab, she seeks the grace of conversion rather than the hot fury of revenge, not yet understanding that this same grace, because of her compassion, already belongs to her . . . as do its rewards.

THE CLOSEST TIE of kinship and courtship can be found in Ellen Gilchrist's story, "Music." Rhoda Manning, with her endless Lucky Strike cigarettes, her "Te Amos," her nerves as taut as a country boy's guitar string, is a throwback to those glittering flapper belles of Zelda Fitzgerald's day, whose evanescence would flicker briefly before vanishing under the stricter codas of ladyhood and marriage. But Rhoda is made of sterner stuff. Actually, she's a throwback to her own father:

Dudley Manning wasn't afraid of Rhoda, even if she was as stubborn as a goat. Dudley Manning wasn't afraid of anything. He had gotten up at dawn every day for years and believed in himself and followed his luck wherever it led him, dragging his sweet southern wife and his children behind him, and now, in his fortieth year, he was about to become a millionaire.

He was about to become a millionaire and he was in love with a beautiful woman who was not his wife and it was the strangest spring he had ever known.

Ironically, Dudley is really the one who is doing the courting here. And what's Rhoda doing? Savoring life, possibly. Storing up enough amorous adventures, enough Te Amos, to be able to throw some back upon the world.

THE STAR IN THE VALLEY

Mary Noailles Murfree

HE FIRST SAW IT in the twilight of a clear October evening. As the earliest planet sprang into the sky, an answering gleam shone red amid the glooms in the valley. A star too it seemed. And later, when the myriads of the fairer, whiter lights of a moonless night were all athrob in the great concave vault bending to the hills, there was something very impressive in that solitary star of earth, changeless and motionless beneath the ever-changing skies.

Chevis never tired of looking at it. Somehow it broke the spell that draws all eyes heavenward on starry nights. He often strolled with his cigar at dusk down to the verge of the crag, and sat for hours gazing at it and vaguely speculating about it. That spark seemed to have kindled all the soul and imagination within him, although he knew well enough its prosaic source, for he had once questioned the gawky mountaineer whose services he had secured as guide through the forest solitudes during this hunting expedition.

"That thar spark in the valley?" Hi Bates had replied, removing the pipe from his lips and emitting a cloud of strong tobacco smoke. "'Tain't nuthin' but the light in Jerry Shaw's house, 'bout haffen mile from the foot of the mounting. Ye pass that thar house when ye goes on the Christel road, what leads down the mounting off the Back-bone. That's Jerry Shaw's house—that's what it is. He's a blacksmith, an' he kin shoe a horse toler'ble well when he ain't drunk, ez he mos'ly is."

"Perhaps that is the light from the forge," suggested Chevis.

"That thar forge ain't run more 'n half the day, let 'lone o' nights. I hev never hearn tell on Jerry Shaw a-workin' o' nights—nor in the daytime nuther, ef he kin get shet of it. No sech no 'count critter 'twixt hyar an' the Settlemint."

So spake Chevis's astronomer. Seeing the star even through the prosaic lens of stern reality did not detract from its poetic aspect. Chevis never failed to watch for it. The first faint glinting in the azure evening sky sent his eyes to that red reflection suddenly aglow in the valley; even when the mists rose above it and hid it from him, he gazed at the spot where it had disappeared, feeling a calm satisfaction to know that it was still shining beneath the cloud-curtain. He encouraged himself in this bit of sentimentality. These unique eventide effects seemed a fitting sequel to the picturesque day, passed in hunting deer, with horn and hounds, through the gorgeous autumnal forest; or perchance in the more exciting sport in some rocky gorge with a bear at bay and the frenzied pack around him; or in the idyllic pleasures of bird-shooting with a thoroughly trained dog; and coming back in the crimson sunset to a well-appointed tent and a smoking supper of venison or wild turkey—the trophies of his skill. The vague dreaminess of his cigar and the charm of that bright bit of color in the night-shrouded valley added a sort of romantic zest to these primitive enjoyments, and ministered to that keen susceptibility of impressions which Reginald

Chevis considered eminently characteristic of a highly wrought mind and nature.

He said nothing of his fancies, however, to his fellow sportsman, Ned Varney, nor to the mountaineer. Infinite as was the difference between these two in mind and cultivation, his observation of both had convinced him that they were alike incapable of appreciating and comprehending his delicate and dainty musings. Varney was essentially a man of this world; his mental and moral conclusions had been adopted in a calm, mercantile spirit, as giving the best return for the outlay, and the market was not liable to fluctuations. And the mountaineer could go no further than the prosaic fact of the light in Jerry Shaw's house. Thus Reginald Chevis was wont to sit in contemplative silence on the crag until his cigar was burnt out, and afterward to lie awake deep in the night, listening to the majestic lyric welling up from the thousand nocturnal voices of these mountain wilds.

During the day, in place of the red light a gauzy little curl of smoke was barely visible, the only sign or suggestion of human habitation to be seen from the crag in all the many miles of long, narrow valley and parallel tiers of ranges. Sometimes Chevis and Varney caught sight of it from lower down on the mountain side, whence was faintly distinguishable the little log-house and certain vague lines marking a rectangular inclosure; near at hand, too, the forge, silent and smokeless. But it did not immediately occur to either of them to theorize concerning its inmates and their lives in this lonely place; for a time not even to the speculative Chevis. As to Varney, he gave his whole mind to the matter in hand—his gun, his dog, his game—and his note-book was as systematic and as romantic as the ledger at home.

It might be accounted an event in the history of that log-hut when Reginald Chevis, after riding past it eighty yards or so, chanced one day to meet a country girl walking toward the house. She did not look up, and he caught only an indistinct glimpse of her face. She spoke to him, however, as she went by, which is the invariable custom with the inhabitants of the sequestered nooks among the encompassing mountains, whether meeting stranger or acquaintance. He lifted his hat in return, with that punctilious courtesy which he made a point of according to persons of low degree. In another moment she had passed down the narrow sandy road, overhung with gigantic trees, and, at a deft, even pace, hardly slackened as she traversed the great log extending across the rushing stream, she made her way up the opposite hill, and disappeared gradually over its brow.

The expression of her face, half-seen though it was, had attracted his attention. He rode slowly along, meditating. "Did she go into Shaw's house, just around the curve of the road?" he wondered. "Is she Shaw's daughter, or some visiting neighbor?"

That night he looked with a new interest at the red star, set like a jewel in the floating mists of the valley.

"Do you know," he asked of Hi Bates, when the three men were seated, after supper, around the camp-fire, which sent lurid tongues of flame and a thousand bright sparks leaping high in the darkness and illumined the vistas of the woods on every side, save where the sudden crag jutted over the valley—"Do you know whether Jerry Shaw has a daughter—a young girl?"

"Ye-es," drawled Hi Bates, disparagingly, "he hev."

A pause ensued. The star in the valley was blotted from sight; the rising mists had crept to the verge of the crag; nay, in the undergrowth fringing the mountain's brink, there were softly clinging white wreaths.

"Is she pretty?" asked Chevis.

"Waal, no, she ain't," said Hi Bates, decisively. "She's a pore, no 'count critter." Then he added, as if he were afraid of being misapprehended, "Not ez thar is any harm in the gal, ye onderstand. She's a mighty good, saft-spoken, quiet sort o' gal, but she's a pore, white-faced, slim little critter. She looks like she hain't got no sort 'n grit in her. She makes me think o' one o' them slim little slips o' willow every time nor I sees her. She hain't got long ter live, I reckon," he concluded, dismally.

Reginald Chevis asked him no more questions about Jerry Shaw's daughter.

Not long afterward, when Chevis was hunting through the deep woods about the base of the mountain near the Christel road, his horse happened to cast a shoe. He congratulated himself upon his proximity to the forge, for there was a possibility that the blacksmith might be at work; according to the account which Hi Bates had given of Jerry Shaw's habits, there were half a dozen chances against it. But the shop was at no great distance, and he set out to find his way back to the Christel road, guided by sundry well-known landmarks on the mountain side: certain great crags hanging above the tree-tops, showing in grander sublimity through the thinning foliage, or beetling bare and grim; a dismantled and deserted hovel, the red-berried vines twining amongst the rotting logs; the full flow of a tumultuous stream making its last leap down a precipice eighty feet high, with yeasty, maddening waves below and a rainbow-crowned crystal sheet above. And here again the curves of the woodland road. As the sound of the falling water grew softer and softer in the distance, till it was hardly more than a drowsy murmur, the faint vibrations of a far-off anvil rang upon the air. Welcome indeed to Chevis, for however enticing might be the long rambles through the redolent October woods with dog and gun, he had no mind to tramp up the mountain to his tent, five miles distant, leading the resisting horse all the way. The afternoon was so clear and so still that the metallic sound penetrated far through the quiet forest. At every curve of the road he expected to see the log-cabin with its rail fence, and beyond the low-hanging chestnut-tree, half its branches resting upon the roof of the little shanty of a blacksmith's shop. After many windings a sharp turn brought him full upon the humble dwelling, with its background of primeval woods and the purpling splendors of the western hills. The chickens were going to roost in a stunted cedar-tree just without the door; an incredibly old man, feeble and bent, sat dozing in the lingering sunshine on the porch; a girl, with a pail on her head, was crossing the road and going down a declivity toward a spring which bubbled up in a cleft of the gigantic rocks that were piled one above another, rising to a great height. A mingled breath of cool, dripping water, sweet-scented fern, and pungent mint greeted him as he passed it. He did not see the girl's face, for she had left the road before he went by, but he recognized the slight figure, with that graceful poise acquired by the prosaic habit of carrying weights upon the head, and its lithe, swaying beauty reminded him of the mountaineer's comparison——a slip of willow.

And now, under the chestnut-tree, in anxious converse with Jerry Shaw, who came out hammer in hand from the anvil, concerning the shoe to be put on Strathspey's left fore-foot, and the problematic damage sustained since the accident. Chevis's own theory occupied some minutes in expounding, and so absorbed his attention that he did not observe, until the horse was fairly under the blacksmith's hands, that, despite Jerry Shaw's unaccustomed industry, this was by no means a red-letter day in his habitual dissipation. He trembled for Strathspey, but it was too late now to interfere. Jerry Shaw was in that stage of drunkenness which is greatly accented by an elaborate affectation of sobriety. His desire that Chevis should consider him perfectly sober was abundantly manifest in his rigidly steady gait, the preternatural gravity in his bloodshot eyes, his sparingness of speech, and the earnestness with which he enunciated the acquiescent formulae which had constituted his share of the conversation. Now and then, controlling his faculties by a great effort, he looked hard at Chevis to discover what doubts might be expressed in his face concerning the genuineness of this staid deportment; and Chevis presently found it best to affect too. Believing that the blacksmith's histrionic attempts in the *rôle* of sober artisan were occupying his attention more than the paring of Strathspey's hoof, which he held between his knees on his leather apron, while the horse danced an animated measure on the other three feet, Chevis assumed an appearance of indifference and strolled away into the shop. He looked about him, carelessly, at the horseshoes hanging on a rod in the rude aperture that served as window, at the wagon-tires, the plowshares, the glowing fire of the forge. The air within was unpleasantly close, and he soon found himself again in the door-way.

"Can I get some water here?" he asked, as Jerry Shaw reentered and began hammering vigorously at the shoe destined for Strathspey.

The resonant music ceased for a moment. The solemn, drunken eyes were slowly turned upon the visitor, and the elaborate affectation of sobriety was again obtrusively apparent in the blacksmith's manner. He rolled up more closely the blue-checked homespun sleeve from his corded hammer-arm, twitched nervously at the single suspender that supported his copper-colored jeans trousers, readjusted his leather apron hanging about his neck, and, casting upon Chevis another glance, replete with a challenging gravity, fell to work upon the anvil, every heavy and well-directed blow telling with the precision of machinery.

The question had hardly been heard before forgotten. At the next interval, when he was going out to fit the horse, Chevis repeated his request.

"Water, did ye say?" asked Jerry Shaw, looking at him with narrowing eyelids, as if to shut out all other contemplation that he might grapple with this problem. "Thar's no fraish water hyar, but ye kin go yander ter the house and ax fur some; or," he added, shading his eyes from the sunlight with his broad, blackened hand, and looking at the huge wall of stone beyond the road, "ye kin go down yander ter the spring, an' ax that thar gal fur a drink."

Chevis took his way, in the last rays of sunshine, across the road and down the declivity in the direction indicated by the blacksmith. A cool gray shadow fell upon him from the heights of the great rocks as he neared them; the narrow path leading from the road grew dank and moist, and presently his feet were sunk in the still green and odorous water-loving weeds, the clumps of fern, and the pungent mint. He did not notice the soft verdure; he did not even see the beautiful vines that hung from earth-filled niches among the rocks, and lent to their forbidding aspect something of a smiling grace; their picturesque grouping, where they had fallen apart to show this sparkling fountain of bright up-springing water, was all lost upon his artistic perceptions. His eyes were fixed on the girl standing beside the spring, her pail filled, but waiting, with a calm, expectant look on her face, as she saw him approaching.

No creature could have been more coarsely habited: a green cotton dress, faded to the faintest hue; rough shoes, just visible beneath her skirts; a dappled gray and brown calico sun-bonnet, thrown aside on a moss-grown bowlder near at hand. But it seemed as if the wild nature about her had been generous to this being toward whom life and fortune had played the niggard. There were opaline lights in her dreamy eyes, which one sees nowhere save in the sunset clouds that brood above dark hills; the golden sunbeams, all faded from the landscape, had left a per-petual reflection in her bronze hair; there was a subtle affinity between her and other pliant, swaying, graceful young things, waving in the moun-tain breezes, fed by the rain and the dew. She was hardly more human to Chevis than certain lissome little woodland flowers, the very names of which he did not know—pure white, star-shaped, with a faint green line threading its way through each of the five delicate petals; he had seen them embellishing the banks of lonely pools, or growing in dank, marshy places in the middle of the unfrequented road, where perhaps it had been mended in a primitive way with a few rotting rails.

"May I trouble you to give me some water?" asked Chevis, prosai-cally enough. She neither smiled nor replied. She took the gourd from the pail, dipped it into the lucent depths of the spring, handed it to him, and stood awaiting its return when he should have finished. The cool, delicious water was drained, and he gave the gourd back. "I am much obliged," he said.

"Ye're welcome," she replied, in a slow, singing monotone. Had the autumn winds taught her voice that melancholoy cadence?

Chevis would have liked to hear her speak again, but the gulf between his station and hers—so undreamed of by her (for the differences of caste are absolutely unknown to the independent mountaineers), so patent to him—could be bridged by few ideas. They had so little in common that for a moment he could think of nothing to say. His cogitation suggested only the inquiry, "Do you live here?" indicating the little house on the other side of the road.

"Yes," she chanted in the same monotone, "I lives hyar."

She turned to lift the brimming pail. Chevis spoke again: "Do you always stay at home? Do you never go anywhere?"

Her eyes rested upon him, with a slight surprise looking out from among their changing lights. "No," she said, after a pause; "I hev no call to go nowhar ez I knows on."

She placed the pail on her head, took the dappled sun-bonnet in her hand, and went along the path with the assured, steady gait and the graceful backward poise of the figure that precluded the possibility of spilling a drop from the vessel.

He had been touched in a highly romantic way by the sweet beauty of this little woodland flower. It seemed hard that so perfect a thing of its kind should be wasted here, unseen by more appreciative eyes than those of bird, or rabbit, or the equally uncultured human beings about her; and it gave him a baffling sense of the mysterious injustice of life to reflect upon the difference in her lot and that of others of her age in higher spheres. He went thoughtfully through the closing shadows to the shop, mounted the re-shod Strathspey, and rode along the rugged ascent of the mountain, gravely pondering on wordly inequalities.

He saw her often afterward, although he spoke to her again but once. He sometimes stopped as he came and went on the Christel road, and sat chatting with the old man, her grandfather, on the porch, sunshiny days, or lounged in the barn-like door of Jerry Shaw's shop talking to the half-drunken blacksmith. He piqued himself on the readiness with which he became interested in these people, entered into their thoughts and feelings, obtained a comprehensive idea of the machinery of life in this wilderness—more complicated than one could readily believe, looking upon the changeless face of the wide, unpopulated expanse of mountain ranges stretching so far beneath that infinite sky. They appealed to him from the basis of their common humanity, he thought, and the pleasure of watching the development of the common human attributes in this peculiar and primitive state of society never palled upon him. He regarded with contempt Varney's frivolous displeasure and annoyance because of Hi Bates's utter insensibility to the difference in their social position, and the necessity of either acquiescing in the supposititious equality or dispensing with the invaluable services of the proud and independent mountaineer; because of the patois of the untutored people, to hear which, Varney was wont to declare, set his teeth on edge; because of their narrow prejudices, their mental poverty, their idle shiftlessness, their uncouth dress and appearance. Chevis flattered himself that he entertained a broader view. He had not even a subacute idea that he looked upon these people and their inner life only as picturesque bits of the mental and moral landscape; that it was an aesthetic and theoretical pleasure their contemplation afforded him; that he was as far as ever from the basis of common humanity.

Sometimes while he talked to the old man on the sunlit porch, the "slip o' willow" sat in the door-way, listening too, but never speaking. Sometimes he would find her with her father at the forge, her fair, ethereal face illumined with an alien and fluctuating brilliancy, shining and fading as the breath of the fire rose and fell. He came to remember that face so well that in a sorry sketch-book, where nothing else was finished, there were several laborious pages lighted up with a faint reflection of its beauty. But he was as much interested perhaps, though less poetically, in that massive figure, the idle blacksmith. He looked at it all from an ideal point of view. The star in the valley was only a brilliant, set in the night landscape, and suggested a unique and pleasing experience.

How should he imagine what luminous and wistful eyes were turned upward to where another star burned—the light of his campfire on the crag; what pathetic, beautiful eyes had learned to watch and wait for that red gleam high on the mountain's brow—hardly below the stars in heaven it seemed! How could he dream of the strange, vague, unreasoning trouble with which his idle comings and goings had clouded that young life, a trouble as strange, as vague, as vast, as the limitless sky above her.

She understood him as little. As she sat in the open door-way, with the flare of the fire behind her, and gazed at the red light shining on the crag, she had no idea of the heights of worldly differences that divided them, more insurmountable than precipices and flying chutes of mountain torrents, and chasms and fissures of the wild ravine: she knew nothing of the life he had left, and of its rigorous artificialties and gradations of wealth and estimation. And with a heart full of pitiable unrealities she looked up at the glittering simulacrum of a star on the crag, while he gazed down on the ideal star in the valley.

The weeks had worn deep into November. Chevis and Varney were thinking of going home; indeed, they talked of breaking camp day after tomorrow and saying a long adieu to wood and mountain and stream. They had had an abundance of good sport and a surfeit of roughing it. They would go back to town and town avocations invigorated by their holiday, and taking with them a fresh and exhilarating recollection of the forest life left so far behind.

It was near dusk, on a dull, cold evening, when Chevis dismounted before the door of the blacksmith's little log-cabin. The chestnut-tree hung desolate and bare on the eaves of the forge; the stream rushed by in swift gray whirlpools under a sullen gray sky; the gigantic wall of broken rocks loomed gloomy and sinister on the opposite side of the road—not so much as a withered leaf of all their vines clung to their rugged surfaces. The mountains had changed color: the nearest ranges were black with the myriads of the grim black branches of the denuded forest; far away they stretched in parallel lines, rising tier above tier, and showing numberless gradations of a dreary, neutral tint, which grew ever fainter in the distance, till merged in the uniform tone of the sombre sky.

Indoors it was certainly more cheerful. A hickory fire dispensed alike warmth and light. The musical whir of a spinning-wheel added its unique charm. From the rafters depended numberless strings of bright red pepper-pods and ears of pop-corn; hanks of woolen and cotton yarn; bunches of medicinal herbs; brown gourds and little bags of seeds. On rude shelves against the wall were ranged cooking utensils, drinking vessels, etc., all distinguished by that scrupulous cleanliness which is a marked feature of the poor hovels of these mountaineers, and in striking contrast to the poor hovels of lowlanders. The rush-bottomed chairs, drawn in a semicircle before the rough, ill-adjusted stones which did duty as hearth were occupied by several men, who seemed to be making the blacksmith a prolonged visit; various members of the family were humbly seated on sundry inverted domestic articles, such as wash-tubs, and splint-baskets made of white oak. There was circulating amoung Jerry Shaw's friends a flat bottle, facetiously denominated "tickler," readily emptied, but as readily replenished from a keg in the corner. Like the widow's cruse of oil, that keg was miraculously never empty. The fact of a still near by in the wild ravine might suggest a reason for its perennial flow. It was a good strong article of apple-brandy, and its effects were beginning to be distinctly visible.

Truly the ethereal woodland flower seemed strangely incongruous with these brutal and uncouth conditions of her life, as she stood at a little distance from this group, spinning at her wheel. Chevis felt a sudden sharp pang of pity for her when he glanced toward her; the next instant he had forgotten it in his interest in her work. It was altogether at variance with the ideas which he had hitherto entertained concerning that humble handicraft. There came across him a vague recollection from his city life that the peasant girls of art galleries and of the lyric stage were wont to sit at the wheel. "But perhaps they were spinning flax," he reflected. This spinning was a matter of walking back and forth with smooth, measured steps and graceful, undulatory motion; a matter, too, of much pretty gesticulation—the thread in one hand, the other regulating the whirl of the wheel. He thought he had never seen attitudes so charming.

Jerry Shaw hastened to abdicate and offer one of the rush-bottomed chairs with the eager hospitality characteristic of these mountaineers—a hospitality that meets a stranger on the threshold of every hut, presses upon him, ungrudgingly, its best, and follows him on his departure with protestations of regret out to the rickety fence. Chevis was more or less known to all of the visitors, and after a little, under the sense of familiarity and the impetus of the apple-brandy, the talk flowed on as freely as before his entrance. It was wilder and more antagonistic to his principles and prejudices than anything he had hitherto heard among these people, and he looked on and listened, interested in this new development of a phase of life which he thought he had sounded from its lowest note to the top of its compass. He was glad to remain; the scene had impressed his cultivated perceptions as an interior by Teniers might have done, and the vehemence and lawlessness of the conversation and the threats of violence had little reality for him; if he thought about the subject under discussion at all, it was with a reassuring conviction that before the plans could be carried out the already intoxicated mountaineers would be helplessly drunk. Nevertheless, he glanced ever and anon at the young girl, loath that she should hear it, lest its virulent, angry bitterness should startle her. She was evidently listening, too, but her fair face was as calm and untroubled as one of the pure white faces of those flower-stars of his early stay in the mountains.

"Them Peels ought n't ter be let live!" exclaimed Elijah Burr, a gigantic fellow, arrayed in brown jeans, with the accompaniments of knife, powder-horn, etc., usual with the hunters of the range; his gun stood, with those of the other guests, against the wall in a corner of the room. "They ought n't ter be let live, an' I'd top off all three of 'em fur the skin an' horns of a deer."

"That thar is a true word," assented Jerry Shaw. "They oughter be run down an' kilt—all three o' them Peels."

Chevis could not forbear a question. Always on the alert to add to his stock of knowledge of men and minds, always analyzing his own inner life and the inner life of those about him, he said, turning to his intoxicated host, "Who are the Peels, Mr. Shaw—if I may ask?"

"Who air the Peels?" repeated Jerry Shaw, making a point of seizing the question. "They air the meanest men in these hyar mountings. Ye might hunt from Copperhead Ridge ter Clinch River, an' the whole spread o' the valley, an' never hear tell o' no sech no 'count critters."

"They ought n't ter be let live! again urged Elijah Burr. "No man ez treats his wife like that dad-burned scoundrel Ike Peel do oughter be let live. That thar woman is my sister an' Jerry Shaw's cousin—an' I shot him down in his own door year afore las'. I shot him ter kill; but somehow 'nother I war that shaky, an' the cussed gun hung fire a-fust, an' that thar pore wife o' his'n screamed an' hollered so, that I never done nuthin' arter all but lay him up for four month an' better for that thar pore critter ter nuss. He'll see a mightly differ nex' time I gets my chance. An' 't ain't fur off," he added threatingly.

"Wouldn't it be better to persuade her to leave him?" suggested Chevis pacifically, without, however, any wild idea of playing peacemaker between fire and tow.

Burr growled a fierce oath, and then was silent.

A slow fellow on the opposite side of the fireplace explained: "Thar's whar all the trouble kem from. She wouldn't leave him, fur all he treated her awful. She said ez how he war mighty good ter her when he warn't drunk. So 'Lijah shot him."

This way of cutting the Gordian knot of domestic difficulties might have proved efficacious but for the shakiness induced by the thrill of fraternal sentiment, the infusion of apple-brandy, the protest of the bone of contention, and the hanging fire of the treacherous gun. Elijah Burr could remember no other failure of aim for twenty years.

"He won't git shet of me that easy agin!" Burr declared, with another pull at the flat tickler. "But ef it hedn't hev been fur what happened las' week, I mought hev let him off fur awhile," he continued, evidently actuated by some curiously distorted sense of duty in the premises. "I oughter hev kilt him afore. But now the cussed critter is a gone coon. Dad-burn the whole tribe!"

Chevis was desirous of knowing what had happened last week. He did not, however, feel justified in asking more questions. But apple-brandy is a potent tongue-loosener, and the unwonted communicativeness of the stolid and silent mountaineers attested its strength in this regard. Jerry Shaw, without inquiry, enlightened him.

"Ye see," he said, turning to Chevis, "'Lijah he thought ez how ef he could git that fool woman ter come ter his house, he could shoot Ike fur his meanness 'thout botherin' of her, an' things would all git easy agin. Waal, he went thar one day when all them Peels, the whole layout, war gone down ter the Settlemint ter hear the rider preach, an' he jes' run away with two of the brats—the littlest ones, ye onderstand—a-thinkin' he mought tole her off from Ike that thar way. We hearn ez how the pore critter war nigh on ter distracted 'bout 'em, but Ike never let her come arter 'em. Leastways, she never kem. Las' week Ike kem fur 'em hisself—him an' them two cussed brothers o' his'n. All 'Lijah's folks war out 'n the way; him an' his boys war off a-huntin', an' his wife hed gone down ter the spring, a haffen mile an' better, a-washin' clothes; nobody war ter the house 'ceptin' them two chillen o' Ikes. An' Ike an' his brothers jes' tuk the chillen away, an' set fire ter the house; an' time 'Lijah's wife got thar, 't war nuthin' but a pile o' ashes. So we've determined ter go up yander ter Laurel Notch, twenty mile along the ridge of the mounting, ter-night, an' wipe out them Peels—'kase they air a-goin' ter move away. That thar wife o' Ike's, what made all the trouble, hev fretted an' fretted at Ike till he hev determined ter break up an' wagon across the range ter Kaintucky, whar his uncle lives in the hills thar. Ike hev gin his cornsent ter go jes' ter pleasure her, ';kase she air mos' crazed ter git Ike away whar 'Lijah can't kill him. Ike's brothers is a-goin', too. I hearn ez how they'll make a start at noon ter-morrer."

"They 'll never start ter Kaintucky ter-morrer," said Burr, grimly. "They 'll git off, afore that, fur hell, stiddier Kaintucky. I hev been a-tryin' ter make out ter shoot that thar man ever sence that thar gal war married ter him, seven year ago—seven year an' better. But what with her a-foolin' round, an' a-talkin,' an' a-goin' on like she war distracted—she run right 'twixt him an' the muzzle of my gun wunst, or I would hev hed him that time fur sure—an' somehow 'nother that critter makes me so shaky with her ways of goin' on that I feel like I hain't got good sense, an' can't git no good aim at nuthin'. Nex' time, though, thar 'll be a differ. She ain't a-goin' ter Kaintucky along of him ter be beat fur nuthin' when he's drunk.''

It was a pitiable picture presented to Chevis's open-eyed imagination—this woman standing for years between the two men she loved: holding back her brother from his vengeance of her wrongs by that subtle influence that shook his aim; and going into exile with her brute of a husband when that influence had waned and failed, and her wrongs were supplemented by deep and irreparable injuries to her brother. And the curious moral attitude of the man: the strong fraternal feeling that alternately nerved and weakened his revengeful hand.

"We air goin' thar 'bout two o'clock ter-night,'' said Jerry Shaw, "and wipe out all three o' them Peels—Ike an' his two brothers.''

"They oughtn't ter be let live,'' reiterated Elijah Burr, moodily. Did he speak to his faintly stirring conscience, or to a woeful premonition of his sister's grief?

"They 'll all three be stiff an' stark afore daybreak,'' resumed Jerry Shaw. "We air all kin ter 'Lijah, an' we air goin' ter holp him top off them Peels. Thar's ten of us an' three o' them, an' we won't hev no trouble 'bout it. An' we'll bring that pore critter, Ike's wife, an' her chillen hyar ter stay. She's welcome ter live along of us till 'Lijah kin fix some sort'n place fur her an' the little chillen. Thar won't be no trouble a-gettin' rid of the men folks, ez thar is ten of us an' three o' them, an' we air goin' ter take 'em in the night.''

There was a protest from an unexpected quarter. The whir of the spinning-wheel was abruptly silenced. "I don't see no sense,'' said Celia Shaw, her singing monotone vibrating in the sudden lull—"I don't see no sense in shootin' folks down like they war nuthin' better nor bear, nor deer, nor suthin' wild. I don't see no sense in it. An' I never did see none.''

There was an astonished pause.

"Shet up, Cely! Shet up!'' exclaimed Jerry Shaw, in mingled anger and surprise. "Them folks ain't no better nor bear, nor sech. They hain't got no right ter live—them Peels."

"No, that they hain't!" said Burr.

"They is powerful no 'count critters, I know," replied the little woodland flower, the firelight bright in her opaline eyes and on the flakes of burnished gold gleaming in the dark masses of her hair. "They is always a-hangin' round the still an' a-gittin' drunk; but I don't see no sense in a-huntin' 'em down an' a-killin' 'em off. 'Pears ter me like they air better nor the dumb ones. I don't see no sense in shootin' 'em."

"Shet up, Cely! Shet up!" reiterated Shaw.

Celia said no more. Reginald Chevis was pleased with this indication of her sensibility; the other women—her mother and grandmother— had heard the whole recital with the utmost indifference, as they sat by the fire monotonously carding cotton. She was beyond her station in sentiment, he thought. However, he was disposed to recant this favorable estimate of her higher nature when, twice afterward, she stopped her work, and, filling the bottle from the keg, pressed it upon her father, despite her unfavorable criticism of the hangers-on of stills. Nay, she insisted. "Drink some more," she said. "Ye hain't got half enough yit." Had the girl no pity for the already drunken creature? She seemed systematically trying to make him even more helpless than he was.

He had fallen into a deep sleep before Chevis left the house, and the bottle was circulating among the other men with a rapidity that boded little harm to the unconscious Ike Peel and his brothers at Laurel Notch, twenty miles away. As Chevis mounted Strathspey he saw the horses of Jerry Shaw's friends standing partly within and partly without the black- smith's shop. They would stand there all night, he thought. It was darker when he commenced the ascent of the mountain than he had anticipated. And what was this driving against his face—rain? No, it was snow. He had not started a moment too soon. But Strathspey, by reason of frequent travel, knew every foot of the way, and perhaps there would only be a flurry. And so he went on steadily up and up the wild, winding road among the great, bare, black trees and the grim heights and chasms. The snow fell fast—so fast and so silently, before he was half-way to the summit he had lost the vague companionship of the sound of his horse's hoofs, now muffled in the thick carpet so suddenly flung upon the ground. Still the snow fell, and when he had reached the mountain's brow the ground was deeply covered, and the whole aspect of the scene was strange. But though obscured by the fast-flying flakes, he knew that down in the bosom of the white valley there glittered still that changeless star.

"Still spinning, I suppose," he said to himself, as he looked toward it and thought of the interior of the log-cabin below. And then he turned into the tent to enjoy his cigar, his aesthetic reveries, and a bottle of wine.

But the wheel was no longer awhirl. Both music and musician were gone. Toiling along the snow-filled mountain ways; struggling with the fierce gusts of wind as they buffeted and hindered her and fluttered derisively among her thin, worn, old garments; shivering as the driving flakes came full into the pale, calm face, and fell in heavier and heavier wreaths upon the dappled calico sun-bonnet; threading her way through unfrequented woodland paths, that she might shorten the distance; now deftly on the verge of a precipice, whence a false step of those coarse, rough shoes would fling her into unimaginable abysses below; now on the sides of steep ravines, falling sometimes with the treacherous, sliding snow, but never faltering; tearing her hands on the shrubs and vines she clutched to help her forward, and bruised and bleeding, but still going on; trembling more than with the cold, but never turning back, when a sudden noise in the terrible loneliness of the sheeted woods suggested the close proximity of a wild beast, or perhaps, to her ignorant, superstitious mind, a supernatural presence—thus she journeyed on her errand of deliverance.

Her fluttering breath came and went in quick gasps; her failing limbs wearily dragged through the deep drifts; the cruel winds untiringly lashed her; the snow soaked through the faded green cotton dress to the chilled white skin—it seemed even to the dull blood coursing feebly through her freezing veins. But she had small thought for herself during those long, slow hours of endurance and painful effort. Her pale lips moved now and then with muttered speculations: how the time went by; whether they had discovered her absence at home; and whether the fleeter horsemen were even now ploughing their way through the longer, winding mountain road. Her only hope was to outstrip their speed. Her prayer—this untaught being!—she had no prayer, except perhaps her life, the life she was so ready to imperil. She had no high, cultured sensibilities to sustain her. There was no instinct stirring within her that might have nerved her to save her father's, or her brother's, or a benefactor's life. She held the creatures that she would have died to warn in low estimation, and spoke of them with reprobation and contempt. She had known no religious training, holding up forever the sublimest ideal. The measureless mountain wilds were not more infinite to her than that great mystery. Perhaps, without any philosophy, she stood upon the basis of a common humanity.

When the silent horsemen, sobered by the chill night air and the cold snow, made their cautious approach to the little porch of Ike Peel's log-hut at Laurel Notch, there was a thrill of dismayed surprise among them to discover the door standing half open, the house empty of its scanty furniture and goods, its owners fled, and the very dogs disappeared; only, on the rough stones before the dying fire, Celia Shaw, falling asleep and waking by fitful starts.

"Jerry Shaw swore ez how he would hev shot that thar gal o' his'n—that thar Cely," Hi Bates said to Chevis and Varney the next day, when he recounted the incident, "only he didn't think she hed her right mind; a-walkin' through this hyar deep snow full fifteen mile—it's fifteen mile by the short cut ter Laurel Notch—ter git Ike Peel's folks off 'fore 'Lijah an' her dad could come up an' settle Ike an' his brothers. Leastways, 'Lijah an' the t'others, fur Jerry hed got so drunk he couldn't go; he war dead asleep till ter-day, when they kem back a-fotchin' the gal with 'em. That thar Cely Shaw never did look ter me like she hed good sense, nohow. Always looked like she war queer an' teched in the head."

There was a furtive gleam of speculation on the dull face of the mountaineer when his two listeners broke into enthusiastic commendation of the girl's high heroism and courage. The man of ledgers swore that he had never heard of anything so fine, and that he himself would walk through fifteen miles of snow and midnight wilderness for the honor of shaking hands with her. There was that keen thrill about their hearts sometimes felt in crowded theatres, responsive to the cleverly simulated heroism of the boards; or in listening to a poet's mid-air song; or in looking upon some grand and ennobling phase of life translated on a great painter's canvas.

Hi Bates thought that perhaps they too were a little "teched in the head."

There had fallen upon Chevis a sense of deep humiliation. Celia Shaw had heard no more of that momentous conversation than he; a wide contrast was suggested. He began to have a glimmering perception that despite all his culture, his sensibility, his yearnings toward humanity, he was not so high a thing in the scale of being; that he had placed a false estimate upon himself. He had looked down on her with a mingled pity for her dense ignorance, her coarse surroundings, her low station, and a dilettante's delight in picturesque effects, and with no recognition of the moral splendors of that star in the valley. A realization, too, was upon him that fine feelings are of most avail as the motive power of fine deeds.

He and his friend went down together to the little log-cabin. There had been only jeers and taunts and reproaches for Celia Shaw from her own people. These she had expected, and she had stolidly borne them. But she listened to the fine speeches of the city-bred men with a vague wonderment on her flower-like face—whiter than ever to-day.

"It was a splendid—a noble thing to do," said Varney, warmly.

"I shall never forget it," said Chevis. "It will always be like a sermon to me."

There was something more that Reginald Chevis never forgot: the look on her face as he turned and left her forever; for he was on his way back to his former life, so far removed from her and all her ideas and imaginings. He pondered long upon that look in her inscrutable eyes—

was it suffering, some keen pang of despair?—as he rode down and down the valley, all unconscious of the heart-break he left behind him. He thought of it often afterward; he never penetrated its mystery.

He heard of her only once again. On the eve of a famous day, when visiting the outposts of a gallant corps, Reginald Chevis happened to recognize in one of the pickets the gawky mountaineer who had been his guide through those autumnal woods so far away. Hi Bates was afterward sought out and honored with an interview in the general's tent; for the accidental encounter had evoked many pleasant reminiscences in Chevis's mind, and among other questions he wished to ask was what had become of Jerry Shaw's daughter.

"She's dead—long ago," answered Hi Bates. "She died afore the winter war over the year ez ye war a-huntin' thar. She never hed good sense ter my way o' thinkin', nohow, an' one night she run away, an' walked 'bout fifteen mile through a big snow-storm. Some say it settled on her chist. Anyhow, she jes' sorter fell away like afterward, an' never held up her head good no more. She always war a slim little critter, an' looked like she war teched in the head."

There are many things that suffer unheeded in those mountains: the birds that freeze on the trees; the wounded deer that leaves its cruel kind to die alone; the despairing, flying fox with its pursuing train of savage dogs and men. And the jutting crag whence had shone the camp-fire she had so often watched—her star, set forever—looked far over the valley beneath, where in one of those sad little rural graveyards she had been laid so long ago.

But Reginald Chevis has never forgotten her. Whenever he sees the earliest star spring into the evening sky, he remembers the answering red gleam of that star in the valley.

THE UGLIEST PILGRIM

Doris Betts

I SIT IN THE bus station, nipping chocolate peel off a Mounds candy bar with my teeth, then pasting the coconut filling to the roof of my mouth. The lump will dissolve there slowly and seep into me the way dew seeps into flowers.

I like to separate flavors that way. Always I lick the salt off cracker tops before taking my first bite.

Somebody sees me with my suitcase, paper sack, and a ticket in my lap. "You going someplace, Violet?"

Stupid. People in Spruce Pine are dumb and, since I look dumb, say dumb things to me. I turn up my face as if to count those dead flies piled under the lightbulb. He walks away—a fat man, could be anybody. I stick out my tongue at his back; the candy oozes down. If I could stop swallowing, it would drip into my lung and I could breathe vanilla.

Whoever it was, he won't glance back. People in Spruce Pine don't like to look at me, full face.

A Greyhound bus pulls in, blows air; the driver stands by the door. He's black-headed, maybe part Cherokee, with heavy shoulders but a weak chest. He thinks well of himself—I can tell that. I open my notebook and copy his name off the metal plate so I can call him by it when he drives me home again. And next week, won't Mr. Wallace Weatherman be surprised to see how well I'm looking!

I choose the front seat behind Mr. Weatherman, settle my bag with the hat in it, then open the lined composition book again. Maybe it's half full of writing. Even the empty pages toward the back have one repeated entry, high, printed off Mama's torn catechism: GLORIFY GOD AND ENJOY HIM FOREVER.

I finish Mr. Weatherman off in my book while he's running his motor and getting us onto the highway. His nose is too broad, his dark eyes too skimpy—nothing in his face I want—but the hair is nice. I write that down, "Black hair?" I'd want it to curl, though, and be soft as a baby's.

Two others are on the bus, a nigger soldier and an old woman whose jaw sticks out like a shelf. There grow, on the backs of her hands, more veins than skin. One fat blue vessel, curling from wrist to knuckle, would be good; so on one page I draw a sample hand and let blood wind across it like a river. I write at the bottom: "Praise God, it is started. May 29, 1969," and turn to a new sheet. The paper's lumpy and I flip back to the thick envelope stuck there with adhesive tape. I can't lose that.

We're driving now at the best speed Mr. Weatherman can make on these winding roads. On my side there is nothing out the bus window but granite rock, jagged and wet in patches. The old lady and the nigger can see red rhododendron on the slope of Roan Mountain. I'd like to own a tight dress that flower color, and breasts to go under it. I write in my notebook, very small, the word "breasts," and turn quickly to another page. AND ENJOY HIM FOREVER.

The soldier bends as if to tie his shoes, but instead zips open a canvas

The Ugliest Pilgrim · *8*7

bag and sticks both hands inside. When finally he sits back, one hand is clenched around something hard. He catches me watching. He yawns and scratches his ribs, but the right fist sets very lightly on his knee, and when I turn he drinks something out of its cup and throws his head quickly back like a bird or a chicken. You'd think I could smell it, big as my nose is.

Across the aisle the old lady says, "You going far?" She shows me a set of tan, artificial teeth.

"Oklahoma."

"I never been there. I hear the trees give out." She pauses so I can ask politely where she's headed. "I'm going to Nashville," she finally says. "The country-music capital of the world. My son lives there and works in the cellophane plant."

I draw in my notebook a box and two arrows. I crisscross the box.

"He's got three children not old enough to be in school yet."

I sit very still, adding new boxes, drawing baseballs in some, looking busy for fear she might bring out their pictures from her big straw pocketbook. The funny thing is she's looking past my head, though there's nothing out that window but rock wall sliding by. I mumble, "It's hot in here."

Angrily she says, "I had eight children myself."

My pencil flies to get the boxes stacked, eight deep, in a pyramid. "Hope you have a nice visit."

"It's not a visit. I maybe will move." She is hypnotized by the stone and the furry moss in its cracks. Her eyes used to be green. Maybe, when young, she was red-haired and Irish. If she'll stop talking, I want to think about trying green eyes with that Cherokee hair. Her lids droop; she looks drowsy. "I am right tired of children," she says, and lays her head back on the white rag they button on these seats.

Now that her eyes are covered, I can study that face—china white, and worn thin as tissue so light comes between her bones and shines through her whole head. I picture the light going around and around her skull, like water spinning in a jar. If I could wait to be eighty, even my face might grind down and look softer. But I'm ready, in case the Preacher mentions that. Did Elisha make Naaman bear into old age his leprosy? Didn't Jesus heal the withered hand, even on Sunday, without waiting for the work week to start? And put back the ear of Malchus with a touch? As soon as Job had learned enough, did his boils fall away?

Lord, I have learned enough.

The old lady sleeps while we roll downhill and up again; then we turn so my side of the bus looks over the valley and its thickety woods where, as a girl, I pulled armloads of galax, fern, laurel, and hemlock to have some spending money. I spent it for magazines full of women with permanent waves. Behind us, the nigger shuffles a deck of cards and deals to himself by fives. Draw poker—I could beat him. My papa showed me, long winter days and nights snowed in on the mountain. He said poker would teach me arithmetic. It taught me there are four ways to make a royal flush, and with two players, it's an even chance one of them holds a pair on the deal. And when you try to draw from a pair to four of a kind, discard the kicker; it helps your odds.

The soldier deals smoothly, using his left hand only with his thumb on top. Papa was good at that. He looks up and sees my whole face with its scar, but he keeps his eyes level as if he has seen worse things; and his left hand drops cards evenly and in rhythm. Like a turtle, laying eggs.

I close my eyes and the riffle of his deck rests me to the next main stop where I write in my notebook: "Praise God for Johnson City, Tennessee, and all the state to come. I am on my way."

AT KINGSPORT, Mr. Weatherman calls rest stop and I go straight through the terminal to the ladies' toilet and look hard at my face in the mirror. I must remember to start the Preacher on the scar first of all— the only thing about me that's even on both sides.

Lord! I am so ugly!

Maybe the Preacher will claim he can't heal ugliness. And I'm going to spread my palms by my ears and show him—this is a crippled face! An infirmity! Would he do for a kidney or liver what he withholds from a face? The Preacher once stuttered, I read someplace, and God bothered with that. Why not me? When the Preacher labors to heal the sick in his Tulsa auditorium, he asks us at home to lay our fingers on the television screen and pray for God's healing. He puts forth his own ten fingers and we match them, pad to pad, on that glass. I have tried that, Lord, and the Power was too filtered and thinned down for me.

I touch my hand now to this cold mirror glass, and cover all but my pimpled chin, or wide nose, or a single red-brown eye. And nothing's too bad by itself. But when they're put together?

I've seen the Preacher wrap his hot, blessed hands on a club foot and cry out, "HEAL!" in his funny way that sounds like the word "Hell" broken into two pieces. Will he not cry out, too, when he sees this poor, clubbed face? I will be to him as Goliath was to David, a need so giant it will drive God to action.

I comb out my pine-needle hair. I think I would like blond curls and Irish eyes, and I want my mouth so large it will never be done with kissing.

The old lady comes in to the toilet and catches me pinching my bent face. She jerks back once, looks sad, then pets me with her twiggy hand. "Listen, honey," she says, "I had looks once. It don't amount to much."

I push right past. Good people have nearly turned me against you, Lord. They open their mouths for the milk of human kindness and boiling oil spews out.

So I'm half running through the terminal and into the café, and I take the first stool and call down the counter, "Tuna-fish sandwich," quick. Living in the mountains, I eat fish every chance I get and wonder what the sea is like. Then I see I've sat down by the nigger soldier. I do not want to meet his gaze, since he's a wonder to me, too. We don't have many black men in the mountains. Mostly they live east in Carolina, on the flatland, and pick cotton and tobacco instead of apples. They seem to me like foreigners. He's absently shuffling cards the way some men twiddle thumbs. On the stool beyond him is a paratrooper, white, and they're talking about what a bitch the army is. Being sent to the same camp has made them friends already.

I roll a dill-pickle slice through my mouth—a wheel, a bitter wheel. Then I start on the sandwich and it's chicken by mistake when I've got chickens all over my backyard.

"Don't bother with the beer," says the black one. "I've got better on the bus." They come to some agreement and deal out cards on the counter.

It's just too much for me. I lean over behind the nigger's back and say to the paratrooper, "I wouldn't play with him." Neither one moves. "He's a mechanic." They look at each other, not at me. "It's a way to cheat on the deal."

The paratrooper sways backward on his stool and stares around out of eyes so blue that I want them, right away, and maybe his pale blond hair. I swallow a crusty half-chewed bite. "One-handed grip; the mechanic's grip. It's the middle finger. He can second-deal and bottom-deal. He can buckle the top card with his thumb and peep."

"I be damn," says the paratrooper.

The nigger spins around and bares his teeth at me, but it's half a grin. "Lady, you want to play?"

I slide my dishes back. "I get mad if I'm cheated."

"And mean when you're mad." He laughs a laugh so deep it makes me retaste that bittersweet chocolate off the candy bar. He offers the deck to cut, so I pull out the center and restack it three ways. A little air blows through his upper teeth. "I'm Grady Fliggins and they call me Flick."

The paratrooper reaches a hand over the counter to shake mine. "Monty Harrill. From near to Raleigh."

"And I'm Violet Karl. Spruce Pine. I'd rather play five-card stud."

By the time the bus rolls on, we've moved to its wider back seat playing serious cards with a fifty-cent ante. My money's sparse, but I'm good and the deck is clean. The old lady settles into my front seat, stiffer than plaster. Sometimes she throws back a hurt look.

The Ugliest Pilgrim · 91

Monty, the paratrooper, plays soft. But Flick's so good he doesn't even need to cheat, though I watch him close. He drops out quick when his cards are bad; he makes me bid high to see what he's got; and the few times he bluffs, I'm fooled. He's no talker. Monty, on the other hand, says often "Whose play is it?" till I know that's his clue phrase for a pair. He lifts his cards close to his nose and gets quiet when planning to bluff. And he'd rather use wild cards but we won't. Ah, but he's pretty, though!

After we've swapped a little money, mostly the paratrooper's, Flick pours us a drink in some cups he stole in Kingsport and asks, "Where'd you learn to play?"

I tell him about growing up on a mountain, high, with Mama dead, and shuffling cards by a kerosene lamp with my papa. When I passed fifteen, we'd drink together, too. Applejack or a beer he made from potato peel.

"And where you headed now?" Monty's windburned in a funny pattern, with pale goggle circles that start high on his cheeks. Maybe it's something paratroopers wear.

"It's a pilgrimage." They lean back with their drinks. "I'm going to see this preacher in Tulsa, the one that heals, and I'm coming home pretty. Isn't that healing?" Their still faces make me nervous. "I'll even trade if he says . . . I'll take somebody else's weak eyes or deaf ears. I could stand limping a little."

The nigger shakes his black head, snickering.

"I tried to get to Charlotte when he was down there with his eight-pole canvas cathedral tent that seats nearly fifteen thousand people, but I didn't have money then. Now what's so funny?" I think for a minute I am going to have to take out my notebook and unglue the envelope and read them all the Scripture I have looked up on why I should be healed. Monty looks sad for me, though, and that's worse. "Let the Lord twist loose my foot or give me a cough, so long as I'm healed of my looks while I'm still young enough—" I stop and tip up my plastic cup. Young enough for you, blue-eyed boy, and your brothers.

"Listen," says Flick in a high voice. "Let me go with you and be there for that swapping." He winks one speckled eye.

"I'll not take black skin, no offense." He's offended, though, and lurches across the moving bus and falls into a far seat. "Well, you as much as said you'd swap it off!" I call. "What's wrong if I don't want it any more than you?"

Monty slides closer. "You're not much to look at," he grants, sweeping me up and down till I nearly glow blue from his eyes. Shaking his head, "And what now? Thirty?"

"Twenty-eight. His drink and his cards, and I hurt Flick's feelings. I didn't mean that." I'm scared, too. Maybe, unlike Job, I haven't learned enough. Who ought to be expert in hurt feelings? Me, that's who.

"And you live by yourself?"

I start to say, "No, there's men falling all over each other going in and out my door." He sees my face, don't he? It makes me call, "Flick? I'm sorry." Not one movement. "Yes. By myself." Five years now, since Papa had heart failure and fell off the high back porch and rolled downhill in the gravel till the hobblebushes stopped him. I found him past sunset, cut from the rocks but not much blood showing. And what there was, dark, and already jellied.

Monty looks at me carefully before making up his mind to say, "That preacher's a fake. You ever see a doctor agree to what he's done?"

"Might be." I'm smiling. I tongue out the last liquor in my cup. I've thought of all that, but it may be what I believe is stronger than him faking. That he'll be electrified by my trust, the way a magnet can get charged against its will. He might be a lunatic or a dope fiend, and it still not matter.

Monty says, "Flick, you plan to give us another drink?"

"No." He acts like he's going to sleep.

"I just wouldn't count on that preacher too much." Monty cleans his nails with a matchbook corner and sometimes gives me an uneasy look. "Things are mean and ugly in this world—I mean *act* ugly, do ugly, be ugly."

The Ugliest Pilgrim · 93

He's wrong. When I leave my house, I can walk for miles and everything's beautiful. Even the rattlesnakes have grace. I don't mind his worried looks, since I'm writing in my notebook how we met and my winnings—a good sign, to earn money on a trip. I like the way the army barbers trim his hair. I wish I could touch it.

"Took one furlough in your mountains. Pretty country. Maybe hard to live in? Makes you feel little." He looks toward Flick and says softer, "Makes you feel like the night sky does. So many stars."

"Some of them big as daisies." It's easy to live in, though. Some mornings a deer and I scare up each other in the brush, and his heart stops, and mine stops. Everything stops till he plunges away. The next pulse beat nearly knocks you down. "Monty, doesn't your hair get lighter in the summers? That might be a good color to ask for in Tulsa. Then I could turn colors like the leaves. Spell your last name for me."

He does, and says I sure am funny. Then he spells Grady Fliggins and I write that, too. He's curious about my book, so I flip through and offer to read him parts. Even with his eyes shut, Flick is listening. I read them about my papa's face, a chunky block face, not much different from the Preacher's square one. After Papa died, I wrote that to slow down how fast I was forgetting him. I tell Monty parts of my lists: that you can get yellow dye out of gopherwood and Noah built his ark from that, and maybe it stained the water. That a cow eating snakeroot might give poison milk. I pass him a pressed maypop flower I'm carrying to Tulsa, because the crown of thorns and the crucifixion nails grow in its center, and each piece of the bloom stands for one of the apostles.

"It's a mollypop vine," says Flick out of one corner of his mouth. "And it makes a green ball that pops when you step on it." He stretches. "Deal you some blackjack?"

For no reason, Monty says, "We oughtn't to let her go."

We play blackjack till supper stop and I write in my book, "Praise God for Knoxville and two new friends." I've not had many friends. At school in the valley, I sat in the back rows, reading, a hand spread on my face. I was smart, too; but if you let that show, you had to stand for the class and present different things.

When the driver cuts out the lights, the soldiers give me a whole seat, and a duffelbag for a pillow. I hear them whispering, first about women, then about me; but after a while I don't hear that anymore.

By the time we hit Nashville, the old lady makes the bus wait while she begs me to stop with her. "Harvey won't mind. He's a good boy." She will not even look at Monty and Flick. "You can wash and change clothes and catch a new bus tomorrow."

"I'm in a hurry. Thank you." I have picked a lot of galax to pay for this trip.

"A girl alone. A girl that maybe feels she's got to prove something?" The skin on her neck shivers. "Some people might take advantage."

Maybe when I ride home under my new face, that will be some risk. I shake my head, and as she gets off she whispers something to Mr. Weatherman about looking after me. It's wasted, though, because a new driver takes his place and he looks nearly as bad as I do—oily-faced, and toad-shaped, with eyeballs a dingy color and streaked with blood. He's the flatlands driver, I guess, because he leans back and drops one warty hand on the wheel and we go so fast and steady you can hardly tell it.

Since Flick is the tops in cards and we're tired of that, it's Monty's turn to brag on his motorcycle. He talks all across Tennessee till I think I could ride one by hearsay alone, that my wrist knows by itself how far to roll the throttle in. It's a Norton and he rides it in Scrambles and Enduro events, in his leathers, with spare parts and tools glued all over him with black electrician's tape.

"So this bastard tells me, 'Zip up your jacket because when I run over you I want some traction.'"

Flick is playing solitaire. "You couldn't get me on one of them killing things."

"One day I'm coming through Spruce Pine, flat out, throw Violet up behind me! We're going to lean all the way through them mountains.

Sliding the right foot and then sliding the left." Monty lays his head back on the seat beside me, rolls it, watches. "How you like that? Take you through creeks and ditches like you was on a skateboard. You can just holler and hang on."

Lots of women have, I bet.

"The Norton's got the best front forks of anybody. It'll nearly roll up a tree trunk and ride down the other side." He demonstrates on the seat back. I keep writing. These are new things, two-stroke and four-stroke, picking your line on a curve, Milwaukee iron. It will all come back to me in the winters, when I reread these pages.

Flick says he rode on a Harley once. "Turned over and got drug. No more."

They argue about what he should have done instead of turning over. Finally Monty drifts off to sleep, his head leaning at me slowly, so I look down on his crisp, light hair. I pat it as easy as a cat would, and it tickles my palm. I'd almost ask them in Tulsa to make me a man if I could have hair like his, and a beard, and feel so different in so many places.

He slides closer in his sleep. One eyebrow wrinkles against my shoulder. Looking our way, Flick smokes a cigarette, then reads some magazine he keeps rolled in his belt. Monty makes a deep noise against my arm as if, while he slept, his throat had cleared itself. I shift and his whole head is on my shoulder now. Its weight makes me breathe shallow.

I rest my eyes. If I should turn, his hair would barely touch my cheek, the scarred one, like a shoebrush. I do turn and it does. For miles he sleeps that way and I almost sleep. Once, when we take a long curve, he rolls against me, and one of his hands drifts up and then drops in my lap. Just there, where the creases are.

I would not want God's Power to turn me, after all, into a man. His breath is so warm. Everywhere, my skin is singing. Praise God for that.

WHEN I GET my first look at the Mississippi River, the pencil goes straight into my pocketbook. How much praise would that take?

"Is the sea like this?"

"Not except they're both water," Flick says. He's not mad anymore. "Tell you what, Vi-oh-LETTE. When Monty picks you up on his cycle" ("sickle," he calls it), "you ride down to the beaches—Cherry Grove, O.D., around there. Where they work the big nets in the fall and drag them up on the sand with trucks at each end, and men to their necks in the surf."

"You do that?"

"I know people that do. And afterward they strip and dress by this big fire on the beach."

And they make chowder while this cold wind is blowing! I know that much, without asking. In a big black pot that sits on that whipping fire. I think they might let me sit with them and stir the pot. It's funny how much, right now, I feel like praising all the good things I've never seen, in places I haven't been.

Everybody has to get off the bus and change in Memphis, and most of them wait a long time. I've taken the long way, coming here; but some of Mama's cousins live in Memphis and might rest me overnight. Monty says they plan to stay the night, too, and break the long trip.

"They know you're coming Violet?" It's Flick says my name that way, in pieces, carefully: Vi-oh-LETTE. Monty is lazier: Viii-lut. They make me feel like more than one.

"I've never even met these cousins. But soon as I call up and tell them who I am and that I'm here . . ."

"We'll stay some hotel tonight and then ride on. Why don't you come with us?" Monty is carrying my scuffed bag. Flick swings the paper sack. "You know us better than them."

"Kin people," grunts Flick, "can be a bad surprise."

Monty is nodding his head. "Only cousin I had got drunk and drove this tractor over his baby brother. Did it on purpose, too." I see by his face that Monty made this up, for my sake.

"Your cousins might not even live here anymore. I bet it's been years since you heard from a one."

"We're picking a cheap hotel, in case that's a worry."

The Ugliest Pilgrim · 97

I never thought they might have moved. "How cheap?"

When Flick says, "Under five," I nod; and my things go right up on their shoulders as I follow them into a Memphis cab. The driver takes for granted I'm Monty's afflicted sister and names a hotel right off. He treats me with pity and good manners.

And the hotel he chooses is cheap, all right, where ratty salesmen with bad territories spend half the night drinking in their rooms. Plastic palm bushes and a worn rug the color of wet cigars. I get Room 210 and they're down the hall in the teens. They stand in my doorway and watch me drop both shoes and walk the bed in bare feet. When Monty opens my window, we can hear some kitchen underneath—a fan, clattering noise, a man's crackly voice singing about the California earthquake.

It scares me, suddenly, to know I can't remember how home sounds. Not one bird call, nor the water over rocks. There's so much you can't save by writing down.

"Smell that grease," says Flick, and shakes his head till his lips flutter. "I'm finding an ice machine. You, Vi-oh-LETTE, come on down in a while."

Monty's got a grin I'll remember if I never write a word. He waves. "Flick and me going to get drunker than my old cousin and put wild things in your book. Going to draw dirty pictures. You come on down and get drunk enough to laugh."

But after a shower, damp in my clean slip, even this bed like a roll of fence wire feels good, and I fall asleep wondering if that rushing noise is a river wind, and how long I can keep it in my mind.

Monty and Flick edge into my dream. Just their voices first, from way downhill. Somewhere in a Shonny Haw thicket. "Just different," Monty is saying. "That's all. Different. Don't make some big thing out of it." He doesn't sound happy. "Nobody else," he says.

Is that Flick singing? No, because the song goes on while his voice says, "Just so . . ." and then some words I don't catch. "It don't hurt"? Or maybe, "You don't hurt"? I hear them climbing my tangled hill, breaking sticks, and knocking the little stones loose. I'm trying to call them which way the path is, but I can't make noise because the Preacher took my voice and put it in a black bag and carried it to a sick little boy in Iowa.

They find the path, anyway. And now they can see my house and me standing little by the steps. I know how it looks from where they are: the wood rained on till the siding's almost silver; and behind the house a wet-weather waterfall that's cut a stream bed downhill and grown pin cherry and bee balm on both sides. The high rock walls by the waterfall are mossy and slick, but I've scraped one place and hammered a mean-looking gray head that leans out of the hillside and stares down the path at whoever comes. I've been here so long by myself that I talk to it sometimes. Right now I'd say, "Look yonder. We've got company at last!" if my voice wasn't gone.

"You can't go by looks," Flick is saying as they climb. He ought to know. Ahead of them, warblers separate and fly out on two sides. Everything moves out of their path if I could just see it—tree frogs and mosquitoes. Maybe the worms drop deeper just before a footstep falls.

"Without the clothes, it's not a hell of a lot improved," says Monty, and I know suddenly they are inside the house with me, inside my very room, and my room today's in Memphis. "There's one thing, though," Monty says, standing over my bed. "Good looks in a woman is almost like a wall. She can use it to shut you outside. You never know what she's like, that's all." He's wearing a T-shirt and his dog tags jingle. "Most of the time I don't even miss knowing that."

And Flick says, disgusted, "I knew that much in grammar school. You sure are slow. It's not the face you screw." If I opened my eyes, I could see him now, behind Monty. He says, "After a while, you don't even notice faces. I always thought, in a crowd, my mother might not pick Daddy out."

"*My* mother could," says Monty. "He was always the one *started* the fight."

I stretch and open my eyes. It's a plain slip, cotton, that I sewed myself and makes me look too white and skinny as a sapling.

"She's waking up."

When I point, Monty hands me the blouse off the doorknob. Flick says they've carried me a soda pop, plus something to spruce it up. They sit stiffly on two hard chairs till I've buttoned on my skirt. I sip the drink, cold but peppery, and prop on the bed pillows. "I dreamed you both came where my house is, on the mountain, and it had rained so the waterfall was working. I felt real proud of that."

After two drinks we go down to the noisy restaurant with that smelly grease. And after that, to a picture show. Monty grins widely when the star comes on the screen. The spit on his teeth shines, even in the dark. Seeing what kind of woman he really likes, black-haired as a gypsy and with a juicy mouth, I change all my plans. My eyes, too, must turn up on the ends and when I bend down my breasts must fall forward and push at each other. When the star does that in the picture, the cowboy rubs his mustache low in the front of her neck.

In the darkness, Monty takes my hand and holds it in his swelling lap. To me it seems funny that my hand, brown and crusty from hoeing and chopping, is harder than his. I guess you don't get calluses rolling a motorcycle throttle. He rubs his thumb up and down my middle finger. Oh, I would like to ride fast behind him, spraddle-legged with my arms wrapped on his belt, and I would lay my face between his sharp shoulder blades.

That night, when I've slept awhile, I hear something brushing the rug in the hall. I slip to my door. It's very dark. I press myself, face first, to the wood. There's breathing on the other side. I feel I get fatter, standing there, than even my own small breasts might now be made to touch. I round both shoulders to see. The movement jars the door and it trembles slightly in its frame.

From the far side, by the hinges, somebody whispers, "Vi-oh-LETTE?"

Now I stand very still. The wood feels cooler on my skin, or else I have grown very warm. Oh, I could love anybody! There is so much of me now, they could line up strangers in the hall and let me hold each one better than he had ever been held before!

Slowly I turn the knob, but Flick's breathing is gone. The corridor's empty. I leave the latch off.

Late in the night, when the noise from the kitchen is over, he comes into my room. I wake when he bumps on a chair, swears, then scrabbles at the footboard.

"Viii-lut?"

I slide up in bed. I'm not ready, not now, but he's here. I spread both arms wide. In the dark he can't tell.

He feels his way onto the bed and he touches my knee and it changes. Stops being just my old knee, under his fingers. I feel the joint heat up and bubble. I push the sheet down.

He comes onto me, whispering something. I reach up to claim him.

One time he stops. He's surprised, I guess, finding he isn't the first. How can I tell him how bad that was? How long ago? The night when the twelfth grade was over and one of them climbed with me all the way home? And he asked. And I thought, *I'm entitled.* Won him a five-dollar bet. Didn't do nothing for me.

But this time I sing out and Monty says, "Shh," in my ear. And he starts over, slow, and makes me whimper one other time. Then he turns sideways to sleep and I try my face there, laid in the nest on his damp back. I reach out my tongue. He is salty and good.

Now there are two things too big for my notebook but praise God! And for the Mississippi, too!

THERE IS NO good reason for me to ride with them all the way to Fort Smith, but since Tulsa is not expecting me, we change my ticket. Monty pays the extra. We ride through the fertile plains. The last of May becomes June and the Arkansas sun is blazing. I am stunned by this heat. At home, night means blankets and even on hot afternoons it may rain and start the waterfall. I lie against my seat for miles without a word.

"What's wrong?" Monty keeps asking; but, under the heat, I am happy. Sleepy with happiness, a lizard on a rock. At every stop Monty's off the bus, bringing me more than I can eat or drink, buying me magazines and gum. I tell him and Flick to play two-handed cards, but mostly Flick lectures him in a low voice about something.

I try to stop thinking of Memphis and think back to Tulsa. I went to the Spruce Pine library to look up Tulsa in their encyclopedia. I thought sure it would tell about the Preacher, and on what street he'd built his Hope and Glory Building for his soul crusades. Tulsa was listed in the *Americana,* Volume 27, Trance to Venial Sin. I got so tickled with that I forgot to write down the rest.

Now, in the hot sun, clogged up with trances and venial sins, I dream under the drone of their voices. For some reason I remember that old lady back in Nashville, moved in with Harvey and his wife and their three children. I hope she's happy. I picture her on Harvey's back porch, baked in the sun like me, in a rocker. Snapping beans.

I've left my pencil in the hotel and must borrow one from Flick to write in my book. I put in, slowly, "This is the day which the Lord hath made." But, before Monty, what kind of days was He sending me? I cross out the line. I have this wish to praise, instead of Him, the littlest things. Honeybees, and the wet slugs under their rocks. A gnat in some farmer's eye.

I give up and hand Flick his pencil. He slides toward the aisle and whispers, "You wish you'd stayed in your mountains?"

I shake my head and a piece of my no-color hair falls into the sunlight. Maybe it even shines.

He spits on the pencil point and prints something inside a gum wrapper. "Here's my address. You keep it. Never can tell."

So I tear the paper in half and give him back mine. He reads it a long time before tucking it away, but he won't send a letter till I do—I can tell that. Through all this, Monty stares out the window. Arkansas rolls out ahead of us like a rug.

Monty has not asked for my address, nor how far uphill I live from

Spruce Pine, though he could ride his motorcycle up to me, strong as its engine is. For a long time he has been sitting quietly, lighting one cigarette off another. This winter, I've got to learn smoking. How to lift my hand up so every eye will follow it to my smooth cheek.

I put Flick's paper in my pocketbook and there, inside, on a round mirror, my face is waiting in ambush for me. I see the curved scar, neat as ever, swoop from the edge of one nostril in rainbow shape across my cheek, then down toward the ear. For the first time in years, pain boils across my face as it did that day. I close my eyes under that red drowning, and see again papa's ax head rise off its locust handle and come floating through the air, sideways, like a gliding crow. And it drops down into my face almost daintily, the edge turned just enough to slash loose a flap of skin the way you might slice straight down on the curve of a melon. My papa is yelling, but I am under a red rain and it bears me down. I am lifted and run with through the wood yard and into the barn. Now I am slumped on his chest and the whipped horse is throwing us down the mountainside, and my head is wrapped in something big as a wet quilt. The doctor groans when he winds if off and I faint while he lifts up my flesh like the flap of a pulpy envelope and sews the white bone out of sight.

Dizzy from the movement of the bus, I snap shut my pocketbook.

Whenever I cry, the first drop quivers there, in the curving scar, and then runs crooked on that track to the ear. I cry straight down on the other side.

I am glad this bus has a toilet. I go there to cool my eyes with wet paper and spit up Monty's chocolate and cola.

When I come out, he's standing at the door with his fist up. "You all right, Viii-lut? You worried or something?"

I see he pities me. In my seat again, I plan the speech I will make at Fort Smith and the laugh I will give. "Honey, you're good," I'll say, laughing, "but the others were better." That ought to do it. I am quieter now than Monty is, practicing it in my mind.

It's dark when we hit Fort Smith. Everybody's face looks shadowed and different. Mine better. Monty's strange. We're saying good-byes very fast. I start my speech twice and he misses it twice.

Then he bends over and offers his own practiced line that I see he's worked up all across Arkansas, "I plan to be right here, Violet, in this bus station. On Monday. All day. You get off your bus when it comes through. Hear me, Viii-lut? I'll watch for you?"

No. He won't watch. Nor I come. "My schedule won't take me this road going back. Bye, Flick. Lots of good luck to both of you."

"Promise me. Like I'm promising."

"Good luck to you, Vi-oh-LETTE." Flick lets his hand fall on my head and it feels as good as anybody's hand.

Monty shoves money at me and I shove it back. "Promise," he says, his voice furious. He tries to kiss me in the hair and I jerk so hard my nose cracks his chin. We stare, blurry-eyed and hurting. He follows Flick down the aisle, calls back, "I'm coming here Monday. See you then, hear? And you get off this bus!"

"No! I won't!"

He yells it twice more. People are staring. He's out of the bus pounding the steel wall by my seat. I'm not going to look. The seats fill up with strangers and we ride away, nobody is talking to anyone else. My nose where I hit it is going to swell—the Preacher will have to throw that in for free. I look back, but he's gone.

The lights in the bus go out again. Outside they bloom thick by the streets, then thinner, then mostly gone as we pass into the countryside. Even in the dark, I can see Oklahoma's mountains are uglier than mine. Knobs and hills, mostly. The bus drives into rain which covers up everything. At home I like that washing sound. We go deeper into the downpour. Perhaps we are under the Arkansas River, after all. It seems I can feel its great weight move over me.

Before daylight, the rain tapers off and here the ground looks dry, even barren. Cattle graze across long fields. In the wind, wheat fields shiver. I can't eat anything all the way to Tulsa. It makes me homesick to see the land grow brighter and flatter and balder. That old lady was right—the trees do give out—and oil towers grow in their place. The glare's in my eyes. I write in my notebook, "Praise God for Tulsa; I am nearly there," but it takes a long time to get the words down.

One day my papa told me how time got slow for him when Mama died. How one week he waded through the creek and it was water, and the next week cold molasses. How he'd lay awake a year between sundown and sunup, and in the morning I'd be a day older and he'd be three hundred and sixty-five.

It works the other way, too. In no time at all, we're into Tulsa without me knowing what we've passed. So many tall buildings. Everybody's running. They rush into taxis before I can get one to wait for me long enough to ask the driver questions. But still I'm speeded to a hotel, and the elevator yanks me to a room quicker than Elijah rode to Heaven. The room's not bad. A Gideon Bible. Inside are lots of dirty words somebody wrote. He must have been feeling bad.

I bathe and dress, trembling from my own speed, and pin on the hat which has traveled all the way from Spruce Pine for this. I feel tired. I go out into the loud streets full of fast cars. Hot metal everywhere. A taxi roars me across town to the Preacher's church.

It looks like a big insurance office, though I can tell where the chapel is by colored glass in the pointed windows. Carved in an arch over the door are the words. "HOPE OF GLORY BUILDING." Right away, something in me sinks. All this time I've been hearing it on TV as the Hope *and* Glory Building. You wouldn't think one word could make that much difference.

Inside the door, there's a list of offices and room numbers. I don't see the Preacher's name. Clerks send me down long, tiled halls, past empty air-conditioned offices. One tells me to go up two flights and ask the fat woman, and the fat woman sends me down again. I'm carrying my notebook in a dry hand, feeling as brittle as the maypop flower.

At last I wait an hour to see some assistant—very close to the Preacher, I'm told. His waiting room is chilly, the leatherette chairs worn down to the mesh. I try to remember how much TB and cancer have passed through this very room and been jerked out of people the way Jesus tore out a demon and flung him into a herd of swine. I wonder what he felt like to the swine.

After a long time, the young man calls me into his plain office—wood desk, wood chairs, shelves of booklets and colored folders. On one wall, a colored picture of Jesus with that fairy ring of light around His head. Across from that, one of His praying hands—rougher than Monty's, smoother than mine.

The young man wears glasses with no rims. In this glare, I am reflected on each lens, Vi-oh-LETTE and Viii-lut. On his desk is a box of postcards of the Hope and Glory Building. *Of* Glory. *Of* Glory.

I am afraid.

I feel behind me for the chair.

The man explains that he is presently in charge. The Preacher's speaking in Tallahassee, his show taped weeks ahead. I never thought of it as a show before. He waits.

I reach inside my notebook where, taped shut, is the thick envelope with everything written down. I knew I could never explain things right. When have I ever been able to tell what I really felt? But it's all in there—my name, my need. The words from the Bible which must argue for me. I did not sit there nights since Papa died, counting my money and studying God's Book, for nothing. Playing solitaire, then going back to search the next page and the next. Stepping outside to rest my eyes on His limitless sky, then back to the Book and the paper, building my case.

He starts to read, turns up his glitter-glass to me once to check how I look, the reads again. His chair must be hard, for he squirms in it, crosses his legs. When he has read every page, he lays the stack down, slowly takes off his glasses, folds them shining into a case. He leaves it open on his desk. Mica shines like that, in the rocks.

Then he looks at me, fully. Oh. He is plain. Almost homely. I nearly expected it. Maybe Samuel was born ugly, so who else would take him but God?

"My child," the man begins, though I'm older than he is, "I understand how you feel. And we will most certainly pray for your spirit . . ."

I shut my eyes against those two flashing faces on his spectacles. "Never mind my spirit." I see he doesn't really understand. I see he will live a long life, and not marry.

"Our Heavenly Father has purpose in all things."

Stubbornly, "Ask Him to set it aside."

"We must all trust His will."

After all these years, isn't it God's turn to trust mine? Could He not risk a little beauty on me? Just when I'm ready to ask, the sober assistant recites, "'Favor is deceitful and beauty is vain.' That's in Proverbs."

And I cry, "'The crooked shall be made straight!' Isaiah said that!" He draws back, as if I had brought the Gideon Bible and struck him with its most disfigured pages. "Jesus healed an impediment in speech. See my impediment! Mud on a blind man's eyes was all He needed! Don't you remember?" But he's read all that. Everything I know on my side lies, written out, under his sweaty hand. Lord, don't let me whine. But I whine, "He healed the ten lepers and only one thanked. Well, I'll thank. I promise. All my life."

He clears his long knotty throat and drones like a bee, "'By the sadness of the countenance the heart is made better.' Ecclesiastes. Seven. Three."

Oh, that's not fair! I skipped those parts, looking for verses that suited me! And it's wrong, besides.

I get up to leave and he asks will I kneel with him? "Let us pray together for that inner beauty."

No, I will not. I go down that hollow hall and past the echoing rooms. Without his help I find the great auditorium, lit through colored glass, with its cross of white plastic and a pinker Jesus molded onto it. I go straight to the pulpit where the Preacher stands. There is nobody else to plead. I ask Jesus not to listen to everything He hears, but to me only.

Then I tell Him how it feels to be ugly, with nothing to look back at you but a deer or an owl. I read Him my paper, out loud, full of His own words.

"I have been praising you, Lord, but it gets harder every year." Maybe that sounds too strong. I try to ease up my tone before the Amens. Then the chapel is very quiet. For one minute I hear the whir of many wings, but it's only a fan inside an air vent.

I go into the streets of Tulsa, where even the shade from a building is hot. And as I walk to the hotel I'm repeating, over and over, "Praise God for Tulsa in spite of everything."

Maybe I say this aloud, since people are staring. But maybe that's only because they've never seen a girl cry crooked in their streets before.

MONDAY MORNING. I have not looked at my face since the pulpit prayer. Who can predict how He might act—with a lightning bolt? Or a melting so slow and tender it could not even be felt?

Now, on the bus, I can touch in my pocketbook the cold mirror glass. Though I cover its surface with prints, I never look down. We ride through the dust and I'm nervous. My pencil is flying: "Be ye therefore perfect as your Heavenly Father is perfect. Praise God for Oklahoma. For Wagoner and Sapulpa and Broken Arrow and every other name on these signs by the road."

Was that the wrong thing to tell Him? My threat that even praise can be withheld? Maybe He's angry. "Praise God for oil towers whether I like them or not." When we pass churches, I copy their names. Praise them all. I want to write, "Bless," but that's *His* job.

We cross the cool Arkansas River. As its damp rises into the bus and touches my face, something wavers there, in the very bottom of each pore; and I clap my rough hands to each cheek. Maybe He's started? How much can He do between here and Fort Smith? If He will?

For I know what will happen. Monty won't come. And I won't stop. That's an end to it.

No, Monty is there. Waiting right now. And I'll go into the bus station on tiptoe and stand behind him. He'll turn with his blue eyes like lamps. *And he won't know me!* If I'm changed. So I will explain myself to him: how this gypsy hair and this juicy mouth is still Violet Karl. He'll say, "Won't old Flick be surprised?" He'll say, "Where is that place you live? Can I come there?"

But if, while I wait and he turns, he should know me by my old face . . . If he should say my name or show by recognition that my name's rising up now in his eyes like something through water . . . I'll be running by then. To the bus. Straight out that door to the Tennessee bus, saying, "Driver, don't let that man on!" It's a very short stop. We'll be pulling out quick. I don't think he'll follow, anyhow.

I don't even think he will come.

One hundred and thirty-one miles to Fort Smith. I wish I could eat.

I try to think up things to look forward to at home. Maybe the sourwoods are blooming early, and the bees have been laying-by my honey. If it's rained enough, my corn might be in tassel. Wouldn't it be something if God took His own sweet time, and I lived on that slope for years and years, getting prettier all the time? And nobody to know?

It takes nearly years and years to get to Fort Smith. My papa knew things about time. I comb out my hair, not looking once to see what color sheddings are caught in the teeth. There's no need feeling my cheek, since my finger expects that scar. I can feel it on me almost anywhere, by memory. I straighten my skirt and lick my lips till the spit runs out.

And they're waiting. Monty at one door of the terminal and Flick at another.

"Ten minutes," the driver says when the bus is parked, but I wait in my seat till Flick gets restless and walks to the cigarette machine. Then I slip through his entrance door and inside the station. Mirrors shine everywhere. On the vending machines and the weight machines and a full-length one by the phone booth. It's all I can do not to look. I pass the ticket window and there's Monty's back at the other door. My face remembers the shape of it. Seeing him there, how he's made, and the

The Ugliest Pilgrim · 109

parts of him fitted, makes me forget how I look. And before I can stop, I call out his name.

Right away, turning, he yells to me "*Viii*-lut!"

So I know. I can look, then, in the wide mirror over a jukebox. Tired as I am and unfed, I look worse than I did when I started from home.

He's laughing and talking. "I been waiting here since daylight scared you wouldn't . . ." but by then I've run past the ugly girl in the glass and I race for the bus, for the road, for the mountain.

Behind me, he calls loudly, "Flick!"

I see that one step in my path like a floating dark blade, but I'm faster this time. I twist by him, into the flaming sun and the parking lot. How my breath hurts!

Monty's between me and my bus, but there's time. I circle the cab-stand, running hard over the asphalt field, with a pain ticking in my side. He calls me. I plunge through the crowd like a deer through fetterbush. But he's running as hard as he can and he's faster than me. And, oh!

Praise God!

He's catching me!

MUSIC

Ellen Gilchrist

RHODA WAS FOURTEEN years old the summer her father dragged her off to Clay County, Kentucky, to make her stop smoking and acting like a movie star. She was fourteen years old, a holy and terrible age, and her desire for beauty and romance drove her all day long and pursued her if she slept.

"Te amo," she whispered to herself in Latin class. "Te amo, Bob Rosen," sending the heat of her passions across the classroom and out through the window and across two states to a hospital room in Saint Louis, where a college boy lay recovering from a series of operations Rhoda had decided would be fatal.

"And you as well must die, beloved dust," she quoted to herself. "Oh, sleep forever in your Latmian cave, Mortal Endymion, darling of the moon," she whispered, and sometimes it was Bob Rosen's lanky body stretched out in the cave beside his saxophone that she envisioned and sometimes it was her own lush, apricot-colored skin growing cold against the rocks in the moonlight.

Rhoda was fourteen years old that spring and her true love had been cruelly taken from her and she had started smoking because there was nothing left to do now but be a writer.

She was fourteen years old and she would sit on the porch at night looking down the hill that led through the small town of Franklin, Kentucky, and think about the stars, wondering where heaven could be in all that vastness, feeling betrayed by her mother's pale Episcopalianism and the fate that had brought her to this small town right in the middle of her sophomore year in high school. She would sit on the porch stuffing chocolate chip cookies into her mouth, drinking endless homemade chocolate milk shakes, smoking endless Lucky Strike cigarettes, watching her mother's transplanted roses move steadily across the trellis, taking Bob Rosen's thin letters in and out of their envelopes, holding them against her face, then going up to the new bedroom, to the soft, blue sheets, stuffed with cookies and ice cream and cigarettes and rage.

"Is that you, Rhoda?" her father would call out as she passed his bedroom. "Is that you, sweetie? Come tell us good night." And she would go into their bedroom and lean over and kiss him.

"You just ought to smell yourself," he would say, sitting up, pushing her away. "You just ought to smell those nasty cigarettes." And as soon as she went into her room he would go downstairs and empty all the ashtrays to make sure the house wouldn't burn down while he was sleeping.

"I've got to make her stop that goddamn smoking," he would say, climbing back into the bed. "I'm goddamned if I'm going to put up with that."

"I'd like to know how you're going to stop it," Rhoda's mother said. "I'd like to see anyone make Rhoda do anything she doesn't want to do. Not to mention that you're hardly ever here."

"Goddammit, Ariane, don't start that this time of night." And he rolled over on his side of the bed and began to plot his campaign against Rhoda's cigarettes.

Dudley Manning wasn't afraid of Rhoda, even if she was as stubborn as a goat. Dudley Manning wasn't afraid of anything. He had gotten up at dawn every day for years and believed in himself and followed his luck wherever it led him, dragging his sweet southern wife and his children behind him, and now, in his fortieth year, he was about to become a millionaire.

He was about to become a millionaire and he was in love with a beautiful woman who was not his wife and it was the strangest spring he had ever known. When he added up the figures in his account books he was filled with awe at his own achievements, amazed at what he had made of himself, and to make up for it he talked a lot about luck and pretended to be humble but deep down inside he believed there was nothing he couldn't do, even love two women at once, even make Rhoda stop smoking.

Both Dudley and Rhoda were early risers. If he was in town he would be waiting in the kitchen when she came down to breakfast, dressed in his khakis, his pens in his pocket, his glasses on his nose, sitting at the table going over his papers, his head full of the clean new ideas of morning.

"How many more days of school do you have?" he said to her one morning, watching her light the first of her cigarettes without saying anything about it.

"Just this week," she said. "Just until Friday. I'm making A's, Daddy. This is the easiest school I've ever been to."

"Well, don't be smart-alecky about it, Rhoda," he said. "If you've got a good mind it's only because God gave it to you."

"God didn't give me anything," she said. "Because there isn't any God."

"Well, let's don't get into an argument about that this morning," Dudley said. "As soon as you finish school I want you to drive up to the mines with me for a few days."

"For how long?" she said.

"We won't be gone long," he said. "I just want to take you to the mines to look things over."

Rhoda french-inhaled, blowing the smoke out into the sunlight coming through the kitchen windows, imagining herself on a tour of her father's mines, the workers with their caps in their hands smiling at her as she walked politely among them. Rhoda liked that idea. She dropped two saccharin tablets into her coffee and sat down at the table, enjoying her fantasy.

"Is that what you're having for breakfast?" he said.

"I'm on a diet," Rhoda said. "I'm on a black coffee diet."

He looked down at his poached eggs, cutting into the yellow with his knife. I can wait, he said to himself. As God is my witness I can wait until Sunday.

Rhoda poured herself another cup of coffee and went upstairs to write Bob Rosen before she left for school.

Dear Bob [the letter began],

School is almost over. I made straight A's, of course, as per your instructions. This school is so easy it's crazy.

They read one of my newspaper columns on the radio in Nashville. Everyone in Franklin goes around saying my mother writes my columns. Can you believe that? Allison Hotchkiss, that's my editor, say she's going to write an editorial about it saying I really write them.

I turned my bedroom into an office and took out the tacky dressing table mother made me and got a desk and put my typewriter on it and made striped drapes, green and black and white. I think you would approve.

Sunday Daddy is taking me to Manchester, Kentucky, to look over the coal mines. He's going to let me drive. He lets me drive all the time. I live for your letters.

Te amo, Rhoda

She put the letter in a pale blue envelope, sealed it, dripped some Toujours Moi lavishly onto it in several places, and threw herself down on her bed.

She pressed her face deep down into her comforter pretending it was Bob Rosen's smooth cool skin. "Oh, Bob, Bob," she whispered to the comforter. "Oh, honey, don't die, don't die, please don't die." She could feel the tears coming. She reached out and caressed the seam of the comforter, pretending it was the scar on Bob Rosen's neck.

The last night she had been with him he had just come home from an operation for a mysterious tumor that he didn't want to talk about. It would be better soon, was all he would say about it. Before long he would be as good as new.

They had driven out of town and parked the old Pontiac underneath a tree beside a pasture. In was September and Rhoda had lain in his arms smelling the clean smell of his new sweater, touching the fresh red scars on his neck, looking out the window to memorize every detail of the scene, the black tree, the September pasture, the white horse leaning against the fence, the palms of his hands, the taste of their cigarettes, the night breeze, the exact temperature of the air, saying to herself over and over, I must remember everything. This will have to last me forever and ever and ever.

"I want you to do it to me," she said. "Whatever it is they do."

"I can't," he said. "I couldn't do that now. It's too much trouble to make love to a virgin." He was laughing. "Besides, it's hard to do it in a car."

"But I'm leaving," she said. "I might not ever see you again."

"Not tonight," he said. "I still don't feel very good, Rhoda."

"What if I come back and visit," she said. "Will you do it then? When you feel better."

"If you still want me to I will," he said. "If you come back to visit and we both want to, I will."

"Do you promise?" she said, hugging him fiercely.

"I promise," he said "On my honor I promise to do it when you come to visit."

But Rhoda was not allowed to go to Saint Louis to visit. Either her mother guessed her intentions or else she seized the opportunity to do what she had been wanting to do all along and stop her daughter from seeing a boy with a Jewish last name.

There were weeks of pleadings and threats. It all ended one Sunday night when Mrs. Manning lost her temper and made the statement that Jews were little peddlers who went through the Delta selling needles and pins.

"You don't know what you're talking about," Rhoda screamed. "He's not a peddler, and I love him and I'm going to love him until I die." Rhoda pulled her arms away from her mother's hands.

"I'm going up there this weekend to see him," she screamed. "Daddy promised me I could and you're not going to stop me and if you try to stop me I'll kill you and I'll run away and I'll never come back."

"You are not going to Saint Louis and that's the end of this conversation and if you don't calm down I'll call a doctor and have you locked up. I think you're crazy, Rhoda. I really do."

"I'm not crazy," Rhoda screamed. "You're the one that's crazy."

"You and your father think you're so smart," her mother said. She was shaking but she held her ground, moving around behind a Queen Anne chair. "Well, I don't care how smart you are, you're not going to get on a train and go off to Saint Louis, Missouri, to see a man when you're only fourteen years old, and that, Miss Rhoda K. Manning, is that."

"I'm going to kill you," Rhoda said. "I really am. I'm going to kill you," and she thought for a moment that she would kill her, but then she noticed her grandmother's Limoges hot chocolate pot sitting on top of the piano holding a spray of yellow jasmine, and she walked over to the piano and picked it up and threw it all the way across the room and smashed it into a wall beside a framed print of "The Blue Boy."

"I hate you," Rhoda said. "I wish you were dead." And while her mother stared in disbelief at the wreck of the sainted hot chocolate pot, Rhoda walked out of the house and got in the car and drove off down the steep driveway. I hate her guts, she said to herself. I hope she cries herself to death.

She shifted into second gear and drove off toward her father's office, quoting to herself from Edna Millay. "Now by this moon, before this moon shall wane, I shall be dead or I shall be with you."

But in the end Rhoda didn't die. Neither did she kill her mother. Neither did she go to Saint Louis to give her virginity to her reluctant lover.

THE SUNDAY OF the trip Rhoda woke at dawn feeling very excited and changed clothes four or five times trying to decide how she wanted to look for her inspection of the mines.

Rhoda had never even seen a picture of a strip mine. In her imagination she and her father would be riding an elevator down into the heart of a mountain where obsequious masked miners were lined up to shake her hand. Later that evening the captain of the football team would be coming over to the hotel to meet her and take her somewhere for a drive.

She pulled on a pair of pink pedal pushers and a long navy blue sweatshirt, threw every single thing she could possibly imagine wearing into a large suitcase, and started down the stairs to where her father was calling for her to hurry up.

Her mother followed her out of the house holding a buttered biscuit on a linen napkin. "Please eat something before you leave," she said. "There isn't a decent restaurant after you leave Bowling Green."

"I told you I don't want anything to eat," Rhoda said. "I'm on a diet." She stared at the biscuit as though it were a coral snake.

"One biscuit isn't going to hurt you," her mother said. "I made you a lunch, chicken and carrot sticks and apples."

"I don't want it," Rhoda said. "Don't put any food in this car, Mother."

"Just because you never eat doesn't mean your father won't get hungry. You don't have to eat any of it unless you want to." Their eyes met. Then they sighed and looked away.

Her father appeared at the door and climbed in behind the wheel of the secondhand Cadillac.

"Let's go, Sweet Sister," he said, cruising down the driveway, turning onto the road leading to Bowling Green and due east into the hill country. Usually this was his favorite moment of the week, starting the long drive into the rich Kentucky hills where his energy and intelligence had created the long black rows of figures in the account books, figures that meant Rhoda would never know what it was to be really afraid or uncertain or powerless.

"How long will it take?" Rhoda asked.

"Don't worry about that," he said. "Just look out the window and enjoy the ride. This is beautiful country we're driving through."

"I can't right now," Rhoda said. "I want to read the new book Allison gave me. It's a book of poems."

She settled down into the seat and opened the book.

Oh, gallant was the first love, and glittering and fine;
The second love was water, in a clear blue cup;
The third love was his, and the fourth was mine.
And after that, I always get them all mixed up.

Oh, God, this is good, she thought. She sat up straighter, wanting to kiss the book. Oh, God, this is really good. She turned the book over to look at the picture of the author. It was a photograph of a small bright face in full profile staring off into the mysterious brightly lit world of a poet's life.

Dorothy Parker, she read. What a wonderful name. Maybe I'll change my name to Dorothy, Dorothy Louise Manning. Dot Manning. Dottie, Dottie Leigh, Dot.

Rhoda pulled a pack of Lucky Strikes out of her purse, tamped it on the dashboard, opened it, extracted a cigarette, and lit it with a gold Ronson lighter. She inhaled deeply and went back to the book.

Her father gripped the wheel, trying to concentrate on the beauty of the morning, the green fields, the small, neat farmhouses, the red barns, the cattle and horses. He moved his eyes from all that order to his fourteen-year-old daughter slumped beside him with her nose buried in a book, her plump fingers languishing in the air, holding a cigarette. He slowed down, pulled the car onto the side of the road, and killed the motor.

"What's wrong?" Rhoda said. "Why are you stopping?"

"Because you are going to put out that goddamn cigarette this very minute and you're going to give me the package and you're not going to smoke another cigarette around me as long as you live," he said.

"I will not do any such thing," Rhoda said. "It's a free country."

"Give me the cigarette, Rhoda," he said. "Hand it here."

"Give me one good reason why I should," she said. But her voice let her down. She knew there wasn't any use in arguing. This was not her soft little mother she was dealing with. This was Dudley Manning, who had been a famous baseball player until he quit when she was born. Who before that had gone to the Olympics on a relay team. There were scrapbooks full of his clippings in Rhoda's house. No matter where the Mannings went those scrapbooks sat on a table in the den. *Manning Hits One Over The Fence,* the headlines read. *Manning Saves The Day. Manning Does It Again.* And he was not the only one. His cousin, Philip Manning, down in Jackson, Mississippi, was famous too. Who was the father of the famous Crystal Manning, Rhoda's cousin who had a fur coat when she was ten. And Leland Manning, who was her cousin Lele's daddy. Leland had been the captain of the Tulane football team before he drank himself to death in the Delta.

Rhoda sighed, thinking of all that, and gave in for the moment. "Give me one good reason and I might," she repeated.

"I don't have to give you a reason for a goddamn thing," he said. "Give the cigarette here, Rhoda. Right this minute." He reached out and took it and she didn't resist. "Goddamn, these things smell awful," he said, crushing it in the ashtray. He reached in her pocketbook and got the package and threw it out the window.

"Only white trash throw things out on the road," Rhoda said. "You'd kill me if I did that."

"Well, let's just be quiet and get to where we're going." He started the motor and drove back out onto the highway. Rhoda crunched down lower in the seat, pretending to read her book. Who cares, she thought. I'll get some as soon as we stop for gas.

Getting cigarettes at filling stations was not as easy as Rhoda thought it was going to be. This was God's country they were driving into now, the hills rising up higher and higher, strange, silent little houses back off the road. Rhoda could feel the eyes looking out at her from behind the silent windows. Poor white trash, Rhoda's mother would have called them. The salt of the earth, her father would have said.

This was God's country and these people took things like children smoking cigarettes seriously. At both places where they stopped there was a sign by the cash register, *No Cigarettes Sold To Minors.*

Rhoda had moved to the backseat of the Cadillac and was stretched out on the seat reading her book. She had found another poem she liked and she was memorizing it.

> *Four be the things I'd be better without,*
> *Love, curiosity, freckles and doubt.*
> *Three be the things I shall never attain,*
> *Envy, content and sufficient champagne.*

Oh, God, I love this book, she thought. *This Dorothy Parker is just like me.* Rhoda was remembering a night when she got drunk in Clarkesville, Mississippi, with her cousin, Baby Gwen Barksdale. They got drunk on tequila LaGrande Conroy brought back from Mexico, and Rhoda had slept all night in the bathtub so she would be near the toilet when she vomited.

She put her head down on her arm and giggled, thinking about waking up in the bathtub. Then a plan occurred to her.

"Stop and let me go to the bathroom," she said to her father. "I think I'm going to throw up."

"Oh, Lord," he said. "I knew you shouldn't have gotten in the backseat. Well, hold on. I'll stop the first place I see." He pushed his hat back off his forehead and began looking for a place to stop, glancing back over his shoulder every now and then to see if she was all right. Rhoda had a long history of throwing up on car trips so he was taking this seriously. Finally he saw a combination store and filling station at a bend in the road and pulled up beside the front door.

"I'll be all right," Rhoda said, jumping out of the car. "You stay here. I'll be right back."

She walked dramatically up the wooden steps and pushed open the screen door. It was so quiet and dark inside she thought for a moment the store was closed. She looked around. She was in a rough, high-ceilinged room with saddles and pieces of farm equipment hanging from the rafters and a sparse array of canned goods on wooden shelves behind a counter. On the counter were five or six large glass jars filled with different kinds of Nabisco cookies. Rhoda stared at the cookie jars, wanting to stick her hand down inside and take out great fistfuls of Lorna Doones and Oreos. She fought off her hunger and raised her eyes to the display of chewing tobacco and cigarettes.

The smells of the store rose up to meet her, fecund and rich, moist and cool, as if the store was an extension of the earth outside. Rhoda looked down at the board floors. She felt she could have dropped a sunflower seed on the floor and it would instantly sprout and take bloom, growing quick, moving down into the earth and upwards toward the rafters.

"Is anybody here?" she said softly, then louder. "Is anybody here?"

A woman in a cotton dress appeared in a door, staring at Rhoda out of very intense, very blue eyes.

"Can I buy a pack of cigarettes from you?" Rhoda said. "My dad's in the car. He sent me to get them."

"What kind of cigarettes you looking for?" the woman said, moving to the space between the cash register and the cookie jars.

"Some Luckies if you have them," Rhoda said. "He said to just get anything you had if you didn't have that."

"They're a quarter," the woman said, reaching behind herself to take the package down and lay it on the counter, not smiling, but not being unkind either.

"Thank you," Rhoda said, laying the quarter down on the counter. "Do you have any matches?"

"Sure," the woman said, holding out a box of kitchen matches. Rhoda took a few, letting her eyes leave the woman's face and some to rest on the jars of Oreos. They looked wonderful and light, as though they had been there a long time and grown soft around the edges.

The woman was smiling now. "You want one of those cookies?" she said. "You want one, you go on and have one. It's free."

"Oh, no thank you," Rhoda said. "I'm on a diet. Look, do you have a ladies' room I can use?"

"It's out back," the woman said. "You can have one of them cookies if you want it. Like I said, it won't cost you nothing."

"I guess I'd better get going," Rhoda said. "My dad's in a hurry. But thank you anyway. And thanks for the matches." Rhoda hurried down the aisle, slipped out the back door and leaned up against the back of the store, tearing the paper off the cigarettes. She pulled one out, lit it, and inhaled deeply, blowing the smoke out in front of her, watching it rise up into the air, casting a veil over the hills that rose up behind and to the left of her. She had never been in such a strange country. It looked as though no one ever did anything to their yards or roads or fences. It looked as though there might not be a clock for miles.

She inhaled again, feeling dizzy and full. She had just taken the cigarette out of her mouth when her father came bursting out of the door and grabbed both of her wrists in his hands.

"Let go of me," she said. "Let go of me this minute." She struggled to free herself, ready to kick or claw or bite, ready for a real fight, but

Ellen Gilchrist · *122*

he held her off. "Drop the cigarette, Rhoda," he said. "Drop it on the ground."

"I'll kill you," she said. "As soon as I get away I'm running away to Florida. Let go of me, Daddy. Do you hear me?"

"I hear you," he said. The veins were standing out on his forehead. His face was so close Rhoda could see his freckles and the line where his false front tooth was joined to what was left of the real one. He had lost the tooth in a baseball game the day Rhoda was born. That was how he told the story. "I lost that tooth the day Rhoda was born," he would say. "I was playing left field against Memphis in the old Crump Stadium. I slid into second and the second baseman got me with his shoe."

"YOU CAN SMOKE all you want to when you get down to Florida," he was saying now. "But you're not smoking on this trip. So you might as well calm down before I drive off and leave you here."

"I don't care," she said. "Go on and leave. I'll just call up Mother and she'll come and get me." She was struggling to free her wrists but she could not move them inside his hands. "Let go of me, you big bully," she added.

"Will you calm down and give me the cigarettes?"

"All right," she said, but the minute he let go of her hands she turned and began to hit him on the shoulders, pounding her fists up and down on his back, not daring to put any real force behind the blows. He pretended to cower under the assault. She caught his eyes and saw that he was laughing at her and she had to fight the desire to laugh with him.

"I'm getting in the car," she said. "I'm sick of this place." She walked grandly around to the front of the store, got into the car, tore open the lunch and began to devour it, tearing the chicken off the bones with her teeth, swallowing great hunks without even bothering to chew them. "I'm never speaking to you again as long as I live," she said, her mouth full of chicken breast. "You are not my father."

"Suits me, Miss Smart-alecky Movie Star," he said, putting his hat back on his head. "Soon as we get home you can head on out for Florida.

You just let me know when you're leaving so I can give you some money for the bus."

"I hate you," Rhoda mumbled to herself, starting in on the homemade raisin cookies. I hate your guts. I hope you go to hell forever, she thought, breaking a cookie into pieces so she could pick out the raisins.

IT WAS LATE afternoon when the Cadillac picked its way up a rocky red clay driveway to a house trailer nestled in the curve of a hill beside a stand of pine trees.

"Where are we doing?" Rhoda said. "Would you just tell me that?"

"We're going to see Maud and Joe Samples," he said. "Joe's an old hand around here. He's my right-hand man in Clay County. Now you just be polite and try to learn something, Sister. These are real folks you're about to meet."

"Why are we going here first?" Rhoda said. "Aren't we going to a hotel?"

"There isn't any hotel," her father said. "Does this look like someplace they'd have hotels? Maud and Joe are going to put you up for me while I'm off working."

"I'm going to stay here?" Rhoda said. "In this trailer?"

"Just wait until you see the inside," her father said. "It's like the inside of a boat, everything all planned out and just the right amount of space for things. I wish your mother'd let me live in a trailer."

They were almost to the door now. A plump smiling woman came out onto the wooden platform and waited for them with her hands on her hips, smiling wider and wider as they got nearer.

"There's Maud," Dudley said. "She's the sweetest woman in the world and the best cook in Kentucky. Hey there, Miss Maud," he called out.

"Mr. D," she said, opening the car door for them. "Joe Samples's been waiting on you all day and here you show up bringing this beautiful girl just like you promised. I've made you some blackberry pies. Come on inside this trailer." Maud smiled deep into Rhoda's face. Her eyes were as blue as the ones on the woman in the store. Rhoda's mother had blue eyes, but not this brilliant and not this blue. These eyes were from another world, another century.

"Come on in and see Joe," Maud said. "He's been having a fit for you to get here."

They went inside and Dudley showed Rhoda all around the trailer, praising the design of trailers. Maud turned on the tiny oven and they had blackberry pie and bread and butter sandwiches and Rhoda abandoned her diet and ate two pieces of the pie, covering it with thick whipped cream.

The men went off to talk business and Maud took Rhoda to a small room at the back of the trailer decorated to match a handmade quilt of the sunrise.

There were yellow ruffled curtains at the windows and a tiny dressing table with a yellow ruffled skirt around the edges. Rhoda was enchanted by the smallness of everything and the way the windows looked out onto layers of green trees and bushes.

Lying on the dresser was a white leather Bible and a display of small white pamphlets, *Alcohol And You, When Jesus Reaches For A Drink, You Are Not Alone, Sorry Isn't Enough, Taking No For An Answer.*

It embarrassed Rhoda even to read the titles of anything as tacky as the pamphlets. But she didn't let on she thought it was tacky, not with Maud sitting on the bed telling her how pretty she was every other second and asking her questions about herself and saying how wonderful her father was.

"We love Mr. D to death," she said. "It's like he was one of our own."

He appeared in the door. "Rhoda, if you're settled in I'll be leaving now," he said. "I've got to drive to Knoxville to do some business but I'll be back here Tuesday morning to take you to the mines." He handed her three twenty-dollar bills. "Here," he said. "In case you need anything."

He left then and hurried out to the car, trying to figure out how long it would take him to get to Knoxville, to where Valerie sat alone in a hotel room waiting for this night they had planned for so long. He felt the sweet hot guilt rise up in his face and the sweet hot longing in his legs and hands.

I'm sorry, Jesus, he thought, pulling out onto the highway. I know it's wrong and I know we're doing wrong. So go on and punish me if you have to but just let me make it there and back before you start in on me.

He set the cruising speed at exactly fifty-five miles an hour and began to sing to himself as he drove.

"Oh, sure as the vine grows around the stump
You're my darling sugar lump," he sang, and;

"Froggy went a-courting and he did ride,
Huhhrummp, Huhhrummp,
Froggy went a-courting and he did ride, Huhhrummp,

What you gonna have for the wedding supper?
Black-eyed peas and bread and butter, Huhhrummp,
huhhrummp . . ."

Rhoda was up and dressed when her father came to get her on Tuesday morning. It was still dark outside but a rooster had begun to crow in the distance. Maud bustled all about the little kitchen making much of them, filling their plates with biscuits and fried eggs and ham and gravy.

Then they got into the Cadillac and began to drive toward the mine. Dudley was driving slowly, pointing out everything to her as they rode along.

"Up on that knoll," he said, "That's where the Traylors live. Rooster Traylor's a man about my age. Last year his mother shot one of the Galtney women for breaking up Rooster's marriage and now the Galtneys have got to shoot someone in the Traylor family."

"That's terrible," Rhoda said.

"No it isn't, Sister," he said, warming into the argument. "These people take care of their own problems."

"They actually shoot each other?" she said. "And you think that's okay? You think that's funny?"

"I think it's just as good as waiting around for some judge and jury to do it for you."

"Then you're just crazy," Rhoda said. "You're as crazy as you can be."

"Well, let's don't argue about it this morning. Come on. I've got something to show you." He pulled the car off the road and they walked into the woods, following a set of bulldozer tracks that made a crude path into the trees. It was quiet in the woods and smelled of pine and sassafras. Rhoda watched her father's strong body moving in front of her, striding along, inspecting everything, noticing everything, commenting on everything.

"Look at this," he said. "Look at all this beauty, honey. Look at how beautiful all this is. This is the real world. Not those goddamn movies and beauty parlors and magazines. This is the world that God made. This is where people are really happy."

"There isn't any God," she said. "Nobody that knows anything believes in God, Daddy. That's just a lot of old stuff . . ."

"I'm telling you, Rhoda," he said. "It breaks my heart to see the way you're growing up." He stopped underneath a tree, took a seat on a log and turned his face to hers. Tears were forming in his eyes. He was famous in the family for being able to cry on cue. "You've just got to learn to listen to someone. You've got to get some common sense in your head. I swear to God, I worry about you all the time." The tears were falling now. "I just can't stand to see the way you're growing up. I don't know where you get all those crazy ideas you come up with."

Rhoda looked down, caught off guard by the tears. No matter how many times he pulled that with the tears she fell for it for a moment. The summer forest was all around them, soft deep earth beneath their feet, morning light falling through the leaves, and the things that passed between them were too hard to understand. Their brown eyes met and locked and after that they were bound to start an argument for no one can bear to be that happy or that close to another human being.

"Well, I'll tell you one thing," Rhoda said. "It's a free country and I can smoke if I want to and you can't keep me from doing it by locking me up in a trailer with some poor white trash."

"What did you say?" he said, getting a look on his face that would have scared a grown man to death. "What did you just say, Rhoda?"

"I said I'm sick and tired of being locked up in that damned old trailer with those corny people and nothing to read but religious magazines. I want to get some cigarettes and I want you to take me home so I can see my friends and get my column written for next week."

"Oh, God, Sister." he said. "Haven't I taught you anything? Maud Samples is the salt of the earth. That woman raised seven children. She knows things you and I will never know as long as we live."

"Well, no she doesn't," Rhoda said. "She's just an old white trash country woman and if Momma knew where I was she'd have a fit."

"Your momma is a very stupid person," he said. "And I'm sorry I ever let her raise you." He turned his back to her then and stalked on out of the woods to a road that ran like a red scar up the side of the mountain. "Come on," he said. "I'm going to take you up there and show you where coal comes from. Maybe you can learn one thing this week."

"I learn things all the time," she said. "I already know more than half the people I know . . . I know . . ."

"Please don't talk anymore this morning," he said. "I'm burned out talking to you."

He put her into a jeep and began driving up the steep unpaved road. In a minute he was feeling better, cheered up by the sight of the big Caterpillar tractors moving dirt. If there was one thing that always cheered him up it was the sight of a big shovel moving dirt. "This is Blue Gem coal," he said. "The hardest in the area. See the layers. Topsoil, then gravel and dirt or clay, then slate, then thirteen feet of pure coal.

Some people think it was made by dinosaurs. Other people think God put it there."

"This is it?" she said. "This is the mine?" It looked like one of his road construction projects. Same yellow tractors, same disorderly activity. The only difference seemed to be the huge piles of coal and a conveyor belt going down the mountain to a train.

"This is it," he said. "This is where they stored the old dinosaurs."

"Well, it is made out of dinosaurs," she said. "There were a lot of leaves and trees and dinosaurs and then they died and the coal and oil is made out of them."

"All right," he said. "Let's say I'll go along with the coal. But tell me this, who made the slate then? Who put the slate right on top of the coal everywhere it's found in the world? Who laid the slate down on top of the dinosaurs?"

"I don't know who put the slate there," she said. "We haven't got that far yet."

"You haven't got that far?" he said. "You mean the scientists haven't got as far as the slate yet? Well, Sister, that's the problem with you folks that evolved out of monkeys. You're still half-baked. You aren't finished like us old dumb ones that God made."

"I didn't say the scientists hadn't got that far," she said. "I just said I hadn't got that far."

"It's a funny thing to me how all those dinosaurs came up here to die in the mountains and none of them died in the farmland," he said. "It sure would have made it a lot easier on us miners if they'd died down there on the flat."

While she was groping around for an answer he went right on. "Tell me this, Sister," he said. "Are any of your monkey ancestors in there with the dinosaurs, or is it just plain dinosaurs? I'd like to know who all I'm digging up . . . I'd like to give credit . . ."

The jeep had come to a stop and Joe was coming toward them, hurrying out of the small tin-roofed office with a worried look on his face. "Mr. D, you better call up to Jellico. Beb's been looking everywhere for you. They had a run-in with a teamster organizer. You got to call him right away.''

"What's wrong?" Rhoda said. "What happened?"

"Nothing you need to worry about, Sister," her father said. He turned to Joe. "Go find Preacher and tell him to drive Rhoda back to your house. You go on now, honey. I've got work to do." He gave her a kiss on the cheek and disappeared into the office. A small shriveled-looking man came limping out of a building and climbed into the driver's seat. "I'm Preacher," he said. "Mr. Joe tole me to drive you up to his place."

"All right," Rhoda said. "I guess that's okay with me." Preacher put the jeep in gear and drove it slowly down the winding rutted road. By the time they got to the bottom Rhoda had thought of a better plan. "I'll drive now," she said. "I'll drive myself to Maud's. It's all right with my father. He lets me drive all the time. You can walk back, can't you?" Preacher didn't know what to say to that. He was an old drunk that Dudley and Joe kept around to run errands. He was so used to taking orders that finally he climbed down out of the jeep and did as he was told. "Show me the way to town," Rhoda said. "Draw me a map. I have to go by town on my way to Maud's." Preacher scratched his head, then bent over and drew her a little map in the dust on the hood. Rhoda studied the map, put the jeep into the first forward gear she could find, and drove off down the road to the little town of Manchester, Kentucky, studying the diagram on the gearshift as she drove.

SHE PARKED BESIDE a boardwalk that led through the main street of town and started off looking for a store that sold cigarettes. One of the stores had dresses in the window. In the center was a red strapless sundress with a white jacket. $6.95, the price tag said. I hate the way I look, she decided. I hate these tacky pants. I've got sixty dollars. I don't have to look like this if I don't want to. I can buy anything I want.

She went inside, asked the clerk to take the dress out of the window, and in a few minutes she emerged from the store wearing the dress and a pair of leather sandals with two-inch heels. The jacket was thrown carelessly over her shoulder like Gene Tierney in *Leave Her to Heaven*. I look great in red, she was thinking, catching a glimpse of herself in a store window. It isn't true that redheaded people can't wear red. She walked on down the boardwalk, admiring herself in every window.

She walked for two blocks looking for a place to try her luck getting cigarettes. She was almost to the end of the boardwalk when she came to a pool hall. She stood in the door looking in, smelling the dark smell of tobacco and beer. The room was deserted except for a man leaning on a cue stick beside a table and a boy with black hair seated behind a cash register reading a book. The boy's name was Johnny Hazard and he was sixteen years old. The book he was reading was *U.S.A.* by John Dos Passos. A woman who came to Manchester to teach poetry writing had given him the book. She had made a dust jacket for it out of brown paper so he could read it in public. On the spine of the jacket she had written *American History*.

"I'd like a package of Lucky Strikes," Rhoda said, holding out a twenty-dollar bill in his direction.

"We don't sell cigarettes to minors," he said. "It's against the law."

"I'm not a minor," Rhoda said. "I'm eighteen. I'm Rhoda Manning. My daddy owns the mine."

"Which mine?" he said. He was watching her breasts as she talked, getting caught up in the apricot skin against the soft red dress.

"The mine," she said. "The Manning mine. I just got here the other day. I haven't been downtown before."

"So, how do you like our town?"

"Please sell me some cigarettes," she said. "I'm about to have a fit for a Lucky."

"I can't sell you cigarettes," he said. "You're not any more eighteen years old than my dog."

"Yes, I am," she said. "I drove here in a jeep, doesn't that prove anything?" She was looking at his wide shoulders and the tough flat chest beneath his plaid shirt.

"Are you a football player?" she said.

"When I have time," he said. "When I don't have to work on the nights they have games."

"I'm a cheerleader where I live," Rhoda said. "I just got elected again for next year."

"What kind of jeep?" he said.

"An old one," she said. "It's filthy dirty. They use it at the mine." She had just noticed the package of Camels in his breast pocket.

"If you won't sell me a whole package, how about selling me one," she said. "I'll give you a dollar for a cigarette." She raised the twenty-dollar bill and laid it down on the glass counter.

He ignored the twenty-dollar bill, opened the cash register, removed a quarter, and walked over to the jukebox. He walked with a precise, balanced sort of cockiness, as if he knew he could walk any way he wanted but had carefully chosen this particular walk as his own. He walked across the room through the rectangle of light coming in the door, walking as though he were the first boy ever to be in the world, the first boy ever to walk across a room and put a quarter into a jukebox. He pushed a button and music filled the room.

Kaw-Liga was a wooden Indian a-standing by the door,
He fell in love with an Indian maid
Over in the antique store.

"My uncle wrote that song," he said, coming back to her. "But it got ripped off by some promoters in Nashville. I'll make you a deal," he said. "I'll give you a cigarette if you'll give me a ride somewhere I have to go."

"All right," Rhoda said. "Where do you want to go?"

"Out to my cousin's," he said. "It isn't far."

"Fine," Rhoda said. Johnny told the lone pool player to keep an eye on things and the two of them walked out into the sunlight, walking together very formally down the street to where the jeep was parked.

"Why don't you let me drive," he said. "It might be easier." She agreed and he drove on up the mountain to a house that looked deserted. He went in and returned carrying a guitar in a case, a blanket, and a quart bottle with a piece of wax paper tied around the top with a rubber band.

"What's in the bottle?" Rhoda said.

"Lemonade, with a little sweetening in it."

"Like whiskey?"

"Yeah. Like whiskey. Do you ever drink it?"

"Sure," she said. "I drink a lot. In Saint Louis we had this club called The Four Roses that met every Monday at Donna Duston's house to get drunk. I thought it up, the club I mean."

"Well, here's your cigarette," he said. He took the package from his pocket and offered her one, holding it near his chest so she had to get in close to take it.

"Oh, God," she said. "Oh, thank you so much. I'm about to die for a ciggie. I haven't had one in days. Because my father dragged me up here to make me stop smoking. He's always trying to make me do something I don't want to do. But it never works. I'm very hardheaded, like him." She took the light Johnny offered her and blew out the smoke in a small controlled stream. "God, I love to smoke," she said.

"I'm glad I could help you out," he said. "Anytime you want one when you're here you just come on over. Look," he said. "I'm going somewhere you might want to see, if you're not in a hurry to get back. You got time to go and see something with me?"

"What is it?" she asked.

"Something worth seeing," he said. "The best thing in Clay County there is to see."

"Sure," she said. "I'll go. I never turn down an adventure. Why not, that's what my cousins in the Delta always say. Whyyyyyyy not." They drove up the mountain and parked and began to walk into the woods along a path. The woods were deeper here than where Rhoda had been that morning, dense and green and cool. She felt silly walking in the woods in the little high-heeled sandals, but she held on to Johnny's hand and followed him deeper and deeper into the trees, feeling grown up and brave and romantic. I'll bet he thinks I'm the bravest girl he ever met, she thought. I'll bet he thinks at last he's met a girl who's not afraid of anything. Rhoda was walking along imagining tearing off a piece of her dress for a tourniquet in case Johnny was bit by a poisonous snake. She was pulling the tourniquet tighter and tighter when the trees opened onto a small brilliant blue pond. The water was so blue Rhoda thought for a moment it must be some sort of trick. He stood there watching her while she took it in.

"What do you think?" he said at last.

"My God," she said. "What is it?"

"It's Blue Pond," he said. "People come from all over the world to see it."

"Who made it?" Rhoda said. "Where did it come from?"

"Springs. Rock springs. No one knows how deep down it goes, but more than a hundred feet because divers have been that far."

"I wish I could swim in it," Rhoda said. "I'd like to jump in there and swim all day."

"Come over here, cheerleader," he said. "Come sit over here by me and we'll watch the light on it. I brought this teacher from New York here last year. She said it was the best thing she'd ever seen in her life. She's a writer. Anyway, the thing she likes about Blue Pond is watching the light change on the water. She taught me a lot when she was here. About things like that."

Rhoda moved nearer to him, trying to hold in her stomach.

"My father really likes this part of the country," she said. "He says people up here are the salt of the earth. He says all the people up here are direct descendants from England and Scotland and Wales. I think he wants us to move up here and stay, but my mother won't let us. It's all because the unions keep messing with his mine that he has to be up here all the time. If it wasn't for the unions everything would be going fine. You aren't for the unions, are you?"

"I'm for myself," Johnny said. "And for my kinfolks." He was tired of her talking then and reached for her and pulled her into his arms, paying no attention to her small resistances, until finally she was stretched out under him on the earth and he moved the dress from her breasts and held them in his hands. He could smell the wild smell of her craziness and after a while he took the dress off and the soft white cotton under-pants and touched her over and over again. Then he entered her with the way he had of doing things, gently and with a good sense of the natural rhythms of the earth.

I'm doing it, Rhoda thought. I'm doing it. This is doing it. This is what it feels like to be doing it.

"This doesn't hurt a bit," she said out loud. "I think I love you, Johnny. I love, love, love you. I've been waiting all my life for you."

"Don't talk so much," he said. "It's better if you stop talking."

And Rhoda was quiet and he made love to her as the sun was leaving the earth and the afternoon breeze moved in the trees. Here was every possible tree, hickory and white oak and redwood and sumac and maple, all in thick foliage now, and he made love to her with great tenderness, forgetting he had set out to fuck the boss's daughter, and he kept on making love to her until she began to tighten around him, not knowing what she was doing, or where she was going, or even that there was anyplace to be going to.

DUDLEY WAS WAITING outside the trailer when she drove up. There was a sky full of cold stars behind him, and he was pacing up and down and talking to himself like a crazy man. Maud was inside the trailer crying her heart out and only Joe had kept his head and was going back and forth from one to the other telling them everything would be all right.

Dudley was pacing up and down talking to Jesus. I know I had it coming, he was saying. I know goddamn well I had it coming. But not her. Where in the hell is she? You get her back in one piece and I'll call Valerie and break it off. I won't see Valerie ever again as long as I live. *But you've got to get me back my little girl. Goddammit, you get me back my girl.*

Then he was crying, his head thrown back and raised up to the stars as the jeep came banging up the hill in third gear. Rhoda parked it and got out and started walking toward him, all bravado and disdain.

Dudley smelled it on her before he even touched her. Smelled it all over her and began to shake her, screaming at her to tell him who it had been. Then Joe came running out from the trailer and threw his hundred and fifty pounds between them, and Maud was right behind him. She led Rhoda into the trailer and put her into bed and sat beside her, bathing her head with a damp towel until she fell asleep.

"I'll find out who it was," Dudley said, shaking his fist. "I'll find out who it was."

"You don't know it was anybody," Joe said. "You don't even know what happened, Mr. D. Now you got to calm down and in the morning we'll find out what happened. More than likely she's just been holed up somewhere trying to scare you."

"I know what happened," Dudley said. "I already know what happened."

"Well, you can find out who it was and you can kill him if you have to," Joe said. "If it's true and you still want to in the morning, you can kill him."

BUT THERE WOULD be no killing. By the time the moon was high, Johnny Hazard was halfway between Lexington, Kentucky, and Cincinnati, Ohio, with a bus ticket he bought with the fifty dollars he'd taken from Rhoda's pocket. He had called the poetry teacher and told her he was coming. Johnny had decided it was time to see the world. After all, that very afternoon a rich cheerleader had cried in his arms and given him her cherry. There was no telling what might happen next.

MUCH LATER THAT night Rhoda woke up in the small room, hearing the wind come up in the trees. The window was open and the moon, now low in the sky and covered with mist, poured a diffused light upon the bed. Rhoda sat up in the bed and shivered. Why did I do that with him? she thought. Why in the world did I do that? But I couldn't help it, she decided. He's so sophisticated and he's so good-looking and he's a wonderful driver and he plays a guitar. She moved her hands along her thighs, trying to remember exactly what it was they had done, trying to remember the details, wondering where she could find him in the morning.

BUT DUDLEY HAD other plans for Rhoda in the morning. By noon she was on her way home in a chartered plane. Rhoda had never been on an airplane of any kind before, but she didn't let on.

"I'm thinking of starting a diary," she was saying to the pilot, arranging her skirt so her knees would show. "A lot of unusual things have been happening to me lately. The boy I love is dying of cancer in Saint Louis. It's very sad, but I have to put up with it. He wants me to write a lot of books and dedicate them to his memory."

The pilot didn't seem to be paying much attention, so Rhoda gave up on him and went back into her own head.

In her head Bob Rosen was alive after all. He was walking along a street in Greenwich Village and passed a bookstore with a window full of her books, many copies stacked in a pyramid with her picture on every cover. He recognized the photograph, ran into the bookstore, grabbed a book, opened it and saw the dedication, *To Bob Rosen, Te Amo Forever, Rhoda.*

Then Bob Rosen, or maybe it was Johnny Hazard, or maybe this unfriendly pilot, stood there on that city street, looking up at the sky, holding the book against his chest, crying and broken-hearted because Rhoda was lost to him forever, this famous author, who could have been his, lost to him forever.

THIRTY YEARS LATER Rhoda woke up in a hotel room in New York City. There was a letter lying on the floor where she had thrown it when she went to bed. She picked it up and read it again. *Take my name off that book,* the letter said. *Imagine a girl with your advantages writing a book like that. Your mother is so ashamed of you.*

Goddamn you, Rhoda thought. Goddamn you to hell. She climbed back into the bed and pulled the pillows over her head. She lay there for a while feeling sorry for herself. Then she got up and walked across the room and pulled a legal pad out of a briefcase and started writing.

Dear Father,

You take my name off those checks you send those television preachers and those goddamn right-wing politicians. That name has come to me from a hundred generations of men and women . . . also, in the future let my mother speak for herself about my work.

Love, Rhoda

P.S. The slate was put there by the second law of thermodynamics. Some folks call it gravity. Other folks call it God.

I guess it was the second law, she thought. It was the second law or the third law or something like that. She leaned back in the chair, looking at the ceiling. Maybe I'd better find out before I mail it.

The Pleasures and
Miseries of Marriage

THE PLEASURES AND MISERIES
OF MARRIAGE

NO INSTITUTION HAS undergone so much change during the course of this century as that of marriage. Southern women writers have often acted as seismographs of the change, pointing out tremors and cracks long before their menfolk realized that anything was amiss. One example is Kate Chopin's novel *The Awakening*, which was brave enough back in 1899 to hint of impending disaster.

On the other hand, marriage as a tradition, as a structure, is still revered in the South, where it represents family, progeny, and values that are passed on from generation to generation.

The first story in this section is by Eudora Welty, who, by virtue of example, has become a spokesperson for the rootedness of narrative.

Place in fiction is the named, identified, concrete, exact and exacting, and therefore credible, gathering-spot of all that has

been felt, is about to be experienced. . . . It seems plain that the art that speaks most clearly, explicitly, directly, and passionately from its place of origin will remain the longest understood. It is through place that we put out roots, wherever birth, chance, fate, or our traveling selves set us down; but where those roots reach toward . . . is the deep and running vein, eternal and consistent and everywhere purely itself—that feeds and is fed by the human understanding.
(from ''Place in Fiction'')

In ''The Wide Net,'' this understanding involves a young married couple dealing with the early throes of pregnancy. (We might expect the wife alone to be dealing with it, but in this case, the husband also has been drawn in.) Ironically, the wide net of the story is controlled by the wife, the husband merely serving as drone to her superior role of Queen Bee.

William Wallace looked down, as though he thought of Hazel with the shining eyes, sitting at home and looking straight before her, like a piece of pure gold, too precious to touch.

Below them the river was glimmering, narrow, soft, and skin-colored, and slowed nearly to stillness. The shining willow trees hung round them. The net that was being drawn out, so old and so long-used, it too looked golden, strung and tied with golden threads.

After all, fertility, the story suggests, is due a certain obeisance, and, like the goddesses of old, the wife demands her sacrifice. Yet there is nothing vituperative in this demand. Though love is two-faced—benign on the one hand, manipulative on the other—care for one another wins out. So does the idea of two people making a home together and creating a history (of which the story of ''the wide net'' will no doubt be part).

IF EUDORA WELTY's view of marriage encapsulates a few brief

hours, Mary Hood's "After Moore" takes the long view. It is a matrimonial epic, observed with precision.

> "According to *Woman's Day*," Rhonda said, "what married couples argue about most is m-o-n-e-y." She had showed Moore that article about credit counseling, with the local phone number already looked up. He threw the magazine out the window.
>
> "Not down, but *up*," Rhonda explained. "I guess it's still on the roof, educating the pigeons."
>
> But he did agree to open a savings account, salt a little away for the boys. "The school says they all test way above average and Scott's maybe a genius," Rhonda told the counselor. "I figure we owe them more than life. I *know* we do. What's life if there's no future in it? What did my parents ever hope for me?"

What's been left out of the story turns out to be just as important as what's been left in—though it's the details in the latter that give us the clues. Personal history becomes the glue that holds the marriage together—history and two people's involvement with one another, for better or for worse . . . until the scales finally tip.

THERE ARE NO scales in Gayl Jones's "White Rat"—no scales, no words of either denial or affection, no gestures, no means of measuring a relationship or even the worth of a human being except by the color and shade of his skin. In this respect, "getting the pigment" is a phrase far more loaded, even, than a girl getting her period.

Reading between the lines—the charged language of rhythm and energy—is the key to interpretation. Within are hidden the dreams, the lies, the truths, the *singularity* of what goes on between men and women.

> "You know my family came down out of the hills, like they was some kind of rain gods, you know, miss'ology. What they teached you bout the Jucifer. Anyway, I knew this nigger what made hisself a priest, you know turned his white color I mean

turned his white collar backwards and dressed up in a monkey suit—you get it?'' He didn't get it. ''Well, he made hisself a priest, but after a while he didn't want to be no priest, so he pronounced hisself.'' The bartender said, ''Renounced.'' ''So he 'nounced hisself and took off his turned-back collar and went back to just being a plain old everyday chi'lins and downhome and ham-hocks and cornpone nigger. And you know what else he did? He got married.''

By the sheer force of voice, Gayl Jones plunges us into a life as different from our own as if it existed on another planet, but at the same time, as familiar as though we spied it through the window next door before the curtains were drawn. There is something raw and vulnerable here that makes the reader feel almost voyeuristic. Maggie and Rat have so many reasons for quitting their marriage that, in the end, we are left wondering why they bother to go on together. We can only deduce that some tie between them still persists, and that this tie has to do with stubborn love and family allegiance. After all, the continuation of marriage means the continuation of the home, and home is not given up lightly.

THE WIDE NET

Eudora Welty

WILLIAM WALLACE JAMIESON's wife Hazel was going to have a
baby. But this was October, and it was six months away, and she acted
exactly as though it would be tomorrow. When he came in the room she
would not speak to him, but would look as straight at nothing as she
could, with her eyes glowing. If he only touched her she stuck out her
tongue or ran around the table. So one night he went out with two of the
boys down the road and stayed out all night. But that was the worst thing
yet, because when he came home in the early morning Hazel had vanished. He went through the house not believing his eyes, balancing with
both hands out, his yellow cowlick rising on end, and then he turned the
kitchen inside out looking for her, but it did no good. Then when he got
back to the front room he saw she had left him a little letter, in an envelope. That was doing something behind someone's back. He took out
the letter, pushed it open, held it out at a distance from his eyes. . . .

After one look he was scared to read the exact words, and he crushed the whole thing in his hand instantly, but what it had said was that she would not put up with him after that and was going to the river to drown herself.

"Drown herself. . . . But she's in mortal fear of the water!"

He ran out front, his face red like the red of the picked cotton field he ran over, and down in the road he gave a loud shout for Virgil Thomas, who was just going in his own house, to come out again. He could just see the edge of Virgil, he had almost got in, he had one foot inside the door.

They met half-way between the farms, under the shade-tree.

"Haven't you had enough of the night?" asked Virgil. There they were, their pants all covered with dust and dew, and they had had to carry the third man home flat between them.

"I've lost Hazel, she's vanished, she went to drown herself."

"Why, that ain't like Hazel," said Virgil.

William Wallace reached out and shook him. "You heard me. Don't you know we have to drag the river?"

"Right this minute?"

"You ain't got nothing to do till spring."

"Let me go set food inside the house and speak to my mother and tell her a story, and I'll come back."

"This will take the wide net," said William Wallace. His eyebrows gathered, and he was talking to himself.

"HOW COME HAZEL to go and do that way?" asked Virgil as they started out.

William Wallace said, "I reckon she got lonesome."

"That don't argue—drown herself for getting lonesome. My mother gets lonesome."

"Well," said William Wallace. "It argues for Hazel."

"How long is it now since you and her was married?"

"Why, it's been a year."

"It don't seem that long to me. A year!"

"It was this time last year. It seems longer," said William Wallace, breaking a stick off a tree in surprise. They walked along, kicking at the flowers on the road's edge. "I remember the day I seen her first, and that seems a long time ago. She was coming along the road holding a little frying-size chicken from her grandma, under her arm, and she had it real quiet. I spoke to her with nice manners. We knowed each other's names, being bound to, just didn't know each other to speak to. I says, 'Where are you taking the fryer?' and she says, 'Mind your manners,' and I kept on till after while she says. 'If you want to walk me home, take littler steps.' So I didn't lose time. It was just four miles across the field and full of blackberries, and from the top of the hill there was Dover below, looking sizeable-like and clean, spread out between the two churches like that. When we got down, I says to her, 'What kind of water's in this well?' and she says, 'The best water in the world.' So I drew a bucket and took out a dipper and she drank and I drank. I didn't think it was that remarkable, but I didn't tell her."

"What happened that night?" asked Virgil.

"We ate the chicken," said William Wallace, "and it was tender. Of course that wasn't all they had. The night I was trying their table out, it sure had good things to eat from one end to the other. Her mama and papa sat at the head and foot and we was face to face with each other across it, with I remember a pat of butter between. They had real sweet butter, with a tree drawed down it, elegant-like. Her mama eats like a man. I had brought her a whole hat-ful of berries and she didn't even pass them to her husband. Hazel, she would leap up and take a pitcher of new milk and fill up the glasses. I had heard how they couldn't have a singing at the church without a fight over her."

"Oh, she's a pretty girl, all right," said Virgil. "It's a pity for the ones like her to grow old, and get like their mothers."

"Another thing will be that her mother will get wind of this and come after me," said William Wallace.

"Her mother will eat you alive," said Virgil.

The Wide Net · *147*

"She's just been watching her chance," said William Wallace. "Why did I think I could stay out all night."

"Just something come over you."

"First it was just a carnival at Carthage, and I had to let them guess my weight . . . and after that . . ."

"It was nice to be sitting on your neck in a ditch singing" prompted Virgil, "in the moonlight. And playing on the harmonica like you can play."

"Even if Hazel did sit home knowing I was drunk, that wouldn't kill her," said William Wallace. "What she knows ain't ever killed her yet. . . . She's smart, too, for a girl," he said.

"She's a lot smarter that her cousins in Beula," said Virgil. "And especially Edna Earle, that never did get to be what you'd call a heavy thinker. Edna Earle could sit and ponder all day on how the little tail of the 'C' got through the 'L' in a Coca-Cola sign."

"Hazel *is* smart," said William Wallace. They walked on. "You ought to see her pantry shelf, it looks like a hundred jars when you open the door. I don't see how she could turn around and jump in the river."

"It's a woman's trick."

"I always behaved before. Till the one night—last night."

"Yes, but the one night," said Virgil. "And she was waiting to take advantage."

"She jumped in the river because she was scared to death of the water and that was to make it worse," he said. "She remembered how I used to have to pick her up and carry her over the oak-log bridge, how she'd shut her eyes and make a dead-weight and hold me round the neck, just for a little creek. I don't see how she brought herself to jump."

"Jumped backwards," said Virgil. "Didn't look."

WHEN THEY TURNED off, it was still early in the pink and green fields. The fumes of morning, sweet and bitter, sprang up where they walked. The insects ticked softly, their strength in reserve; butterflies chopped the air, going to the east, and the birds flew carelessly and sang by fits and starts, not the way they did in the evening in sustained and drowsy songs.

"It's a pretty *day* for sure," said William Wallace. "It's a pretty *day* for it."

"I don't see a sign of her ever going along here," said Virgil.

"Well," said William Wallace. "She wouldn't have dropped anything. I never saw a girl to leave less signs of where she's been."

"Not even a plum seed," said Virgil, kicking the grass.

In the grove it was so quiet that once William Wallace gave a jump, as if he could almost hear a sound of himself wondering where she had gone. A descent of energy came down on him in the thick of the woods and he ran at a rabbit and caught it in his hands.

"Rabbit . . . Rabbit . . ." He acted as if he wanted to take it off to himself and hold it up and talk to it. He laid a palm against its pushing heart. "Now . . . There now . . ."

"Let her go, William Wallace, let her go." Virgil, chewing on an elderberry whistle he had just made, stood at his shoulder: "What do you want with a live rabbit?"

William Wallace squatted down and set the rabbit on the ground but held it under his hand. It was a little, old, brown rabbit. It did not try to move. "See there?"

"Let her go."

"She can go if she wants to, but she don't want to."

Gently he lifted his hand. The round eye was shining at him sideways in the green gloom.

"Anybody can freeze a rabbit, that wants to," said Virgil. Suddenly he gave a far-reaching blast on the whistle, and the rabbit went in a streak. "Was you out catching cotton-tails, or was you out catching your wife?" he said, taking the turn to the open fields. "I come along to keep you on the track."

"WHO'LL WE GET, now?" They stood on top of a hill and William Wallace looked critically over the countryside. "Any of the Malones?"

The Wide Net · *149*

"I was always scared of the Malones," said Virgil. "Too many of them."

"This is my day with the net, and they would have to watch out," said William Wallace. "I reckon some Malones, and the Doyles, will be enough. The six Doyles and their dogs, and you and me, and two little nigger boys is enough, with just a few Malones."

"That ought to be enough," said Virgil, "no matter what."

"I'll bring the Malones, and you bring the Doyles," said William Wallace, and they separated at the spring.

When William Wallace came back, with a string of Malones just showing behind him on the hilltop, he found Virgil with the two little Rippen boys waiting behind him, solemn little towheads. As soon as he walked up, Grady, the one in front, lifted his hand to signal silence and caution to his brother Brucie who began panting merrily and untrustworthily behind him.

Brucie bent readily under William Wallace's hand-pat, and gave him a dreamy look out of the tops of his round eyes, which were pure green-and-white like clover tops. William Wallace gave him a nickel. Grady hung his head; his white hair lay in a little tail in the nape of his neck.

"Let's let them come," said Virgil.

"Well, they can come then, but if we keep letting everybody come it is going to be too many," said William Wallace.

"They'll appreciate it, those little-old boys," said Virgil. Brucie held up at arm's length a long red thread with a bent pin tied on the end; and a look of helpless and intense interest gathered Grady's face like a drawstring—his eyes, one bright with a sty, shone pleadingly under his white bangs, and he snapped his jaw and tried to speak. . . . "Their papa was drowned in the Pearl River," said Virgil.

There was a shout from the gully.

"Here come all the Malones," cried William Wallace. "I asked four of them would they come, but the rest of the family invited themselves."

"Did you ever see a time when they didn't," said Virgil. "And yonder from the other direction comes the Doyles, still with biscuit crumbs on their cheeks, I bet, now it's nothing to do but eat as their mother said."

"If two little niggers would come along now, or one big nigger," said William Wallace. And the words were hardly out of his mouth when two little Negro boys came along, going somewhere, one behind the other, stepping high and gay in their overalls, as though they waded in honeydew to the waist.

"Come here, boys. What's your names?"

"Sam and Robbie Bell."

"Come along with us, we're going to drag the river."

"You hear that Robbie Bell?" said Sam.

They smiled.

The Doyles came noiselessly, their dogs made all the fuss. The Malones, eight giants with great long black eyelashes, were already stamping the ground and pawing each other, ready to go. Everybody went up together to see Doc.

Old Doc owned the wide net. He had a house on top of the hill and he sat and looked out from a rocker on the front porch.

"CLIMB THE HILL and come in!" he began to intone across the valley. "Harvest's over . . . slipped up on everybody . . . cotton's picked, gone to the gin . . . hay cut . . . molasses made around here. . . . Big explosion's over, supervisors elected, some pleased, some not. . . . We're hearing talk of war!"

When they got closer, he was saying, "Many's been saved at revival, twenty-two last Sunday including a Doyle, ought to counted two. Hope they'll be a blessing to Dover community besides a shining star in Heaven. Now what?" he asked, for they had arrived and stood gathered in front of the steps.

"If nobody is using your wide net, could we use it?" asked William Wallace.

"You just used it a month ago," said Doc. "It ain't your turn."

Virgil jogged William Wallace's arm and cleared his throat. "This time is kind of special," he said. "We got reason to think William Wallace's wife Hazel is in the river, drowned."

"What reason have you got to think she's in the river drowned?" asked Doc. He took out his old pipe. "I'm asking the husband."

"Because she's not in the house," said William Wallace.

"Vanished?" and he knocked out the pipe.

"Plum vanished."

"Of course a thousand things could have happened to her," said Doc, and he lighted the pipe.

"Hand him up the letter, William Wallace," said Virgil. "We can't wait around till Doomsday for the net while Doc sits back thinkin'."

"I tore it up, right at the first," said William Wallace. "But I know it by heart. It said she was going to jump straight in the Pearl River and that I'd be sorry."

"Where do you come in, Virgil?" asked Doc.

"I was in the same place William Wallace sat on his neck in, all night, and done as much as he done, and come home the same time."

"You-all were out cuttin' up, so Lady Hazel has to jump in the river, is that it? Cause and effect? Anybody want to argue with me? Where do these others come in, Doyles, Malones, and what not?"

"Doc is the smartest man around," said William Wallace, turning to the solidly waiting Doyles, "but it sure takes time."

"These are the ones that's collected to drag the river for her," said Virgil.

"Of course I am not going on record to say so soon that *I* think she's drowned," Doc said, blowing out blue smoke.

"Do you think . . ." William Wallace mounted a step, and his hands both went into fists. "Do you think she was *carried off?*"

"Now that's the way to argue, see it from all sides," said Doc promptly. "But who by?"

Some Malone whistled, but not so you could tell which one.

"There's no booger around the Dover section that goes around carrying off young girls that's married," stated Doc.

"She was always scared of the Gypsies." William Wallace turned scarlet. "She'd sure turn her ring around on her finger if she passed one, and look in the other direction so they couldn't see she was pretty and carry her off. They come in the end of summer."

"Yes, there are the Gypsies, kidnappers since the world began. But was it to be you that would pay the grand ransom?" asked Doc. He pointed his finger. They all laughed then at how clever old Doc was and clapped William Wallace on the back. But that turned into a scuffle and they fell to the ground.

"Stop it, or you can't have the net," said Doc. "You're scaring my wife's chickens."

"It's time we was gone," said William Wallace.

The big barking dogs jumped to lean their front paws on the men's chests.

"My advice remains, Let well enough alone," said Doc. "Whatever this mysterious event will turn out to be, it has kept one woman from talking a while. However, Lady Hazel is the prettiest girl in Mississippi, you've never seen a prettier one and you never will. A golden-haired girl." He got to his feet with the nimbleness that was always his surprise, and said, "I'll come along with you."

THE PATH THEY always followed was the Old Natchez Trace. It took them through the deep woods and led them out down below on the Pearl River, where they could begin dragging it upstream to a point near Dover. They walked in silence around William Wallace, not letting him carry anything, but the net dragged heavily and the buckets were full of clatter in a place so dim and still.

Once they went through a forest of cucumber trees and came up on a high ridge. Grady and Brucie who were running ahead all the way stopped in their tracks; a whistle had blown and far down and far away a long freight train was passing. It seemed like a little festival procession, moving with the slowness of ignorance or a dream, from distance to distance, the tiny pink and gray cars like secret boxes. Grady was counting the cars to himself, as if he could certainly see each one clearly, and Brucie watched his lips, hushed and cautious, the way he would watch a bird drinking. Tears suddenly came to Grady's eyes, but it could only be because a tiny man walked along the top of the train, walking and moving on top of the moving train.

They went down again and soon the smell of the river spread over the woods, cool and secret. Every step they took among the great walls of vines and among the passion-flowers started up a little life, a little flight.

"We're walking along in the changing-time," said Doc. "Any day now the change will come. It's going to turn from hot to cold, and we can kill the hog that's ripe and have fresh meat to eat. Come one of these nights and we can wander down here and tree a nice possum. One Jack Frost will be pinching things up. Old Mr. Winter will be standing in the door. Hickory tree there will be yellow. Sweet-gum red, hickory yellow, dogwood red, sycamore yellow." He went along rapping the tree trunks with his knuckle. "Magnolia and live-oak never die. Remember that. Persimmons will all get fit to eat, and the nuts will be dropping like rain all through the woods here. And run, little quail, run, for we'll be after you too."

They went on and suddenly the woods opened upon light, and they had reached the river. Everyone stopped, but Doc talked on ahead as though nothing had happened. "Only today," he said, "today, in October sun, it's all gold—sky and tree and water. Everything just before it changes looks to be made of gold."

William Wallace looked down, as though he thought of Hazel with the shining eyes, sitting at home and looking straight before her, like a piece of pure gold, too precious to touch.

Below them the river was glimmering, narrow, soft, and skin-colored, and slowed nearly to stillness. The shining willow trees hung round them. The net that was being drawn out, so old and so long-used, it too looked golden, strung and tied with golden threads.

Standing still on the bank, all of a sudden William Wallace, on whose word they were waiting, spoke up in a voice of surprise. "What is the name of this river?"

They looked at him as if he were crazy not to know the name of the river he had fished in all his life. But a deep frown was on his forehead, as if he were compelled to wonder that people had come to call this river, or to think there was a mystery in the name of a river they all knew so well, the same as if it were some great far torrent of waves that dashed through the mountains somewhere, and almost as if it were a river in some dream, for they could not give him the name of that.

"Everybody knows Pearl River is named the Pearl River," said Doc.

A bird note suddenly bold was like a stone thrown into the water to sound it.

"It's deep here," said Virgil, and jogged William Wallace. "Remember?"

William Wallace stood looking down at the river as if it were still a mystery to him. There under his feet which hung over the bank it was transparent and yellow like an old bottle lying in the sun, filling with light.

Doc clattered all his paraphernalia.

Then all of a sudden all the Malones scattered jumping and tumbling down the bank. They gave their loud shout. Little Brucie started after them, and looked back.

"Do you think she jumped?" Virgil asked William Wallace.

II

SINCE THE NET was so wide, when it was all stretched it reached from bank to bank of the Pearl River, and the weights should hold it all the way to the bottom. Juglike sounds filled the air, splashes lifted in the sun, and the party began to move upstream. The Malones with great groans swam and pulled near the shore, the Doyles swam and pushed from behind with Virgil to tell them how to do it best; Grady and Brucie with his thread and pin trotted along the sandbars hauling buckets and lines. Sam and Robbie Bell, naked and bright, guided the old oarless rowboat that always drifted at the shore, and in it, sitting up tall with his hat on, was Doc—he went along without ever touching water and without ever taking his eyes off the net. William Wallace himself did everything but most of the time he was out of sight, swimming about under water or diving, and he had nothing to say any more.

The dogs chased up and down, in and out of the water, and in and out of the woods.

"Don't let her get too heavy, boys," Doc intoned regularly, every few minutes, "and she won't let nothing through."

"She won't let nothing through, she won't let nothing through," chanted Sam and Robbie Bell, one at his front and one at his back.

The sandbars were pink or violet drifts ahead. Where the light fell on the river, in a wandering from shore to shore, it was leaf-shaped spangles that trembled softly, while the dark of the river was calm. The willow trees leaned overhead under muscadine vines, and their trailing leaves hung like waterfalls in the morning air. The thing that seemed like silence must have been the endless cry of all the crickets and locusts in the world, rising and falling.

Every time William Wallace took hold of a big eel that slipped the net, the Malones all yelled, "Rassle with him, son!"

"Don't let her get too heavy, boys," said Doc.

"This is hard on catfish," William Wallace said once.

There were big and little fishes, dark and bright, that they caught, good ones and bad ones, the same old fish.

"This is more shoes that I ever saw got together in any store," said Virgil when they emptied the net to the bottom. "Get going!" he shouted in the next breath.

The little Rippens who had stayed ahead in the woods stayed ahead on the river. Brucie, leading them all, made small jumps and hops as he went, sometimes on one foot, sometimes on the other.

The winding river looked old sometimes, when it ran wrinkled and deep under high banks where the roots of trees hung down, and sometimes it seemed to be only a young creek, shining with the colors of wildflowers. Sometimes sandbars in the shapes of fishes lay nose to nose across, without the track of even a bird.

"Here comes some alligators," said Virgil. "Let's let them by."

They drew out on the shady side of the water, and three big alligators and four middle-sized ones went by, taking their own time.

"Look at their great big old teeth!" called a shrill voice. It was Grady making his only outcry, and the alligators were not showing their teeth at all.

"The better to eat folks with," said Doc from his boat, looking at him severely.

"Doc, you are bound to declare all you know," said Virgil. "Get going!"

When they started off again the first thing they caught in the net was the baby alligator.

"That's just what we wanted!" cried the Malones.

They set the little alligator down on a sandbar and he squatted perfectly still; they could hardly tell when it was he started to move. They watched with set faces his incredible mechanics, while the dogs after one bark stood off in inquisitive humility, until he winked.

"He's ours!" shouted all the Malones. "We're taking him home with us!"

"He ain't nothing but a little-old baby," said William Wallace.

The Malones only scoffed, as if he might be only a baby but he looked like the oldest and worst lizard.

"What are you going to do with him?" asked Virgil.

"Keep him."

"I'd be more careful what I took out of this net," said Doc.

"Tie him up and throw him in the bucket," the Malones were saying to each other, while Doc was saying "Don't come running to me and ask me what to do when he gets big."

They kept catching more and more fish, as if there was no end in sight.

"Look, a string of lady's beads," said Virgil. "Here, Sam and Robbie Bell."

Sam wore them around his head, with a knot over his forehead and loops around his ears, and Robbie Bell walked behind and stared at them.

In a shadowy place something white flew up. It was a heron, and it went away over the dark treetops. William Wallace followed it with his eyes and Brucie clapped his hands, but Virgil gave a sigh, as if he knew that when you go looking for what is lost, everything is a sign.

An eel slid out of the net.

"Rassle with him, son!" yelled the Malones. They swam like fiends.

"The Malones are in it for the fish," said Virgil.

It was about noon that there was a little rustle on the bank.

"Who is that yonder?" asked Virgil, and he pointed to a little under-sized man with short legs and a little straw hat with a band around it, who was following along on the other side of the river.

"Never saw him and don't know his brother," said Doc.

Nobody had ever seen him before.

"Who invited you?" cried Virgil hotly. "Hi . . . !" and he made signs for the little undersized man to look at him, but he would not.

"Looks like a crazy man, from here," said the Malones.

"Just don't pay any attention to him and maybe he'll go away," advised Doc.

But Virgil had already swum across and was up on the other bank. He and the stranger could be seen exchanging a word apiece and then Virgil put out his hand the way he would pat a child and patted the stranger to the ground. The little man got up again just as quickly, lifted his shoulders, turned around, and walked away with his hat tilted over his eyes.

When Virgil came back he said, "Little-old man claimed he was harmless as a baby. I told him to just try horning in on this river and anything in it."

"What did he look like up close?" asked Doc.

"I wasn't studying how he looked," said Virgil. "But I don't like anybody to come looking at me that I am not familiar with." And he shouted, "Get going!"

"Things are moving in too great a rush," said Doc.

Brucie darted ahead and ran looking into all the bushes, lifting up their branches and looking underneath.

"Not one of the Doyles has spoke a word," said Virgil.

"That's because they're not talkers," said Doc.

All day William Wallace kept diving to the bottom. Once he dived down and down into the dark water, where it was so still that nothing stirred, not even a fish, and so dark that it was no longer the muddy world of the upper river but the dark clear world of deepness, and he must have believed this was the deepest place in the whole Pearl River, and if she was not here she would not be anywhere. He was gone such a long time that the others stared hard at the surface of the water, through which the bubbles came from below. So far down and all alone, had he found Hazel? Had he suspected down there, like some secret, the real, the true trouble that Hazel had fallen into, about which words in a letter could not speak . . . how (who knew?) she had been filled to the brim with that elation that they all remembered, like their own secret, the elation that comes of great hopes and changes, sometimes simply of the harvest time, that comes with a little course of its own like a tune to run in the head, and there was nothing she could do about it—they knew—and so it had turned into this? It could be nothing but the old trouble that William Wallace was finding out, reaching and turning in the gloom of such depths.

"Look down yonder," said Grady softly to Brucie.

He pointed to the surface, where their reflections lay colorless and still side by side. He touched his brother gently as though to impress him.

"That's you and me," he said.

Brucie swayed precariously over the edge, and Grady caught him by the seat of his overalls. Brucie looked, but showed no recognition. Instead, he backed away, and seemed all at once unconcerned and spiritless, and pressed the nickel William Wallace had given him into his palm, rubbing it into his skin. Grady's inflamed eyes rested on the brown water. Without warning he saw something . . . perhaps the image in the river seemed to be his father, the drowned man—with arms open, eyes open, mouth open. . . . Grady stared and blinked, again something wrinkled up his face.

And when William Wallace came up it was in an agony from submersion, which seemed an agony of the blood and of the very heart, so woeful he looked. He was staring and glaring around in astonishment, as if a long time had gone by, away from the pale world where the brown light of the sun and the river and the little party watching him trembled before his eyes.

"What did you bring up?" somebody called—was it Virgil?

One of his hands was holding fast to a little green ribbon of plant, root and all. He was surprised, and let it go.

It was afternoon. The trees spread softly, the clouds hung wet and tinted. A buzzard turned a few slow wheels in the sky, and drifted upwards. The dogs promenaded the banks.

"It's time we ate fish," said Virgil.

ON A WIDE sandbar on which seashells lay they dragged up the haul and built a fire.

Then for a long time among clouds of odors and smoke, all half-naked except Doc, they cooked and ate catfish. They ate until the Malones groaned and all the Doyles stretched out on their faces, though for long after, Sam and Robbie Bell sat up to their own little table on a cypress stump and ate on and on. Then they all were silent and still, and one by one fell asleep.

"There ain't a thing better than fish," muttered William Wallace. He lay stretched on his back in the glimmer and shade of trampled sand. His sunburned forehead and cheeks seemed to glow with fire. His eyelids fell. The shadow of a willow branch dipped and moved over him. "There is nothing in the world as good as . . . fish. The fish of Pearl River." Then slowly he smiled. He was asleep.

But it seemed almost at once that he was leaping up, and one by one up sat the others in their ring and looked at him, for it was impossible to stop and sleep by the river.

"You're feeling as good as you felt last night," said Virgil, setting his head on one side.

"The excursion is the same when you go looking for your sorrow as when you go looking for your joy," said Doc.

But William Wallace answered none of them anything, for he was leaping all over the place and all, over them and the feast and the bones of the feast, trampling the sand, up and down, and doing a dance so crazy that he would die next. He took a big catfish and hooked it to his belt buckle and went up and down so that they all hollered, and the tears of laughter streaming down his cheeks made him put his hand up, and the two days' growth of beard began to jump out, bright red.

But all of a sudden there was an even louder cry, something almost like a cheer, from everybody at once, and all pointed fingers moved from William Wallace to the river. In the center of three light-gold rings across the water was lifted first an old hoary head ("It has whiskers!" a voice cried) and then in an undulation loop after loop and hump after hump of a long dark body, until there were a dozen rings of ripples, one behind the other, stretching all across the river, like a necklace.

"The King of the Snakes!" cried all the Malones at once, in high tenor voices and leaning together.

"The King of the Snakes," intoned old Doc in his profound bass.

"He looked you in the eye."

William Wallace stared back at the King of the Snakes with all his might.

It was Brucie that darted forward, dangling his little thread with the pin tied to it, going toward the water.

"That's the King of the Snakes!" cried Grady, who always looked after him.

Then the snake went down.

The little boy stopped with one leg in the air, spun around on the other, and sank to the ground.

"Git up," Grady whispered. "It was just the King of the Snakes. He went off whistling. Git up. It wasn't a thing but the King of the Snakes."

Brucie's green eyes opened, his tongue darted out, and he sprang up; his feet were heavy, his head light, and he rose like a bubble coming to the surface.

Then thunder like a stone loosened and rolled down the bank.

THEY ALL STOOD unwilling on the sandbar, holding to the net. In the eastern sky were the familiar castles and the round towers to which they were used, gray, pink, and blue, growing darker and filling with thunder. Lightning flickered in the sun along their thick walls. But in the west the sun shone with such a violence that in an illumination like a long-prolonged glare of lightning the heavens looked black and white; all color left the world, the goldenness of everything was like a memory, and only heat, a kind of glamor and oppression, lay on their heads. The thick heavy trees on the other side of the river were brushed with mile-long streaks of silver, and a wind touched each man on the forehead. At the same time there was a long roll of thunder that began behind them, came up and down mountains and valleys of air, passed over their heads, and left them listening still. With a small, near noise a mockingbird followed it, the little white bars of its body flashing over the willow trees.

"We are here for a storm now," Virgil said. "We will have to stay till it's over."

They retreated a little, and hard drops fell in the leathery leaves at their shoulders and about their heads.

"Magnolia's the loudest tree there is in a storm," said Doc.

Then the light changed the water, until all about them the woods in the rising wind seemed to grow taller and blow inward together and suddenly turn dark. The rain struck heavily. A huge tail seemed to lash through the air and the river broke in a wound of silver. In silence the party crouched and stooped beside the trunk of the great tree, which in the push of the storm rose full of a fragrance and unyielding weight. Where they all stared, past their tree, was another tree, and beyond that another and another, all the way down the bank of the river, all towering and darkened in the storm.

"The outside world is full of endurance," said Doc. "Full of endurance."

Robbie Bell and Sam squatted down low and embraced each other from the start.

"Runs in our family to get struck by lightnin'," said Robbie Bell. "Lightnin' drawed a pitchfork right on our grandpappy's cheek, stayed till he died. Pappy got struck by some bolts of lightnin' and was dead three days, dead as that-there axe."

There was a succession of glares and crashes.

"This'n's goin' to be either me or you," said Sam. "Here come a little bug. If he go to the left, be me, and to the right, be you."

But at the next flare a big tree on the hill seemed to turn into fire before their eyes, every branch, twig, and leaf, and a purple cloud hung over it.

"Did you hear that crack?" asked Robbie Bell. "That were its bones."

"Why do you little niggers talk so much!" said Doc. "Nobody's profiting by this information."

"We always talks this much," said Sam "but now everybody so quiet, they hears us."

The great tree, split and on fire, fell roaring to earth. Just at its moment of falling, a tree like it on the opposite bank split wide open and fell in two parts.

"Hope they ain't goin' to be no balls of fire come rollin' over the water and fry all the fishes with they scales on," said Robbie Bell.

The water in the river had turned purple and was filled with sudden currents and whirlpools. The little willow trees bent almost to its surface, bowing one after another down the bank and almost breaking under the storm. A great curtain of wet leaves was borne along before a blast of wind, and every human being was covered.

"Now us got scales," wailed Sam. "Us is the fishes."

"Hush up, little-old colored children," said Virgil. "This isn't the way to act when somebody takes you out to drag a river."

"Poor lady's-ghost, I bet it is scareder than us," said Sam.

"All I hoping is, us don't find her!" screamed Robbie Bell.

William Wallace bent down and knocked their heads together. After that they clung silently in each other's arms, the two black heads resting, with wind-filled cheeks and tight-closed eyes, one upon the other until the storm was over.

"Right over yonder is Dover," said Virgil. "We've come all the way. William Wallace, you have walked on a sharp rock and cut your foot open."

III

IN DOVER IT had rained, and the town looked somehow like new. The wavy heat of late afternoon came down from the watertank and fell over everything like shiny mosquito-netting. At the wide place where the road was paved and patched with tar, it seemed newly embedded with Coca-Cola tops. The old circus posters on the store were nearly gone, only bits, the snowflakes of white horses, clinging to its side. Morning-glory vines started almost visibly to grow over the roofs and cling round the ties of the railroad track, where bluejays lighted on the rails, and umbrella chinaberry trees hung heavily over the whole town, dripping intermittently upon the tin roofs.

Each with his counted fish on a string the members of the river-dragging party walked through the town. They went toward the town well, and there was Hazel's mother's house, but no sign of her yet coming out. They all drank a dipper of the water, and still there was not a soul on the street. Even the bench in front of the store was empty, except for a little corn-shuck doll.

But something told them somebody had come, for after one moment people began to look out of the store and out of the post-office. All the bird dogs woke up to see the Doyle dogs and such a large number of men and boys materialize suddenly with such a big catch of fish, and they ran out barking. The Doyle dogs joyously barked back. The bluejays flashed up and screeched above the town, whipping through their tunnels in the chinaberry trees. In the café a nickel clattered inside a music box and a love song began to play. The whole town of Dover began to throb in its wood and tin, like an old tired heart, when the men walked through once more, coming around again and going down the street carrying the fish, so drenched, exhausted, and muddy that no one could help but admire them.

William Wallace walked through the town as though he did not see anybody or hear anything. Yet he carried his great string of fish held high where it could be seen by all. Virgil came next, imitating William Wallace exactly, then the modest Doyles crowded by the Malones, who were holding up their alligator, tossing it in the air, even, like a father tossing his child. Following behind and pointing authoritatively at the ones in front strolled Doc, with Sam and Robbie Bell still chanting in his wake. In and out of the whole little line Grady and Brucie jerked about. Grady, with his head ducked, and stiff as a rod, walked with a springy limp; it made him look forever angry and unapproachable. Under his breath he was whispering, "Sty, sty, git out of my eye, and git on somebody passin' by." He traveled on with narrowed shoulders, and kept his eye unerringly upon his little brother, wary and at the same time proud, as though he held a flying June-bug on a string. Brucie, making a twanging noise with his lips, had shot forth again, and he was darting rapidly everywhere at once, delighted and tantalized, running in circles around William Wallace, pointing to his fish. A frown of pleasure like the print of a bird's

foot was stamped between his faint brows, and he trotted in some unknown realm of delight.

"Did you ever see so many fish?" said the people in Dover.

"How much are your fish, mister?"

"Would you sell your fish?"

"Is that all the fish in Pearl River?"

"How much you sell them all for? Everybody's?"

"Three dollars," said William Wallace suddenly, and loud.

The Malones were upon him and shouting, but it was too late.

And just as William Wallace was taking the money in his hand,
Hazel's mother walked solidly out of her front door and saw it.

"You can't head her mother off," said Virgil. "Here she comes in
full bloom."

But William Wallace turned his back on her, that was all, and on
everybody, for that matter, and that was the breaking-up of the party.

JUST AS THE sun went down, Doc climbed his back steps, sat in his
chair on the back porch where he sat in the evenings, and lighted his
pipe. William Wallace hung out the net and came back and Virgil was
waiting for him, so they could say good evening to Doc.

"All in all," said Doc, when they came up, "I've never been on a
better river-dragging, or seen better behavior. If it took catching catfish
to move the Rock of Gibraltar, I believe this outfit could move it."

"Well, we didn't catch Hazel," said Virgil.

"What did you say?" asked Doc.

"He don't really pay attention," said Virgil. "I said, 'We didn't catch
Hazel.'"

"Who says Hazel was to be caught?" asked Doc "She wasn't in
there. Girls don't like the water—remember that. Girls don't just haul
off and go jumping in the river to get back at their husbands. They got
other ways."

"Didn't you ever think she was in there?" asked William Wallace.
"The whole time?"

"Nary once," said Doc.

"He's just smart," said Virgil, putting his hand on William Wallace's arm. "It's only because we didn't find her that he wasn't looking for her."

"I'm beholden to you for the net, anyway," said William Wallace.

"You're welcome to borry it again," said Doc.

ON THE WAY home Virgil kept saying, "Calm down, calm down, William Wallace."

"If he wasn't such an old skinny man I'd have wrung his neck for him," said William Wallace. "He had no business coming."

"He's too big for his britches," said Virgil. "Don't nobody know everything. And just because it's his net. Why does it have to be his net?"

"If it wasn't for being polite to old men, I'd have skinned him alive," said William Wallace.

"I guess he don't really know nothing about wives at all, his wife's so deaf," said Virgil.

"He don't know Hazel," said William Wallace. "I'm the only man alive knows Hazel: would she jump in the river or not, and I say she would. She jumped in because I was sitting on the back of my neck in a ditch singing, and that's just what she ought to done. Doc ain't got no right to say one word about it."

"Calm down, calm down, William Wallace," said Virgil.

"If it had been you that talked like that, I'd have broke every bone in your body," said William Wallace. "Just let you talk like that. You're my age and size."

"But I ain't going to talk like that," said Virgil. "What have I done the whole time but keep this river-dragging going straight and running even, without no hitches? You couldn't have drug the river a foot without me."

"What are you talking about! Without who!" cried William Wallace. "This wasn't your river-dragging! It wasn't your wife!" He jumped on Virgil and they began to fight.

"Let me up." Virgil was breathing heavily.

"Say it was my wife. Say it was my river-dragging."

"Yours!" Virgil was on the ground with William Wallace's hand putting dirt in his mouth.

"Say it was my net."

"Your net!"

"Get up then."

They walked along getting their breath, and smelling the honeysuckle in the evening. On a hill William Wallace looked down, and at the same time there went drifting by the sweet sounds of music outdoors. They were having the Sacred Harp Sing on the grounds of an old white church glimmering there at the crossroads, far below. He stared away as if he saw it minutely, as if he could see a lady in white take a flowered cover off the organ, which was set on a little slant in the shade, dust the keys, and start to pump and play. . . . He smiled faintly, as he would at his mother, and at Hazel, and at the singing women in his life, now all one young girl standing up to sing under the trees the oldest and longest ballads there were.

Virgil told him good night and went into his own house and the door shut on him.

When he got to his own house, William Wallace saw to his surprise that it had not rained at all. But there, curved over the roof, was something he had never seen before as long as he could remember, a rainbow at night. In the light of the moon, which had risen again, it looked small and of gauzy material, like a lady's summer dress, a faint veil through which the stars showed.

He went up on the porch and in at the door, and all exhausted he had walked through the front room and through the kitchen when he heard his name called. After a moment, he smiled, as if no matter what he might have hoped for in his wildest heart, it was better than that to hear his name called out in the house. The voice came out of the bedroom.

"What do you want?" he yelled, standing stock-still.

Then she opened the bedroom door with the old complaining creak, and there she stood. She was not changed a bit.

"How do you feel?" he said.

"I feel pretty good. Not too good," Hazel said, looking mysterious.

"I cut my foot," said William Wallace, taking his shoe off so she could see the blood.

"How in the world did you do that?" she cried, with a step back.

"Dragging the river. But it don't hurt any longer."

"You ought to have been more careful," she said. "Supper's ready and I wondered if you would ever come home, or if it would be last night all over again. Go and make yourself fit to be seen," she said, and ran away from him.

After supper they sat on the front steps a while.

"Where were you this morning when I came in?" asked William Wallace when they were ready to go in the house.

"I was hiding," she said. "I was still writing on the letter. And then you tore it up."

"Did you watch me when I was reading it?"

"Yes, and you could have put out your hand and touched me, I was so close."

But he bit his lip, and gave her a little tap and slap, and then turned her up and spanked her.

"Do you think you will do it again?" he asked.

"I'll tell my mother on you for this!"

"Will you do it again?"

"No!" she cried.

"Then pick yourself up off my knee."

It was just as if he had chased her and captured her again. She lay smiling in the crook of his arm. It was the same as any other chase in the end.

"I will do it again if I get ready," she said. "Next time will be different, too."

Then she was ready to go in, and rose up and looked out from the top step, out across their yard where the China tree was and beyond, into the dark fields where the lightning-bugs flickered away. He climbed to his feet too and stood beside her, with the frown on his face, trying to look where she looked. And after a few minutes she took him by the hand and led him into the house, smiling as if she were smiling down on him.

AFTER MOORE

Mary Hood

I

RHONDA COULD DIVIDE her whole life into *before* and *after* Moore.
She was fifteen when they met, and thirty now. She had gone to the
Buckhorn Club with a carload of older friends and a fake ID in her pocket
just in case. Moore, a manufacturer's rep, had been standing alone at the
bar, thirtyish, glancing indifferently around, looking familiar. Her friends
kept daring her, and after a few beers Rhonda threaded through the
crowd to ask him:

"You think you're Ted Turner or something?"

It is true he cultivated the likeness, in style and posture, the neat
silver-shot mustache, the careless curve of gold around his lean wrist, the
insolence: his calculating, damn-all eyes focused always on the inner, driving dream. Because she had been searching so long for her mysteriously

lost father, a trucker, she thought she preferred men rougher, blue collar, not white silk, monogrammed. For his part, he knew he was dancing with danger. Still, or perhaps because of that, Moore drew her to him, so close he could reach around her, slip his hands into the back pockets of her jeans, and ask: "You ever wear a dress, jailbait?" They were slow-dancing, legs between, not toe-to-toe.

"I take my pants off sometimes," Rhonda said. She was pretty fast for fifteen, but not fast enough. That was when and how it began, with her wanting someone, and him wanting anyone. Love was all they knew to call it.

"My problem is I'm a romantic," Moore said.

"I guess I still love him, but so what?" Rhonda told the counselor. They had sought professional help toward the bitter end. The family counselor listened and listened.

"I got married when I was fifteen," Rhonda explained. "A case of *had to*. . . . Three babies in five years, tell me what chance I had?" And Moore with such ingrained tastes and habits—sitting for barbershop shaves, manicures, spitshines on his Italian shoes. "What he paid out in tips would've kept all three babies in Pampers," Rhonda grieved, "except he didn't believe in throwaway diapers, said it was throwing away money." But he couldn't stand to be around when she laundered cloth diapers, either, and when it rained—before she bought her dryer at a yard sale—and she had to hang them indoors on strings all over the house, and the steam rose as she ironed them dry, Moore would leave. "He just doesn't have the stomach for baby business," Rhonda said.

Moore said "I never hit her. If she says I did, she's lying."

"He had this *list*," she told the counselor. "A scorecard. All the women he's had." She found it the day Chip and Scott ran away.

The boys had made up their beds to look as though they were still asleep in them, body-shaping the pillows, arranging the sheets. They slipped out the window and dropped to the sour bare ground, not to be missed for hours. When Moore slept in on Saturdays, the duplex had to stay holy dark, Sabbath still, and no cartoons. "Boring," the boys remembered. Rhonda made sure there were always library books around, but Chip and Scott weren't readers then. They saw the window as a good way out. "We had a loose screen," Scott told the counselor.

"You've got a loose screw," Chip told Scott. He didn't see getting friendly with the counselor, who had classified him, already, as a "tough case." Chip lay low in his chair, legs spraddled, heels dug in, arms behind his head as he gazed at the ceiling tiles. He was the one most like Moore.

Corey said, "We had fun."

Scott said, "Not you. You were a baby in the crib. Just Chip and me."

Corey told the counselor, "Chip's the oldest."

"*Numero uno,*" Chip agreed. The boys were talking to the counselor on their own, by themselves. Rhonda and Moore sat in the waiting room.

"It wasn't *running away,*" Scott explained. "We were just goofing around."

Corey said, "I bet Mom yelled."

"Mom's okay," Scott said.

Corey agreed. "I like her *extremely.* I guess I love her."

Chip said, "Oh boy."

"Moore came after us," Scott said. It had been years but the shock and awe were still fresh.

"God yes," Chip said. "He gave us Sam Hell all the way home." And it is true that Moore had stripped off his belt and leathered their bare legs right up the stairs and into the apartment.

"It was summer," Scott said. "No Six Flags that year, no nothing."

"They thought you were kidnapped," Corey said, in that slow way he had, as though truth were a matter of diction. "Mom worries about dumb stuff," he told the counselor. "During tornado season she writes our names on our legs in Magic Marker . . ."

"And we have to wear seat belts," Scott added.

"And keep the car doors locked *at all times.*"

"That was because of Moore trying to snatch us that time and go to California, but that's okay now," Chip said. "He was just drunk."

"We call him Moore because that's his name," Corey explained. "He says, 'Is *Son* your name? Well *Daddy's* not mine . . .'"

"He tells the waitresses we're his brothers," Chip said.

"He belted us because he thought we ripped off his wallet," Scott said. "That was why."

"Which we damn well did not," Chip pointed out.

Rhonda had found it in the laundry box, in Moore's jogging pants pocket, where he'd left it. "That's when it hit the fan," Rhonda said. She had looked through the contents, not spying, "just exercising a wifely prerogative," and behind the side window, with his driver's license and Honest Face, there had been the record of his conquests, a little book with names and dates.

"I was number seventy-eight," Rhonda said. Not the last one on the list by any means.

When the family counselor spoke to them one-on-one, they talked freely enough, but when they gathered as a group again, reconvening in the semicircled chairs, a cagey silence fell. The counselor, thus at bay, tested their solidarity, fired shots into it, harking for ricochet or echo. Were they closed against each other, or him? He left the room, to see. In the hall, he listened. There was nothing to overhear but their unbroken, patient, absolute silences, each with its own truth, as though they were dumb books on a shelf. He did not necessarily know how to open them, to read them to each other.

"It can't all be up to *me,*" he warned, going back in, as they looked up, hoping it would be easy, or over soon.

II

MOORE HAD SAID, "All right, then, let's split," more than once when the bills and grievances piled up on Rhonda's heart and she made suggestions. Moore called it "nagging." Sometimes Moore did leave them, not just on business. Perhaps after a fight, always after a payday. He'd be back, though, sooner or later.

"A man like Moore can be gone a week or so and then whistle on

Mary Hood · 174

back home like he's been out for a haircut," Rhonda said. "In the meantime, he'll never stop to drop his lucky quarter into a phone and call collect to say he's still alive and itching." On a moment's notice he'd fly to Vegas, the Bahamas, Atlantic City, anywhere he could gamble. He never took his family.

"We'd cramp his style," Rhonda said. "He's the sort of man that needs more than one woman."

MOORE HAD BEEN the one to say, "Let's split, then," but in all those years Rhonda had been the one who had actually walked out with full intentions of never coming back. The first time had been early on, while Chip was still an only child, in that rocky beginning year, long before Rhonda discovered that she was number 78, Rosalind was number 122, and Moore was still counting. Rhonda took Chip and drove away, rode as far as she could till she ran out of gas. She had no money, and the only thing in her pocket besides Chip's pacifier was the fake ID she had used to get into the clubs. Her learner's permit had expired while she was on the maternity ward.

When she had burned up all the gas, she nosed the coasting station wagon over the berm and into a ditch, and ran the battery down with the dome light and radio. This was a side road heading generally toward Alabama, and not much traffic passed. She told the ones who stopped she was fine, didn't need help. When things got dark and quiet, she and the baby slept. It was good weather that time, so they were fairly comfortable. By morning Moore had had the state patrol track them down. They had to be towed out.

"God, he loved that Volvo," Rhonda said.

THE ONLY OTHER time she had left him she had learned better than to take his wheels. She walked, rolling Chip along in the stroller. Scott, baby number two, was due in three months. Rhonda headed for the church.

"You know, just to hide out," Rhonda explained, "till I could figure what to do next. The last place he'd look.'' She didn't count on its being locked. It was raining so she pushed the baby back on down the road to Starvin' Marvin's and bought a cup of coffee. She gave the baby her nondairy creamer, loaded her cup with sugar, and nursed the steam till the rain let up. Then she headed on home.

"Moore don't know about that time," Rhonda said. "He never even missed us."

She said, "Don't expect me to be fair. The kids love him. Ask them. They think he's Jesus Christ, Santa Claus, and Rambo all rolled into one. But you ask me, I'll give you an earful. I'll try for facts, but I can't help my feelings."

She said, "Between jobs he'd get so low he'd cry." Moore was always jumping to a better job, and when the glamour wore off, he'd jump again, sometimes with no place to land.

"I've only been fired three times for my temper," Moore said. "The real reason is I drink a little sometimes. But I never lost a client or a sale. When I did, I made it up on the next one. They've got no kick! Anywhere I go I can get a top job in one day. You kidding? My résumé's solid gold. People like me. They remember me. They trust me."

"He has a bad habit of talking up to his bosses," Rhonda said. "Says all men are created equal and he isn't in the goddamned Marines any more and don't have to call no SOB *sir*."

"I've got an 'attitude,'" Moore said.

One layoff with him home underfoot every day, Rhonda took up gardening. "I got a real kick out of digging in the dirt. Anything, just to stay out of his reach. If he wasn't yelling at me and the kids, he was wanting to talk, as in 'Lay down, I think I love you.' We didn't need any more rug rats!"

She made a beautiful garden that year. There was even time for a pumpkin vine to bear fruit. She trained it around a little cage of rabbit fence filled with zinnias. "Pretty as a quilt," she said. "I'd go out there and rake leaves, pull weeds, plant stuff for spring. . . . You have to look ahead, put out a little hope, even if you rent." They were always moving. They rented their furniture and TV.

"Someday I'm going to have my own place, great big yard. Put down roots a mile deep. My house is going to suffer, but that yard'll look like a dream come true. I'm tired of praising other women's glads!"

She and her babies would stay outdoors till moonlight, working, enjoying the air, steering clear of Moore's moods. She was still a teenager herself, more like their baby-sitter than their mother. They played in the leaves, piling them, jumping in, scattering them around by the arm-loads. "The way Moore spends money," Rhonda said. "Fast as he can rake it in."

He never did without anything nice he could owe for. "You've got to go into debt to get ahead," he'd tell Rhonda. But somehow they never could get enough ahead to put a down payment on a house of their own.

"According to *Woman's Day*," Rhonda said, "what married couples argue about most is m-o-n-e-y." She had showed Moore that article about credit counseling, with the local phone number already looked up. He threw the magazine out the window.

"Not down, but *up*," Rhonda explained. "I guess it's still on the roof, educating the pigeons."

But he did agree to open a savings account, salt a little away for the boys. "The school says they all test way above average and Scott's maybe a genius," Rhonda told the counselor. "I figure we owe them more than life. I *know* we do. What's life if there's no future in it? What did my parents ever hope for me?"

With the opening of the savings account, and the balance slowly growing, Rhonda had begun to feel that they were on their way. Then that fall the tax bill came.

"See, we rent," Rhonda told the counselor. "No property taxes on that. But here was this bill for taxes on a lot in Breezewater Estates! Waterfront high-dollar location." Rhonda couldn't believe it. Since it was

After Moore · 177

near her birthday, she guessed that Moore had meant it to be a surprise. She didn't want to wait. "I tooled up that day, while the kids were still in school, just to sneak a peek. Wouldn't you?"

She drove along hoping for a shade tree or two. "An oak," she decided. "If there wasn't one, we'd plant an acorn. There was plenty of time for it to grow." But when she got there, there was no oak, just pines and a trailer. "Not a house trailer, but a little bitty camper," Rhonda said. No one was home. "But there was sexy laundry of the female persuasion dripping on the line," Rhonda said. Patio lamps shaped like ice-cream cones, a barbecue cooker on wheels, and a name on the mail in the mailbox: *Rosalind.*

"I won't say her last name," Rhonda said. "Why blame her? She'd be as shocked to learn about me as I was to learn about her."

Rhonda laughed. "I knew it wouldn't last either. Maybe not past first frost. That trailer had 'Summer Romance' and 'Temporary Insanity' and 'Repossess' written all over it."

Rosalind was Moore's 122nd true love.

"That's how Moore is," Rhonda said. "He can't help it."

She had driven straight home in her Fury, a rattling old clunker she never washed, believing that the dirt helped hold it together. "I could poke my finger through the rust," she said, "but not the mud." Moore hated the whole idea of that car. She had had to cut a few budgetary corners to achieve it—buying it from Moore's father at his auto-salvage yard—and from spare parts made its fenders whole again, though of unmatching colors. She paid cash, like any customer off the street.

"No favors," she told her father-in-law. "Except don't tell Moore."

For six months she kept the car a secret, parking it down the block. But when they moved away from there, she had to explain it to Moore when the car showed up on their new street. It wasn't the sort of car you can overlook. She told him his father had made her a deal on it, for two hundred dollars. Actually, she had paid three-fifty, but the extra had gone for transmission seals, retreads, and a new battery. The muffler was shot and the car blew smoke, rumbled and shook in idle, and when she gave it some gas, the U-joint clunked.

"You're a goddamn redneck," Moore had yelled, over the racket. "I don't want to see that car in my driveway!" He stood between her and his leased BMW.

"Like rust was contagious," Rhonda said.

ALL THE WAY home from discovering Rosalind's little trailer Rhonda thought up ways to pay Moore back for the rotten surprise, for using up their savings to make another woman happy. She considered cutting off the sleeves of his cashmere sweaters, or filling his shoes with dog mess. He was particular about his shoes. . . . "He'll pay out more for one pair than he gives me for a week's groceries."

Moore said, "I'd rather go without lunch for a month than walk on crappy leather."

"He threw the slippers the boys bought him for Christmas in the fireplace. J.C. Penney, not junk! They burned. I couldn't even take them back for credit on our revolving charge," Rhonda said.

"In my line of life," Moore said, "you have to impress people into respecting you. I don't mean pimp flash. I mean class. What people can *see*: tailoring, jewelry, gloves, car. . . . Look at my hands, like a surgeon's. And I've got a great smile. A fair country voice too; I could've been a singer. I could've been a lot of things; that's why I can sell: I have sympathy. I'm a great listener."

Rhonda said, "I don't know why I wasted my breath arguing with him when he came home that night. And the funny thing is, we didn't really argue about Rosalind at all. We argued about money. So I guess *Woman's Day* is pretty much on the ball."

Moore had said, "That bank account was my money. I earned it."

Rhonda said, "I earned it too."

Moore said, "Housekeeping?" with a mean look around the kitchen: greasy dishes piled in the cold suds, laundry heaped on the dining table for sorting, and no supper underway.

Thus the stage was set for the final argument, with shots fired.

III

COREY, THEIR AIM-to-please baby, the one they all called Mister Personality now he was nine, told the counselor, "Mom tried to kill Moore, so he left."

Chip said, "In your ear, Corey," but Corey didn't take the warning, just went right on, adding:

"It was Moore's gun. He had to buy another one. She stole it and kept it. It's on top of the refrigerator in the cake box."

"It's not loaded," Chip said.

"That's what Moore said," Scott pointed out. "Then pow! pow! pow!

"She only fired twice," Chip said. He had watched, the bedroom door open a pajama button wide, his left eye taking it all in, from the first slug Rhonda fired into the shag rug between Moore's ankles to the way the taillights looked as Moore headed west.

"I probably shouldn't have drunk those three strawberry daiquiris made with Campbell's tomato soup," Rhonda said, with her wild, unrueful laugh, "but we were out of frozen strawberries." She was a good shot, even when hammered with vodka. That was exactly where she had aimed. She raised the gun a little, between Moore's knees and belt buckle. "Dead center," she warned. "Don't dare me."

When she and Moore had gone to the firing range so he could teach her how to handle a gun, her scores had been sharpshooter quality. His were not.

"An off day," he had said. "Too much caffeine." He didn't give up coffee, but he didn't take her there again either. It was the only thing in their life so far she had been better at than him. "Except holding a grudge," Moore said.

Moore never took her anywhere much after they were married. She was no asset, pregnant. Before, they had gone to clubs and races. He liked the horses, but he'd bet on anything running, walking, or flying, any sport, so long as there was action. He'd scratch up the cash to lay down even if he had to pawn something. When he'd win big, he'd spend big. "You've got to live up to your luck," Moore said. He didn't like anything cheap or secondhand.

"Like my car," Rhonda said. "I used up my Fury in the demolition derby, so I've got me a Heavy Chevy now, a Nova with a 355 engine. That's what I race. Moore's dad is helping me keep it tuned." She had only been stock-car racing a year, just since Moore left. She had found a job as a waitress at the VFW, working from two in the afternoon till one at night—"No way to keep my health," she agreed, "but I had bills to pay off." She had got them whittled down to five hundred dollars by hoarding her tips and with what she saved on rent by moving in with Moore's father, in the trailer at the junkyard. "It's easier on the boys, anyway," she said. "They can ride the bus to school, and I know there'll be someone there to meet with them when they get home, even if I'm at work.

"What I really wanted to do," Rhonda said, "was drive an over-the-road truck. You know my daddy was a gear-jammer, and I'm still not satisfied with what I know about that story. I'm not even convinced he's dead." She thought he might be out there somewhere, and maybe she could find him, in the truck stops, rest areas, coffee shops. "I'd know him," she said. "Something like that, you know in your heart." In any other city she and Moore had ever traveled to, she had slipped away in cafés, gas stations, or motel lobbies to check the phone directory, furtively flipping through the pages, hoping for news. She wore that questing look on her face, always searching the crowds, every stranger a candidate. Moore didn't understand. He called it flirting. They had more than one fight about it.

"Can you picture it? *Him* jealous of *me?* Maybe I did a little shopping, but I never bought any. I'm no cheat," she said. "All I ever wanted was a man who'd be there for the kids, be a real daddy, not run out on me. And here I am living out my life like history repeating itself.

"So how can I go on the road, full time, with three kids to raise? I can't leave them—don't I know how that feels? They count plenty in my plans, and they know it." Her brother was in prison in Texas.

"Nine to life at Huntsville," she explained. "He's no letter writer." And her mother had dropped out of sight two marriages ago. With no family, and no diploma, she had chosen the best she could, and made the most of her chances. When she read that poster for the demolition derby out at the dirt track, prize purse of one thousand—"That's a one, followed by three zeroes," Rhonda marveled—she had decided to go for it.

Moore said, "I have a bad habit of not taking her seriously, you know? Like night school. She was all fired up over that, too, but she didn't stick with it. I thought racing would be the same way."

Rhonda had dropped out of night school, never getting even close to an equivalency diploma because she was so off and on about attendance. Moore didn't like watching the boys while she was gone, and there was no nursery at the school. The boys made him feel tied down, nervous, even if they slept through.

"I'd give them beer for supper," Rhonda said. The baby would take it right from the bottle and hope for seconds. "They were good babies," Rhonda said. "And they were *his,* but so far as I know, he never once changed a soak-ass diaper or cleaned up any puke but his own." Night school hadn't worked out.

"Nowadays, they let girls go back to high school when they get married. Regular classes, every day. I don't know if I would have, even if I could have. Maybe just gone back once to show my rings." It was Moore's first wife's diamond. "I knew I was number two, and that he had a past, but I thought I was woman enough to handle anything that came up. I don't mean that dirty. . . . Well, maybe. I was pretty cocky back then, before I knew he was keeping score."

She had painted her number—78— on the racer's door. "My first demolition derby was my last. I said to myself, 'Rhonda, why spend your life mostly in reverse, taking cheap shots and being blindsided? That's too much like everyday life.' I decided right then I was going to race.''

"It's just like Rhonda to think she can get ahead by going in circles," Moore said. "And my old man—Christ!—this is his second childhood."

Rhonda said, "Did he tell you that he thinks his daddy and I are a number? He came back from California and found that I was living there at the salvage yard and flung a fit."

"Did Rhonda tell you that she's living with my old man now?" Moore had returned home in a van. He drove it over to the auto salvage to ask his father if he could crash there a couple of days, "Just till I got back on my feet," Moore said. "The van's a home away from home, I just needed a water spigot to hook to and somewhere to plug in my extension cord. There they all were, one big happy family, churning out to see me like peasants around the Pope. Chip had grown. He was as tall as I am, and Corey wasn't sure if he knew me anymore . . .''

Rhonda said, "He didn't have a word for me. He told his daddy, 'I was just going to plug into your outlet, to charge my batteries. God knows you've been doing a little plugging into mine.' He said it right in front of the boys!" Rhonda said, heating up all over again.

Moore's father said, trying to joke them past the awkward moment, but only making it worse, "She's got her pick of dozens of good-looking guys every night at work, why should she settle for a one-armed, gut-busted, short-peckered old-timer with a gap in his beard?" The gap came from a welding accident years before. Moore didn't stick around to listen to his father or Rhonda explain. He backed the van out and headed away, fast, taking the three boys with him.

"I saw those California plates vanishing down Dayton Road and all I could think was: *kidnapping*." She called the state patrol first, "and then every damn number in the world, and threw the book at him," Rhonda explained.

"She hoodooed me," Moore said. "I don't just mean the writ. She visits palm readers. She's put some sort of hex on my love life. I'm telling you, since that afternoon, nothing. As in, zero, *nada*. It's not just the equipment, it's the want-to. I'm seeing a doc. He says it's in my head, says if I lay off the booze and keep up my jogging program—''

"They got Moore back on the road at the wring-out clinic," Rhonda said. "He's looking one hundred percent better."

"—I'll be good as new in no time. I've just got to take it easy on myself for a while. Avoid challenging and competitive situations. I'm not even working as a rep any more. I'm a plain old nine-to-five jerk clerk for B. Dalton. Just till I get my feet back on the ground. Something's better than nothing. You'd be surprised at what-all you can learn from books. I'm reading more now than I did in all my life before, a book a night. What else do I have to do, you know?"

"He was gone a *year*," Rhonda said, "and he never sent back one penny of child support, one birthday hello, one Merry Christmas. I'm lucky his daddy helped us out, or we'd have been on food stamps from day one." It was Moore's father she had called the night of their battle when Rhonda fired those two shots, the first one burning into the carpet and the second—because Rhonda's attention wandered an instant before she pulled the trigger—breaking the picture window and their lease. His father came right over, asking no questions, taking no sides, with a stapler and a roll of three-mil plastic garden mulch to tack over the empty window frame. By then, Rhonda had thrown all of Moore's stuff out onto the lawn and was praying for rain.

IV

"MOORE'S DAD IS so special," Rhonda said. "He loves the kids like they were his own, and they get a kick out of him too. But I quit going over there to see him when Moore was along. We'd go on weekdays instead. Mainly, Moore just hated going, but he didn't like it when we left him home, either. When he's ticked off like that, it's a pain."

Moore liked things better than he found them at the salvage yard. The junk dealer made jokes about Moore's exalted tastes, saying things like, "You must've hatched from the wrong egg. If we didn't favor, I'd say the hospital must've pulled a switch on us as to babies, but they won't take you back now, so I guess we're stuck." And he'd offer Moore a can of beer.

Moore always brought his own brand, imported. "Green-bottle beer" is what Rhonda called it. He wouldn't drink Old Milwaukee. "A pretty good brew if you ask me," Rhonda said.

Moore used the Old Milwaukee cans for target practice, out behind the junkyard office. "All they're good for," he said.

"He'd have been a better shot if he'd have worn his glasses," Rhonda said, "but heaven forbid anyone seeing him in glasses!"

"Sure I wear a gun," Moore told the therapist he was seeing about sexual dysfunction. "While I'm breathing I'm toting. It's legal. I don't go around ventilating people. I just want a little respect, you know? Who's going to argue with a gun?"

Rhonda had hated it when Moore used to shoot up the beer cans in the junkyard. The way it sounded when he missed and the bullet shattered glass in one of the junked cars. The way Moore laughed. Rhonda wouldn't let the boys play outside when he was like that. She made them stay in, watching TV. Moore's father stationed himself at the door, apparently looking at the clouds, talking about the weather like he was a farmer. He had all sorts of instruments on his roof and kept records—wind speed, humidity, barometric pressure, records for high and low, precipitation—and called the television weathermen to correct them when they made a bad forecast. "It was his hobby," Rhonda said, "till he took up racing. He'd talk about clouds while Moore shot those cans through the heart like they were Commies. And the kids would have the TV going full blast. It was crazy. And his daddy just fretting, saying, 'Looks like a son of mine would have sense enough to come in out of the rain.'" Moore got as wild as the weather, sometimes, and he'd stand out in the open, defying the lightning and the kudzu. Every year the vines and weeds grew nearer, creeping over the acres toward the trailer on the hill, turning the pines into topiary jungles. On the junkyard's cyclone fence the boys had helped their grandfather spell out HUBCAPS in glittering wheelcovers, and on the pole by the office a weathered flag lifted and drooped in the breezes. This was the flag honoring Moore's brother, who was still listed officially as missing in action. It had, over the years, faded like their hopes.

"Moore and him were jarheads—"

"—leathernecks—"

"*Marines*," the boys told the counselor.

"His name's on the wall—"

"—in Washington—"

"—D.C."

Moore's father still wore the Remember bracelet. "It's kind of late to start forgetting," he said.

When the boys would beg him to tell about the war, Moore wouldn't say much. He took them to any movie about Vietnam, though.

"We've seen *Rambo* twice, and we're going again," Corey said.

Scott said: "Moore says it's about time—"

"—about *damn* time—" Chip said.

"—we won that war."

MOORE'S MOTHER HAD died, not suddenly, and too soon, shortly after Moore and the Marines parted ways. She had, some said, grieved herself into a state. She insisted to the last that she was really ill. She consulted physicians and surgeons in clinic after clinic about the pain. Finally, she found a surgeon who would listen. "Tell us where it hurts and that's where we'll cut," he said.

She lay on the bed and wept, to be understood and taken seriously at last. Her continuing hospitalization and petition finally convinced the Marines to release Moore, on a hardship. He was supposed to be needed at the junkyard. In his fury at how she had manipulated events, Moore hadn't even come home. The junkyard to him was no future. Within two years she had died, her last surgery—elective—being the removal of her navel, after which the pain finally stopped, and so did she. Moore had married by then, and he and his first wife Lana, the stewardess, were on a holiday when the news came of his mother's death. He didn't fly back.

"So far as I know, he's never even been to her grave," Rhonda said. "I ask him, 'You want me to run by there and put some flowers or something?' He never did."

After Moore's mother died, Moore's father sold their house in Paulding and moved into the little trailer on the hilltop at the junkyard. He narrowed his interest in life to the weather and his customers. He paid his bills and filed his taxes. He didn't look for much more out of life. He had pretty well gone to seed when Moore brought Rhonda by for the first time, just married.

Rhonda waded right in. "I'm gonna call you Daddy," she said, "because I never had a real one." She hugged him fiercely, and didn't shy away from his rough beard, his cud of tobacco, or the stump of his left arm. He never would tell her how he lost it. "I'm no hero," is all he'd say. He let her wonder, through all those years—making her silly guesses, calling him in the middle of the night when she thought of some new way it might have happened, driving by in her ratty old car with the boys, teasing, joking, giving him something to look forward to. Gradually he got interested in things again, like a candle that gutters and then steadies and burns tall. She had to remind him not to keep buying the boys bicycles for every birthday, spoiling them, quick to make them happy, generous with his time and his money. He had been so sure his usefulness was over, he took his second chance seriously.

"Second childhood, I'm telling you," Moore said. "A classic case. I thought when Mom cooled that was going to be the end of him. It was a real shock, you know, coming so soon after my brother bought it in Nam. We were in New Mexico when we heard she had died. Or maybe it was Brazil. Anyway, I wired roses. My mom loved roses. She's where I get my romantic side. Not from my old man, that's for damn sure. Hardy peasant stock."

"Moore's daddy stood by me through some rough times, I'll say that much," Rhonda told the counselor. "I never had to wonder if he'd show up. Like that night after Moore left us and went to California—"

"I wasn't having as much fun as she thought," Moore said. "It's dog-eat-dog out there."

"—and Corey had some kind of breathing attack and turned blue. I thought my baby was dead!" When she looked up to see who was coming so fast down the hall, praying it would be Moore—"though that would be a miracle," Rhonda said—that he had somehow got her frantic message and for once come running: it hadn't been Moore. It had been his father instead.

"I was glad to see him, but it wasn't the same, you know? I just bawled."

"Aw, hell, honey," he told her, "He'll be back. If he can't make it to the funeral, he's bound to send an armload of roses."

"MAYBE, RIGHT THEN, I could have fallen for him, you know? For being there, and being strong, and laughing at heartache," Rhonda said. "But we didn't screw up a good thing. We're still friends, the way it ought to be. He's always been my friend, the only one I ever had, in my corner every round." And now on her team, as she raced.

"I like winning," she said. "The night I won my first race—not demolition derby, but out on the track, running against the others— maybe that was the best night of my life so far. Except the night Moore and I made Corey. I'll still have to call that one the best. He's the only one where it was love, not lust. I still feel good about him."

V

"THEY LIKE MOORE better than they do me," Rhonda said. "He can give them stuff—trail bikes, waterbeds, tapes. When they're fourteen, they can get him to go to court and ask for a modification in the custody. They can live with him full time. Chip's old enough now."

"The other day," Moore told the counselor, "Corey was dressing on the run, as usual, and as he passed I called him back. 'What's that written on your shirt?' He's always into something. He looked. 'Just my name,' he said and headed on out the door . . .''

"His *name*," Moore said. "C-o-r-e-y." Moore shook his head. "I thought his name was spelled with a *K!* Can you believe it? He's ten years old, and I didn't even know how to spell his name. That's when it hit me. That's when I started thinking."

VI

"I'M PRETTY MUCH self-contained," Moore said.

"He doesn't even have a permanent address!" Rhonda said. "He blew in from the West Coast in that van—"

"Listen," Moore said, "we're talking custom conversion here, not telephone-company surplus. I've sunk 23K in this buggy already." He had pictures of it, inside and out, to show to anyone who cared to see. "Take my word for it, the ladies looooove powder blue shag."

"—with status plates: SEMPRFI—" Rhonda said.

"There are no ex-Marines," Moore said.

"—and a bumper sticker: *If this rig is rockin', don't bother knockin'.*"

Chip said, "Corey thought that meant if the radio was playing too loud!"

"Why do grown-ups act that way?" Corey said.

"You want to know something funny? Rhonda thinks Lana—my first wife—is still around . . . as in, 'not dead.' She thought—all those years—I was divorced."

Lana had died in a plane crash. Not even Moore's father knew much about Lana. She and Moore hadn't been married but a few months. They had been good months, though. They had known each other for about a year, had been flying on Lana's pass—"The airlines give great incentives"—as husband and wife, and they decided to make it official. They married on one of their trips, and it was on their honeymoon that word came of Moore's mother dying.

"I knew I wasn't a jinx or anything. It's luck, and being home wouldn't have saved my mom. But I really took it hard when Lana died.

She begged me to go with her. She didn't want to fly that day. They called her to fill in for another stewardess. She went, of course. Part of the deal. Duty. She was a class act, head to heel. Natural blond, a lady. She could blush, you know?

"I flipped my lucky quarter—go with her to Orlando or sleep in?—and I still don't know if I won, or lost.

"Don't tell Rhonda what I said about Lana's being dead. She thinks we're divorced. All those years we were married, I told Rhonda I had to pay seventy-five a week alimony. Great little alibi. Kept me in incidentals. I spread it around. I never saved a thing for myself. It all went. I blew Lana's insurance in one week at Vegas. Let me tell you, they're crooked as hell out there, luck doesn't enter into it."

After Lana died, Moore drifted. He didn't see his father again till he married Rhonda and brought her by the junkyard.

"I don't know why I did that," Moore said. "Like I was asking his blessing or something. Maybe I just wanted a witness, this time. Lana was like a dream. None of my family had ever met her. That's why when she died, I just said, 'It's over.' I didn't want any sympathy. I've got a strong mind. I can control my emotions. I'm no quiche-eater, no hugger. . . . I never told anyone, but I put Lana's ashes right there on my mother's grave. I went out there at night, there's no guard, it's just a walk-over. They'd have got along, if anyone could. Lana knew how to treat people. She was Playmate caliber."

After that, Moore didn't think he'd ever feel good again, or want to. "But a man has to get out, meet people, take an interest." Rhonda happened along at the right moment. "Bing-o," Moore said. "I'm not saying it was a case of something's better than nothing—I had my pick—but I'm not saying I didn't fall for her either. It was more a case of body than soul. She could be pretty cute.

"Whatever it was, it was no meeting of minds. It was a struggle all the way, to teach her anything about style. All we had in common at first was the kids. I took her to the museum once. So what did she ask the guide? *'Where's the clown paintings?'* And she laughed over Golden Books like she was a second-grader herself. She never got tired of reading stories to the boys. Said it would make them smarter."

"In my whole life, nobody ever read me a book," Rhonda said. "How much time does it take?"

"She saved Green Stamps for a year to get that damn serene picture, big as a coffee table—white horse, red barn, kids on a tire swing, ducks on a pond, daisies, the whole deal. I wish you could see it! We were married—what, twelve, thirteen years?—"

"Fourteen years," Rhonda said. "We were together fourteen years."

"—and I couldn't teach her a thing."

VIII

"I LEARNED HOW to fix appliances," Rhonda said.

She said, "I took remedial English my first course in night school. After that I picked small-appliance repair and automotive. I didn't tell Moore. I said I was flunking history. History couldn't teach me how to wind a watch, must less fix one. You can save a lot of money if you repair things yourself. The library has what they call troubleshooter's guides. I'd look it up, order the parts, get whatever it was going again, and charge Moore what Sears would've charged me for a service call, thirty-five dollars for driving up in the yard! Not to mention labor. I fixed Moore's adding machine one time. Those guys make eighty-five dollars an hour . . .

"I learned all sorts of little tricks to help out our budget. Moore never suspected half of it. Including me doing his shirts laundry-style. He wanted them just so. But on hangers, not folded. But if he had wanted them folded on cardboard and in those little bags, I'd have figured a way. He never knew the difference. He paid me what the cleaners charge. What I saved like that—including laundry, couponing, repairs, and cigarettes—went into a special fund. He was always running out of cigarettes. He'd give me money and say 'Rhonda, run to the store and get me some Kents.' I got to thinking. I started buying a pack ahead of time just to save me running to the store, besides which I didn't like him smoking—we'd made a New Year's resolution when I was pregnant with Corey that we'd both quit, and I did, but he didn't. I made him do his smoking outside, not in the house, and yet here I was hiding them for his convenience. What was in it for me? If I think long enough, I'll find an angle. After I wouldn't let him smoke in the house, he kept his cigarettes in the car. I started going out there and taking a pack from his carton, just one pack—and when he ran out, I'd sell it back to him! It all added up. I'm a patient person, generally.

"Anyhow, that's the way I saved enough for the encyclopedia set. I didn't order it right away. I went to the library and asked them which one was best, no doubt about it. It's a good thing I *am* a patient person; they aren't giving those *Britannica*s away. When they finally arrived, I told the boys, 'Anything you ever need to know, begin looking right here.' I told them, 'You won't hurt my feelings any if you wear these out.' They do pretty good about homework, but in the summers, forget it. Scott's the only bookworm I've got. He was reading me about the Appalachian Mountains while I ironed the other day. Did you know, as mountains go, they're *young?*

"I told Moore I won the encyclopedias at a raffle. 'Pearls before swine,' he said. But I could tell he was pleased. He respects knowledge a lot.

"He wanted me to learn. He bought me *The Joy of Cooking,* and that's serious cooking, you know? A page and a half just for pie crust! And what kind of weather is it, and all that hoodoo before you make a meringue. . . . He didn't think much of my cooking but I kept trying."

"If she ever loses the can opener she'll starve to death," Moore said.

"When Moore had clients over, everything had to be per-fect-o. We had honest-to-god butter and cloth napkins. Wine in little mugs on stalks, what-do-you-call-'ems? Goblets, yeah. I told Moore I wasn't going to wheel the food in under pan lids, like at the hospital, but everything else was just what he wanted. The night we got friendly and made Corey, I had cooked Christmas dinner for his crowd. And they didn't show up.

Not one of them. Moore thought it was a reflection on him. I said 'Invite someone else, look at all this food!'

"He said, 'Nobody else rates.' I said, 'How about your dad?' and he finally said okay and went on down to the Quik-Shop to use the pay phone. Ours was disconnected a lot. I had a system on how to pay the bills: rent, electric, water, car payment, Gulf, Visa. Phone was the last on my list, and some months, like when insurance came due, no way I could stretch income to cover outgo. That's why I got so upset at the fancy dress he bought me to wear for entertaining. There I was in that lah-de-dah deal—he wanted me to look high-dollar for his friends: 'No goddamn jeans,' he said—and I could've cried to think what-all he spent on it, and the food too. He went wild when he did the shopping. Anything he wanted, he'd reach for.

"That party dress was something else. I don't know what you call that kind of merchandise; I'm no lady. Light-colored stuff, nothing you'd choose for a funeral or anything. Maybe I could wear it to get married in again. There's just so much you can do in an outfit like that."

IX

"IF SHE GETS married again, I won't have to pay alimony, will I? I'm only pulling down minimum wage now," Moore said, "but still I'm saving some. That's better than I've ever done in my whole life. I figured it the other night at Gamblers Anonymous: in the twenty years I've been on my own, since the Marines, I've pissed away half a million dollars. That's conservative.

"Listen, since California, I've tried it all: I've been dried out, shrunk, reformed, recovered, Rolfed, revived, acupunctured, hypnotized, and chiropractically adjusted. I've knocked around some: look at me. And I was no Eagle Scout to begin with. The doctor says it's natural to slow down. . . . I just don't want to chase it much anymore. I've got something else on my mind, believe it or not. I'm taking an evening course at the vocational school: blueprint reading. Look at my hands!

"Chip's already saying he's going in the Marines when he's seventeen if I'll sign for him. That'd kill Rhonda. She's been making plans since day one. She's such a pissant about money, but I have to hand it to her, she's never been lost a day in her life. She's got this inner map, and she knows which way is *ahead.*

"I was the firstborn son, just like Chip, and I can see a lot of myself in him. He wants to be the leader, set the pace, push things right to the edge, and over. At that age, you don't think about death, or even getting old. I want to tell him things, but why should he listen? Did I? I left home on the run when I was seventeen, and never looked back. I guess I thought the clock would stand still if I kept moving.

"I'm not worrying about any of it. One day at a time and all that crap, you know?"

X

"I DON'T TRUST him, he's up to something," Rhonda told her Creative Divorce group. She and Moore had been officially divorced— "I've got it in writing," she said—for two months now, and he had completely dropped out of sight, paying child support on time, but not —as he had done before the final decree—driving by the house at all hours, or tailing her as she went to work or shopping, or calling to ask the boys if she was alone, or seeing someone else. "He was even hassling my boyfriend," Rhonda said, "the one who drives a dozer." Rhonda liked him a lot.

"Jake don't tell me how to drive or dress," she said. She was back on her feet again, had her own place—having moved out of the junkyard, living now in a rented cottage with Chip and Scott and Corey. "So far, Chip hasn't talked Moore into filing for custody," Rhonda said. "Things are going too smooth," Rhonda said. She didn't see Moore all summer. She raced well, and when she won the Enduro, she got her picture in the local paper. She clipped the article and sent it to Moore in care of his lawyer.

She had cried her eyeliner off. "I looked more like a loser than a winner, but they spelled my name right," she said. She used a red pen and circled the car's number—78—and wrote across the picture: BET ON ME!

"I don't know why I did that," Rhonda said.

Then Moore called her at work.

It was her busiest time of night, and she told them to tell him she couldn't leave her post. He called again, in an hour.

"What if I buy a house?" he said.

She said, "You never talked like that when we were married, don't bother now," and hung up. Hard.

Moore called again, in a couple of weeks. "I sold the van," he told her.

"To pay off gambling debts," Rhonda guessed, even though Moore swore he wasn't gambling anymore, or drinking either. "He's definitely up to something."

TOWARD HALLOWEEN HE drove over to the VFW in an old flatbed Ford.

"Used," Rhonda marveled. "Moore bought a used truck!"

"What if I *build* a house?" Moore said. His credit was still so bad, he couldn't find a bank willing to take a chance. By then, he had completed the blueprint course at Vo-Tech, and had ordered plans from Lowe's.

When she wouldn't talk to him about it, he said "Just come on out to the parking lot and see . . ."

When she didn't even let him finish asking her, he yelled "Just walk out to the parking lot, goddammit! I'm not asking you to go to North Carolina . . ." Heads turned, and Moore sat back down, his face in his hands.

He wouldn't leave. He took a booth and ordered supper and waited. He didn't eat much, Rhonda noticed. The boys told her he had an ulcer. He didn't look much different, only a little more silver-haired. He had a tan like he'd been working outdoors, and he was thin. "Wiry, not thin," she realized. He looked strong enough. She told her boss, as she left on break to go out with Moore to the parking lot to see the truck, "If I'm not back here in five minutes, call the Law."

Moore was so proud of that Ford, Rhonda tried to be nice. Conversationally, she pointed out, "I don't get it. It's just an old truck, tilting over under a load of—"

"—cement bags. That's for the footers," Moore said. "I'm doing all the work myself." He had books and books on carpentry. He read late into the night, and dreamed about permits and codes.

"He's building a house," Rhonda told her boss when she went back to work. "Who's the lucky girl?" he asked. Everybody laughed. Rhonda hadn't kept much about her divorce a secret, including Moore's list. Everybody knew why her race car was number 78.

"I talk too much," Rhonda said, for the hundredth time.

"She was vaccinated with a phonograph needle," Moore used to say.

ALL THAT FALL he worked on the house. His father helped too, in the evenings—not on weekends, when Rhonda needed him at the speedway. The boys were over there every afternoon now. They'd come home and report: "Roof's on." Or, "There's going to be a ceiling fan." Or, "You oughta see the fishing dock!"

Moore called her at work. She kept her phone unplugged at home, so she could sleep during the days. She had gotten used to nightshift hours, and didn't even mind sleeping in direct sunlight, but she couldn't stand noise. Moore told her, "Chip's getting pretty good with that drywall stuff, you oughta come see. . . ."

"Not now, not ever, not negotiable," Rhonda said.

"It's finished," Moore told her at Christmas.

"You bet," Rhonda said.

There was a party going on at the VFW, and she could hardly hear him on the phone. ". . . you always wanted," Moore was saying, when Rhonda hung up.

She told her boss as she went back to work, "What I always wanted wasn't much."

XI

RHONDA WAS FIVE days away from marrying Jake—his mother had already taught her to crochet placemats left-handed—when Moore fell through the glass while recaulking the hall skylight. "If he'd just done it right the first time," Rhonda said.

Instead, she spent what would have been her wedding day at Tri-County Hospital, watching Moore breathe. He wasn't very good at it, but better than he had been at first, when they flew him in by Med-Evac, on life support. He lay unconscious in intensive care for three days, and the first thing he said when he woke was, "Don't tell my wife."

Rhonda, hearing that, drew her own conclusions as to what he had been dreaming about while in a coma.

After they moved Moore to a private room, Rhonda went back to work. Moore had a week to go before they could remove the stitches, and he was still in traction. Rhonda told her boss, with some satisfaction, "It'd tear the heart right out of your chest to see him like that."

As she went by the bulletin board after signing in, she ripped the wedding invitation for her and Jake from under its pushpins, and dropped in the trash. The jukebox was playing "You're a Hard Dog to Keep under the Porch."

"I hate that tune," Rhonda said. Nobody laughed.

XII

TO CLEAN UP the glass in Moore's hallway, Rhonda borrowed a pair of heavy leather work gloves from Jake. "Keep 'em," Jake said. It sounded final. Rhonda said, "I'll get back to you," but how could she mean it? She had the boys to see to, and work, and the racing season, just beginning. And there was Moore . . .

Nothing had been done at Moore's house to clean up after the accident. Rhonda and Moore's father managed to staple plastic over the skylight.

"Reminds me of old times," Rhonda said, thinking of the night she had run Moore off at gunpoint and shot out the picture window in the duplex on Elm Terrace. Her laugh echoed hollow in Moore's empty rooms. Moore hadn't bought furniture yet. When Rhonda turned the key and first looked in—she had not been out to see the house before— she said, "This place looks like 'early marriage.'" She was determined not to be impressed.

There was no way, that many days past its drying, to get all of Moore's blood off the hall floor. She scrubbed at it till her head ached and her hands trembled. Finally she stood up and said, "I've got a scatter rug that'll cover it," and added that to her list.

Rhonda felt funny just being there. Not because of the bloodstains on the floor—one handprint perfectly clear where he had lain broken— but rather on account of the house being built on that very lot where Moore had installed Rosalind in her little love-nest camper.

Rhonda took Moore's last two Tylenol. His medicine chest had only shaving supplies, a bottle of ulcer medication, and cold remedies. She drank from his glass. While she was waiting to feel better, she made his bed and hung up his clothes, checking out his closet as she did—hardly enough stuff to fill a suitcase—and examining the titles of his books— mostly paperbacks, mostly how-tos—and prowling shamelessly through the cabinets. She was amazed to see generic labels. Most of the kitchen drawers were empty, sweet-smelling new wood. She dampened a rag and wiped sawdust out of one. When she found his revolver, she spun the cylinder—it wasn't loaded—and put it back. She researched the garbage in the cans outside, marveling: "Even his Pepsi's decaffeinated."

She found not one drop of Southern Comfort, and no green bottles . . .

IT HAD BEEN the imported beer that finally told Rhonda where to look for Moore's paycheck, in the closing moments of their marriage, when he had countered her arguments about Rosalind by saying, "You're such a pissant accountant, you'll find this money in fifteen minutes. . . ." He endorsed and hid his whole paycheck. It was Rhonda's for the keeping if she could find it. He gave her a week, not fifteen minutes. "Seven days," he said.

Rhonda had torn the house apart. Not while Moore was home, watching, but during the days, while he was at work. Sometimes she felt that he could see her, frantic, down on her hands and knees, reaching under the sofa, standing on a chair to look on top of the hutch, probing with her flashlight under the kitchen sink, searching the shoebag, laundry box, flour and sugar canisters. She'd have the house put back together when he came home at night. He'd walk in and head for the refrigerator, stirring through the utensils drawer till he found the can opener, prying the cap off the beer and sighing after the first quenching. He never asked, "Did you find it?" and she never volunteered, "No, dammit," but he knew, by Wednesday, that she still hadn't lucked across it. She had to ask him for money for a loaf of bread and some milk. "For the boys."

"I gave you all I had," he said, with that smile she wanted, always, to slap off his face.

Thursday night he brought three paper hats from the Varsity Drive-In. "For the boys." They loved those Varsity hot dogs, but Moore didn't bring any home, just the hats. "I had lunch there," he explained. "Hot dogs wouldn't have kept." Corey cried and had to be sent to bed. Moore was mean in little ways like that, when he had been drinking. And it occurred to Rhonda, on Friday, as her week was about up, that Moore might not even have hidden the check. He might have spent it all, and how would she ever know? It made her crazy to think that. She was rubbing lotion on the carpet burns on her knees—the "treasure hunt" had taken its toll on her nerves and flesh—when Moore drove home. She ran to the kitchen, and was washing dishes when Moore strode by to get his beer. The rule was: Nobody messes with Moore till he gets his beer. "I don't want to be greeted by what broke, who died, or where the dog threw up," Moore always said. Driving the perimeter home left him jumpy. Sometimes he went jogging. This time he didn't. He said, after his first swallow, "The week's up."

Rhonda didn't even turn to look at him. What need? She could see his grinning reflection in the window. Before he tipped back his head to chug the last of the Heineken, he added, so smoothly she knew he had been pleasing himself thinking up the words all the miles home, "Since you haven't spent what I gave you last week, why should I give you any more?"

She said, "How do I know you even hid it?" He had lied before. Hadn't she looked everywhere? Turned the house upside down? With the boys helping, like it was a game? Even behind the pictures on the walls, in the hems of the curtains, in the box of Tide . . .

"You always were a lazy slut," he said, laughing. He drained that bottle and reached for another—sixteen a night; he was just beginning. As he raised it to his lips, Rhonda figured out the hiding place. Just like that.

"That's when I knew," she said later. But she waited till Moore had padded into the living room and shoved his recliner back, staring at the world news through his toes, before she made sure.

She opened the door to the freezer compartment—it always needed defrosting, it was the job she hated most—and reached for his special beer mug. He had had a pair of them, so one could be in use, and one on ice, at all times. But she had broken one washing it, and after that, Moore said, "Hands off." He never drank from the bottle, always from that mug. "So why had he been pulling on the bottles all week?" Rhonda asked herself, just as she retrieved the answer from the frost. There it was: the endorsed check, dry and negotiable in a baggie. She took it out quick and banked it, with a little shiver, in her bra.

She needed time to think, to make plans. But he noticed, somehow, that the power balance had shifted. Maybe it was the way she unzipped her purse and slipped her car key off the larger ring and into her pocket. She pretended she was getting a stick of gum. He couldn't have known better, she was so cool. She even turned and offered him a stick, the pack covering the palmed car key. Maybe it was her lighthearted laugh. He looked sharp. Something gave her away. He scrambled to his feet and headed for the kitchen, returning in a moment, incredulous. "You found it."

"You betcha," she said, patting her chest.

"Let me kiss it good-bye, then" he said, reaching for her with both hands.

That's when Rhonda hooked the gun from his armpit holster. Without yelling—the boys were working on homework in the next room—she warned, "Back off."

Moore grabbed her pocketbook and swung it at her, missing, but spilling the wallet and other stuff all over the rug. He snatched up her billfold and dumped it. Pennies rolled under the sofa. She put out her foot and stopped a quarter. By then he had torn her checks into confetti and tossed them at her, and was bending her credit cards into modern art. "Try making it without me," he said. He slapped at the gun. "It's not loaded," he said.

"That lie could cost you," she said, and fired right between his feet.

"IF CHIP HADN'T opened the bedroom door there's no telling what might've happened next," Rhonda said, to no one in particular. She was sitting on the fishing dock, her feet dangling in the cool lake. She slipped her sneakers back on and started for the house. Moore's father was still on the ladder, stapling weather stripping around the skylight.

"We'll just make it," she called up to him.

They headed back to town to meet the school bus.

"Do you realize," she said at the outskirts, "he's got nineteen windows needing curtains, plus that weird kitchen door?"

XIII

OF COURSE, THIS thing led to that. That's how home improvements go. The counselor had warned them, even before they filed formally for divorce, that what can't be argued or bettered, in therapy, is indifference. "No use pretending it's over when it isn't," the counselor said.

"Or it ain't when it is," Rhonda pointed out.

Her lawyer, when she asked him about it, had said, "I've seen clients replaying their vows in candlelit churches the night before heading for divorce court in the morning. And I've seen newly divorced couples get back together before the ink dries on the final decree."

"Then they're fools," Rhonda said.

She said, "Not me, not for Moore."

"Something's different," Moore said, on homecoming, looking around, easing through the doorways on his crutches. Six more weeks in a walking cast, then therapy. "Then back to normal."

"God forbid," Rhonda said, when she heard that.

THOSE SIX WEEKS passed somehow. One Saturday Rhonda looked up on her final lap as she raced by in her Nova: Moore and the boys were in the stands, ketchup and chili on their identical T-shirts, red dust on their identical hats, waving mustardy hands, yelling, "Stand on it!" as she roared by. She didn't take the checkered flag, though. She finished third. Cooling off in the pits, she didn't even open the long florist's box Moore handed to her. She laid it on the fender, saying, uneagerly, "Roses."

"Did it ever occur to you—" Moore began.

By then, Corey had the ribbon off and was saying "Look, Mom."

"I could hardly believe my eyes" Rhonda told her boss. "I could've puked."

It was Levolor blinds for that weird kitchen door, custom-made, custom-colored, with an airbrush painting on them of Rhonda's racer, a red Chevy with 78 on the door and a driver looking out, looking very much like Rhonda, giving the thumbs-up sign.

"Happy Mother's Day!" they said. Moore's father had the card. He'd sat on it, and it was pretty well bent, but its wishes were intact.

"AT THAT POINT, there wasn't a thing I could do to stop it," Rhonda was telling the doctor. "I know it sounds crazy, but he should've started right then building another room on the house. It was just a matter of time." How could she explain it any better than that? Was it her fault? Her resolution had failed in a slow leak, not a dam break, but still, the reservoir was empty. "Full circle," she said to the nurse, a fan of docudramas, who had no more sense than to ask, "Rape?"

Rhonda said, "The fortune-teller swore my next husband's name would start with a J."

"Will it?"

"Yeah," Rhonda said. "Jerk."

When she came fuming back from the doctor's, her worst suspicion—pregnancy—confirmed, she told Moore, "I should've killed you when I had the chance."

Moore laughed. "You don't mean that," he said.

WHITE RAT

Gayl Jones

I LEARNED WHERE she was when Cousin Willie come down home and said Maggie sent for her but told her not to tell nobody where she was, especially me, but Cousin Willie come and told me anyway cause she said I was the lessen two evils and she didn't like to see Maggie stuck up in the room up there like she was. I asked her what she mean like she was. Willie said that she was pregnant by J.T. J.T. the man she run off with because she said I treat her like dirt. And now Willie say J.T. run off and left her after he got her knocked up. I asked Willie where she was. Willie said she was up in that room over Babe Lawson's. She told me not to be surprised when I saw her looking real bad. I said I wouldn't be least surprised. I asked Willie she think Maggie come back. Willie say she better.

The room was dirty and Maggie looked worser than Willie say she going to look. I knocked on the door but there weren't no answer so I just opened the door and went in and saw Maggie laying on the bed turned up against the wall. She turnt around when I come in but she didn't say nothing. I said Maggie we getting out a here. So I got the bag she brung when she run away and put all her loose things in it and just took her by the arm and brung her on home. You couldn't tell nothing was in her belly though.

I been taking care of little Henry since she been gone but he three and a half years old and ain't no trouble since he can play hisself and know what it mean when you hit him on the ass when he do something wrong.

Maggie don't say nothing when we get in the house. She just go over to little Henry. He sleeping in the front room on the couch. She go over to little Henry and bend down and kiss him on the cheek and then she ask me have I had supper and when I say naw she go back in the kitchen and start fixing it. We sitting at the table and nobody saying nothing but I feel I got to say something.

"You can go head and have the baby," I say. "I give him my name."

I say it meaner than I want to. She just look up at me and don't say nothing. Then she say, "He ain't yours."

I say, "I know he ain't mine. But don't nobody else have to know. Even the baby. He don't even never have to know."

She just keep looking at me with her big eyes that don't say nothing, and then she say, "You know. I know."

She look down at her plate and go on eating. We don't say nothing no more and then when she get through she clear up the dishes and I just go round front and sit out on the front porch. She don't come out like she used to before she start saying I treat her like dirt, and then when I go on in the house to go to bed, she hunched up on her side, with her back to me, so I just take my clothes off and get on in the bed on my side.

MAGGIE A LIGHT yeller woman with chicken-scratch hair. That what my mama used to call it, chicken-scratch hair, cause she say there weren't enough hair for a chicken to scratch around in. If it weren't for her hair she look like she was a white woman, a light yeller white woman though. Anyway, when we was coming up somebody say, "Woman cover you hair if you ain't go'n' straighten' it. Look like chicken scratch." Sometime they say look like chicken shit, but they don't tell them to cover it no more, so they wear it like it is. Maggie wears hers like it is.

Me, I come from a family of white-looking niggers, some of 'em, my mama, my daddy musta been; my half daddy he weren't. Come down from the hills round Hazard, Kentucky, most of them and claimed nigger cause somebody grandmammy way back there was. First people I know ever claim nigger, 'cept my mama say my daddy hate hoogies (up north I hear they call em honkies) worser than anybody. She say cause he look like he one hisself and then she laugh. I laugh too but I didn't know why she laugh. She say when I come, I look just like a little white rat, so tha's why some a the people I hang aroun with call me "White Rat." When little Henry come he look just like a little white rabbit, but don't nobody call him "White Rabbit," they just call him little Henry. I guess the other jus' ain't took. I tried to get them to call him little White Rabbit, but Maggie say naw, cause she say when he grow up he develop a complex, what with the problem he got already. I say what you come at me for with this a complex and then she say, Nothin, jus' something I heard on the radio on one of them edgecation morning shows. And then I say, Aw. And then she say, Anyway by the time he get seven or eight he probably get the pigment and be dark, cause some of her family was. So I say where I heard somewhere where the chil'ren couldn't be no darker'n the darkest of the two parent and bout the best he could do would be high yeller like she was. And then she say how her sister Lucky got the pigment when she was bout seven and come out real dark. I tell her, Well y'all's daddy was dark. And she say, Yeah. Anyway, I guess she still think little Henry gonna get the pigment when he get to be seven or eight, and told me about all these people come out lighter'n I was and got the pigment fore they growed up.

Gayl Jones · *206*

Like I told you my relatives come down out of the hills and claimed nigger, but only people that believe 'em is people that got to know 'em and people that know 'em, so I usually just stay around with people I know and go in some joint over to Versailles or up to Lexington or down over in Midway where they know me cause I don't like to walk in no place where they say, "What's that white man doing in here?" They probably say "yap"—that the Kentucky word for honky. Or "What that yap doing in here with that nigger woman?" So I jus' keep to the places where they know me. I member when I was young me and the other niggers used to ride around in these cars, and when we go to some town where they don't know "White Rat" everybody look at me like I'm some hoogie, but I don't pay them no mind. 'Cept sometime it hard not to pay em no mind cause I hate the hoogie much as they do, much as my daddy did. I drove up to this filling station one time and these other niggers drove up at the same time, they mighta even drove up a little ahead a me, but this filling station man come up to me first and bent down and said, "I wait on you first, 'fore I wait on them niggers," and then he laugh. And then I laugh and say, "You can wait on them first. I'm a nigger too." He don't say nothing. He just look at me like he thought I was crazy. I don't remember who he wait on first. But I guess he be careful next time who he say nigger to, even somebody got blond hair like me, most which done passed over anyhow. That, or the way things been go'n, go'n be trying to pass back. I member once all us was riding around one Saturday night, I must a been bout twenty-five then, close to forty now, but we was driving around, all us drunk cause it was Saturday, and Shotgun, he was driving and probably drunker'n a skunk and drunken the rest of us hit up on this police car and the police got out and by that time Shotgun done stop, and the police come over and told all us to get out the car, and he looked us over, he didn't have to do much looking because he probably smell it before he got there, but he looked us all over and say he gonna haul us all in for being drunk and disord'ly. He say, "I'm gone haul all y'all in." And I say, "Haul y'all all." Everybody laugh, but he don't hear me cause he over to his car ringing up the police station to have them send the wagon out. He turn his back to us cause he know we wasn goin nowhere. Didn't have to call but one man cause the only people in the whole Midway police station is Fat Dick and Skinny Dick, Buster Crab and Mr. Willie. Sometime we call Buster, Crab Face too, and Mr. Willie is John Willie, but everybody call him Mr. Willie cause the name just took. So Skinny Dick come out with the wagon and hauled us all in. So they didn't know me well as I knew them. Thought I was some hoogie jus' run around with the niggers instead of be one of them. So they put my cousin Covington, cause he dark, in the cell with Shotgun and the other niggers, and they put me in the cell with the white men. So I'm drunker'n a skunk and I'm yellin', Let me outa here I'm a nigger too. And Crab Face say, "If you a nigger I'm a Chinee." And I keep rattling the bars and saying, "Cov, they got me in here with the white men. Tell 'em I'm a nigger too," and Cov yell back, "He a nigger too," and then they all laugh, all the niggers laugh, the hoogies they laugh too, but for a different reason, and Cov say, "Tha's what you get for being drunk and orderly." And I say, "Put me in there with the niggers too, I'm a nigger too." And then one of the white men, he's sitting over in his corner say, "I ain't never heard of a white man want to be a nigger. 'Cept maybe for the nigger women." So I look around at him and haul off cause I'm goin hit him and then some man grab me and say, "He keep a blade," but that don't make me no difrent and I say, "A spade don't need a blade." But then he get his friend to help hole me and then he call Crab Face to come get me out a the cage. So Crab Face come and get me out a the cage and put me in a cage by myself and say, "When you get out a here you can run around with the niggers all you want, but while you in here you ain't getting no niggers." By now I'm more sober so I jus' say, "My cousin's a nigger." And he say, "My cousin a monkey's uncle."

By that time Grandy come. Cause Cov took his free call but didn't nobody else. Grandy's Cov's grandmama. She my grandmama too on my stepdaddy's side. Anyway, Grandy come and she say, "I want my *two* sons." And he take her over to the nigger cage and say, "Which two?" and she say, "There one of them," and points to Cov'ton. "But I don't see t'other one." And Crab Face say, "Well, if you don't see him I don't see him." Cov'ton just standing there grinning and don't say nothing. I don't say nothing. I'm just waiting. Grandy ask, "Cov, where Rat?" Sometime she just call me Rat and leave the "White" off. Cov say, "They put him in the cage with the white men." Crab Face standing there looking funny now. His back to me, but I figure he looking funny now. Grandy says, "Take me to my other boy, I want to see my other boy." I don't think Crab Face want her to know he thought I was white so he don't say nothing. She just standing there looking up at him cause he tall and fat and she short and fat. Crab Face finally say, "I put him in a cell by hisself cause he started a ruckus." He point over to me, and she turn and see me and frown. I'm just sitting there. She look back at Crab Face and say, "I want them both out." "That be about five dollars apiece for the both of them for disturbing the peace." That what Crab Face say. I'm sitting there thinking he a poet and don't know it. He a bad poet and don't know it. Grandy say she pay it if it take all her money, which it probably did. So the police let Cov and me out. And Shotgun waving. Some of the others already settled. Didn't care if they got out the next day. I wouldn't a cared neither, but Grandy say she didn' like to see nobody in a cage, specially her own. I say I pay her back. Cov say he pay her back too. She say we can both pay her back if we just stay out a trouble. So we got together and pay her next week's grocery bill.

Well, that was one 'sperience. I had others, but like I said, now I jus' about keep to the people I know and that know me. The only other big 'sperience was when me and Maggie tried to get married. We went down to the courthouse and fore I even said a word, the man behind the glass cage look up at us and say "Round here nigger don't marry white." I don't say nothing, just standing up there looking at him and he looking like a white toad, and I'm wondering if they call him "white toad," more likely "white turd." But I just keep looking at him. Then he the one get tired a looking first and he say, "Next." I'm thinking I want to reach in that little winder and pull him right out of that little glass cage. But I don't. He say again, "Around here nigger don't marry white." I say, "I'm a nigger. Nigger marry nigger, don't they?" He just look at me like he think I'm crazy. I say, "I got rel'tives blacker'n your shit. Ain't you never heard a niggers what look like they white?" He just look at me like I'm a nigger too, and tell me where to sign.

Then we get married and I bring her over here to live in this house in Huntertown ain't got but three rooms and a outhouse, that's where we always lived, seems like to me, all us Hawks, cept the ones come down from the mountains way back yonder, cept they don't count no more anyway. I keep telling Maggie it get harder and harder to be a white nigger now specially since it don't count no more how much white blood you got in you, in fact, it make you worser for it. I said nowadays sted a walking around like you something special people look at you, after they find out what you are if you like me, like you some kind a bad news that you had something to do with. I tell em I aint had nothing to do with the way I come out. They ack like they like you better if you go on ahead and try to pass, cause least then they know how to feel about you. Cept nowadays everybody want to be a nigger, or it getting that way. I tell Maggie she got it made, cause at least she got that chicken-shit hair, but all she answer is, "That why you treat me like chicken shit." But tha's only since we been having our troubles.

Little Henry the cause a our troubles. I tell Maggie I ain't changed since he was borned, but she say I have. I always say I been a hard man, kind of quick-tempered. A hard man to crack like one of them walnuts. She say all it take to crack a walnut is your teeth. She say she put a walnut between her teeth and it crack not even need a hammer. So I say I'm a nigger-toe nut then. I ask her if she ever seen one of them nigger-toe nuts they the toughest nuts to crack. She say, "A nigger-toe nut is black. A white nigger-toe nut be easy to crack." Then I don't say nothing and she keep saying I changed cause I took to drink. I tell her I drink before I married her. She say then I start up again. She say she don't like it when

I drink cause I'm quicker tempered than when I ain't drunk. She say I come home drunk and say things and then go sleep and then the next morning forget what I say. She won't tell me what I say. I say, "You a woman scart of words. Won't do nothing." She say she ain't scart of words. She say one of these times I might not jus' say something. I might *do* something. Short time after she say that was when she run off with J.T.

Reason I took to drink again was because little Henry was borned clubfooted. I tell the truth in the beginning I blamed Maggie, cause I herited all those hill man's superstitions and nigger superstitions too, and I said she didn't do something right when she was carrying him or she did something she shouldn't oughta did or looked at something she shouldn't oughta looked at like some cows fucking or something. I'm serious. I blamed her. Little Henry come out looking like a little club-footed rabbit. Or some rabbits being birthed or something. I said there weren't never nothing like that in my family ever since we been living on this earth. And they must have come from her side. And then I said cause she had more of whatever it was in her than I had in me. And then she said that brought it all out. All that stuff I been hiding up inside me cause she said I didn't hated them hoogies like my daddy did and I just been feeling I had to live up to something he set and the onliest reason I married her was because she was the lightest and brightest nigger woman I could get and still be nigger. Once that nigger start to lay it on me she jus' kept it up till I didn't feel nothing but start to feeling what she say, and then I even told her I was leaving and she say, "What about little Henry?" And I say, "He's your nigger." And then it was like I didn't know no other word but nigger when I was going out that door.

I found some joint and went in it and just start pouring the stuff down. It weren't no nigger joint neither, it was a hoogie joint. First time in my life I ever been in a hoogie joint too, and I kept thinking a nigger woman did it. I wasn't drunk enough *not* to know what I was saying neither. I was sitting up to the bar talking to the tender. He just standing up there, wasn nothing special to him, he probably weren't even lisen cept but with one ear. I say, "I know this nigger. You know I know the niggers. (He just nod but don't say nothing.) Know them close. You know what I mean. Know them like they was my own. Know them where you s'pose to know them." I grinned at him like he was s'pose to know them too. "You know my family came down out of the hills, like they was some kind of rain gods, you know, miss'ology. What they teached you bout the Juicifer. Anyway, I knew this nigger what made hisself a priest, you know turned his white color I mean turned his white collar backwards and dressed up in a monkey suit—you get it?" He didn't get it. "Well, he made hisself a priest, but after a while he didn't want to be no priest, so he pronounced hisself." The bartender said, "Renounced." "So he 'nounced hisself and took off his turned-back collar and went back to just being a plain old everyday chi'lins and downhome and ham-hocks and cornpone nigger. And you know what else he did? He got married. Yeah the nigger what once was a priest got married. Once took all them vows of cel'bacy come and got married. Got married so he could come." I laugh. He don't. I got evil. "Well, he come awright. He come and she come too. She come and had a baby. And you know what else? The baby come too. Ha. No ha? The baby come out clubfooted. So you know what he did? He didn't blame his wife he blamed hisself. The nigger blamed hisself cause he said the God put a curse on him for goin' agin his vows. He said the God put a curse on him cause he took his vows of cel'bacy, which mean no fuckin', cept everybody know what *they* do, and went agin his vows of cel'bacy and married a nigger woman so he could do what every ord'narry onery person was doing and the Lord didn't just put a curse on him. He said he could a stood that. But the Lord carried the curse clear over the the next gen'ration and put a curse on his little baby boy who didn do nothing in his whole life . . . cept come." I laugh and laugh. Then when I quit laughing I drink some more, and then when I quit drinking I talk some more. "And you know something else?" I say. This time he say, "No." I say, "I knew another priest what took the vows, only this priest was white. You wanta know what happen to him. He broke his vows same as the nigger and got married same as the nigger. And they had a baby too. Want to know what happen to him?'' ''What?'' ''He come out a nigger.''

Then I get so drunk I can't go no place but home. I'm thinking it's the Hawks' house, not hers. If anybody get throwed out it's her. She the nigger. I'm goin' fool her. Throw her right *out* the bed if she in it. But then when I get home I'm the one that's fool. Cause she gone *and* little Henry gone. So I guess I just badmouthed the walls like the devil till I jus' layed down and went to sleep. The next morning little Henry come back with a neighbor woman but Maggie don't come. The woman hand over little Henry, and I ask her, ''Where Maggie?'' She looked at me like she think I'm the devil and say, ''I don't know, but she lef' me this note to give to you.'' So she jus' give me the note and went. I open the note and read. She write like a chicken too, I'm thinking, chicken scratch. I read: ''I run off with J.T. cause he been wanting me to run off with him and I ain't been wanting to tell now. I'm send little Henry back cause I just took him away last night cause I didn't want you to be doing nothing you regrit in the morning.'' So I figured she figured I got to stay sober if I got to take care of myself and little Henry. Little Henry didn't say nothing and I didn't say nothing. I just put him on in the house and let him play with hisself.

That was two months ago. I ain't take a drop since. But last night Cousin Willie come and say where Maggie was and now she moving around in the kitchen and feeding little Henry and I guess when I get up she feed me. I get up and get dressed and go in the kitchen. She say when the new baby come we see whose fault it was. J.T. blacker'n a lump of coal.

Maggie keep saying, ''When the baby come we see who fault it was.'' It's two more months now that I been look at her, but I still don't see no belly change.

The Weight of the Past

THE WEIGHT OF THE PAST

THE BLAKEAN NOTION that the past, present, and future can exist in the same moment is hardly new to anyone brought up on the Old Testament; southerners understand that the present is rarely absolute. When echoes from the past threaten to destroy family bonds, the situation becomes (in the words of Flannery O'Connor in another context) "loaded." This dynamism is reflected in much southern fiction, even though it is often skillfully muted.

The first story in this section, Ellen Glasgow's "Dare's Gift," was published in 1923, though written a few years earlier when "the War" was still a vivid memory in everyone's mind and tales of Yankee viciousness were being handed down from parent to child. Although emotions at times may seem excessively melodramatic, remember that southern aristocrats often identified with the ancient Greeks—in this case, Antigone and Electra.

One more note: Miss Glasgow herself admitted her debt to Edgar Allan Poe, especially to his "Fall of the House of Usher," whose ghostly, and ghastly, echoes can be heard in "Dare's Gift."

To this day—for Mildred has been strangely reticent about Dare's Gift—I do not know whether her pallor was due to the shade in which we walked or whether, at the instant when I turned to her, she was visited by some intuitive warning against the house we were approaching. Even after a year the events of Dare's Gift are not things I can talk over with Mildred; and, for my part, the occurrence remains, like the house in its grove of cedars, wrapped in an impenetrable mystery.

GHOSTS ALSO EXIST in "First Dark," by Elizabeth Spencer, but they—or it, or he—seem to be bearing a different message (for isn't bearing messages the job of ghosts?). From the beginning, Spencer hitches up ghost to family history, or vice versa, and they stay hitched through the rest of the story, no matter how hard one of them pulls and tugs on the other.

She was a girl whom no ordinary description would fit. One would have to know first of all who she was: Frances Harvey. After that, it was all right for her to be a little odd-looking, with her reddish hair that curled back from her brow, her light eyes, and her high, pale temples. This is not the material for being pretty, but in Frances Harvey it was what could sometimes be beauty. Her family home was laden with history that nobody but the Harveys could remember. It would have been on a Pilgrimage if Richton had had one. Frances still lived in it, looking after an invalid mother.

"What were you-all talking about?" she wanted to know.

"About that ghost they used to tell about . . ."

During the course of the story, Spencer holds various elements of the past up to scrutiny: one is the undefined racial guilt of Frances Harvey (as representative of aristocratic Richton) toward the "ghost"; another is Tom Beavers's bitter memory of Mrs. Harvey's cruelty to him as a child; still another is the Harvey house itself with all its meaningful family history—a history that is delicately poised between enrichment and deprivation. The author describes this balance beautifully:

> In Richton, the door to the past was always wide open, and what came in through it and went out of it had made people "different." But it scarcely ever happens, even in Richton, that one is able to see the precise moment when fact becomes faith, when life turns into legend, and people start to bend their finest loyalties to make themselves bemused custodians of the grave.

Rejection of the past, Spencer seems to be saying, does not alter its potency—its possibility for affecting the present and future—which will continue no matter who is aware of it.

AWARENESS IS ONE of the major themes of Bobbie Ann Mason's story "Shiloh": who is aware, and who isn't? Norma Jean Moffitt is, or trying to be, in comparison to husband Leroy, who is clueless about his wife, and life in general. Their history together includes a tragedy: the death of an infant.

> Now that Leroy is home all the time, they sometimes feel awkward around each other, and Leroy wonders if one of them should mention the child. He has the feeling that they are waking up out of a dream together—that they must create a new marriage, start afresh. They are lucky they are still married. Leroy has read that for most people losing a child destroys the marriage—or else he heard this on *Donahue*. He can't always remember where he learns things anymore.

Since "Dare's Gift" an important change has taken place. The past now consists of television talk shows and sitcoms: here lie the memories, the points of reference. Norma Jean and Leroy—at her mother Mabel's instigation, and in an attempt to find some legitimate tie to the past—visit the Civil War battlefield at Shiloh. The trip is not a success. Leroy is disappointed: "He thought it would look like a golf course." Norma Jean is merely bored. She and Leroy have a picnic; she tells him that she wants to leave him. Next day—as if believing that the connection will save his marriage—Leroy tries desperately to instill history into his own life:

> He can only think of that war as a board game with plastic soldiers. Leroy almost smiles, as he compares the Confederates' daring attack on the Union camps and Virgil Mathis's raid on the bowling alley. General Grant, drunk and furious, shoved the Southerners back to Corinth, where Mabel and Jet Beasley were married years later, when Mabel was still thin and good-looking.

Whether Norma Jean and Leroy will find a way of salvaging their relationship is a minor point here. The story ends with the realization that the past is in grave danger of being displaced altogether. Norma Jean and Leroy will never be its saviors—but perhaps the reader will. In this respect, "Shiloh" is a very profound story indeed.

DARE'S GIFT

Ellen Glasgow

A YEAR HAS PASSED, and I am beginning to ask myself if the thing actually happened? The whole episode, seen in clear perspective, is obviously incredible. There are, of course, no haunted houses in this age of science; there are merely hallucinations, neurotic symptoms, and optical illusions. Any one of these practical diagnoses would, no doubt, cover the impossible occurrence, from my first view of that dusky sunset on James River to the erratic behavior of Mildred during the spring we spent in Virginia. There is—I admit it readily!—a perfectly rational explanation of every mystery. Yet, while I assure myself that the supernatural has been banished, in the evil company of devils, black plagues, and witches, from this sanitary century, a vision of Dare's Gift, amid its clustering cedars under the shadowy arch of the sunset, rises before me, and my feeble scepticism surrenders to that invincible spirit of darkness. For once in my life—the ordinary life of a corporation lawyer in Washington—the impossible really happened.

It was the year after Mildred's first nervous breakdown, and Drayton, the great specialist in whose care she had been for some months, advised me to take her away from Washington until she recovered her health. As a busy man I couldn't spend the whole week out of town; but if we could find a place near enough—somewhere in Virginia! we both exclaimed, I remember—it would be easy for me to run down once a fortnight. The thought was with me when Harrison asked me to join him for a week's hunting on James River; and it was still in my mind, though less distinctly, on the evening when I stumbled alone, and for the first time, on Dare's Gift.

I had hunted all day—a divine day in October—and at sunset, with a bag full of partridges, I was returning for the night to Chericoke, where Harrison kept his bachelor's house. The sunset had been wonderful; and I had paused for a moment with my back to the bronze sweep of the land, when I had a swift impression that the memories of the old river gathered around me. It was at this instant—I recall even the trivial detail that my foot caught in a brier as I wheeled quickly about—that I looked past the sunken wharf on my right, and saw the garden of Dare's Gift falling gently from its almost obliterated terraces to the scalloped edge of the river. Following the steep road, which ran in curves through a stretch of pines and across an abandoned pasture or two, I came at last to an iron gate and a grassy walk leading, between walls of box, to the open lawn planted in elms. With that first glimpse the Old World charm of the scene held me captive. From the warm red of its brick walls to the pure Colonial lines of its doorway, and its curving wings mantled in roses and ivy, the house stood there, splendid and solitary. The rows of darkened windows sucked in without giving back the last flare of daylight; the heavy cedars crowding thick up the short avenue did not stir as the wind blew from the river; and above the carved pineapple on the roof, a lonely bat was wheeling high against the red disc of the sun. While I had climbed the rough road and passed more slowly between the marvelous walls of the box, I had told myself that the place must be Mildred's and mine at any cost. On the upper terrace, before several crude modern additions to the wings, my enthusiasm gradually ebbed, though I still asked myself incredulously, "Why have I never heard of it? To whom does it belong? Has it a name as well known in Virginia as Shirley or Brandon?" The house was of great age, I knew, and yet from obvious signs I discovered that it was not too old to be lived in. Nowhere could I detect a hint of decay or dilapidation. The sound of cattle bells floated up from a pasture somewhere in the distance. Through the long grass on the lawn little twisted paths, like sheep tracks, wound back and forth under the fine old elms, from which a rain of bronze leaves fell slowly and ceaselessly in the wind. Nearer at hand, on the upper terrace, a few roses were blooming; and when I passed between two marble urns on the right of the house, my feet crushed a garden of "simples" such as our grandmothers used to grow.

As I stepped on the porch I heard a child's voice on the lawn, and a moment afterwards a small boy, driving a cow, appeared under the two cedars at the end of the avenue. At sight of me he flicked the cow with the hickory switch he held and bawled, "Ma! thar's a stranger out here, an' I don't know what he wants."

At his call the front door opened, and a woman in a calico dress, with a sunbonnet pushed back from her forehead, came out on the porch.

"Hush yo' fuss, Eddy!" she remarked authoritatively. "He don't want nothin'." Then, turning to me, she added civilly, "Good evenin', suh. You must be the gentleman who is visitin' over at Chericoke?"

"Yes, I am staying with Mr. Harrison. You know him, of course?"

"Oh, Lordy, yes. Everybody aroun' here knows Mr. Harrison. His folks have been here goin' on mighty near forever. I don't know what me and my children would come to it if wa'n't for him. He is gettin' me my divorce now. It's been three years and mo' sence Tom deserted me."

"Divorce?" I had not expected to find this innovation on James River.

"Of course it ain't the sort of thing anybody would want to come to. But if a woman in the State ought to have one easy, I reckon it's me. Tom went off with another woman—and she my own sister—from this very house—''

"From this house—and, by the way, what is the name of it?''

"Name of what? This place? Why, it's Dare's Gift. Didn't you know it? Yes, suh, it happened right here in this very house, and that, too, when we hadn't been livin' over here mo' than three months. After Mr. Duncan got tired and went away he left us as caretakers, Tom and me, and I asked Tilly to come and stay with us and help me look after the children. It came like a lightning stroke to me, for Tom and Tilly had known each other all their lives, and he'd never taken any particular notice of her till they moved over here and began to tend the cows together. She wa'n't much for beauty, either. I was always the handsome one of the family—though you mightn't think it now, to look at me— and Tom was the sort that never could abide red hair—''

"And you've lived at Dare's Gift ever since?" I was more interested in the house than in the tenant.

"I didn't have nowhere else to go, and the house has got to have a caretaker till it is sold. It ain't likely that anybody will want to rent an out-of-the-way place like this—though now that automobiles have come to stay that don't make so much difference.''

"Does it still belong to the Dares?''

"Naw, suh; they had to sell it at auction right after the war on account of mortgages and debts—old Colonel Dare died the very year Lee surrendered, and Miss Lucy she went off somewhere to strange parts. Sence their day it has belonged to so many different folks that you can't keep account of it. Right now it's owned by a Mr. Duncan, who lives out in California. I don't know that he'll ever come back here—he couldn't get on with the neighbors—and he is trying to sell it. No wonder, too, a great big place like this, and he ain't even a Virginian—''

"I wonder if he would let it for a season?" It was then, while I stood there in the brooding dusk of the doorway, that the idea of the spring at Dare's Gift first occurred to me.

Ellen Glasgow · 224

"If you want it, you can have it for 'most nothing, I reckon. Would you like to step inside and go over the rooms?"

That evening at supper I asked Harrison about Dare's Gift, and gleaned the salient facts of its history.

"Strange to say, the place, charming as it is, has never been well known in Virginia. There's historical luck, you know, as well as other kinds, and the Dares—after that first Sir Roderick, who came over in time to take a stirring part in Bacon's Rebellion, and, tradition says, to betray his leader—have never distinguished themselves in the records of the State. The place itself, by the way, is about a fifth of the original plantation of three thousand acres, which was given—though I imagine there was more in that than appears in history—by some Indian chief of forgotten name to this notorious Sir Roderick. The old chap—Sir Roderick, I mean—seems to have been something of a fascinator in his day. Even Governor Berkeley, who hanged half the colony, relented, I believe, in the case of Sir Roderick, and that unusual clemency gave rise, I suppose, to the legend of the betrayal. But, however that may be, Sir Roderick had more miraculous escapes than John Smith himself, and died at last in his bed at the age of eighty from overeating cherry pie."

"And now the place has passed away from the family?"

"Oh, long ago—though not so long, after all, when one comes to think of it. When the old Colonel died the year after the war, it was discovered that he had mortgaged the farm up to the last acre. At that time real estate on James River wasn't regarded as a particularly profitable investment, and under the hammer Dare's Gift went for a song."

"Was the Colonel the last of his name?"

"He left a daughter—a belle, too, in her youth, my mother says—but she died—at least I think she did—only a few months after her father."

Coffee was served on the veranda, and while I smoked my cigar and sipped my brandy—Harrison had an excellent wine cellar—I watched the full moon shining like a yellow lantern through the diaphanous mist on the river. Downshore, in the sparkling reach of the water, an immense cloud hung low over the horizon, and between the cloud and the river a band of silver light quivered faintly, as if it would go out in an instant.

"It is over there, isn't it?"—I pointed to the silver light—"Dare's Gift, I mean."

"Yes, it's somewhere over yonder—five miles away by the river, and nearly seven by the road."

"It is the dream of a house, Harrison, and there isn't too much history attached to it—nothing that would make a modern beggar ashamed to live in it."

"By Jove! so you are thinking of buying it?" Harrison was beaming. "It is downright ridiculous, I declare, the attraction that place has for strangers. I never knew a Virginian who wanted it; but you are the third Yankee of my acquaintance—and I don't know many—who has fallen in love with it. I searched the title and drew up the deed for John Duncan exactly six years ago—though I'd better not boast of that transaction, I reckon."

"He still owns it, doesn't he?"

"He still owns it, and it looks as if he would continue to own it unless you can be persuaded to buy it. It is hard to find purchasers for these old places, especially when the roads are uncertain and they happen to be situated on the James River. We live too rapidly in these days to want to depend on a river, even on a placid old fellow like the James."

"Duncan never really lived here, did he?"

"At first he did. He began on quite a royal scale; but, somehow, from the very start things appeared to go wrong with him. At the outset he prejudiced the neighbors against him—I never knew exactly why—by putting on airs, I imagine, and boasting about his money. There is something in the Virginia blood that resents boasting about money. However that may be, he hadn't been here six months before he was at odds with every living thing in the county, white, black, and spotted—for even the dogs snarled at him. Then his secretary—a chap he had picked up starving in London, and had trusted absolutely for years—made off with a lot of cash and securities, and that seemed the last straw in poor Duncan's ill luck. I believe he didn't mind the loss half so much—he refused to prosecute the fellow—as he minded the betrayal of confidence. He told me, I remember, before he went away, that it had spoiled Dare's Gift for him. He said he had a feeling that the place had come too high; it had cost him his belief in human nature."

"Then I imagine he'd be disposed to consider an offer?"

"Oh, there isn't a doubt of it. But, if I were you, I shouldn't be too hasty. Why not rent the place for the spring months? It's beautiful here in the spring, and Duncan has left furniture enough to make the house fairly comfortable."

"Well, I'll ask Mildred. Of course Mildred must have the final word in the matter."

"As if Mildred's final word would be anything but a repetition of yours!" Harrison laughed slyly—for the perfect harmony in which we lived had been for ten years a pleasant jest among our friends. Harrison had once classified wives as belonging to two distinct groups—the group of those who talked and knew nothing about their husbands' affairs, and the group of those who knew everything and kept silent. Mildred, he had added politely, had chosen to belong to the latter division.

The next day I went back to Washington, and Mildred's first words to me in the station were,

"Why, Harold, you look as if you had bagged all the game in Virginia!"

"I look as if I had found just the place for you!"

When I told her about my discovery, her charming face sparkled with interest. Never once, not even during her illness, had she failed to share a single one of my enthusiasms; never once, in all the years of our marriage, had there been so much as a shadow between us. To understand the story of Dare's Gift, it is necessary to realize at the beginning all that Mildred meant and means in my life.

Well, to hasten my slow narrative, the negotiations dragged through most of the winter. At first, Harrison wrote me, Duncan couldn't be found, and a little later that he was found, but that he was opposed, from some inscrutable motive, to the plan of renting Dare's Gift. He wanted to sell it outright, and he'd be hanged if he'd do anything less than get the place clean off his hands. "As sure as I let it"—Harrison sent me his letter—"there is going to be trouble, and somebody will come down on me for damages. The damned place has cost me already twice as much as I paid for it."

In the end, however—Harrison has a persuasive way—the arrangements were concluded. "Of course," Duncan wrote after a long silence, "Dare's Gift may be as healthy as heaven. I may quite as easily have contracted this confounded rheumatism, which makes life a burden, either in Italy or from too many cocktails. I've no reason whatever for my dislike for the place; none, that is, except the incivility of my neighbors—where, by the way, did you Virginians manufacture your reputation for manners?—and my unfortunate episode with Paul Grymes. That, as you remark, might, no doubt, have occurred anywhere else, and if a man is going to steal he could have found all the opportunities he wanted in New York or London. But the fact remains that one can't help harboring associations, pleasant or unpleasant, with the house in which one has lived, and from start to finish my associations with Dare's Gift are frankly unpleasant. If, after all, however, your friend wants the place, and can afford to pay for his whims—let him have it! I hope to Heaven he'll be ready to buy it when his lease has run out. Since he wants it for a hobby, I suppose one place is as good as another; and I can assure him that by the time he has owned it for a few years—especially if he undertakes to improve the motor road up to Richmond—he will regard a taste for Chinese porcelain as an inexpensive diversion." Then, as if impelled by a twist of ironic humor, he added, "He will find the shooting good anyhow."

By early spring Dare's Gift was turned over to us—Mildred was satisfied, if Duncan wasn't—and on a showery day in April, when drifting clouds cast faint gauzy shadows over the river, our boat touched at the old wharf, where carpenters were working, and rested a minute before steaming on the Chericoke Landing five miles away. The spring was early that year—or perhaps the spring is always early on James River. I remember the song of birds in the trees; the veil of bright green over the distant forests; the broad reach of the river scalloped with silver; the dappled sunlight on the steep road which climbed from the wharf to the iron gates; the roving fragrance from lilacs on the lower terrace; and, surmounting all, the two giant cedars which rose like black crags against the changeable blue of the sky—I remember these things as distinctly as if I had seen them this morning.

We entered the wall of box through a living door, and strolled up the grassy walk from the lawn to the terraced garden. Within the garden the air was perfumed with a thousand scents—with lilacs, with young box, with flags and violets and lilies, with aromatic odors from the garden of "simples," and with the sharp sweetness of sheep-mint from the mown grass on the lawn.

"This spring is fine, isn't it?" As I turned to Mildred with the question, I saw for the first time that she looked pale and tired—or was it merely the green light from the box wall that fell over her features? "The trip has been too much for you. Next time we'll come by motor."

"Oh, no, I had a sudden feeling of faintness. It will pass in a minute. What an adorable place, Harold!"

She was smiling again with her usual brightness, and as we passed from the box wall to the clear sunshine on the terrace her face quickly resumed its natural color. To this day—for Mildred has been strangely reticent about Dare's Gift—I do not know whether her pallor was due to the shade in which we walked or whether, at the instant when I turned to her, she was visited by some intuitive warning against the house we were approaching. Even after a year the events of Dare's Gift are not things I can talk over with Mildred; and, for my part, the occurrence remains, like the house in its grove of cedars, wrapped in an impenetrable mystery. I don't in the least pretend to know how or why the thing happened. I only know that it did happen—that it happened, word for word as I record it. Mildred's share in it will, I think, never become clear to me. What she felt, what she imagined, what she believed, I have never asked her. Whether the doctor's explanation is history or fiction, I do not attempt to decide. He is an old man, and old men, since Biblical times, have seen visions. There were places in his story where it seemed to me that he got historical data a little mixed—or it may be that his memory failed him. Yet, in spite of his liking for romance and his French education, he is without constructive imagination—at least he says that he is without it—and the secret of Dare's Gift, if it is not fact, could have sprung only from the ultimate chaos of imagination.

But I think of these things a year afterwards, and on that April morning the house stood there in the sunlight, presiding over its grassy terraces with an air of gracious and intimate hospitality. From the symbolic pineapple on its sloping roof to the twittering sparrows that flew in and out of its ivied wings, it reaffirmed that first flawless impression. Flaws, of course, there were in the fact, yet the recollection of it to-day—the garnered impression of age, of formal beauty, of clustering memories—is one of exquisite harmony. We found later, as Mildred pointed out, architectural absurdities—wanton excrescences in the modern additions, which had been designed apparently with the purpose of providing space at the least possible cost of material and labor. The rooms, when we passed through the fine old doorway, appeared cramped and poorly lighted; broken pieces of the queer mullioned window, where the tracery was of wood, not stone, had been badly repaired, and much of the original detail work of the mantels and cornices had been blurred by recent disfigurements. But these discoveries came afterwards. The first view of the place worked like a magic spell—like an intoxicating perfume—on our senses.

"It is just as if we had stepped into another world," said Mildred, looking up at the row of windows, from which the ivy had been carefully clipped. "I feel as if I had ceased to be myself since I left Washington." Then she turned to meet Harrison, who had ridden over to welcome us.

We spent a charming fortnight together at Dare's Gift—Mildred happy as a child in her garden, and I satisfied to lie in the shadow of the box wall and watch her bloom back to health. At the end of the fortnight I was summoned to an urgent conference in Washington. Some philanthropic busybody, employed to nose out corruption, had scented legal game in the affairs of the Atlantic & Eastern Railroad, and I had been retained as special counsel by that corporation. The fight would be long, I knew—I had already thought of it as one of my great cases—and the evidence was giving me no little anxiety. "It is my last big battle," I told Mildred, as I kissed her good-bye on the steps. "If I win, Dare's Gift shall be your share of the spoils; if I lose—well, I'll be like any other general who has met a better man in the field."

"Don't hurry back, and don't worry about me. I am quite happy here."

"I shan't worry, but all the same I don't like leaving you. Remember, if you need advice or help about anything, Harrison is always at hand."

"Yes, I'll remember."

With this assurance I left her standing in the sunshine, with the windows of the house staring vacantly down on her.

When I try now to recall the next month, I can bring back merely a turmoil of legal wrangles. I contrived in the midst of it all to spend two Sundays with Mildred, but I remember nothing of them except the blessed wave of rest that swept over me as I lay on the grass under the elms. On my second visit I saw that she was looking badly, though when I commented on her pallor and the darkened circles under her eyes, she laughed and put my anxious questions aside.

"Oh, I've lost sleep, that's all," she answered, vaguely, with a swift glance at the house. "Did you ever think how many sounds there are in the country that keep one awake?"

As the day went on I noticed, too, that she had grown restless, and once or twice while I was going over my case with her—I always talked over my cases with Mildred because it helped to clarify my opinions— she returned with irritation to some obscure legal point I had passed over. The flutter of her movements—so unlike my calm Mildred—disturbed me more than I confessed to her, and I made up my mind before night that I would consult Drayton when I went back to Washington. Though she had always been sensitive and impressionable, I had never seen her until that second Sunday in a condition of feverish excitability.

In the morning she was so much better that by the time I reached Washington I forgot my determination to call on her physician. My work was heavy that week—the case was developing into a direct attack upon the management of the road—and in seeking evidence to rebut the charges of illegal rebates to the American Steel Company, I stumbled by accident upon a mass of damaging records. It was a clear case of somebody having blundered—or the records would not have been left for me to discover—and with disturbed thoughts I went down for my third visit to Dare's Gift. It was in my mind to draw out of the case, if an honorable way could be found, and I could barely wait until dinner was over before I unburdened my conscience to Mildred.

"The question has come to one of personal honesty." I remember that I was emphatic. "I've nosed out something real enough this time. There is material for a dozen investigations in Dowling's transactions alone."

The exposure of the Atlantic & Eastern Railroad is public property by this time, and I needn't resurrect the dry bones of that deplorable scandal. I lost the case, as everyone knows; but all that concerns me in it today is the talk I had with Mildred on the darkening terrace at Dare's Gift. It was a reckless talk, when one comes to think of it. I said, I know, a great deal that I ought to have kept to myself; but, after all, she is my wife; I had learned in ten years that I could trust her discretion, and there was more than a river between us and the Atlantic & Eastern Railroad.

Well, the sum of it is that I talked foolishly, and went to bed feeling justified in my folly. Afterwards I recalled that Mildred had been very quiet, though whenever I paused she questioned me closely, with a flash of irritation as if she were impatient of my slowness or my lack of lucidity. At the end she flared out for a moment into the excitement I had noticed the week before; but at the time I was so engrossed in my own affairs that this scarcely struck me as unnatural. Not until the blow fell did I recall the hectic flush in her face and the quivering sound of her voice, as if she were trying not to break down and weep.

It was long before either of us got to sleep that night, and Mildred moaned a little under her breath as she sank into unconsciousness. She was not well, I knew, and I resolved again that I would see Drayton as soon as I reached Washington. Then, just before falling asleep, I became acutely aware of all the noises of the country which Mildred said had kept her awake—of the chirping of the crickets in the fireplace, of the fluttering of swallows in the chimney, of the sawing of innumerable insects in the night outside, of the croaking of frogs in the marshes, of the distant solitary hooting of an owl, of the whispering sound of wind in the leaves, of the stealthy movement of a myriad creeping lives in the ivy. Through the open window the moonlight fell in a milk-white flood, and in the darkness the old house seemed to speak with a thousand voices. As I dropped off I had a confused sensation—less a perception than an apprehension—that all these voices were urging me to something—somewhere—

The next day I was busy with a mass of evidence—dull stuff, I remember. Harrison rode over for luncheon, and not until late afternoon, when I strolled out, with my hands full of papers, for a cup of tea on the terrace, did I have a chance to see Mildred alone. Then I noticed that she was breathing quickly, as if from a hurried walk.

"Did you go to meet the boat, Mildred?"

"No, I've been nowhere—nowhere. I've been on the lawn all day," she answered sharply—so sharply that I looked at her in surprise.

In the ten years that I had lived with her I had never before seen her irritated without cause—Mildred's disposition, I had once said, was as flawless as her profile—and I had for the first time in my life that baffled sensation which comes to men whose perfectly normal wives reveal flashes of abnormal psychology. Mildred wasn't Mildred, that was the upshot of my conclusions; and, hang it all! I didn't know any more than Adam what was the matter with her. There were lines around her eyes, and her sweet mouth had taken an edge of bitterness.

"Aren't you well, dear?" I asked.

"Oh, I'm perfectly well," she replied, in a shaking voice, "only I wish you would leave me alone!" And then she burst into tears.

While I was trying to comfort her the servant came with the tea things, and she kept him about some trivial orders until the big touring car of one of our neighbors rushed up the drive and halted under the terrace.

In the morning Harrison motored up to Richmond with me, and on the way he spoke gravely of Mildred.

"Your wife isn't looking well, Beckwith. I shouldn't wonder if she were a bit seedy—and if I were you I'd get a doctor to look at her. There is a good man down at Chericoke Landing—old Palham Lakeby. I don't care if he did get his training in France half a century ago; he knows more than your half-baked modern scientists."

"I'll speak to Drayton this very day," I answered, ignoring his suggestion of the physician. "You have seen more of Mildred this last month than I have. How long have you noticed that she isn't herself?"

"A couple of weeks. She is usually so jolly, you know." Harrison had played with Mildred in his childhood. "Yes, I shouldn't lose any time over the doctor. Though, of course, it may be only the spring," he added, reassuringly.

"I'll drop by Drayton's office on my way uptown," I replied, more alarmed by Harrison's manner than I had been by Mildred's condition.

But Drayton was not in his office, and his assistant told me that the great specialist would not return to town until the end of the week. It was impossible for me to discuss Mildred with the earnest young man who discoursed so eloquently of the experiments in the Neurological Institute, and I left without mentioning her, after making an appointment for Saturday morning. Even if the consultation delayed my return to Dare's Gift until the afternoon, I was determined to see Drayton, and, if possible, take him back with me. Mildred's last nervous breakdown had been too serious for me to neglect this warning.

I was still worrying over that case—wondering if I could find a way to draw out of it—when the catastrophe overtook me. It was on Saturday morning, I remember, and after a reassuring talk with Drayton, who had promised to run down to Dare's Gift for the coming weekend, I was hurrying to catch the noon train for Richmond. As I passed through the station, one of the *Observer*'s sensational "war extras" caught my eye, and I stopped for an instant to buy the paper before I hastened through the gate to the train. Not until we had started, and I had gone back to the dining car, did I unfold the pink sheets and spread them out on the table before me. Then, while the waiter hung over me for the order, I felt the headlines on the front page slowly burn themselves into my brain—for, instead of the news of the great French drive I was expecting, there flashed back at me, in large type, the name of the opposing counsel in the case against the Atlantic & Eastern. The *Observer*'s "extra" battened not on the war this time, but on the gross scandal of the railroad; and the front page of the paper was devoted to a personal interview with Herbert Tremaine, the great Tremaine, that philanthropic busybody who had first scented corruption. It was all there, every ugly detail—every secret proof of the illegal transactions on which I had stumbled. It was all there, phrase for phrase, as I alone could have told it—as I alone, in my folly, had told it to Mildred. The Atlantic & Eastern had been betrayed, not privately, not secretly, but in large type in the public print of a sensational newspaper. And not only the road! I also had been betrayed—betrayed so wantonly, so irrationally, that it was like an incident out of melodrama.

It was conceivable that the simple facts might have leaked out through other channels, but the phrases, the very words of Tremaine's interview, were mine.

The train had started; I couldn't have turned back even if I had wanted to do so. I was bound to go on, and some intuition told me that the mystery lay at the end of my journey. Mildred had talked indiscreetly to someone, but to whom? Not to Harrison, surely! Harrison, I knew, I could count on, and yet whom had she seen except Harrison? After my first shock the absurdity of the thing made me laugh aloud. It was all as ridiculous, I realized, as it was disastrous! It might so easily not have happened. If only I hadn't stumbled on those accursed records! If only I had kept my mouth shut about them! If only Mildred had not talked unwisely to someone! But I wonder if there was ever a tragedy so inevitable that the victim, in looking back, could not see a hundred ways, great or small, of avoiding or preventing it?—a hundred trivial incidents which, falling differently, might have transformed the event into pure comedy?

The journey was unmitigated torment. In Richmond the car did not meet me, and I wasted half an hour in looking for a motor to take me to Dare's Gift. When at last I got off, the road was rougher than ever, plowed into heavy furrows after the recent rains, and filled with mud-holes from which it seemed we should never emerge. By the time we puffed exhaustedly up the rocky road from the river's edge, and ran into the avenue, I had worked myself into a state of nervous apprehension bordering on panic. I don't know what I expected, but I think I shouldn't have been surprised if Dare's Gift had lain in ruins before me. Had I found the house leveled to ashes by a divine visitation, I believe I should have accepted the occurrence as within the bounds of natural phenomena.

But everything—even the young peacocks on the lawn—was just as I had left it. The sun, setting in a golden ball over the pineapple on the roof, appeared as unchangeable, while it hung there in the glittering sky, as if it were made of metal. From the somber dusk of the wings, where the ivy lay like a black shadow, the clear front of the house, with its formal doorway and its mullioned windows, shone with an intense brightness, the last beams of sunshine lingering there before they faded into the profound gloom of the cedars. The same scents of roses and sage and mown grass and sheep-mint hung about me; the same sounds—the croaking of frogs and the sawing of katydids—floated up from the low grounds; the very books I had been reading lay on one of the tables on the terrace, and the front door still stood ajar as if it had not closed since I passed through it.

I dashed up the steps, and in the hall Mildred's maid met me. "Mrs. Beckwith was so bad that we sent for the doctor—the one Mr. Harrison recommended. I don't know what it is, sir, but she doesn't seem like herself. She talks as if she were quite out of her head."

"What does the doctor say?"

"He didn't tell me. Mr. Harrison saw him. He—the doctor, I mean—has sent a nurse, and he is coming again in the morning. But she isn't herself, Mr. Beckwith. She says she doesn't want you to come to her—"

"Mildred!" I had already sprung past the woman, calling the beloved name aloud as I ran up the stairs.

In her chamber, standing very straight, with hard eyes, Mildred met me. "I had to do it, Harold," she said coldly—so coldly that my outstretched arms fell to my sides. "I had to tell all I knew."

"You mean you told Tremaine—you wrote to him—you, Mildred?"

"I wrote to him—I had to write. I couldn't keep it back any longer. No, don't touch me. You must not touch me. I had to do it. I would do it again."

Then it was, while she stood there, straight and hard, and rejoiced because she had betrayed me—then it was that I knew that Mildred's mind was unhinged.

"I had to do it. I would do it again," she repeated, pushing me from her.

Dare's Gift · 237

II

ALL NIGHT I sat by Mildred's bedside, and in the morning, without having slept, I went downstairs to meet Harrison and the doctor.

"You must get her away, Beckwith," began Harrison with a curious, suppressed excitement. "Dr. Lakeby says she will be all right again as soon as she gets back to Washington."

"But I brought her away from Washington because Drayton said it was not good for her."

"I know, I know." His tone was sharp, "But it's different now. Dr. Lakeby wants you to take her back as soon as you can."

The old doctor was silent while Harrison spoke, and it was only after I had agreed to take Mildred away tomorrow that he murmured something about "bromide and chloral," and vanished up the staircase. He impressed me then as a very old man—old not so much in years as in experience, as if, living there in that flat and remote country, he had exhausted all human desires. A leg was missing, I saw, and Harrison explained that the doctor had been dangerously wounded in the battle of Seven Pines, and had been obliged after that to leave the army and take up again the practice of medicine.

"You had better get some rest," Harrison said, as he parted from me. "It is all right about Mildred, and nothing else matters. The doctor will see you in the afternoon, when you have had some sleep, and have a talk with you. He can explain things better than I can."

Some hours later, after a profound slumber, which lasted well into the afternoon, I waited for the doctor by the tea table, which had been laid out on the upper terrace. It was a perfect afternoon—a serene and cloudless afternoon in early summer. All the brightness of the day gathered on the white porch and the red walls, while the clustering shadows slipped slowly over the box garden to the lawn and the river.

I was sitting there, with a book I had not even attempted to read, when the doctor joined me; and while I rose to shake hands with him I received again the impression of weariness, of pathos and disappointment, which his face had given me in the morning. He was like sun-dried fruit, I thought, fruit that has ripened and dried under the open sky, not withered in tissue paper.

Declining my offer of tea, he sat down in one of the wicker chairs, selecting, I noticed, the least comfortable among them, and filled his pipe from a worn leather pouch.

"She will sleep all night," he said; "I am giving her bromide every three hours, and tomorrow you will be able to take her away. In a week she will be herself again. These nervous natures yield quickest to the influence, but they recover quickest also. In a little while this illness, as you choose to call it, will have left no mark upon her. She may even have forgotten it. I have known this to happen."

"You have known this to happen?" I edged my chair nearer.

"They all succumb to it—the neurotic temperament soonest, the phlegmatic one later—but they all succumb to it in the end. The spirit of the place is too strong for them. The surrender to the thought of the house—to the psychic force of its memories—"

"There are memories, then? Things have happened here?"

"All old houses have memories, I suppose. Did you ever stop to wonder about the thoughts that must have gathered within walls like these?—to wonder about the impressions that must have lodged in the bricks, in the crevices, in the timber and the masonry? Have you ever stopped to think that these multiplied impressions might create a current of thought—a mental atmosphere—an inscrutable power of suggestion?"

"Even when one is ignorant? When one does not know the story?"

"She may have heard scraps of it from the servants—who knows? One can never tell how traditions are kept alive. Many things have been whispered about Dare's Gift; some of these whispers may have reached her. Even without her knowledge she may have absorbed the suggestion; and some day, with that suggestion in her mind, she may have gazed too long at the sunshine on these marble urns before she turned back into the haunted rooms where she lived. After all, we know so little, so

Dare's Gift · 239

pitifully little about these things. We have only touched, we physicians, the outer edges of psychology. The rest lies in darkness—''

I jerked him up sharply. "The house, then, is haunted?''

For a moment he hesitated. "The house is saturated with a thought. It is haunted by treachery.''

"You mean something happened here?''

"I mean—'' He bent forward, groping for the right word, while his gaze sought the river, where a golden web of mist hung midway between sky and water. "I am an old man, and I have lived long enough to see every act merely as the husk of an idea. The act dies; it decays like the body, but the idea is immortal. The thing that happened at Dare's Gift was over fifty years ago, but the thought of it still lives—still utters its profound and terrible message. The house is a shell, and if one listens long enough one can hear in its heart the low murmur of the past—of that past which is but a single wave of the great sea of human experience—''

"But the story?'' I was becoming impatient of his theories. After all, if Mildred was the victim of some phantasmal hypnosis, I was anxious to meet the ghost who had hypnotized her. Even Drayton, I reflected, keen as he was about the fact of mental suggestion, would never have regarded seriously the suggestion of a phantom. And the house looked so peaceful—so hospitable in the afternoon light.

"The story? Oh, I am coming to that—but of late the story has meant so little to me beside the idea. I like to stop by the way. I am getting old, and an amble suits me better than too brisk a trot—particularly in this weather—''

Yes, he was getting old. I lit a fresh cigarette and waited impatiently. After all, this ghost that he rambled about was real enough to destroy me, and my nerves were quivering like harp strings.

"Well, I came into the story—I was in the very thick of it, by accident, if there is such a thing as accident in this world of incomprehensible laws. The Incomprehensible! That has always seemed to me the supreme fact of life, the one truth overshadowing all others—the truth that we know nothing. We nibble at the edges of the mystery, and the great Reality—the Incomprehensible—is still untouched, undiscovered. It unfolds hour by hour, day by day, creating, enslaving, killing us, while we painfully gnaw off—what? A crumb or two, a grain from that vastness which envelops us, which remains impenetrable—''

Again he broke off, and again I jerked him back from his reverie.

''As I have said, I was placed, by an act of Providence, or of chance, in the very heart of the tragedy. I was with Lucy Dare on the day, the unforgettable day, when she made her choice—her heroic or devilish choice, according to the way one has been educated. In Europe a thousand years ago such an act committed for the sake of religion would have made her a saint; in New England, a few centuries past, it would have entitled her to a respectable position in history—the little history of New England. But Lucy Dare was a Virginian, and in Virginia—except in the brief, exalted Virginia of the Confederacy—the personal loyalties have always been esteemed beyond the impersonal. I cannot imagine us as a people canonizing a woman who sacrificed the human ties for the superhuman—even for the divine. I cannot imagine it, I repeat; and so Lucy Dare—though she rose to greatness in that one instant of sacrifice—has not even a name among us today. I doubt if you can find a child in the State who has ever heard of her—or a grown man, outside of this neighborhood, who could give you a single fact of her history. She is as completely forgotten as Sir Roderick, who betrayed Bacon—she is forgotten because the thing she did, though it might have made a Greek tragedy, was alien to the temperament of the people among whom she lived. Her tremendous sacrifice failed to arrest the imagination of her time. After all, the sublime cannot touch us unless it is akin to our ideal; and though Lucy Dare was sublime, according to the moral code of the Romans, she was a stranger to the racial soul of the South. Her memory died because it was the bloom of an hour—because there was nothing in the soil of her age for it to thrive on. She missed her time; she is one of the mute inglorious heroines of history; and yet, born in another century, she might have stood side by side with Antigone——'' For an instant he paused. "But she has always seemed to me diabolical," he added.

"What she did, then, was so terrible that it has haunted the house ever since?" I asked again, for, wrapped in memories, he had lost the thread of his story.

"What she did was so terrible that the house has never forgotten. The thought in Lucy Dare's mind during those hours while she made her choice has left an ineffaceable impression on the things that surrounded her. She created in the horror of that hour an unseen environment more real, because more spiritual, than the material fact of the house. You won't believe this, of course—if people believed in the unseen as in the seen, would life be what it is?"

The afternoon light slept on the river; the birds were mute in the elm trees; from the garden of herbs at the end of the terrace an aromatic fragrance rose like invisible incense.

"To understand it all, you must remember that the South was dominated, was possessed by an idea—the idea of the Confederacy. It was an exalted idea—supremely vivid, supremely romantic—but, after all, it was only an idea. It existed nowhere within the bounds of the actual unless the souls of its devoted people may be regarded as actual. But it is the dream, not the actuality, that commands the noblest devotion, the completest self-sacrifice. It is the dream, the ideal, that has ruled mankind from the beginning.

"I saw a great deal of the Dares that year. It was a lonely life I led after I lost my leg at Seven Pines and dropped out of the army, and, as you may imagine, a country doctor's practice in wartimes was far from lucrative. Our one comfort was that we were all poor, that we were all starving together; and the Dares—there were only two of them, father and daughter—were as poor as the rest of us. They had given their last coin to the government—had poured their last bushel of meal into the sacks of the army. I can imagine the superb gesture with which Lucy Dare flung her dearest heirloom—her one remaining brooch or pin—

into the bare coffers of the Confederacy. She was a small woman, pretty rather than beautiful—not the least heroic in build—yet I wager that she was heroic enough on that occasion. She was a strange soul, though I never so much as suspected her strangeness while I knew her—while she moved among us with her small oval face, her gentle blue eyes, her smoothly banded hair, which shone like satin in the sunlight. Beauty she must have had in a way, though I confess a natural preference for queenly women; I dare say I should have preferred Octavia to Cleopatra, who, they tell me, was small and slight. But Lucy Dare wasn't the sort to blind your eyes when you first looked at her. Her charm was like a fragrance rather than a color—a subtle fragrance that steals into the senses and is the last thing a man ever forgets. I knew half a dozen men who would have died for her—and yet she gave them nothing, nothing, barely a smile. She appeared cold—she who was destined to flame to life in an act. I can see her distinctly as she looked then, in that last year—grave, still, with the curious, unearthly loveliness that comes to pretty women who are underfed—who are slowly starving for bread and meat, for bodily nourishment. She had the look of one dedicated—as ethereal as a saint, and yet I never saw it at the time; I only remember it now, after fifty years, when I think of her. Starvation, when it is slow, not quick—when it means, not acute hunger, but merely lack of the right food, of the blood-making, nerve-building elements—starvation like this often plays strange pranks with one. The visions of the saints, the glories of martyrdom, come to the underfed, the anemic. Can you recall one of the saints—the genuine sort—whose regular diet was roast beef and ale?

"Well, I have said that Lucy Dare was a strange soul, and she was, though to this day I don't know how much of her strangeness was the result of improper nourishment, of too little blood to the brain. Be that as it may, she seems to me when I look back on her to have been one of those women whose characters are shaped entirely by external events—who are the playthings of circumstance. There are many such women. They move among us in obscurity—reserved, passive, commonplace—and we never suspect the spark of fire in their natures until it flares up at the touch of the unexpected. In ordinary circumstances Lucy Dare would have been ordinary, submissive, feminine, domestic; she adored children. That she possessed a stronger will than the average Southern girl, brought up in the conventional manner, none of us—least of all I, myself—ever imagined. She was, of course, intoxicated, obsessed, with the idea of the Confederacy; but, then, so were all of us. There wasn't anything unusual or abnormal in that exalted illusion. It was the common property of our generation. . . .

"Like most noncombatants, the Dares were extremists, and I, who had got rid of a little of my bad blood when I lost my leg, used to regret sometimes that the Colonel—I never knew where he got his title—was too old to do a share of the actual fighting. There is nothing that takes the fever out of one so quickly as a fight; and in the army I had never met a hint of this concentrated, vitriolic bitterness towards the enemy. Why, I've seen the Colonel, sitting here on this terrace, and crippled to the knees with gout, grow purple in the face if I spoke so much as a good word for the climate of the North. For him, and for the girl, too, the Lord had drawn a divine circle round the Confederacy. Everything inside of that circle was perfection; everything outside of it was evil. Well, that was fifty years ago, and his hate is all dust now; yet I can sit here, where he used to brood on this terrace, sipping his blackberry wine—I can sit here and remember it all as if it were yesterday. The place has changed so little, except for Duncan's grotesque additions to the wings, that one can scarcely believe all these years have passed over it. Many an afternoon just like this I've sat here, while the Colonel nodded and Lucy knitted for the soldiers, and watched these same shadows creep down the terrace and that mist of light—it looks just as it used to—hang there over the James. Even the smell from those herbs hasn't changed. Lucy used to keep her little garden at the end of the terrace, for she was fond of making essences and beauty lotions. I used to give her all the prescriptions I could find in old books I read—and I've heard people say that she owed her wonderful white skin to the concoctions she brewed from shrubs and herbs. I couldn't convince them that lack of meat, not lotions, was responsible for the pallor—pallor was all the fashion then—that they admired and envied."

He stopped a minute, just long enough to refill his pipe, while I glanced with fresh interest at the garden of herbs.

"It was a March day when it happened," he went on presently; "cloudless, mild, with the taste and smell of spring in the air. I had been at Dare's Gift almost every day for a year. We had suffered together, hoped, feared, and wept together, hungered and sacrificed together. We had felt together the divine, invincible sway of an idea.

"Stop for a minute and picture to yourself what it is to be of a war and yet not in it; to live in imagination until the mind becomes inflamed with the vision; to have no outlet for the passion that consumes one except the outlet of thought. Add to this the fact that we really knew nothing. We were as far away from the truth, stranded here on our river, as if we had been anchored in a canal on Mars. Two men—one crippled, one too old to fight—and a girl—and the three living for a country which in a few weeks would be nothing—would be nowhere—not on any map of the world. . . .

"When I look back now it seems to me incredible that at that time any persons in the Confederacy should have been ignorant of its want of resources. Yet remember we lived apart, remote, unvisited, out of touch with realities, thinking the one thought. We believed in the ultimate triumph of the South with that indomitable belief which is rooted not in reason, but in emotion. To believe had become an act of religion; to doubt was rank infidelity. So we sat there in our little world, the world of unrealities, bounded by the river and the garden, and talked from noon till sunset about our illusion—not daring to look a single naked fact in the face—talking of plenty when there were no crops in the ground and no flour in the storeroom, prophesying victory while the Confederacy was in her death struggle. Folly! All folly, and yet I am sure even now that we were sincere, that we believed the nonsense we were uttering. We believed, I have said, because to doubt would have been far too horrible. Hemmed in by the river and the garden, there wasn't anything left for us to do—since we couldn't fight—but believe. Someone has said, or ought to have said, that faith is the last refuge of the inefficient. The twin devils of famine and despair were at work in the country, and we sat there—we three, on this damned terrace—and prophesied about the second president of the Confederacy. We agreed, I remember, that Lee would be the next president. And all the time, a few miles away, the demoralization of defeat was abroad, was around us, was in the air. . . .

"It was a March afternoon when Lucy sent for me, and while I walked up the drive—there was not a horse left among us, and I made all my rounds on foot—I noticed that patches of spring flowers were blooming in the long grass on the lawn. The air was as soft as May, and in the woods at the back of the house buds of maple trees ran like a flame. There were, I remember, leaves—dead leaves, last year's leaves—everywhere, as if, in the demoralization of panic, the place had been forgotten, had been untouched since autumn. I remember rotting leaves that gave like moss underfoot; dried leaves that stirred and murmured as one walked over them; black leaves, brown leaves, wine-colored leaves, and the still glossy leaves of the evergreens. But they were everywhere—in the road, over the grass on the lawn, beside the steps, piled in wind drifts against the walls of the house.

"On the terrace, wrapped in shawls, the old Colonel was sitting; and he called out excitedly, 'Are you bringing news of a victory?' Victory! when the whole country had been scraped with a fine-tooth comb for provisions.

"'No, I bring no news except that Mrs. Morson has just heard of the death of her youngest son in Petersburg. Gangrene, they say. The truth is the men are so ill-nourished that the smallest scratch turns to gangrene—'

"'Well, it won't be for long—not for long. Let Lee and Johnston get together and things will go our way with a rush. A victory or two, and the enemy will be asking for terms of peace before the summer is over.'

"A lock of his silver-white hair had fallen over his forehead, and pushing it back with his clawlike hand, he peered up at me with his little nearsignted eyes, which were of a peculiar burning blackness, like the eyes of some small enraged animal. I can see him now as vividly as if I had left him only an hour ago, and yet it is fifty years since then—fifty years filled with memories and with forgetfulness. Behind him the warm red of the bricks glowed as the sunshine fell, sprinkled with shadows, through the elm boughs. Even the soft wind was too much for him, for he shivered occasionally in his blanket shawls, and coughed the dry, hacking cough which had troubled him for a year. He was a shell of a man—a shell vitalized and animated by an immense, an indestructible illusion. While he sat there, sipping his blackberry wine, with his little fiery dark eyes searching the river in hope of something that would end his interminable expectancy, there was about him a fitful somber gleam of romance. For him the external world, the actual truth of things, had vanished—all of it, that is, except the shawl that wrapped him and the glass of blackberry wine he sipped. He had died already to the material fact, but he lived intensely, vividly, profoundly, in the idea. It was the idea that nourished him, that gave him his one hold on reality.

"'It was Lucy who sent for you,' said the old man presently. 'She has been on the upper veranda all day overlooking something—the sunning of winter clothes, I think. She wants to see you about one of the servants—a sick child, Nancy's child, in the quarters.'

"'Then I'll find her,' I answered readily, for I had, I confess, a mild curiosity to find out why Lucy had sent for me.

"She was alone on the upper veranda, and I noticed that she closed her Bible and laid it aside as I stepped through the long window that opened from the end of the hall. Her face, usually so pale, glowed now with a wan illumination, like ivory before the flame of a lamp. In this illumination her eyes, beneath delicately penciled eyebrows, looked unnaturally large and brilliant, and so deeply, so angelically blue that they made me think of the Biblical heaven of my childhood. Her beauty, which had never struck me sharply before, pierced through me. But it was her fate—her misfortune perhaps—to appear commonplace, to pass unrecognized, until the fire shot from her soul.

"'No, I want to see you about myself, not about one of the servants.'

"At my first question she had risen and held out her hand—a white, thin hand, small and frail as a child's.

"'You are not well, then?' I had known from the first that her starved look meant something.

"'It isn't that; I am quite well.' She paused a moment, and then looked at me with a clear shining gaze. 'I have had a letter,' she said.

"'A letter?' I have realized since how dull I must have seemed to her in that moment of excitement, of exaltation.

"'You didn't know. I forgot that you didn't know that I was once engaged—long ago—before the beginning of the war. I cared a great deal—we both cared a great deal, but he was not one of us; he was on the other side—and when the war came, of course there was no question. We broke if off; we had to break it off. How could it have been possible to do otherwise?'

"'How, indeed!' I murmured; and I had a vision of the old man downstairs on the terrace, of the intrepid and absurd old man.

"'My first duty is to my country,' she went on after a minute, and the words might have been spoken by her father. 'There has been no thought of anything else in my mind since the beginning of the war. Even if peace comes I can never feel the same again—I can never forget that he has been a part of all we have suffered—of the thing that has made us suffer. I could never forget—I can never forgive.'

"Her words sound strange now, you think, after fifty years; but on that day, in this house surrounded by dead leaves, inhabited by an inextinguishable ideal—in this country, where the spirit had fed on the body until the impoverished brain reacted to transcendent visions—in this place, at that time, they were natural enough. Scarcely a woman of the South but would have uttered them from her soul. In every age one ideal enthralls the imagination of mankind; it is in the air; it subjugates the will; it enchants the emotions. Well, in the South fifty years ago this ideal was patriotism; and the passion of patriotism, which bloomed like some red flower, the flower of carnage, over the land, had grown in Lucy Dare's soul into an exotic blossom.

"Yet even today, after fifty years, I cannot get over the impression she made upon me of a woman who was, in the essence of her nature, thin and colorless. I may have been wrong. Perhaps I never knew her. It is not easy to judge people, especially women, who wear a mask by instinct. What I thought lack of character, of personality, may have been merely reticence; but again and again there comes back to me the thought that she never said or did a thing—except the one terrible thing—that one could remember. There was nothing remarkable that one could point to about her. I cannot recall either her smile or her voice, though both were sweet, no doubt, as the smile and the voice of a Southern woman would be. Until that morning on the upper veranda I had not noticed that her eyes were wonderful. She was like a shadow, a phantom, that attains in one supreme instant, by one immortal gesture, union with reality. Even I remember her only by that one lurid flash.

"'And you say you have had a letter?'

"'It was brought by one of the old servants—Jacob, the one who used to wait on him when he stayed here. He was a prisoner. A few days ago he escaped. He asked me to see him—and I told him to come. He wishes to see me once again before he goes North—forever—' She spoke in gasps in a dry voice. Never once did she mention his name. Long afterwards I remembered that I had never heard his name spoken. Even today I do not know it. He also was a shadow, a phantom—a part of the encompassing unreality.

"'And he will come here?'

"For a moment she hesitated; then she spoke quite simply, knowing that she could trust me.

"'He is here. He is in the chamber beyond.' She pointed to one of the long windows that gave on the veranda. 'The blue chamber at the front.'

"I remember that I made a step towards the window when her voice arrested me. 'Don't go in. He is resting. He is very tired and hungry.'

" 'You didn't send for me, then, to see him?'

" 'I sent for you to be with father. I knew you would help me—that you would keep him from suspecting. He must not know, of course. He must be kept quiet.'

" 'I will stay with him,' I answered, and then, 'Is that all you wish to say to me?'

" 'That is all. It is only for a day or two. He will go on in a little while, and I can never see him again. I do not wish to see him again.'

"I turned away, across the veranda, entered the hall, walked the length of it, and descended the staircase. The sun was going down in a ball—just as it will begin to go down in a few minutes—and as I descended the stairs I saw it through the mullioned window over the door—huge and red and round above the black cloud of the cedars.

"The old man was still on the terrace. I wondered vaguely why the servants had not brought him indoors; and then, as I stepped over the threshold, I saw that a company of soldiers—Confederates—had crossed the lawn and were already gathering about the house. The commanding officer—I was shaking hands with him presently—was a Dare, a distant cousin of the Colonel's, one of those excitable, nervous, and slightly theatrical natures who become utterly demoralized under the spell of any violent emotion. He had been wounded at least a dozen times, and his lean, sallow, still handsome features had the greenish look which I had learned to associate with chronic malaria.

"When I look back now I can see it ail as a part of the general disorganization—of the fever, the malnutrition, the complete demoralization of panic. I know now that each man of us was facing in his soul defeat and despair; and that we—each one of us—had gone mad with the thought of it. In a little while, after the certainty of failure had come to us, we met it quietly—we braced our souls for the issue; but in those last weeks defeat had all the horror, all the insane terror of a nightmare, and all the vividness. The thought was like a delusion from which we fled, and which no flight could put farther away from us.

"Have you ever lived, I wonder, from day to day in that ever-present and unchanging sense of unreality, as if the moment before you were but an imaginary experience which must dissolve and evaporate before the touch of an actual event? Well, that was the sensation I had felt for days, weeks, months, and it swept over me again while I stood there, shaking hands with the Colonel's cousin, on the terrace. The soldiers, in their ragged uniforms, appeared as visionary as the world in which we had been living. I think now that they were as ignorant as we were of the things that had happened—that were happening day by day to the army. The truth is that it was impossible for a single one of us to believe that our heroic army could be beaten even by unseen powers—even by hunger and death.

"'And you say he was a prisoner?' It was the old man's quavering voice, and it sounded avid for news, for certainty.

"'Caught in disguise. Then he slipped through our fingers.' The cousin's tone was querulous, as if he were irritated by loss of sleep or of food. 'Nobody knows how it happened. Nobody ever knows. But he has found out things that will ruin us. He has plans. He has learned things that mean the fall of Richmond if he escapes.'

"Since then I have wondered how much they sincerely believed—how much was simply the hallucination of fever, of desperation? Were they trying to bully themselves by violence into hoping? Or had they honestly convinced themselves that victory was still possible? If one only repeats a phrase often and emphatically enough one comes in time to believe it; and they had talked so long of that coming triumph, of the established Confederacy, that it had ceased to be, for them at least, merely a phrase. It wasn't the first occasion in life when I had seen words bullied—yes, literally bullied into beliefs.

"Well, looking back now after fifty years, you see, of course, the weakness of it all, the futility. At that instant, when all was lost, how could any plans, any plotting have ruined us? It seems irrational enough now—a dream, a shadow, that belief—and yet not one of us but would have given our lives for it. In order to understand you must remember that we were, one and all, victims of an idea—of a divine frenzy.

"'And we are lost—the Confederacy is lost, you say, if he escapes?'

"It was Lucy's voice; and turning quickly, I saw that she was standing in the doorway. She must have followed me closely. It was possible that she had overheard every word of the conversation.

"'If Lucy knows anything, she will tell you. There is no need to search the house,' quavered the old man, 'she is my daughter.'

"'Of course we wouldn't search the house—not Dare's Gift,' said the cousin. He was excited, famished, malarial, but he was a gentleman, every inch of him.

"He talked on rapidly, giving details of the capture, the escape, the pursuit. It was all rather confused. I think he must have frightfully exaggerated the incident. Nothing could have been more unreal than it sounded. And he was just out of a hospital—was suffering still, I could see, from malaria. While he drank his blackberry wine—the best the house had to offer—I remember wishing that I had a good dose of quinine and whiskey to give him.

"The narrative lasted a long time; I think he was glad of a rest and of the blackberry wine and biscuits. Lucy had gone to fetch food for the soldiers; but after she had brought it she sat down in her accustomed chair by the old man's side and bent her head over her knitting. She was a wonderful knitter. During all the years of the war I seldom saw her without her ball of yarn and her needles—the long wooden kind that the women used at the time. Even after the dusk fell in the evenings the click of her needles sounded in the darkness.

"'And if he escapes it will mean the capture of Richmond?' she asked once again when the story was finished. There was no hint of excitement in her manner. Her voice was perfectly toneless. To this day I have no idea what she felt—what she was thinking.

"'If he gets away it is the ruin of us—but he won't get away. We'll find him before morning.'

"Rising from his chair, he turned to shake hands with the old man before descending the steps. 'We've got to go on now. I shouldn't have stopped if we hadn't been half starved. You've done us a world of good, Cousin Lucy. I reckon you'd give your last crust to the soldiers?'

"'She'd give more than that,' quavered the old man. 'You'd give more than that, wouldn't you, Lucy?'

"'Yes, I'd give more than that,' repeated the girl quietly, so quietly that it came as a shock to me—like a throb of actual pain in the midst of a nightmare—when she rose to her feet and added, without a movement, without a gesture, 'You must not go, Cousin George. He is upstairs in the blue chamber at the front of the house.'

"For an instant surprise held me speechless, transfixed, incredulous; and in that instant I saw a face—a white face of horror and disbelief— look down on us from one of the side windows of the blue chamber. Then, in a rush it seemed to me the soldiers were everywhere, swarming over the terrace, into the hall, surrounding the house. I had never imagined that a small body of men in uniforms, even ragged uniforms, could so possess and obscure one's surroundings. The three of us waited there—Lucy had sat down again and taken up her knitting—for what seemed hours, or an eternity. We were still waiting—though, for once, I noticed, the needles did not click in her fingers—when a single shot, followed by a volley, rang out from the rear of the house, from the veranda that looked down on the grove of oaks and the kitchen.

"Rising, I left them—the old man and the girl—and passed from the terrace down the little walk which led to the back. As I reached the lower veranda one of the soldiers ran into me.

"'I was coming after you,' he said, and I observed that his excitement had left him. 'We brought him down while he was trying to jump from the veranda. He is there now on the grass.'

"The man on the grass was quite dead, shot through the heart; and while I bent over to wipe the blood from his lips, I saw him for the first time distinctly. A young face, hardly more than a boy—twenty-five at the most. Handsome, too, in a poetic and dreamy way; just the face, I thought, that a woman might have fallen in love with. He had dark hair, I remember, though his features have long ago faded from my memory. What will never fade, what I shall never forget, is the look he wore— the look he was still wearing when we laid him in the old graveyard next day—a look of mingled surprise, disbelief, terror, and indignation.

"I had done all that I could, which was nothing, and rising to my feet, I saw for the first time that Lucy had joined me. She was standing perfectly motionless. Her knitting was still in her hands, but the light had gone from her face, and she looked old—old and gray—beside the glowing youth of her lover. For a moment her eyes held me while she spoke as quietly as she had spoken to the soldiers on the terrace.

"'I had to do it,' she said. 'I would do it again.'"

Suddenly, like the cessation of running water, or of wind in the treetops, the doctor's voice ceased. For a long pause we stared in silence at the sunset; then, without looking at me, he added slowly:

"Three weeks later Lee surrendered and the Confederacy was over."

THE SUN HAD slipped, as if by magic, behind the tops of the cedars, and dusk fell quickly, like a heavy shadow, over the terrace. In the dimness a piercing sweetness floated up from the garden of herbs, and it seemed to me that in a minute the twilight was saturated with fragrance. Then I heard the cry of a solitary whippoorwill in the graveyard, and it sounded so near that I started.

"So she died of the futility, and her unhappy ghost haunts the house?"

"No, she is not dead. It is not her ghost; it is the memory of her act that has haunted the house. Lucy Dare is still living. I saw her a few months ago."

"You saw her? You spoke to her after all these years?"

He had refilled his pipe, and the smell of it gave me a comfortable assurance that I was living here, now, in the present. A moment ago I had shivered as if the hand of the past, reaching from the open door at my back, had touched my shoulder.

"I was in Richmond. My friend Beverly, an old classmate, had asked me up for a weekend, and on Saturday afternoon, before motoring into the country for supper, we started out to make a few calls which had been left over from the morning. For a doctor, a busy doctor, he had always seemed to me to possess unlimited leisure, so I was not surprised when a single visit sometimes stretched over twenty-five minutes. We had stopped several times, and I confess that I was getting a little impatient when he remarked abruptly while he turned his car into a shady street,

"'There is only one more. If you don't mind, I'd like you to see her. She is a friend of yours, I believe.'

"Before us, as the car stopped, I saw a red-brick house, very large, with green shutters, and over the wide door, which stood open, a sign reading 'St. Luke's Church Home.' Several old ladies sat, half asleep, on the long veranda; a clergyman, with a prayer book in his hand, was just leaving; a few pots of red geraniums stood on little green wicker stands; and from the hall, through which floated the smell of freshly baked bread, there came the music of a Victrola—sacred music, I remember. Not one of these details escaped me. It was as if every trivial impression was stamped indelibly in my memory by the shock of the next instant.

"In the center of the large, smoothly shaven lawn an old woman was sitting on a wooden bench under an ailanthus tree which was in blossom. As we approached her, I saw that her figure was shapeless, and that her eyes, of a faded blue, had the vacant and listless expression of the old who have ceased to think, who have ceased even to wonder or regret. So unlike was she to anything I had ever imagined Lucy Dare could become, that not until my friend called her name and she glanced up from the muffler she was knitting—the omnipresent dun-colored muffler for the war relief associations—not until then did I recognize her.

"'I have brought an old friend to see you, Miss Lucy.'

"She looked up, smiled slightly, and after greeting me pleasantly, relapsed into silence. I remembered that the Lucy Dare I had known was never much of a talker.

"Dropping on the bench at her side, my friend began asking her about her sciatica, and, to my surprise, she became almost animated. Yes, the pain in her hip was better—far better than it had been for weeks. The new medicine had done her a great deal of good; but her fingers were getting rheumatic. She found trouble holding her needles. She couldn't knit as fast as she used to.

"Unfolding the end of the muffler, she held it out to us. 'I have managed to do twenty of these since Christmas. I've promised fifty to the War Relief Association by autumn, and if my fingers don't get stiff I can easily do them.'

"The sunshine falling through the ailanthus tree powdered with dusty gold her shapeless, relaxed figure and the dun-colored wool of the muffler. While she talked her fingers flew with the click of the needles—older fingers than they had been at Dare's Gift, heavier, stiffer, a little knotted in the joints. As I watched her the old familiar sense of strangeness, of encompassing and hostile mystery, stole over me.

"When we rose to go she looked up, and, without pausing for an instant in her knitting, said, gravely, 'It gives me something to do, this work for the Allies. It helps to pass the time, and in an Old Ladies' Home one has so much time on one's hands.'

"Then, as we parted from her, she dropped her eyes again to her needles. Looking back at the gate, I saw that she still sat there in the faint sunshine—knitting—knitting—"

"And you think she has forgotten?"

He hesitated, as if gathering his thoughts. "I was with her when she came back from the shock—from the illness that followed—and she had forgotten. Yes, she has forgotten, but the house has remembered."

Pushing back his chair, he rose unsteadily on his crutch, and stood staring across the twilight which was spangled with fireflies. While I waited I heard again the loud cry of the whippoorwill.

"Well, what could one expect?" he asked, presently. "She had drained the whole of experience in an instant, and there was left to her only the empty and withered husks of the hours. She had felt too much ever to feel again. After all," he added slowly, "it is the high moments that make a life, and the flat ones that fill the years."

First Dark

Elizabeth Spencer

WHEN TOM BEAVERS started coming back to Richton, Mississippi, on weekends, after the war was over, everybody in town was surprised and pleased. They had never noticed him much before he paid them this compliment; now they could not say enough nice things. There was not much left in Richton for him to call family—just his aunt who had raised him, Miss Rita Beavers, old as God, ugly as sin, deaf as a post. So he must be fond of the town, they reasoned; certainly it was a pretty old place. Far too many young men had left it and never come back at all.

He would drive in every Friday night from Jackson, where he worked. All weekend, his Ford, dusty of flank, like a hard-ridden horse, would sit parked down the hill near Miss Rita's old wire front gate, which sagged from the top hinge and had worn a span in the ground. On Saturday morning, he would head for the drugstore, then the post office;

then he would be observed walking here and there around the streets under the shade trees. It was as though he were looking for something.

He wore steel taps on his heels, and in the still the click of them on the sidewalks would sound across the big front lawns and all the way up to the porches of the houses, where two ladies might be sitting behind a row of ferns. They would identify him to one another, murmuring in their fine little voices, and say it was just too bad there was nothing here for young people. It was just a shame they didn't have one or two more old houses, here, for a Pilgrimage—look how Natchez had waked up.

One Saturday morning in early October, Tom Beavers sat at the counter in the drugstore and reminded Totsie Poteet, the drugstore clerk, of a ghost story. Did he remember the strange old man who used to appear to people who were coming into Richton along the Jackson road at twilight—what they called "first dark"?

"Sure I remember," said Totsie. "Old Cud'n Jimmy Wiltshire used to tell us about him every time we went 'possum hunting. I could see him plain as I can see you, the way he used to tell it. Tall, with a top hat on, yeah, and waiting in the weeds alongside the road ditch, so'n you couldn't tell if he wasn't taller than any mortal man could be, because you couldn't tell if he was standing down in the ditch or not. It would look like he just grew up out of the weeds. Then he'd signal to you."

"Them that stopped never saw anybody," said Tom Beavers, stirring his coffee. "There were lots of folks besides Mr. Jimmy that saw him."

"There was, let me see . . ." Totsie enumerated others—some men, some women, some known to drink, others who never touched a drop. There was no way to explain it. "There was that story the road gang told. Do you remember, or were you off at school? It was while they were straightening the road out to the highway—taking the curves out and building a new bridge. Anyway, they said that one night at quitting time, along in the winter and just about dark, this old guy signaled to some of 'em. They said they went over and he asked them to move a bulldozer they had left across the road, because he had a wagon back behind on a little dirt road, with a sick nigger girl in it. Had to get to the doctor and this was the only way. They claimed they knew didn't nobody live back there on that little old road, but niggers can come from anywhere. So they moved the bulldozer and cleared back a whole lot of other stuff, and waited and waited. Not only didn't no wagon ever come, but the man that had stopped them, he was gone, too. They was right shook up over it. You never heard that one?"

"No, I never did." Tom Beavers said this with his eyes looking up over his coffee cup, as though he sat behind a hand of cards. His lashes and brows were heavier than was ordinary, and worked as a veil might, to keep you away from knowing exactly what he was thinking.

"They said he was tall and had a hat on." The screen door flapped to announce a customer, but Totsie kept on talking. "But whether he was a white man or a real light-colored nigger they couldn't say. Some said one and some said another. I figured they'd been pulling on the jug a little earlier than usual. You know why? I never heard of *our* ghost *saying* nothing. Did you, Tom?"

He moved away on the last words, the way a clerk will, talking back over his shoulder and ahead of him to his new customer at the same time, as though he had two voices and two heads. "And what'll it be today, Miss Frances?"

The young woman standing at the counter had a prescription already out of her bag. She stood with it poised between her fingers, but her attention was drawn toward Tom Beavers, his coffee cup, and the conversation she had interrupted. She was a girl whom no ordinary description would fit. One would have to know first of all who she was: Frances Harvey. After that, it was all right for her to be a little odd-looking, with her reddish hair that curled back from her brow, her light eyes, and her high, pale temples. This is not the material for being pretty, but in Frances Harvey it was what could sometimes be beauty. Her family home was laden with history that nobody but the Harveys could remember. It would have been on a Pilgrimage if Richton had had one. Frances still lived in it, looking after an invalid mother.

"What were you-all talking about?" she wanted to know.

"About that ghost they used to tell about," said Totsie, holding out his hand for the prescription. "The one people used to see just outside of town, on the Jackson road."

"But why?" she demanded. "Why were you talking about him?"

"Tom, here——" the clerk began, but Tom Beavers interrupted him.

"I was asking because I was curious," he said. He had been studying her from the corner of his eye. Her face was beginning to show the wear of her mother's long illness, but that couldn't be called change. Changing was something she didn't seem to have done, her own style being the only one natural to her.

"I was asking," he went on, "because I saw him." He turned away from her somewhat too direct gaze and said to Totsie Poteet, whose mouth had fallen open, "It was where the new road runs close to the old road, and as far as I could tell he was right on the part of the old road where people always used to see him."

"But when?" Frances Harvey demanded.

"Last night," he told her. "Just around first dark. Driving home."

A wealth of quick feeling came up in her face. "So did I! Driving home from Jackson! I saw him, too!"

FOR SOME PEOPLE, a liking for the same phonograph record or for Mayan archaeology is enough of an excuse to get together. Possibly, seeing the same ghost was no more than that. Anyway, a week later, on Saturday at first dark, Frances Harvey and Tom Beavers were sitting together in a car parked just off the highway, near the spot where they agreed the ghost had appeared. The season was that long, peculiar one between summer and fall, and there were so many crickets and tree frogs going full tilt in their periphery that their voices could hardly be distinguished from the background noises, though they both would have heard a single footfall in the grass. An edge of autumn was in the air at night, and Frances had put on a tweed jacket at the last minute, so the smell of moth balls was in the car, brisk and most unghostlike.

But Tom Beavers was not going to forget the value of the ghost, whether it put in an appearance or not. His questions led Frances into reminiscence.

"No, I never saw him before the other night," she admitted. "The Negroes used to talk in the kitchen, and Regina and I—you know my sister Regina—would sit there listening, scared to go and scared to stay. Then finally going to bed upstairs was no relief, either, because sometimes Aunt Henrietta was visiting us, and *she'd* seen it. Or if she wasn't visiting us, the front room next to us, where she stayed, would be empty, which was worse. There was no way to lock ourselves in, and besides, what was there to lock out? We'd lie all night like two sticks in bed, and shiver. Papa finally had to take a hand. He called us in and sat us down and said that the whole thing was easy to explain—it was all automobiles. What their headlights did with the dust and shadows out on the Jackson road. 'Oh, but Sammie and Jerry!' we said, with great big eyes, sitting side by side on the sofa, with our tennis shoes flat on the floor."

"Who were Sammie and Jerry?" asked Tom Beavers.

"Sammie was our cook. Jerry was her son, or husband, or something. Anyway, they certainly didn't have cars. Papa called them in. They were standing side by side by the bookcase, and Regina and I were on the sofa—four pairs of big eyes, and Papa pointing his finger. Papa said, 'Now, you made up these stories about ghosts, didn't you?' 'Yes, sir,' said Sammie. 'We made them up.' 'Yes, sir,' said Jerry. 'We sho did.' 'Well, then, you can just stop it,' Papa said. 'See how peaked these children look?' Sammie and Jerry were terribly polite to us for a week, and we got in the car and rode up and down the Jackson road at first dark to see if the headlights really did it. But we never saw anything. We didn't tell Papa, but headlights had nothing whatever to do with it."

"You had your own *car* then?" He couldn't believe it.

"Oh no!" She was emphatic. "We were too young for that. Too young to drive, really, but we did anyway."

She leaned over to let him give her cigarette a light, and saw his hand tremble. Was he afraid of the ghost or of her? She would have to stay away from talking family.

Frances remembered Tommy Beavers from her childhood—a small boy going home from school down a muddy side road alone, walking right down the middle of the road. His old aunt's house was at the bottom of a hill. It was damp there, and the yard was always muddy, with big fat chicken tracks all over it, like Egyptian writing. How did Frances know? She could not remember going there, ever. Miss Rita Beavers was said to order cold ham, mustard, bread, and condensed milk from the grocery store. "I doubt if that child ever has anything hot," Frances's mother had said once. He was always neatly dressed in the same knee pants, high socks, and checked shirt, and sat several rows ahead of Frances in study hall, right in the middle of his seat. He was three grades behind her; in those days, that much younger seemed very young indeed. What had happened to his parents? There was some story, but it was not terribly interesting, and, his people being of no importance, she had forgotten.

"I think it's past time for our ghost," she said. "He's never out so late at night."

"He gets hungry, like me," said Tom Beavers. "Are you hungry, Frances?"

They agreed on a highway restaurant where an orchestra played on weekends. Everyone went there now.

From the moment they drew up on the graveled entrance, cheerful lights and a blare of music chased the spooks from their heads. Tom Beavers ordered well and danced well, as it turned out. Wasn't there something she had heard about his being "smart"? By "smart," Southerners mean intellectual, and they say it in an almost condescending way, smart being what you are when you can't be anything else, but it is better, at least, than being nothing. Frances Harvey had been away enough not to look at things from a completely Southern point of view, and she was encouraged to discover that she and Tom had other things in common besides a ghost, though all stemming, perhaps, from the imagination it took to see one.

First Dark · *263*

They agreed about books and favorite movies and longing to see more plays. She signed that life in Richton was so confining, but he assured her that Jackson could be just as bad; *it* was getting to be like any Middle Western city, he said, while Richton at least had a sense of the past. This was the main reason, he went on, gaining confidence in the jumble of commonplace noises—dishes, music, and a couple of drinkers chattering behind them—that he had started coming back to Richton so often. He wanted to keep a connection with the past. He lived in a modern apartment, worked in a soundproof office—he could be in any city. But Richton was where he had been born and raised, and nothing could be more old-fashioned. Too many people seemed to have their lives cut in two. He was earnest in desiring that this should not happen to him.

"You'd better be careful," Frances said lightly. Her mood did not incline her to profound conversation. "There's more than one ghost in Richton. You may turn into one yourself, like the rest of us."

"It's the last thing I'd think of you," he was quick to assure her.

Had Tommy Beavers really said such a thing, in such a natural, charming way? Was Frances Harvey really so pleased? Not only was she pleased but, feeling warmly alive amid the music and small lights, she agreed with him. She could not have agreed with him more.

"I HEAR THAT Thomas Beavers has gotten to be a very attractive man," Frances Harvey's mother said unexpectedly one afternoon.

Frances had been reading aloud—Jane Austen this time. Theirs was one house where the leather-bound sets were actually read. In Jane Austen, men and women seesawed back and forth for two or three hundred pages until they struck a point of balance; then they got married. She had just put aside the book, at the end of a chapter, and risen to lower the shade against the slant of afternoon sun. "Or so Cud'n Jennie and Mrs. Giles Antley and Miss Fannie Stapleton have been coming and telling you," she said.

"People talk, of course, but the consensus is favorable," Mrs. Harvey said. "Wonders never cease; his mother ran away with a brush salesman. But nobody can make out what he's up to, coming back to Richton."

"Does he have to be 'up to' anything?" Frances asked.

"Men are always up to something," said the old lady at once. She added, more slowly, "In Thomas's case, maybe it isn't anything it oughtn't to be. They say he reads a lot. He may just have taken up with some sort of idea."

Frances stole a long glance at her mother's face on the pillow. Age and illness had reduced the image of Mrs. Harvey to a kind of caricature, centered on a mouth that Frances could not help comparing to that of a fish. There was a tension around its rim, as though it were outlined in bone, and the underlip even stuck out a little. The mouth ate, it took medicine, it asked for things, it gasped when breath was short, it commented. But when it commented, it ceased to be just a mouth and became part of Mrs. Harvey, that witty tyrant with the infallible memory for the right detail, who was at her terrible best about men.

"And what could he be thinking of?" she was wont to inquire when some man had acted foolishly. No one could ever defend accurately the man in question, and the only conclusion was Mrs. Harvey's; namely, that he wasn't thinking, if, indeed, he could. Although she had never been a belle, never a flirt, her popularity with men was always formidable. She would be observed talking marathons with one in a corner, and could you ever be sure, when they both burst into laughter, that they had not just exchanged the most shocking stories? "Of course, *he*—" she would begin later, back with the family, and the masculinity that had just been encouraged to strut and preen a little was quickly shown up as idiotic. Perhaps Mrs. Harvey hoped by this method to train her daughters away from a lot of sentimental nonsense that was their birthright as pretty Southern girls in a house with a lawn that moonlight fell on and that was often lit also by Japanese lanterns hung for parties. "Oh, he's not like that, Mama!" the little girls would cry. They were already alert for heroes who would ride up and cart them off. "Well, then, you watch," she would say. Sure enough, if you watched, she would be right.

First Dark · 265

Mrs. Harvey's younger daughter, Regina, was a credit to her mother's long campaign; she married well. The old lady, however, never tired of pointing out behind her son-in-law's back that his fondness for money was ill-concealed, that he had the longest feet she'd ever seen, and that he sometimes made grammatical errors.

Her elder daughter, Frances, on a trip to Europe, fell in love, alas! The gentleman was of French extraction but Swiss citizenship, and Frances did not marry him, because he was already married—that much filtered back to Richton. In response to a cable, she had returned home one hot July in time to witness her father's wasted face and last weeks of life. That same September, the war began. When peace came, Richton wanted to know if Frances Harvey would go back to Europe. Certain subtly complicated European matters, little understood in Richton, seemed to be obstructing Romance; one of them was probably named Money. Meanwhile, Frances's mother took to bed, in what was generally known to be her last illness.

So no one crossed the ocean, but eventually Tom Beavers came up to Mrs. Harvey's room one afternoon, to tea.

Though almost all her other faculties were seriously impaired, in ear and tongue Mrs. Harvey was as sound as a young beagle, and she could still leave a more interesting conversation than most people who go about every day and look at the world. She was of the old school of Southern lady talkers; she vexed you with no ideas, she tried to protect you from even a moment of silence. In the old days, when a bright company filled the downstairs rooms, she could keep the ball rolling amongst a crowd. Everyone—all the men especially—got their word in, but the flow of things came back to her. If one of those twenty-minutes-to-or-after silences fell—and even with her they did occur—people would turn and look at her daughter Frances. "And what do you think?" some kind-eyed gentleman would ask. Frances did not credit that she had the sort of face people would turn to, and so did not know how to take advantage of it. What did she think? Well, to answer that honestly took a moment of reflection—a fatal moment, it always turned out. Her mother would be up instructing the maid, offering someone an ashtray or another goody, or remarking outright, "Frances is so timid. She never says a word."

Tom Beavers stayed not only past teatime that day but for a drink as well. Mrs. Harvey was induced to take a glass of sherry, and now her bed became her enormous throne. Her keenest suffering as an invalid was occasioned by the absence of men. "What is a house without a man in it?" she would often cry. From her eagerness to be charming to Frances's guest that afternoon, it seemed that she would have married Tom Beavers herself if he had asked her. The amber liquid set in her small four-sided glass glowed like a jewel, and her diamond flashed; she had put on her best ring for the company. What a pity no longer to show her ankle, that delicious bone, so remarkably slender for so ample a frame.

Since the time had flown so, they all agreed enthusiastically that Tom should wait downstairs while Frances got ready to go out to dinner with him. He was hardly past the stair landing before the old lady was seized by such a fit of coughing that she could hardly speak. "It's been—it's been too much—too *much* for me!" she gasped out.

But after Frances had found the proper sedative for her, she was calmed, and insisted on having her say.

"Thomas Beavers has a good job with an insurance company in Jackson," she informed her daughter, as though Frances were incapable of finding out anything for herself. "He makes a good appearance. He is the kind of man"—she paused—"who would value a wife of good family." She stopped, panting for breath. It was this complimenting a man behind his back that was too much for her—as much out of character, and hence as much of a strain, as if she had got out of bed and tried to tap dance.

"Heavens, Mama," Frances said, and almost giggled.

At this, the old lady, thinking the girl had made light of her suitor, half screamed at her, "Don't be so critical, Frances! You can't be so critical of men!" and fell into an even more terrible spasm of coughing. Frances had to lift her from the pillow and hold her straight until the fit passed and her breath returned. Then Mrs. Harvey's old, dry, crooked, ineradicably feminine hand was laid on her daughter's arm, and when she spoke again she shook the arm to emphasize her words.

"When your father knew he didn't have long to live," she whispered, "we discussed whether to send for you or not. You know you were his favorite, Frances. 'Suppose our girl is happy over there,' he said. 'I wouldn't want to bring her back on my account.' I said you had to have the right to choose whether to come back or not. You'd never forgive us, I said, if you didn't have the right to choose."

Frances could visualize this very conversation taking place between her parents; she could see them, decorous and serious, talking over the fact of his approaching death as though it were a piece of property for agreeable disposition in the family. She could never remember him without thinking, with a smile, how he used to come home on Sunday from church (he being the only one of them who went) and how, immediately after hanging his hat and cane in the hall, he would say, "Let all things proceed in orderly progression to their final confusion. How long before dinner?" No, she had to come home. Some humor had always existed between them—her father and her—and humor, of all things, cannot be betrayed.

"I meant to go back," said Frances now. "But there was the war. At first I kept waiting for it to be over. I still wake up at night sometimes thinking, I wonder how much longer before the war will be over. And then—" She stopped short. For the fact was that her lover had been married to somebody else, and her mother was the very person capable of pointing that out to her. Even in the old lady's present silence she heard the unspoken thought, and got up nervously from the bed, loosing herself from the hand on her arm, smoothing her reddish hair where it was inclined to straggle. "And then he wrote me that he had gone back to his wife. Her family and his had always been close, and the war brought them back together. This was in Switzerland—naturally, he couldn't stay on in Paris during the war. There were the children, too—all of them were Catholic. Oh, I do understand how it happened."

Mrs. Harvey turned her head impatiently on the pillow. She dabbed at her moist upper lip with a crumpled linen handkerchief; her diamond flashed once in motion. "War, religion, wife, children—yes. But men do what they want to."

Could anyone make Frances as angry as her mother could? "Believe what you like then! You always know so much better than I do. *You* would have managed things somehow. Oh, you would have had your way!"

"Frances," said Mrs. Harvey, "I'm an old woman." The hand holding the handkerchief fell wearily, and her eyelids dropped shut. "If you should want to marry Thomas Beavers and bring him here, I will accept it. There will be no distinctions. Next, I suppose, we will be having his old deaf aunt for tea. I hope she has a hearing aid. I haven't got the strength to holler at her."

"I don't think any of these plans are necessary, Mama."

The eyelids slowly lifted. "None?"

"None."

Mrs. Harvey's breathing was as audible as a voice. She spoke, at last, without scorn, honestly. "I cannot bear the thought of leaving you alone. You, nor the house, nor your place in it—alone. I foresaw Tom Beavers here! What has he got that's better than you and this place? I knew he would come!"

Terrible as her mother's meanness was, it was not half so terrible as her love. Answering nothing, explaining nothing, Frances stood without giving in. She trembled, and tears ran down her cheeks. The two women looked at each other helplessly across the darkening room.

IN THE CAR, later that night, Tom Beavers asked, "Is your mother trying to get rid of me?" They had passed an unsatisfactory evening, and he was not going away without knowing why.

"No, it's just the other way around," said Frances, in her candid way. "She wants you so much she'd like to eat you up. She wants you in the house. Couldn't you tell?"

"She once chased me out of the yard," he recalled.

"Not really!"

They turned into Harvey Street (that was actually the name of it), and when he had drawn the car up before the dark front steps, he related the incident. He told her that Mrs. Harvey had been standing just there in the yard, talking to some visitor who was leaving by inches, the way ladies used to—ten minutes' more talk for every forward step. He, a boy not more than nine, had been crossing a corner of the lawn where a faint path had already been worn; he had had nothing to do with wearing the path and had taken it quite innocently and openly. "You, boy!" Mrs. Harvey's fan was an enormous painted thing. She had furled it with a clack so loud he could still hear it. "You don't cut through my yard again! Now, you stop where you are and you go all the way back around by the walk, and don't you ever do that again." He went back and all the way around. She was fanning comfortably as he passed. "Old Miss Rita Beavers's nephew," he heard her say, and though he did not speak of it now to Frances, Mrs. Harvey's rich tone had been as stuffed with wickedness as a fruitcake with goodies. In it you could have found so many things: that, of course, he didn't know any better, that he was poor, that she knew his first name but would not deign to mention it, that she meant him to understand all this and more. Her fan was probably still somewhere in the house, he reflected. If he ever opened the wrong door, it might fall from above and brain him. It seemed impossible that nowadays he could even have the chance to open the wrong door in the Harvey house. With its graceful rooms and big lawn, its camellias and magnolia trees, the house had been one of the enchanted castles of his childhood, and Frances and Regina Harvey had been two princesses running about the lawn one Saturday morning drying their hair with big white towels and not noticing when he passed.

There was a strong wind that evening. On the way home, Frances and Tom had noticed how the night was streaming, but whether with mist or dust or the smoke from some far-off fire in the dry winter woods they could not tell. As they stood on the sidewalk, the clouds raced over them, and moonlight now and again came through. A limb rubbed against a high cornice. Inside the screened area of the porch, the swing jangled in its iron chains. Frances's coat blew about her, and her hair blew. She felt herself to be no different from anything there that the wind was blowing on, her happiness of no relevance in the dark torrent of nature.

"I can't leave her, Tom. But I can't ask you to live with her, either. Of all the horrible ideas! She'd make demands, take all my time, laugh at you behind your back—she has to run everything. You'd hate me in a week."

He did not try to pretty up the picture, because he had a feeling that it was all too accurate. Now, obviously, was the time she should go on to say there was no good his waiting around through the years for her. But hearts are not noted for practicality, and Frances stood with her hair blowing, her hands stuck in her coat pockets, and did not go on to say anything. Tom pulled her close to him—in, as it were, out of the wind.

"I'll be coming by next weekend, just like I've been doing. And the next one, too," he said. "We'll just leave it that way, if it's OK with you."

"Oh yes, it is, Tom!" Never so satisfied to be weak, she kissed him and ran inside.

He stood watching on the walk until her light flashed on. Well, he had got what he was looking for; a connection with the past, he had said. It was right upstairs, a splendid old mass of dictatorial female flesh, thinking about him. Well, they could go on, he and Frances, sitting on either side of a sickbed, drinking tea and sipping sherry with streaks of gray broadening on their brows, while the familiar seasons came and went. So he thought. Like Frances, he believed that the old lady had a stranglehold on life.

Suddenly, in March, Mrs. Harvey died.

A HEAVY SPRING funeral, with lots of roses and other scented flowers in the house, is the worst kind of all. There is something so recklessly fecund about a south Mississippi spring that death becomes just another word in the dictionary, along with swarms of others, and even so pure and white a thing as a gardenia has too heavy a scent and may suggest decay. Mrs. Harvey, amid such odors, sank to rest with a determined pomp, surrounded by admiring eyes.

While Tom Beavers did not "sit with the family" at this time, he was often observed with the Harveys, and there was whispered speculation among those who were at the church and the cemetery that the Harvey house might soon come into new hands, "after a decent interval." No one would undertake to judge for a Harvey how long an interval was decent.

Frances suffered from insomnia in the weeks that followed, and at night she wandered about the spring-swollen air of the old house, smelling now spring and now death. "Let all things proceed in orderly progression to their final confusion." She had always thought that the final confusion referred to death, but now she began to think that it could happen any time; that final confusion, having found the door ajar, could come into a house and show no inclination to leave. The worrisome thing, the thing it all came back to, was her mother's clothes. They were numerous, expensive, and famous, and Mrs. Harvey had never discarded any of them. If you opened a closet door, hatboxes as big as crates towered above your head. The shiny black trim of a great shawl stuck out of a wardrobe door just below the lock. Beneath the lid of a cedar chest, the bright eyes of a tippet were ready to twinkle at you. And the jewels! Frances's sister had restrained her from burying them all on their mother, and had even gone off with a wad of them tangled up like fishing tackle in an envelope, on the ground of promises made now and again in the course of the years.

("Regina," said Frances, "what else were you two talking about besides jewelry?" "I don't remember," said Regina, getting mad.

"Frances makes me so mad," said Regina to her husband as they were driving home. "I guess I can love Mama and jewelry, too. Mama certainly loved *us* and jewelry, too.")

One afternoon, Frances went out to the cemetery to take two wreaths sent by somebody who had "just heard." She drove out along the winding cemetery road, stopping the car a good distance before she reached the gate, in order to walk through the woods. The dogwood was beautiful that year. She saw a field where a house used to stand but had burned down; its cedar trees remained, and two bushes of bridal wreath marked where the front gate had swung. She stopped to admire the clusters of white bloom massing up through the young, feathery leaf and stronger now than the leaf itself. In the woods, the redbud was a smoke along shadowy ridges, and the dogwood drifted in layers, like snow suspended to give you all the time you needed to wonder at it. But why, she wondered, do they call it bridal *wreath?* It's not a wreath but a little bouquet. Wreaths are for funerals, anyway. As if to prove it, she looked down at the two she held, one in each hand. She walked on, and such complete desolation came over her that it was more of a wonder than anything in the woods—more, even, than death.

As she returned to the car from the two parallel graves, she met a thin, elderly, very light-skinned Negro man in the road. He inquired if she would mind moving her car so that he could pass. He said that there was a sick colored girl in his wagon, whom he was driving in to the doctor. He pointed out politely that she had left her car right in the middle of the road. "Oh, I'm terribly sorry," said Frances, and hurried off toward the car.

That night, reading late in bed, she thought, I could have given her a ride into town. No wonder they talk about us up North. A mile into town in a wagon! She might have been having a baby. She became conscience-stricken about it—foolishly so, she realized, but if you start worrying about something in a house like the one Frances Harvey lived in, in the dead of night, alone, you will go on worrying about it until dawn. She was out of sleeping pills.

She remembered having bought a fresh box of sedatives for her mother the day before she died. She got up and went into her mother's closed room, where the bed had been dismantled for airing, its wooden parts propped along the walls. On the closet shelf she found the shoe box into which she had packed away the familiar articles of the bedside table. Inside she found the small enameled-cardboard box, with the date and prescription inked on the cover in Totsie Poteet's somewhat prissy handwriting, but the box was empty. She was surprised, for she realized that her mother could have used only one or two of the pills. Frances was so determined to get some sleep that she searched the entire little store of things in the shoe box quite heartlessly, but there were no pills. She returned to her room and tried to read, but could not, and so smoked instead and stared out at the dawn-blackening sky. The house sighed. She could not take her mind off the Negro girl. If she died . . . When it was light, she dressed and got into the car.

In town, the postman was unlocking the post office to sort the early mail. "I declare," he said to the rural mail carrier who arrived a few minutes later, "Miss Frances Harvey is driving herself crazy. Going back out yonder to the cemetery, and it not seven o'clock in the morning."

"Aw," said the rural deliveryman skeptically, looking at the empty road.

"That's right. I was here and seen her. You wait there, you'll see her come back. She'll drive herself nuts. Them old maids like that, left in them old houses—crazy and sweet, or crazy and mean, or just plain crazy. They just ain't locked up like them that's down in the asylum. That's the only difference."

"Miss Frances Harvey ain't no more than thirty-two, -three years old."

"Then she's just got more time to get crazier in. You'll see."

THAT DAY WAS Friday, and Tom Beavers, back from Jackson, came up Frances Harvey's sidewalk, as usual, at exactly a quarter past seven in the evening. Frances was not "going out" yet, and Regina had telephoned her long distance to say that "in all probability" she should not be receiving gentlemen "in." "What would Mama say?" Regina asked. Frances said she didn't know, which was not true, and went right on cooking dinners for Tom every weekend.

In the dining room that night, she sat across one corner of the long table from Tom. The useless length of polished cherry stretched away from them into the shadows as sadly as a road. Her plate pushed back, her chin resting on one palm, Frances stirred her coffee and said, "I don't know what on earth to do with all of Mama's clothes. I can't give them away, I can't sell them, I can't burn them, and the attic is full already. What can I do?"

"You look better tonight," said Tom.

"I slept," said Frances. "I slept and slept. From early this morning until just 'while ago. I never slept so well."

Then she told him about the Negro near the cemetery the previous afternoon, and how she had driven back out there as soon as dawn came, and found him again. He had been walking across the open field near the remains of the house that had burned down. There was no path to him from her, and she had hurried across ground uneven from old plowing and covered with the kind of small, tender grass it takes a very skillful mule to crop. "Wait!" she had cried. "Please wait!" The Negro had stopped and waited for her to reach him. "Your daughter?" she asked, out of breath.

"Daughter?" he repeated.

"The colored girl that was in the wagon yesterday. She was sick, you said, so I wondered. I could have taken her to town in the car, but I just didn't think. I wanted to know, how is she? Is she very sick?"

He had removed his old felt nigger hat as she approached him. "She a whole lot better, Miss Frances. She going to be all right now." Then he smiled at her. He did not say thank you, or anything more. Frances turned and walked back to the road and the car. And exactly as though the recovery of the Negro girl in the wagon had been her own recovery, she felt the return of a quiet breath and a steady pulse, and sensed the blessed stirring of a morning breeze. Up in her room, she had barely time to draw an old quilt over her before she fell asleep.

"When I woke, I knew about Mama," she said now to Tom. By the deepened intensity of her voice and eyes, it was plain that this was the important part. "It isn't right to say I *knew*," she went on, "because I had known all the time—ever since last night. I just realized it, that's all. I realized she had killed herself. It had to be that."

He listened soberly through the story about the box of sedatives. "But why?" he asked her. "It maybe looks that way, but what would be her reason for doing it?"

"Well, you see—" Frances said, and stopped.

Tom Beavers talked quietly on. "She didn't suffer. With what she had, she could have lived five, ten, who knows how many years. She was well cared for. Not hard up, I wouldn't say. Why?"

The pressure of his questioning could be insistent, and her trust in him, even if he was nobody but old Miss Rita Beavers's nephew, was well-nigh complete. "Because of you and me," she said, finally. "I'm certain of it, Tom. She didn't want to stand in our way. She never knew how to express love, you see." Frances controlled herself with an effort.

He did not reply, but sat industriously balancing a match folder on the tines of an unused serving fork. Anyone who has passed a lonely childhood in the company of an old deaf aunt is not inclined to doubt things hastily, and Tom Beavers would not have said he disbelieved anything Frances had told him. In fact, it seemed only too real to him. Almost before his eyes, that imperial, practical old hand went fumbling for the pills in the dark. But there had been much more to it than just love, he reflected. Bitterness, too, and pride, and control. And humor, perhaps, and the memory of a frightened little boy chased out of the yard by a twitch of her fan. Being invited to tea was one thing; suicide was quite another. Times had certainly changed, he thought.

But, of course, he could not say that he believed it, either. There was only Frances to go by. The match folder came to balance and rested on the tines. He glanced up at her, and a chill walked up his spine, for she was too serene. Cheek on palm, a lock of reddish hair fallen forward, she was staring at nothing with the absorbed silence of a child, or of a sweet, silver-haired old lady engaged in memory. Soon he might find that more and more of her was vanishing beneath this placid surface.

Elizabeth Spencer · 276

He himself did not know what he had seen that Friday evening so many months ago—what the figure had been that stood forward from the roadside at the tilt of the curve and urgently waved an arm to him. By the time he had braked and backed, the man had disappeared. Maybe it had been somebody drunk (for Richton had plenty of those to offer), walking it off in the cool of the woods at first dark. No such doubts had occurred to Frances. And what if he told her now the story Totsie had related of the road gang and the sick Negro girl in the wagon? Another labyrinth would open before her; she would never get out.

In Richton, the door to the past was always wide open, and what came in through it and went out of it had made people "different." But it scarcely ever happens, even in Richton, that one is able to see the precise moment when fact becomes faith, when life turns into legend, and people start to bend their finest loyalties to make themselves bemused custodians of the grave. Tom Beavers saw that moment now, in the profile of this dreaming girl, and he knew there was no time to lose.

He dropped the match folder into his coat pocket. "I think we should be leaving, Frances."

"Oh well, I don't know about going out yet," she said. "People criticize you so. Regina even had the nerve to telephone. Word had got all the way to her that you came here to have supper with me and we were alone in the house. When I tell the maid I want biscuits made up for two people, she looks like 'What would yo' mama say?'"

"I mean," he said, "I think it's time we left for good."

"And never came back?" It was exactly like Frances to balk at going to a movie but seriously consider an elopement.

"Well, never is a long time. I like to see about Aunt Rita every once in a great while. She can't remember from one time to the next whether it's two days or two years since I last came."

She glanced about the walls and at the furniture, the pictures, and the silver. "But I thought you would want to live here, Tom. It never occurred to me. I know it never occurred to Mama . . . This house . . . It can't be just left."

First Dark · 277

"It's a fine old house," he agreed. "But what would you do with all your mother's clothes?"

Her freckled hand remained beside the porcelain cup for what seemed a long time. He waited and made no move toward her; he felt her uncertainty keenly, but he believed that some people should not be startled out of a spell.

"It's just as you said," he went on, finally. "You can't give them away, you can't sell them, you can't burn them, and you can't put them in the attic, because the attic is full already. So what are you going to do?"

Between them, the single candle flame achieved a silent altitude. Then, politely, as on any other night, though shaking back her hair in a decided way, she said, "Just let me get my coat, Tom."

She locked the door when they left, and put the key under the mat—a last obsequy to the house. Their hearts were bounding ahead faster than they could walk down the sidewalk or drive off in the car, and, mindful, perhaps, of what happened to people who did, they did not look back.

Had they done so, they would have seen that the Harvey house was more beautiful than ever. All unconscious of its rejection by so mere a person as Tom Beavers, it seemed, instead, to have got rid of what did not suit it, to be free, at last, to enter with abandon the land of mourning and shadows and memory.

SHILOH

Bobbie Ann Mason

LEROY MOFFIT's wife, Norma Jean, is working on her pectorals. She lifts three-pound dumbbells to warm up, then progresses to a twenty-pound barbell. Standing with her legs apart, she reminds Leroy of Wonder Woman.

"I'd give anything if I could just get these muscles to where they're real hard," says Norma Jean. "Feel this arm. It's not as hard as the other one."

"That's 'cause you're right-handed," says Leroy, dodging as she swings the barbell in an arc.

"Do you think so?"

"Sure."

Leroy is a truckdriver. He injured his leg in a highway accident four months ago, and his physical therapy, which involves weights and a pulley, prompted Norma Jean to try building herself up. Now she is attending a bodybuilding class. Leroy has been collecting temporary disability since his tractor-trailer jackknifed in Missouri, badly twisting his left leg in its socket. He has a steel pin in his hip. He will probably not be able to drive his rig again. It sits in the backyard, like a gigantic bird that has flown home to roost. Leroy has been home in Kentucky for three months, and his leg is almost healed, but the accident frightened him and he does not want to drive any more long hauls. He is not sure what to do next. In the meantime, he makes things from craft kits. He started by building a miniature log cabin from notched Popsicle sticks. He varnished it and placed it on the TV set, where it remains. It reminds him of a rustic Nativity scene. Then he tried string art (sailing ships on black velvet), a macramé owl kit, a snap-together B-17 Flying Fortress, and a lamp made out of a model truck, with a light fixture screwed in the top of the cab. At first the kits were diversions, something to kill time, but now he is thinking about building a full-scale log house from a kit. It would be considerably cheaper than building a regular house, and besides, Leroy has grown to appreciate how things are put together. He has begun to realize that in all the years he was on the road he never took time to examine anything. He was always flying past scenery.

"They won't let you build a log cabin in any of the new subdivisions," Norma Jean tells him.

"They will if I tell them it's for you," he says, teasing her. Ever since they were married, he has promised Norma Jean he would build her a new home one day. They have always rented, and the house they live in is small and nondescript. It does not even feel like a home, Leroy realizes now.

Norma Jean works at the Rexall drugstore, and she has acquired an amazing amount of information about cosmetics. When she explains to Leroy the three stages of complexion care, involving creams, toners, and moisturizers, he thinks happily of other petroleum products—axle grease, diesel fuel. This is a connection between him and Norma Jean. Since he has been home, he has felt unusually tender about his wife and guilty over his long absences. But he can't tell what she feels about him.

Norma Jean has never complained about his traveling; she has never made hurt remarks, like calling his truck a "widow-maker." He is reasonably certain she has been faithful to him, but he wishes she would celebrate his permanent homecoming more happily. Norma Jean is often startled to find Leroy at home, and he thinks she seems a little disappointed about it. Perhaps he reminds her too much of the early days of their marriage, before he went on the road. They had a child who died as an infant, years ago. They never speak about their memories of Randy, which have almost faded, but now that Leroy is home all the time, they sometimes feel awkward around each other, and Leroy wonders if one of them should mention the child. He has the feeling that they are waking up out of a dream together—that they must create a new marriage, start afresh. They are lucky they are still married. Leroy has read that for most people losing a child destroys the marriage—or else he heard this on *Donahue*. He can't always remember where he learns things anymore.

At Christmas, Leroy bought an electric organ for Norma Jean. She used to play piano when she was in high school. "It don't leave you," she told him once. "It's like riding a bicycle."

The new instrument had so many keys and buttons that she was bewildered by it at first. She touched the keys tentatively, pushed some buttons, then pecked out "Chopsticks." It came out in an amplified foxtrot rhythm, with marimba sounds.

"It's an orchestra!" she cried.

The organ had a pecan-look finish and eighteen preset chords, with optional flute, violin, trumpet, clarinet, and banjo accompaniments. Norma Jean mastered the organ almost immediately. At first she played Christmas songs. Then she bought *The Sixties Songbook* and learned every tune in it, adding variations to each of the rows of brightly colored buttons.

"I didn't like these old songs back then," she said. "But I have this crazy feeling I missed something."

"You didn't miss a thing," said Leroy.

Shiloh · 281

Leroy likes to lie on the couch and smoke a joint and listen to Norma Jean play "Can't Take My Eyes Off You" and "I'll Be Back." He is back again. After fifteen years on the road, he is finally settling down with the woman he loves. She is still pretty. Her skin is flawless. Her frosted curls resemble pencil trimmings.

NOW THAT LEROY has come home to stay, he notices how much the town has changed. Subdivisions are spreading across western Kentucky like an oil slick. The sign at the edge of town says "Pop: 11,500"— only seven hundred more than it said twenty years before. Leroy can't figure out who is living in all the new houses. The farmers who used to gather around the courthouse square on Saturday afternoons to play checkers and spit tobacco juice have gone. It has been years since Leroy has thought about the farmers, and they have disappeared without his noticing.

Leroy meets a kid named Stevie Hamilton in the parking lot at the new shopping center. While they pretend to be strangers meeting over a stalled car, Stevie tosses an ounce of marijuana under the front seat of Leroy's car. Stevie is wearing orange jogging shoes and a T-shirt that says CHATTAHOOCHEE SUPER-RAT. His father is a prominent doctor who lives in one of the expensive subdivisions in a new white-columned brick house that looks like a funeral parlor. In the phone book under his name there is a separate number, with the listing "Teenagers."

"Where do you get this stuff?" asks Leroy. "From your pappy?"

"That's for me to know and you to find out," Stevie says. He is slit-eyed and skinny.

"What else you got?"

"What you interested in?"

"Nothing special. Just wondered."

Leroy used to take speed on the road. Now he has to go slowly. He needs to be mellow. He leans back against the car and says, "I'm aiming to build me a log house, soon as I get time. My wife, though, I don't think she likes the idea."

"Well, let me know when you want me again," Stevie says. He has a cigarette in his cupped palm, as though sheltering it from the wind. He takes a long drag, then stomps it on the asphalt and slouches away.

Stevie's father was two years ahead of Leroy in high school. Leroy is thirty-four. He married Norma Jean when they were both eighteen, and their child Randy was born a few months later, but he died at the age of four months and three days. He would be about Stevie's age now. Norma Jean and Leroy were at the drive-in, watching a double feature (*Dr. Strangelove* and *Lover Come Back*), and the baby was sleeping in the backseat. When the first movie ended, the baby was dead. It was the sudden infant death syndrome. Leroy remembers handing Randy to a nurse at the emergency room, as though he were offering her a large doll as a present. A dead baby feels like a sack of flour. "It just happens sometimes," said the doctor, in what Leroy always recalls as a nonchalant tone. Leroy can hardly remember the child anymore, but he still sees vividly a scene from *Dr. Strangelove* in which the President of the United States was talking in a folksy voice on the hot line to the Soviet premier about the bomber accidentally headed toward Russia. He was in the War Room, and the world map was lit up. Leroy remembers Norma Jean standing catatonically beside him in the hospital and himself thinking: Who is this strange girl? He had forgotten who she was. Now scientists are saying that crib death is caused by a virus. Nobody knows anything, Leroy thinks. The answers are always changing.

When Leroy gets home from the shopping center, Norma Jean's mother, Mabel Beasley, is there. Until this year, Leroy has not realized how much time she spends with Norma Jean. When she visits, she inspects the closets and then the plants, informing Norma Jean when a plant is droopy or yellow. Mabel calls the plants "flowers," although there are never any blooms. She always notices if Norma Jean's laundry is piling up. Mabel is a short, overweight woman whose tight, brown-dyed curls look more like a wig than the actual wig she sometimes wears. Today she has brought Norma Jean an off-white dust ruffle she made for the bed; Mabel works in a custom-upholstery shop.

"This is the tenth one I made this year," Mabel says. "I got started and couldn't stop."

"It's real pretty," says Norma Jean.

"Now we can hide things under the bed," says Leroy, who gets along with his mother-in-law primarily by joking with her. Mabel has never really forgiven him for disgracing her by getting Norma Jean pregnant. When the baby died, she said that fate was mocking her.

"What's that thing?" Mabel says to Leroy in a loud voice, pointing to a tangle of yarn on a piece of canvas.

Leroy holds it up for Mabel to see. "It's my needlepoint," he explains. "This is a *Star Trek* pillow cover."

"That's what a woman would do," says Mabel. "Great day in the morning!"

"All the big football players on TV do it," he says.

"Why, Leroy, you're always trying to fool me. I don't believe you for one minute. You don't know what to do with yourself—that's the whole trouble. Sewing!"

"I'm aiming to build us a log house," says Leroy. "Soon as my plans come."

"Like *heck* you are," says Norma Jean. She takes Leroy's needlepoint and shoves it into a drawer. "You have to find a job first. Nobody can afford to build now anyway."

Mabel straightens her girdle and says, "I still think before you get tied down y'all ought to take a little run to Shiloh."

"One of these days, Mama," Norma Jean says impatiently.

Mabel is talking about Shiloh, Tennessee. For the past few years, she has been urging Leroy and Norma Jean to visit the Civil War battleground there. Mabel went there on her honeymoon—the only real trip she ever took. Her husband died of a perforated ulcer when Norma Jean was ten, but Mabel, who was accepted into the United Daughters of the Confederacy in 1975, is still preoccupied with going back to Shiloh.

"I've been to kingdom come and back in that truck out yonder,"

Leroy says to Mabel, "but we never yet set foot in that battleground. Ain't that something? How did I miss it?"

"It's not even that far," Mabel says.

After Mabel leaves, Norma Jean reads to Leroy from a list she has made. "Things you could do," she announces. "You could get a job as a guard at Union Carbide, where they'd let you set on a stool. You could get on at the lumberyard. You could do a little carpenter work, if you want to build so bad. You could——"

"I can't do something where I'd have to stand up all day."

"You ought to try standing up all day behind a cosmetics counter. It's amazing that I have strong feet, coming from two parents that never had strong feet at all." At the moment Norma Jean is holding on to the kitchen counter, raising her knees one at a time as she talks. She is wearing two-pound ankle weights.

"Don't worry," says Leroy. "I'll do something."

"You could truck calves to slaughter for somebody. You wouldn't have to drive any big old truck for that."

"I'm going to build you this home," says Leroy. "I want to make you a real home."

"I don't want to live in any log cabin."

"It's not a cabin. It's a house."

"I don't care. It looks like a cabin."

"You and me together could lift those logs. It's just like lifting weights."

Norma Jean doesn't answer. Under her breath, she is counting. Now she is marching through the kitchen. She is doing goose steps.

BEFORE HIS ACCIDENT, when Leroy came home he used to stay in the house with Norma Jean, watching TV in bed and playing cards. She would cook fried chicken, picnic ham, chocolate pie—all his favorites. Now he is home alone much of the time. In the mornings, Norma Jean disappears, leaving a cooling place in the bed. She eats a cereal called

Body Buddies, and she leaves the bowl on the table, with the soggy tan balls floating in a milk puddle. He sees things about Norma Jean that he never realized before. When she chops onions, she stares off into a corner, as if she can't bear to look. She puts on her house slippers almost precisely at nine o'clock every evening and nudges her jogging shoes under the couch. She saves bread heels for the birds. Leroy watches the birds at the feeder. He notices the peculiar way goldfinches fly past the window. They close their wings, then fall, then spread their wings to catch and lift themselves. He wonders if they close their eyes when they fall. Norma Jean closes her eyes when they are in bed. She wants the lights turned out. Even then, he is sure she closes her eyes.

He goes for long drives around town. He tends to drive a car rather carelessly. Power steering and an automatic shift make a car feel so small and inconsequential that his body is hardly involved in the driving process. His injured leg stretches out comfortably. Once or twice he has almost hit something, but even the prospect of an accident seems minor in a car. He cruises the new subdivisions, feeling like a criminal rehearsing for a robbery. Norma Jean is probably right about a log house being inappropriate here in the new subdivisions. All the houses look grand and complicated. They depress him.

One day when Leroy comes home from a drive he finds Norma Jean in tears. She is in the kitchen making a potato and mushroom-soup casserole, with grated-cheese topping. She is crying because her mother caught her smoking.

"I didn't hear her coming. I was standing here puffing away pretty as you please," Norma Jean says, wiping her eyes.

"I knew it would happen sooner or later," says Leroy, putting his arm around her.

"'She don't know the meaning of the word 'knock,'" says Norma Jean. "It's a wonder she hadn't caught me years ago."

"Think of it this way," Leroy says. "What if she caught me with a joint?"

"You better not let her!" Norma Jean shrieks. "I'm warning you, Leroy Moffitt!"

"I'm just kidding. Here, play me a tune. That'll help you relax."

Norma Jean puts the casserole in the oven and sets the timer. Then she plays a ragtime tune, with horns and banjo, as Leroy lights up a joint and lies on the couch, laughing to himself about Mabel's catching him at it. He thinks of Stevie Hamilton—a doctor's son pushing grass. Everything is funny. The whole town seems crazy and small. He is reminded of Virgil Mathis, a boastful policeman Leroy used to shoot pool with. Virgil recently led a drug bust in a back room at a bowling alley, where he seized ten thousand dollars' worth of marijuana. The newspaper had a picture of him holding up the bags of grass and grinning widely. Right now, Leroy can imagine Virgil breaking down the door and arresting him with a lungful of smoke. Virgil would probably have been alerted to the scene because of all the racket Norma Jean is making. Now she sounds like a hard-rock band. Norma Jean is terrific. When she switches to a Latin-rhythm version of "Sunshine Superman," Leroy hums along. Norma Jean's foot goes up and down, up and down.

"Well, what do you think?" Leroy says, when Norma Jean pauses to search through her music."

"What do I think about what?"

His mind has gone blank. Then he says, "I'll sell my rig and build us a house." That wasn't what he wanted to say. He wanted to know what she thought—what she *really* thought— about them.

"Don't start in on that again," says Norma Jean. She begins playing "Who'll Be the Next in Line?"

Leroy used to tell hitchhikers his whole life story—about his travels, his hometown, the baby. He would end with a question: "Well, what do you think?" It was just a rhetorical question. In time, he had the feeling that he'd been telling the same story over and over to the same hitchhikers. He quit talking to hitchhikers when he realized how his voice sounded—whining and self-pitying, like some teenage-tragedy song.

Now Leroy has the sudden impulse to tell Norma Jean about himself, as if he had just met her. They have known each other so long they have forgotten a lot about each other. They could become reacquainted. But when the oven timer goes off and she runs to the kitchen, he forgets why he wants to do this.

THE NEXT DAY, Mabel drops by. It is Saturday and Norma Jean is cleaning. Leroy is studying the plans of his log house, which have finally come in the mail. He has them spread out on the table—big sheets of stiff blue paper, with diagrams and numbers printed in white. While Norma Jean runs the vacuum, Mabel drinks coffee. She sets her coffee cup on a blueprint.

"I'm just waiting for time to pass," she says to Leroy, drumming her fingers on the table.

As soon as Norma Jean switches off the vacuum, Mabel says in a loud voice, "Did you hear about the datsun dog that killed the baby?"

Norma Jean says, "The word is 'dachshund.'"

"They put the dog on trial. It chewed the baby's legs off. The mother was in the next room all the time." She raises her voice. "They thought it was neglect."

Norma Jean is holding her ears. Leroy manages to open the refrigerator and get some Diet Pepsi to offer Mabel. Mabel still has some coffee and she waves away the Pepsi.

"Datsuns are like that," Mabel says. "They're jealous dogs. They'll tear a place to pieces if you don't keep an eye on them."

"You better watch out what you're saying, Mabel," says Leroy.

"Well, facts is facts."

Leroy looks out the window at his rig. It is like a huge piece of furniture gathering dust in the backyard. Pretty soon it will be an antique. He hears the vacuum cleaner. Norma Jean seems to be cleaning the living room rug again.

Later, she says to Leroy, "She just said that about the baby because she caught me smoking. She's trying to pay me back."

"What are you talking about?" Leroy says, nervously shuffling blueprints.

"You know good and well," Norma Jean says. She is sitting in a kitchen chair with her feet up and her arms wrapped around her knees. She looks small and helpless. She says, "The very idea, her bringing up a subject like that! Saying it was neglect."

"She didn't mean that," Leroy says.

"She might not have *thought* she meant it. She always says things like that. You don't know how she goes on."

"But she didn't really mean it. She was just talking."

Leroy opens a king-sized bottle of beer and pours it into two glasses, dividing it carefully. He hands a glass to Norma Jean and she takes it from him mechanically. For a long time, they sit by the kitchen window watching the birds at the feeder.

Something is happening. Norma Jean is going to night school. She has graduated from her six-week bodybuilding course and now she is taking an adult-education course in composition at Paducah Community College. She spends her evenings outlining paragraphs.

"First you have a topic sentence," she explains to Leroy. "Then you divide it up. Your secondary topic has to be connected to your primary topic."

To Leroy, this sounds intimidating. "I never was any good in English," he says.

"It makes a lot of sense."

"What are you doing this for, anyhow?"

She shrugs. "It's something to do." She stands up and lifts her dumbbells a few times.

"Driving a rig, nobody cared about my English."

"I'm not criticizing your English."

Norma Jean used to say, "If I lose ten minutes' sleep, I just drag all day." Now she stays up late, writing compositions. She got a B on her first paper—a how-to theme on soup-based casseroles. Recently Norma Jean has been cooking unusual foods— tacos, lasagna, Bombay chicken.

Shiloh · 289

She doesn't play the organ anymore, though her second paper was called "Why Music Is Important to Me." She sits at the kitchen table, concentrating on her outlines, while Leroy plays with his log house plans, practicing with a set of Lincoln Logs. The thought of getting a truckload of notched, numbered logs scares him, and he wants to be prepared. As he and Norma Jean work together at the kitchen table, Leroy has the hopeful thought that they are sharing something, but he knows he is a fool to think this. Norma Jean is miles away. He knows he is going to lose her. Like Mabel, he is just waiting for time to pass.

One day, Mabel is there before Norma Jean gets home from work, and Leroy finds himself confiding in her. Mabel, he realizes, must know Norma Jean better than he does.

"I don't know what's got into that girl," Mabel says. "She used to go to bed with the chickens. Now you say she's up all hours. Plus her a-smoking. I like to died."

"I want to make her this beautiful home," Leroy says, indicating the Lincoln Logs. "I don't think she even wants it. Maybe she was happier with me gone."

"She don't know what to make of you, coming home like this."

"Is that it?"

Mabel takes the roof off his Lincoln Log cabin. "You couldn't get *me* in a log cabin," she says. "I was raised in one. It's no picnic, let me tell you."

"They're different now," says Leroy.

"I tell you what," Mabel says, smiling oddly at Leroy.

"What?"

"Take her on down to Shiloh. Y'all need to get out together, stir a little. Her brain's all balled up over them books."

Leroy can see traces of Norma Jean's features in her mother's face. Mabel's worn face has the texture of crinkled cotton, but suddenly she looks pretty. It occurs to Leroy that Mabel has been hinting all along that she wants them to take her with them to Shiloh.

Bobbie Ann Mason · 290

"Let's all go to Shiloh," he says. "You and me and her. Come Sunday."

Mabel throws up her hands in protest. "Oh, no, not me. Young folks want to be by theirselves."

When Norma Jean comes in with groceries, Leroy says excitedly, "Your mama here's been dying to go to Shiloh for thirty-five years. It's about time we went, don't you think?"

"I'm not going to butt in on anybody's second honeymoon," Mabel says.

"Who's going on a honeymoon, for Christ's sake?" Norma Jean says loudly.

"I never raised no daughter of mine to talk that-a-way," Mabel says.

"You ain't seen nothing yet," says Norma Jean. She starts putting away boxes and cans, slamming cabinet doors.

"There's a log cabin at Shiloh," Mabel says. "It was there during the battle. There's bullet holes in it."

"When are you going to *shut up* about Shiloh, Mama?" asks Norma Jean.

"I always thought Shiloh was the prettiest place, so full of history," Mabel goes on. "I just hoped y'all could see it once before I die, so you could tell me about it." Later, she whispers to Leroy, "You do what I said. A little change is what she needs."

"YOUR NAME MEANS 'the king,'" Norma Jean says to Leroy that evening. He is trying to get her to go to Shiloh, and she is reading a book about another century.

"Well, I reckon I ought to be right proud."

"I guess so."

"Am I still king around here?"

Norma Jean flexes her biceps and feels them for hardness. "I'm not fooling around with anybody, if that's what you mean," she says.

"Would you tell me if you were?"

"I don't know."

"What does *your* name mean?"

"It was Marilyn Monroe's real name."

"No kidding!"

"Norma comes from the Normans. They were invaders," she says. She closes her book and looks hard at Leroy. "I'll go to Shiloh with you if you'll stop staring at me."

ON SUNDAY, NORMA Jean packs a picnic and they go to Shiloh. To Leroy's relief, Mabel says she does not want to come with them. Norma Jean drives, and Leroy, sitting beside her, feels like some boring hitchhiker she has picked up. He tries some conversation, but she answers him in monosyllables. At Shiloh, she drives aimlessly through the park, past bluffs and trails and steep ravines. Shiloh is an immense place, and Leroy cannot see it as a battleground. It is not what he expected. He thought it would look like a golf course. Monuments are everywhere, showing through the thick clusters of trees. Norma Jean passes the log cabin Mabel mentioned. It is surrounded by tourists looking for bullet holes.

"That's not the kind of log house I've got in mind," says Leroy apologetically.

"I know *that*."

"This is a pretty place. Your mama was right."

"It's OK," says Norma Jean. "Well, we've seen it. I hope she's satisfied."

They burst out laughing together.

At the park museum, a movie on Shiloh is shown every half hour, but they decide that they don't want to see it. They buy a souvenir Confederate flag for Mabel, and then they find a picnic spot near the cemetery. Norma Jean has brought a picnic cooler, with pimiento sandwiches, soft drinks, and Yodels. Leroy eats a sandwich and then smokes a joint, hiding it behind the picnic cooler. Norma Jean has quit smoking altogether. She is picking cake crumbs from the cellophane wrapper, like a fussy bird.

Leroy says, "So the boys in gray ended up in Corinth. The Union soldiers zapped 'em finally. April 7, 1862."

They both know that he doesn't know any history. He is just talking about some of the historical plaques they have read. He feels awkward, like a boy on a date with an older girl. They are still just making conversation.

"Corinth is where Mama eloped to," says Norma Jean.

They sit in silence and stare at the cemetery for the Union dead and, beyond, at a tall cluster of trees. Campers are parked nearby, bumper to bumper, and small children in bright clothing are cavorting and squealing. Norma Jean wads up the cake wrapper and squeezes it tightly in her hand. Without looking at Leroy, she says, "I want to leave you."

Leroy takes a bottle of Coke out of the cooler and flips off the cap. He holds the bottle poised near his mouth but cannot remember to take a drink. Finally he says, "No, you don't."

"Yes, I do."

"I won't let you."

"You can't stop me."

"Don't do me that way."

Leroy knows Norma Jean will have her own way. "Didn't I promise to be home from now on?" he says.

"In some ways, a woman prefers a man who wanders," says Norma Jean. "That sounds crazy, I know."

"You're not crazy."

Leroy remembers to drink from his Coke. Then he says, "Yes, you *are* crazy. You and me could start all over again. Right back at the beginning."

"We *have* started all over again," says Norma Jean. "And this is how it turned out."

"What did I do wrong?"

"Nothing."

"Is this one of those women's lib things?" Leroy asks.

"Don't be funny."

The cemetery, a green slope dotted with white markers, looks like a subdivision site. Leroy is trying to comprehend that his marriage is breaking up, but for some reason he is wondering about white slabs in a graveyard.

"Everything was fine till Mama caught me smoking," says Norma Jean, standing up. "That set something off."

"What are you talking about?"

"She won't leave me alone—*you* won't leave me alone." Norma Jean seems to be crying, but she is looking away from him. "I feel eighteen again. I can't face that all over again." She starts walking away. "No, it *wasn't* fine. I don't know what I'm saying. Forget it."

Leroy takes a lungful of smoke and closes his eyes as Norma Jean's words sink in. He tries to focus on the fact that thirty-five hundred soldiers died on the grounds around him. He can only think of that war as a board game with plastic soldiers. Leroy almost smiles, as he compares the Confederates' daring attack on the Union camps and Virgil Mathis's raid on the bowling alley. General Grant, drunk and furious, shoved the Southerners back to Corinth, where Mabel and Jet Beasley were married years later, when Mabel was still thin and good-looking. The next day, Mabel and Jet visited the battleground, and then Norma Jean was born, and then she married Leroy and they had a baby, which they lost, and now Leroy and Norma Jean are here at the same battleground. Leroy knows he is leaving out a lot. He is leaving out the insides of history. History was always just names and dates to him. It occurs to him that building a house out of logs is similarly empty—too simple. And the real inner workings of a marriage, like most of history, have escaped him. Now he sees that building a log house is the dumbest idea he could have had. It was clumsy of him to think Norma Jean would want a log house. It was a crazy idea. He'll have to think of something else, quickly. He will wad the blueprints into tight balls and fling them into the lake. Then he'll get moving again. He opens his eyes. Norma Jean has moved away and is walking through the cemetery, following a serpentine brick path.

Leroy gets up to follow his wife, but his good leg is asleep and his bad leg still hurts him. Norma Jean is far away, walking rapidly toward the bluff by the river, and he tries to hobble toward her. Some children run past him, screaming noisily. Norma Jean has reached the bluff, and she is looking out over the Tennessee River. Now she turns toward Leroy and waves her arms. Is she beckoning to him? She seems to be doing an exercise for her chest muscles. The sky is unusually pale—the color of the dust ruffle Mabel made for their bed.

Settings, Customs, and Artifacts

Settings, Customs, and Artifacts

THE ORDER OF "settings, customs, and artifacts" suggests, or should suggest, a certain linkage between the three. Their relationships are never fixed, but keep shifting as traditions shift, as history is reinterpreted, as public and private concerns change.

But perhaps setting holds precedence over the other two because, without it, customs and artifacts would have little significance. After finishing Flannery O'Connor's ironically titled story, "Good Country People," for instance, the reader might ponder these questions: What value does a Bible have for a Zulu warrior? What meaning would a wooden leg have . . . even for a one-legged Amazon princess? Would she use it as a means of rebelling against her mother's hypocritical gentility? Would it turn her into a freak in the minds of those around her? Would it become a symbol for her own hardness of soul, and finally would it be used against her by someone with a soul harder than her own? Artifacts require customs to confer meaning upon them, just as customs require a setting.

The setting of "Good Country People" is placed squarely within the Bible Belt South where a social caste system exists alongside a strong (and often conflicting) sense of religious principles. The tensions come from the caste differences between Mrs. Hopewell and Mrs. Freeman (which Mrs. Hopewell works hard to ignore), the caste differences between the Hopewells and the Bible salesman (which Mrs. Hopewell tries to gloss over), the difference between the daughter (Joy) whom Mrs. Hopewell hoped for and the daughter (Hulga) she got, and the confused notion about what Christian behavior entails.

She stood up and said, "Well, young man, I don't want to buy a Bible and I smell my dinner burning."

He didn't get up. He began to twist his hands and looking down at them, he said softly, "Well lady, I'll tell you the truth—not many people want to buy one nowadays and besides, I know I'm real simple. I don't know how to say a thing but to say it. I'm just a country boy." He glanced up into her unfriendly face. "People like you don't like to fool with country people like me."

"Why!" she cried, "good country people are the salt of the earth! Besides, we all have different ways of doing, it takes all kinds to make the world go 'round. That's life!"

"You said a mouthful," he said.

"Why, I think there aren't enough good country people in the world!" she said, stirred. "I think that's what's wrong with it!"

His face had brightened. "I didn't inraduce myself," he said. "I'm Manley Pointer from out in the country around Willohobie, not even from a place, just from near a place."

"You wait a minute," she said. "I have to see about my

dinner." She went out to the kitchen and found Joy standing near the door where she had been listening.

"Get rid of the salt of the earth," she said, "and let's eat."

Mrs. Hopewell gave her a pained look and turned the heat down under the vegetables. "*I* can't be rude to anybody," she murmured and went back into the parlor.

The end brings a revelation of evil. O'Connor was never a writer to hang back from depicting Evil Incarnate—in fact her genius was to be able to suggest its complicated and insidious nature without once making it ambiguous.

Note the part that Mrs. Freeman's daughters, Glynese and Carramae, play in the plot although they never actually appear. It is a story in which every word counts—as O'Connor insisted that it must in short stories—and where everything has a doubly ironic meaning, which, she said, is what "saves a story from being short."

ALICE WALKER'S "EVERYDAY USE" deals in irony, too, by dramatizing the way in which the value of artifacts fluctuates radically over the generations—the despised object of yesteryear becoming today's prized icon: the homely quilt metamorphosing into a tapestry, the top of the churn into a table centerpiece.

The story also gently spoofs a certain trendiness in the search for identity, especially when Dee returns to her birthplace with more changed than her appearance:

> "Well," I say. "Dee."
>
> "No, Mama," she says. "Not 'Dee,' Wangero Leewanika Kemanjo!"
>
> "What happened to 'Dee'?" I wanted to know.
>
> "She's dead," Wangero said. "I couldn't bear it any longer, being named after the people who oppress me."
>
> "You know as well as me you was named after your aunt

Dicie,' I said. Dicie is my sister. She named Dee. We called her "Big Dee" after Dee was born.

"But who was *she* named after?" asked Wangero.

"I guess after Grandma Dee," I said.

"And who was she named after?" asked Wangero.

"Her mother," I said, and saw Wangero was getting tired. . . .

At the opposite end of the spectrum from Wangero is her younger sister, Maggie, a burn victim, who is about to marry a local boy. Because of her care and patience and rootedness, Maggie understands her antecedents in a far more profound sense than her sister. Involved in this understanding is memory, the crux of identity. As much as any story in the anthology, Walker shows how home and homeland are inextricably bound to a person's soul.

THE WOODEN LEG that is so important in "Good Country People" reemerges in "Yellow Ribbons"—except now the leg is plastic and attached to (or disattached from) an ex-Vietnam "roustabout"—but is he? Just as identity and the surprise of identity play a role in the O'Connor story, so they do in "Yellow Ribbons"—the roustabout pretending to be less sensitive than he really is, the girl Destry, less vulnerable. But here the resemblance ends. "Yellow Ribbons" is also about the redemptive quality of human attachment even in the face of various kinds of disintegration. The subplot juxtaposes the visual culture with the literate culture, including fairy tales and poetry—and there are hints that the South, along with the rest of the country, has turned into a vast show biz enterprise with customs and traditions borrowed from television and film.

On the bus, he'd turned to the young girl who plopped down beside him. "Begging your pardon, miss, but I'm about to do something you might be too squeamish to witness."

"What's that?" She barely glanced up from the movie magazine she was rifling through.

"I'm about to remove this here artificial limb." He tapped on the polyethylene kneecap with his thumbnail.

But the girl was fascinated, especially when she found out that he'd been wounded in a mine explosion near the Cambodian border. "But I didn't lose my leg until fairly recently." He could have added that he'd lost his wife at the same time. "I mean, it was *here,* there just wasn't any feeling in it."

"Like Jon Voigt," she said, lending him her manicure scissors to snip away his pants leg. "Did you see *Coming Home?*"

"No'm, I don't get to too many movies, especially war movies."

"Oh, my lord, I couldn't live without movies!" the girl said.

The theme that ties these three stories together is an implied questioning of expectations surrounding the southern homeplace: Is a rigid compliance too much to pay for familial security and support? In times of change, should we be more cautious about letting go of certain values? How does the rebel manage to live in a place where his emerging ethical sense clashes with the one around him?

The thrust of the question depends largely upon the time frame, which ranges from the fifties ("Good Country People") through the sixties and seventies ("Everyday Use"), and into the Reagan and post-Reagan years of the eighties and early nineties ("Yellow Ribbons").

GOOD COUNTRY PEOPLE

Flannery O'Connor

BESIDES THE NEUTRAL expression that she wore when she was alone, Mrs. Freeman had two others, forward and reverse, that she used for all her human dealings. Her forward expression was steady and driving, like the advance of a heavy truck. Her eyes never swerved to left or right but turned as the story turned as if they followed a yellow line down the center of it. She seldom used the other expression because it was not often necessary for her to retract a statement, but when she did, her face came to a complete stop, there was an almost imperceptible movement of her black eyes, during which they seemed to be receding, and then the observer would see that Mrs. Freeman, though she might stand there as real as several grain sacks thrown on top of each other, was no longer there in spirit. As for getting anything across to her when this was the case, Mrs. Hopewell had given it up. She might talk her head off. Mrs. Freeman could never be brought to admit herself wrong on any point.

She would stand there and if she could be brought to say anything, it was something like, "Well, I wouldn't of said it was and I wouldn't of said it wasn't," or letting her gaze range over the top kitchen shelf where there was an assortment of dusty bottles, she might remark, "I see you ain't ate many of them figs you put up last summer."

They carried on their most important business in the kitchen at breakfast. Every morning Mrs. Hopewell got up at seven o'clock and lit her gas heater and Joy's. Joy was her daughter, a large blonde girl who had an artificial leg. Mrs. Hopewell thought of her as a child though she was thirty-two years old and highly educated. Joy would get up while her mother was eating and lumber into the bathroom and slam the door, and before long, Mrs. Freeman would arrive at the back door. Joy would hear her mother call, "Come on in," and then they would talk for a while in low voices that were indistinguishable in the bathroom. By the time Joy came in, they had usually finished the weather report and were on one or the other of Mrs. Freeman's daughters, Glynese or Carramae. Joy called them Glycerin and Caramel. Glynese, a redhead, was eighteen and had many admirers; Carramae, a blonde, was only fifteen but already married and pregnant. She could not keep anything on her stomach. Every morning Mrs. Freeman told Mrs. Hopewell how many times she had vomited since the last report.

Mrs. Hopewell liked to tell people that Glynese and Carramae were two of the finest girls she knew and that Mrs. Freeman was a *lady* and that she was never ashamed to take her anywhere or introduce her to anybody they might meet. Then she would tell how she had happened to hire the Freemans in the first place and how they were a godsend to her and how she had had them four years. The reason for her keeping them so long was that they were not trash. They were good country people. She had telephoned the man whose name they had given as a reference and he had told her that Mr. Freeman was a good farmer but that his wife was the nosiest woman ever to walk the earth. "She's got to be into everything," the man said. "If she don't get there before the dust settles, you can bet she's dead, that's all. She'll want to know all your business. I

Good Country People · 305

can stand him real good," he had said, "but me nor my wife neither could have stood that woman one more minute on this place." That had put Mrs. Hopewell off for a few days.

She had hired them in the end because there were no other applicants but she had made up her mind beforehand exactly how she would handle the woman. Since she was the type who had to be into everything, then, Mrs. Hopewell had decided, she would not only let her be into every- thing, she would *see to it* that she was into everything—she would give her the responsibility of everything, she would put her in charge. Mrs. Hopewell had no bad qualities of her own but she was able to use other people's in such a constructive way that she never felt the lack. She had hired the Freeman's and she had kept them four years.

Nothing is perfect. This was one of Mrs. Hopewell's favorite sayings. Another was: that is life! And still another, the most important, was: well, other people have their opinions too. She would make these state- ments, usually at the table, in a tone of gentle insistence as if no one held them but her, and the large hulking Joy, whose constant outrage had obliterated every expression from her face, would stare just a little to the side of her, her eyes icy blue, with the look of someone who has achieved blindness by an act of will and means to keep it.

When Mrs. Hopewell said to Mrs. Freeman that life was like that, Mrs. Freeman would say, "I always said so myself." Nothing had been arrived at by anyone that had not first been arrived at by her. She was quicker than Mr. Freeman. When Mrs. Hopewell said to her after they had been on the place a while, "You know, you're the wheel behind the wheel," and winked, Mrs. Freeman had said, "I know it. I've always been quick. It's some that are quicker than others."

"Everybody is different," Mrs. Hopewell said.

"Yes, most people is," Mrs. Freeman said.

"It takes all kinds to make the world."

"I always said it did myself."

The girl was used to this kind of dialogue for breakfast and more of it for dinner; sometimes they had it for supper too. When they had no guest they ate in the kitchen because that was easier. Mrs. Freeman always managed to arrive at some point during the meal and to watch them finish it. She would stand in the doorway if it were summer but in the winter she would stand with one elbow on top of the refrigerator and look down on them, or she would stand by the gas heater, lifting the back of her skirt slightly. Occasionally she would stand against the wall and roll her head from side to side. At no time was she in any hurry to leave. All this was very trying on Mrs. Hopewell but she was a woman of great patience. She realized that nothing is perfect and that in the Freemans she had good country people and that if, in this day and age, you get good country people, you had better hang on to them.

She had had plenty of experience with trash. Before the Freemans she had averaged one tenant family a year. The wives of these farmers were not the kind you would want to be around you for very long. Mrs. Hopewell, who had divorced her husband long ago, needed someone to walk over the fields with her; and when Joy had to be impressed for these services, her remarks were usually so ugly and her face so glum that Mrs. Hopewell would say, "If you can't come pleasantly, I don't want you at all," to which the girl, standing square and rigid-shouldered with her neck thrust slightly forward, would reply, "If you want me, here I am—LIKE I AM."

Mrs. Hopewell excused this attitude because of the leg (which had been shot off in a hunting accident when Joy was ten). It was hard for Mrs. Hopewell to realize that her child was thirty-two now and that for more than twenty years she had had only one leg. She thought of her still as a child because it tore her heart to think instead of the poor stout girl in her thirties who had never danced a step or had any *normal* good times. Her name was really Joy but as soon as she was twenty-one and away from home, she had had it legally changed. Mrs. Hopewell was certain that she had thought and thought until she had hit upon the ugliest name in any language. Then she had gone and had the beautiful name, Joy, changed without telling her mother until after she had done it. Her legal name was Hulga.

When Mrs. Hopewell thought the name, Hulga, she thought of the broad blank hull of a battleship. She would not use it. She continued to call her Joy, to which the girl responded but in a purely mechanical way.

Hulga had learned to tolerate Mrs. Freeman who saved her from taking walks with her mother. Even Glynese and Carramae were useful when they occupied attention that might otherwise have been directed at her. At first she had thought she could not stand Mrs. Freeman for she had found that it was not possible to be rude to her. Mrs. Freeman would take on strange resentments and for days together she would be sullen but the source of her displeasure was always obscure; a direct attack, a positive leer, blatant ugliness to her face—these never touched her. And without warning one day, she began calling her Hulga.

She did not call her that in front of Mrs. Hopewell, who would have been incensed but when she and the girl happened to be out of the house together, she would say something and add the name Hulga to the end of it, and the big spectacled Joy-Hulga would scowl and redden as if her privacy had been intruded upon. She considered the name her personal affair. She had arrived at it first purely on the basis of its ugly sound and then the full genius of its fitness had struck her. She had a vision of the name working like the ugly sweating Vulcan who stayed in the furnace and to whom, presumably, the goddess had to come when called. She saw it as the name of her highest creative act. One of her major triumphs was that her mother had not been able to turn her dust into Joy, but the greater one was that she had been able to turn it herself into Hulga. However, Mrs. Freeman's relish for using the name only irritated her. It was as if Mrs. Freeman's beady steel-pointed eyes had penetrated far enough behind her face to reach some secret fact. Something about her seemed to fascinate Mrs. Freeman and then one day Hulga realized that it was the artificial leg. Mrs. Freeman had a special fondness for the details of secret infections, hidden deformities, assaults upon children. Of diseases, she preferred the lingering or incurable. Hulga had heard Mrs. Hopewell give her the details of the hunting accident, how the leg had been literally blasted off, how she had never lost consciousness. Mrs. Freeman could listen to it any time as if it had happened an hour ago.

When Hulga stumped into the kitchen in the morning (she could walk without making the awful noise but she made it—Mrs. Hopewell was certain—because it was ugly-sounding), she glanced at them and did not speak. Mrs. Hopewell would be in her red kimono with her hair tied around her head in rags. She would be sitting at the table, finishing her breakfast and Mrs. Freeman would be hanging by her elbow outward from the refrigerator, looking down at the table. Hulga always put her eggs on the stove to boil and then stood over them with her arms folded, and Mrs. Hopewell would look at her—a kind of indirect gaze divided between her and Mrs. Freeman—and would think that if she would only keep herself up a little, she wouldn't be so bad looking. There was nothing wrong with her face that a pleasant expression wouldn't help. Mrs. Hopewell said that people who looked on the bright side of things would be beautiful even if they were not.

Whenever she looked at Joy this way, she could not help but feel that it would have been better if the child had not taken the Ph.D. It had certainly not brought her out any and now that she had it, there was no more excuse for her to go to school again. Mrs. Hopewell thought it was nice for girls to go to school to have a good time but Joy had "gone through." Anyhow, she would not have been strong enough to go again. The doctors had told Mrs. Hopewell that with the best of care, Joy might see forty-five. She had a weak heart. Joy had made it plain that if it had not been for this condition, she would be far from these red hills and good country people. She would be in a university lecturing to people who knew what she was talking about. And Mrs. Hopewell could very well picture her there, looking like a scarecrow and lecturing to more of the same. Here she went about all day in a six-year-old skirt and a yellow sweat shirt with a faded cowboy on a horse embossed on it. She thought this was funny; Mrs. Hopewell thought it was idiotic and showed simply that she was still a child. She was brilliant but she didn't have a grain of sense. It seemed to Mrs. Hopewell that every year she grew less like other people and more like herself—bloated, rude, and squint-eyed. And she said such strange things! To her own mother she had said—without warning, without excuse, standing up in the middle of a meal with her face purple and her mouth half full— "Woman! do you ever look inside? Do you ever look inside and see what you are *not*? God!" she had cried sinking down again and staring at her plate, "Malebranche was right: we are not our own light. We are not our own light!" Mrs. Hopewell had no idea to this day what brought that on. She had only made the remark, hoping Joy would take it in, that a smile never hurt anyone.

The girl had taken the Ph.D. in philosophy and this left Mrs. Hopewell at a complete loss. You could say, "My daughter is a nurse," or "My daughter is a school teacher," or even, "My daughter is a chemical engineer." You could not say, "My daughter is a philosopher." That was something that had ended with the Greeks and Romans. All day Joy sat on her neck in a deep chair, reading. Sometimes she went for walks but she didn't like dogs or cats or birds or flowers or nature or nice young men. She looked at nice young men as if she could smell their stupidity.

One day Mrs. Hopewell had picked up one of the books the girl had just put down and opening it at random, she read, "Science, on the other hand, has to assert its soberness and seriousness afresh and declare that it is concerned solely with what-is. Nothing—how can it be for science anything but a horror and a phantasm? If science is right, then one thing stands firm: science wishes to know nothing of nothing. Such is after all the strictly scientific approach to Nothing. We know it by wishing to know nothing of Nothing." These words had been underlined with a blue pencil and they worked on Mrs. Hopewell like some evil incantation in gibberish. She shut the book quickly, and went out of the room as if she were having a chill.

This morning when the girl came in, Mrs. Freeman was on Carramae. "She thrown up four times after supper," she said, "and was up twict in the night after three o'clock. Yesterday she didn't do nothing but ramble in the bureau drawer. All she did. Stand up there and see what she could run up on."

"She's got to eat," Mrs. Hopewell muttered, sipping her coffee, while she watched Joy's back at the stove. She was wondering what the child had said to the Bible salesman. She could not imagine what kind of a conversation she could possibly have had with him.

He was a tall gaunt hatless youth who had called yesterday to sell them a Bible. He had appeared at the door, carrying a large black suitcase that weighted him so heavily on one side that he had to brace himself against the door facing. He seemed on the point of collapse but he said in a cheerful voice, "Good morning, Mrs. Cedars!" and set the suitcase down on the mat. He was not a bad-looking young man though he had on a bright blue suit and yellow socks that were not pulled up far enough. He had prominent face bones and a streak of sticky-looking brown hair falling across his forehead.

"I'm Mrs. Hopewell," she said.

"Oh!" he said, pretending to look puzzled but with his eyes sparkling. "I saw it said 'The Cedars,' on the mailbox so I thought you was Mrs. Cedars!" and he burst out in a pleasant laugh. He picked up the satchel and under cover of a pant, he fell forward into her hall. It was rather as if the suitcase had moved first, jerking him after it. "Mrs. Hopewell!" he said and grabbed her hand. "I hope you are well!" and he laughed again and then all at once his face sobered completely. He paused and gave her a straight earnest look and said, "Lady, I've come to speak of serious things."

"Well, come in," she muttered, none too pleased because her dinner was almost ready. He came into the parlor and sat down on the edge of a straight chair and put the suitcase between his feet and glanced around the room as if he were sizing her up by it. Her silver gleamed on the two sideboards; she decided he had never been in a room as elegant as this.

"Mrs. Hopewell," he began, using her name in a way that sounded almost intimate, "I know you believe in Chrustian service."

"Well yes," she murmured.

"I know," he said and paused, looking very wise with his head cocked on one side, "that you're a good woman. Friends have told me."

Mrs. Hopewell never liked to be taken for a fool. "What are you selling?" she asked.

"Bibles," the young man said and his eye raced around the room before he added, "I see you have no family Bible in your parlor, I see that is the one lack you got!"

Mrs. Hopewell could not say, "My daughter is an atheist and won't let me keep the Bible in the parlor." She said, stiffening slightly, "I keep my Bible by my bedside." This was not the truth. It was in the attic somewhere.

"Lady," he said, "the word of God ought to be in the parlor."

"Well, I think that's a matter of taste," she began. "I think . . ."

"Lady," he said, "for a Chrustian, the word of God ought to be in every room in the house besides in his heart. I know you're a Chrustian because I can see it in every line of your face."

She stood up and said, "Well, young man, I don't want to buy a Bible and I smell my dinner burning."

He didn't get up. He began to twist his hands and looking down at them, he said softly, "Well lady, I'll tell you the truth—not many people want to buy one nowadays and besides, I know I'm real simple. I don't know how to say a thing but to say it. I'm just a country boy." He glanced up into her unfriendly face. "People like you don't like to fool with country people like me!"

"Why!" she cried, "good country people are the salt of the earth! Besides, we all have different ways of doing, it takes all kinds to make the world go 'round. That's life!"

"You said a mouthful," he said.

"Why, I think there aren't enough good country people in the world!" she said, stirred. "I think that's what's wrong with it!"

His face had brightened. "I didn't inraduce myself," he said. "I'm

Manley Pointer from out in the country around Willohobie, not even from a place, just from near a place."

"You wait a minute," she said. "I have to see about my dinner." She went out to the kitchen and found Joy standing near the door where she had been listening.

"Get rid of the salt of the earth," she said, "and let's eat."

Mrs. Hopewell gave her a pained look and turned the heat down under the vegetables. "*I* can't be rude to anybody," she murmured and went back into the parlor.

He had opened the suitcase and was sitting with a Bible on each knee.

"You might as well put those up," she told him. "I don't want one."

"I appreciate your honesty," he said. "You don't see any more real honest people unless you go way out in the country."

"I know," she said, "real genuine folks!" Through the crack in the door she heard a groan.

"I guess a lot of boys come telling you they're working their way through college," he said, "but I'm not going to tell you that. Somehow," he said, "I don't want to go to college. I want to devote my life to Chrustian service. See," he said, lowering his voice, "I got this heart condition. I may not live long. When you know it's something wrong with you and you may not live long, well then, lady . . ." He paused, with his mouth open, and stared at her.

He and Joy had the same condition! She knew that her eyes were filling with tears but she collected herself quickly and murmured, "Won't you stay for dinner? We'd love to have you!" and was sorry the instant she heard herself say it.

"Yes mam," he said in an abashed voice, "I would sher love to do that!"

Joy had given him one look on being introduced to him and then throughout the meal had not glanced at him again. He had addressed several remarks to her, which she had pretended not to hear. Mrs. Hopewell could not understand deliberate rudeness, although she lived with it, and she felt she had always to overflow with hospitality to make up for Joy's lack of courtesy. She urged him to talk about himself and he did. He said he was the seventh child of twelve and that his father had been crushed under a tree when he himself was eight year old. He had been crushed very badly, in fact, almost cut in two and was practically not recognizable. His mother had got along the best she could by hard working and she had always seen that her children went to Sunday School and that they read the Bible every evening. He was now nineteen year old and he had been selling Bibles for four months. In that time he had sold seventy-seven Bibles and had the promise of two more sales. He wanted to become a missionary because he thought that was the way you could do most for people. "He who losest his life shall find it," he said simply and he was so sincere, so genuine and earnest that Mrs. Hopewell would not for the world have smiled. He prevented his peas from sliding onto the table by blocking them with a piece of bread which he later cleaned his plate with. She could see Joy observing sidewise how he handled his knife and fork and she saw too that every few minutes, the boy would dart a keen appraising glance at the girl as if he were trying to attract her attention.

After dinner Joy cleared the dishes off the table and disappeared and Mrs. Hopewell was left to talk with him. He told her again about his childhood and his father's accident and about various things that had happened to him. Every five minutes or so she would stifle a yawn. He sat for two hours until finally she told him she must go because she had an appointment in town. He packed his Bibles and thanked her and prepared to leave, but in the doorway he stopped and wrung her hand and said that not on any of his trips had he met a lady as nice as her and he asked if he could come again. She had said she would always be happy to see him.

Joy had been standing in the road, apparently looking at something in the distance, when he came down the steps toward her, bent to the side with his heavy valise. He stopped where she was standing and confronted her directly. Mrs. Hopewell could not hear what he said but she trembled to think what Joy would say to him. She could see that after a minute Joy said something and that then the boy began to speak again, making an excited gesture with his free hand. After a minute Joy said something else at which the boy began to speak once more. Then to her amazement, Mrs. Hopewell saw the two of them walk off together, toward the gate. Joy had walked all the way to the gate with him and Mrs. Hopewell could not imagine what they had said to each other, and she had not yet dared to ask.

Mrs. Freeman was insisting upon her attention. She had moved from the refrigerator to the heater so that Mrs. Hopewell had to turn and face her in order to seem to be listening. "Glynese gone out with Harvey Hill again last night," she said. "She had this sty."

"Hill," Mrs. Hopewell said absently, "is that the one who works in the garage?"

"Nome, he's the one that goes to chiropracter school," Mrs. Freeman said. "She had this sty. Been had it two days. So she says when he brought her in the other night he says, 'Lemme get rid of that sty for you,' and she says, 'How?' and he says, 'You just lay yourself down acrost the seat of that car and I'll show you.' So she done it and he popped her neck. Kept on a-popping it several times until she made him quit. This morning," Mrs. Freeman said, "she ain't got no sty. She ain't got no traces of a sty."

"I never heard of that before," Mrs. Hopewell said.

"He ast her to marry him before the Ordinary," Mrs. Freeman went on, "and she told him she wasn't going to be married in no *office*."

"Well, Glynese is a fine girl," Mrs. Hopewell said. "Glynese and Carramae are both fine girls."

"Carramae said, when her and Lyman was married, Lyman said it sure felt sacred to him. She said he said he wouldn't take five hundred dollars for being married by a preacher."

"How much would he take?" the girl asked from the stove.

"He said he wouldn't take five hundred dollars," Mrs. Freeman repeated.

"Well we all have work to do," Mrs. Hopewell said.

"Lyman said it just felt more sacred to him," Mrs. Freeman said. "The doctor wants Carramae to eat prunes. Says instead of medicine. Says them cramps is coming from pressure. You know where I think it is?"

"She'll be better in a few weeks," Mrs. Hopewell said.

"In the tube," Mrs. Freeman said. "Else she wouldn't be as sick as she is."

Hulga had cracked her two eggs into a saucer and was bringing them to the table along with a cup of coffee that she had filled too full. She sat down carefully and began to eat, meaning to keep Mrs. Freeman there by questions if for any reason she showed an inclination to leave. She could perceive her mother's eye on her. The first roundabout question would be about the Bible salesman and she did not wish to bring it on. "How did he pop her neck?" she asked.

Mrs. Freeman went into a description of how he had popped her neck. She said he owned a '55 Mercury but that Glynese said she would rather marry a man with only a '36 Plymouth who would be married by a preacher. The girl asked what if he had a '32 Plymouth and Mrs. Freeman said what Glynese had said was a '36 Plymouth.

Mrs. Hopewell said there were not many girls with Glynese's common sense. She said what she admired in those girls was their common sense. She said that reminded her that they had had a nice visitor yesterday, a young man selling Bibles. "Lord," she said, "he bored me to death but he was so sincere and genuine I couldn't be rude to him. He was just good country people, you know," she said, "—just the salt of the earth."

"I seen him walk up," Mrs. Freeman said, "and then later—I seen him walk off," and Hulga could feel the slight shift in her voice, the slight insinuation, that he had not walked off alone, had he? Her face remained expressionless but the color rose into her neck and she seemed to swallow it down with the next spoonful of egg. Mrs. Freeman was looking at her as if they had a secret together.

"Well, it takes all kinds of people to make the world go 'round," Mrs. Hopewell said. "It's very good we aren't all alike."

"Some people are more alike than others," Mrs. Freeman said.

Hulga got up and stumped, with about twice the noise that was necessary, into her room and locked the door. She was to meet the Bible salesman at ten o'clock at the gate. She had thought about it half the night. She had started thinking of it as a great joke and then she had begun to see profound implications in it. She had lain in bed imagining dialogues for them that were insane on the surface but that reached below to depths that no Bible salesman would be aware of. Their conversation yesterday had been of this kind.

He had stopped in front of her and had simply stood there. His face was bony and sweaty and bright, with a little pointed nose in the center of it, and his look was different from what it had been at the dinner table. He was gazing at her with open curiosity, with fascination, like a child watching a new fantastic animal at the zoo, and he was breathing as if he had run a great distance to reach her. His gaze seemed somehow familiar, but she could not think where she had been regarded with it before. For almost a minute he didn't say anything. Then on what seemed an insuck of breath, he whispered, "You ever ate a chicken that was two days old?"

The girl looked at him stonily. He might have just put this question up for consideration at the meeting of a philosophical association. "Yes," she presently replied as if she had considered it from all angles.

"It must have been mighty small!" he said triumphantly and shook all over with little nervous giggles, getting very red in the face, and subsiding finally into his gaze of complete admiration, while the girl's expression remained exactly the same.

"How old are you?" he asked softly.

She waited some time before she answered. Then in a flat voice she said, "Seventeen."

His smiles came in succession like waves breaking on the surface of a little lake. "I see you got a wooden leg," he said. "I think you're real brave. I think you're real sweet."

The girl stood blank and solid and silent.

"Walk to the gate with me," he said. "You're a brave sweet little thing and I liked you the minute I seen you walk in the door."

Hulga began to move forward.

"What's your name?" he asked, smiling down on the top of her head.

"Hulga," she said.

"Hulga," he murmured, "Hulga. Hulga. I never heard of anybody name Hulga before. You're shy, aren't you, Hulga?" he asked.

She nodded, watching his large red hand on the handle of the giant valise.

"I like girls that wear glasses," he said. "I think a lot. I'm not like these people that a serious thought don't ever enter their heads. It's because I may die."

"I may die too," she said suddenly and looked up at him. His eyes were very small and brown, glittering feverishly.

"Listen," he said, "don't you think some people was meant to meet on account of what all they got in common and all? Like they both think serious thoughts and all?" He shifted the valise to his other hand so that the hand nearest her was free. He caught hold of her elbow and shook it a little. "I don't work on Saturday," he said. "I like to walk in the woods and see what Mother Nature is wearing. O'er the hills and far away. Picnics and things. Couldn't we go on a pic-nic tomorrow? Say yes, Hulga," he said and gave her a dying look as if he felt his insides about to drop out of him. He had even seemed to sway slightly toward her.

During the night she had imagined that she seduced him. She imagined that the two of them walked on the place until they came to the storage barn beyond the two back fields and there, she imagined, that things came to such a pass that she very easily seduced him and that then, of course, she had to reckon with his remorse. True genius can get an idea across even to an inferior mind. She imagined that she took his remorse in hand and changed it into a deeper understanding of life. She took all his shame away and turned it into something useful.

She set off for the gate at exactly ten o'clock, escaping without drawing Mrs. Hopewell's attention. She didn't take anything to eat, forgetting that food is usually taken on a picnic. She wore a pair of slacks and a dirty white shirt, and as an afterthought, she had put some Vapex on the collar of it since she did not own any perfume. When she reached the gate no one was there.

She looked up and down the empty highway and had the furious feeling that she had been tricked, that he had only meant to make her walk to the gate after the idea of him. Then suddenly he stood up, very tall, from behind a bush on the opposite embankment. Smiling, he lifted his hat which was new and wide-brimmed. He had not worn it yesterday and she wondered if he had bought it for the occasion. It was toast-colored with a red and white band around it and was slightly too large for him. He stepped from behind the bush still carrying the black valise. He had on the same suit and the same yellow socks sucked down in his shoes from walking. He crossed the highway and said, "I knew you'd come!"

The girl wondered acidly how he had known this. She pointed to the valise and asked, "Why did you bring your Bibles?"

He took her elbow, smiling down on her as if he could not stop. "You can never tell when you'll need the word of God, Hulga," he said. She had a moment in which she doubted that this was actually happening and then they began to climb the embankment. They went down into the pasture toward the woods. The boy walked lightly by her side, bouncing on his toes. The valise did not seem to be heavy today; he even swung it. They crossed half the pasture without saying anything and then, putting his hand easily on the small of her back, he asked softly, "Where does your wooden leg join on?"

She turned an ugly red and glared at him and for an instant the boy looked abashed. "I didn't mean you no harm," he said. "I only meant you're so brave and all. I guess God takes care of you."

"No," she said, looking forward and walking fast, "I don't even believe in God."

At this he stopped and whistled. "No!" he exclaimed as if he were too astonished to say anything else.

She walked on and in a second he was bouncing at her side, fanning with his hat. "That's very unusual for a girl," he remarked, watching her out of the corner of his eye. When they reached the edge of the wood, he put his hand on her back again and drew her against him without a word and kissed her heavily.

The kiss, which had more pressure than feeling behind it, produced that extra surge of adrenaline in the girl that enables one to carry a packed trunk out of a burning house, but in her, the power went at once to the brain. Even before he released her, her mind, clear and detached and ironic anyway, was regarding him from a great distance, with amusement but with pity. She had never been kissed before and she was pleased to discover that it was an unexceptional experience and all a matter of the mind's control. Some people might enjoy drain water if they were told it was vodka. When the boy, looking expectant but uncertain, pushed her gently away, she turned and walked on, saying nothing as if such business, for her, were common enough.

He came along panting at her side, trying to help her when he saw a root that she might trip over. He caught and held back the long swaying blades of thorn vine until she had passed beyond them. She led the way and he came breathing heavily behind her. Then they came out on a sunlit hillside, sloping softly into another one a little smaller. Beyond, they could see the rusted top of the old barn where the extra hay was stored.

The hill was sprinkled with small pink weeds. "Then you ain't saved?" he asked suddenly, stopping.

The girl smiled. It was the first time she had smiled at him at all. "In my economy," she said, "I'm saved and you are damned, but I told you I didn't believe in God."

Nothing seemed to destroy the boy's look of admiration. He gazed at her now as if the fantastic animal at the zoo had put its paw through the bars and given him a loving poke. She thought he looked as if he wanted to kiss her again and she walked on before he had the chance.

"Ain't there somewheres we can sit down sometime?" he murmured, his voice softening toward the end of the sentence.

"In that barn," she said.

They made for it rapidly as if it might slide away like a train. It was a large two-story barn, cool and dark inside. The boy pointed up the ladder that led into the loft and said, "It's too bad we can't go up there."

"Why can't we?" she asked.

"Yer leg," he said reverently.

The girl gave him a contemptuous look and putting both hands on the ladder, she climbed it while he stood below, apparently awestruck. She pulled herself expertly through the opening and then looked down at him and said, "Well, come on if you're coming," and he began to climb the ladder, awkwardly bringing the suitcase with him.

"We won't need the Bible," she observed.

"You never can tell," he said, panting. After he had got into the loft, he was a few seconds catching his breath. She had sat down in a pile of straw. A wide sheath of sunlight, filled with dust particles, slanted over her. She lay back against a bale, her face turned away, looking out the front opening of the barn where hay was thrown from a wagon into the loft. The two pink-speckled hillsides lay back against a dark ridge of woods. The sky was cloudless and cold blue. The boy dropped down by her side and put one arm under her and the other over her and began methodically kissing her face, making little noises like a fish. He did not remove his hat but it was pushed far enough back not to interfere. When her glasses got in his way, he took them off of her and slipped them into his pocket.

The girl at first did not return any of the kisses but presently she began to and after she had put several on his cheek, she reached his lips and remained there, kissing him again and again as if she were trying to draw all the breath out of him. His breath was clear and sweet like a child's and the kisses were sticky like a child's. He mumbled about loving her and about knowing when he first seen her that he loved her, but the mumbling was like the sleepy fretting of a child being put to sleep by his mother. Her mind, throughout this, never stopped or lost itself for a second to her feelings. "You ain't said you loved me none," he whispered finally, pulling back from her. "You got to say that."

She looked away from him off into the hollow sky and then down at a black ridge and then down farther into what appeared to be two green swelling lakes. She didn't realize he had taken her glasses but this landscape could not seem exceptional to her for she seldom paid any close attention to her surroundings.

"You got to say it," he repeated. "You got to say you love me."

She was always careful how she committed herself. "In a sense," she began, "if you use the word loosely, you might say that. But it's not a word I use. I don't have illusions. I'm one of those people who see *through* to nothing."

The boy was frowning. "You got to say it. I said it and you got to say it," he said.

The girl looked at him almost tenderly. "You poor baby," she murmured. "It's just as well you don't understand," and she pulled him by the neck, face-down, against her. "We are all damned," she said, "but some of us have taken off our blindfolds and see that there's nothing to see. It's a kind of salvation."

The boy's astonished eyes looked blankly through the ends of her hair. "Okay," he almost whined, "but do you love me or don'tcher?"

"Yes," she said and added, "in a sense. But I must tell you something. There mustn't be anything dishonest between us." She lifted his head and looked him in the eye. "I am thirty years old," she said. "I have a number of degrees."

The boy's look was irritated but dogged. "I don't care," he said. "I don't care a thing about what all you done. I just want to know if you love me or don'tcher?" and he caught her to him and wildly planted her face with kisses until she said, "Yes, yes."

"Okay then," he said, letting her go. "Prove it."

She smiled, looking dreamily out on the shifty landscape. She had seduced him without even making up her mind to try. "How?" she asked, feeling that he should be delayed a little.

He leaned over and put his lips to her ear. "Show me where your wooden leg joins on," he whispered.

The girl uttered a sharp little cry and her face instantly drained of color. The obscenity of the suggestion was not what shocked her. As a child she had sometimes been subject to feelings of shame, but education had removed the last traces of that as a good surgeon scrapes for cancer; she would no more have felt it over what he was asking than she would have believed in his Bible. But she was as sensitive about the artificial leg as a peacock about his tail. No one ever touched it but her. She took care of it as someone else would his soul, in private and almost with her own eyes turned away. "No," she said.

"I known it," he muttered, sitting up. "You're just playing me for a sucker."

"Oh no!" she cried. "It joins on at the knee. Only at the knee. Why do you want to see it?"

The boy gave her a long penetrating look. "Because," he said, "it's what makes you different. You ain't like anybody else."

She sat staring at him. There was nothing about her face or her round freezing-blue eyes to indicate that this had moved her; but she felt as if her heart had stopped and left her mind to pump her blood. She decided that, for the first time in her life she was face to face with real innocence. This boy, with an instinct that came from beyond wisdom, had touched the truth about her. When after a minute, she said in a hoarse high voice, "All right," it was like surrendering to him completely. It was like losing her own life and finding it again, miraculously, in his.

Very gently he began to roll the slack leg up. The artificial limb, in a white sock and brown flat shoe, was bound in a heavy material like canvas and ended in an ugly jointure where it was attached to the stump. The boy's face and his voice were entirely reverent as he uncovered it and said, "Now show me how to take it off and on."

She took it off for him and put it back on again and then he took it off himself, handling it as tenderly as if it were a real one. "See!" he said with a delighted child's face. "Now I can do it myself!"

"Put it back on," she said. She was thinking that she would run away with him and that every night he would take the leg off and every morning put it back on again. "Put it back on," she said.

"Not yet," he murmured, setting it on its foot out of her reach. "Leave it off for a while. You got me instead."

She gave a little cry of alarm but he pushed her down and began to kiss her again. Without the leg she felt entirely dependent on him. Her brain seemed to have stopped thinking altogether and to be about some other function that it was not very good at. Different expressions raced back and forth over her face. Every now and then the boy, his eyes like two steel spikes, would glance behind him where the leg stood. Finally she pushed him off and said, "Put it back on me now."

"Wait," he said. He leaned the other way and pulled the valise toward him and opened it. It had a pale blue spotted lining and there were only two Bibles in it. He took one of these out and opened the cover of it. It was hollow and contained a pocket flask of whiskey, a pack of cards, and a small blue box with printing on it. He laid these out in front of her one at a time in an evenly spaced row, like one presenting offerings at the shrine of a goddess. He put the blue box in her hand. THIS PRODUCT TO BE USED ONLY FOR THE PREVENTION OF DISEASE, she read, and dropped it. The boy was unscrewing the top of the flask. He stopped and pointed, with a smile, to the deck of cards. It was not an ordinary deck but one with an obscene picture on the back of each card. "Take a swig," he said, offering her the bottle first. He held it in front of her, but like one mesmerized, she did not move.

Her voice when she spoke had an almost pleading sound. "Aren't you," she murmured, "aren't you just good country people?"

The boy cocked his head. He looked as if he were just beginning to understand that she might be trying to insult him. "Yeah," he said, curling his lip slightly, "but it ain't held me back none. I'm as good as you any day in the week."

"Give me my leg," she said.

He pushed it farther away with his foot. "Come on now, let's begin to have us a good time," he said coaxingly. "We ain't got to know one another good yet."

"Give me my leg!" she screamed and tried to lunge for it but he pushed her down easily.

"What's the matter with you all of a sudden?" he asked, frowning as he screwed the top on the flask and put it quickly back inside the Bible. "You just a while ago said you didn't believe in nothing. I thought you was some girl!"

Her face was almost purple. "You're a Christian!" she hissed. "You're a fine Christian! You're just like them all—say one thing and do another. You're a perfect Christian, you're . . ."

The boy's mouth was set angrily. "I hope you don't think," he said in a lofty indignant tone, "that I believe in that crap! I may sell Bibles but I know which end is up and I wasn't born yesterday and I know where I'm going!"

"Give me my leg!" she screeched. He jumped up so quickly that she barely saw him sweep the cards and the blue box back into the Bible and throw the Bible into the valise. She saw him grab the leg and then she saw it for an instant slanted forlornly across the inside of the suitcase with a Bible at either side of its opposite ends. He slammed the lid shut and snatched up the valise and swung it down the hole and then stepped through himself.

When all of him had passed but his head, he turned and regarded her with a look that no longer had any admiration in it. "I've gotten a lot of interesting things," he said. "One time I got a woman's glass eye this way. And you needn't to think you'll catch me because Pointer ain't really my name. I use a different name at every house I call at and don't stay nowhere long. And I'll tell you another thing, Hulga," he said, using the name as if he didn't think much of it, "you ain't so smart. I been believing in nothing ever since I was born!" and then the toast-colored hat disappeared down the hole and the girl was left, sitting on the straw in the dusty sunlight. When she turned her churning face toward the opening, she saw his blue figure struggling successfully over the green speckled lake.

Mrs. Hopewell and Mrs. Freeman, who were in the back pasture, digging up onions, saw him emerge a little later from the woods and head across the meadow toward the highway. "Why, that looks like that nice dull young man that tried to sell me a Bible yesterday," Mrs. Hopewell said, squinting. "He must have been selling them to the Negroes back in there. He was so simple," she said, "but I guess the world would be better off if we were all that simple."

Mrs. Freeman's gaze drove forward and just touched him before he disappeared under the hill. Then she returned her attention to the evil-smelling onion shoot she was lifting from the ground. "Some can't be that simple," she said. "I know I never could."

for your grandmama

EVERYDAY USE

Alice Walker

I WILL WAIT for her in the yard that Maggie and I made so clean and
wavy yesterday afternoon. A yard like this is more comfortable than most
people know. It is not just a yard. It is like an extended living room.
When the hard clay is swept clean as a floor and the fine sand around the
edges lined with tiny, irregular grooves, anyone can come and sit and
look up into the elm tree and wait for the breezes that never come inside
the house.

Maggie will be nervous until after her sister goes: she will stand
hopelessly in corners, homely and ashamed of the burn scars down her
arms and legs, eyeing her sister with a mixture of envy and awe. She
thinks her sister has held life always in the palm of one hand, that "no"
is a word that the world never learned to say to her.

YOU'VE NO DOUBT seen those TV shows where the child who has

"made it" is confronted, as a surprise, by her own mother and father, tottering in weakly from backstage. (A pleasant surprise, of course: What would they do if parent and child came on the show only to curse out and insult each other?) On TV mother and child embrace and smile into each other's faces. Sometimes the mother and father weep, the child wraps them in her arms and leans across the table to tell how she would not have made it without their help. I have seen these programs.

Sometimes I dream a dream in which Dee and I are suddenly brought together on a TV program of this sort. Out of a dark and soft-seated limousine I am ushered into a bright room filled with many people. There I meet a smiling, gray, sporty man like Johnny Carson who shakes my hand and tells me what a fine girl I have. Then we are on the stage and Dee is embracing me with tears in her eyes. She pins on my dress a large orchid, even though she has told me once that she thinks orchids are tacky flowers.

In real life I am a large, big-boned woman with rough, man-working hands. In the winter I wear flannel nightgowns to bed and overalls during the day. I can kill and clean a hog as mercilessly as a man. My fat keeps me hot in zero weather. I can work outside all day, breaking ice to get water for washing; I can eat pork liver cooked over the open fire minutes after it comes steaming from the hog. One winter I knocked a bull calf straight in the brain between the eyes with a sledgehammer and had the meat hung up to chill before nightfall. But of course all this does not show on television. I am the way my daughter would want me to be: a hundred pounds lighter, my skin like an uncooked barley pancake. My hair glistens in the hot bright lights. Johnny Carson has much to do to keep up with my quick and witty tongue.

But that is a mistake. I know even before I wake up. Who ever knew a Johnson with a quick tongue? Who can even imagine me looking a strange white man in the eye? It seems to me I have talked to them always with one foot raised in flight, with my head turned in whichever way is farthest from them. Dee, though. She would always look anyone in the eye. Hesitation was no part of her nature.

Alice Walker • 328

"HOW DO I look, Mama?" Maggie says, showing just enough of her thin body enveloped in pink skirt and red blouse for me to know she's there, almost hidden by the door.

"Come out into the yard," I say.

Have you ever seen a lame animal, perhaps a dog run over by some careless person rich enough to own a car, sidle up to someone who is ignorant enough to be kind to him? That is the way my Maggie walks. She has been like this, chin on chest, eyes on ground, feet in shuffle, ever since the fire that burned the other house to the ground.

Dee is lighter than Maggie, with nicer hair and a fuller figure. She's a woman now, though sometimes I forget. How long ago was it that the other house burned? Ten, twelve years? Sometimes I can still hear the flames and feel Maggie's arms sticking to me, her hair smoking and her dress falling off her in little black papery flakes. Her eyes seemed stretched open, blazed open by the flames reflected in them. And Dee. I see her standing off under the sweet gum tree she used to dig gum out of; a look of concentration on her face as she watched the last dingy gray board of the house fall in toward the red-hot brick chimney. Why don't you do a dance around the ashes? I'd wanted to ask her. She had hated the house that much.

I used to think she hated Maggie, too. But that was before we raised the money, the church and me, to send her to Augusta to school. She used to read to us without pity; forcing words, lies, other folks' habits, whole lives upon us two, sitting trapped and ignorant underneath her voice. She washed us in a river of make-believe, burned us with a lot of knowledge we didn't necessarily need to know. Pressed us to her with the serious way she read, to shove us away at just the moment, like dimwits, we seemed about to understand.

Dee wanted nice things. A yellow organdy dress to wear to her graduation from high school; black pumps to match a green suit she'd made from an old suit somebody gave me. She was determined to stare down any disaster in her efforts. Her eyelids would not flicker for minutes at a time. Often I fought off the temptation to shake her.

At sixteen she had a style of her own: and knew what style was.

I NEVER HAD an education myself. After second grade the school was closed down. Don't ask me why: in 1927 colored asked fewer questions than they do now. Sometimes Maggie reads to me. She stumbles along good-naturedly but can't see well. She knows she is not bright. Like good looks and money, quickness passed her by. She will marry John Thomas (who has mossy teeth in an earnest face) and then I'll be free to sit here and I guess just sing church songs to myself. Although I never was a good singer. Never could carry a tune. I was always better at a man's job. I used to love to milk till I was hooked in the side in '49. Cows are soothing and slow and don't bother you, unless you try to milk them the wrong way.

I have deliberately turned my back on the house. It is three rooms, just like the one that burned, except the roof is tin; they don't make shingle roofs any more. There are no real windows, just some holes cut in the sides, like the portholes in a ship, but not round and not square, with rawhide holding the shutters up on the outside. This house is in a pasture, too, like the other one. No doubt when Dee sees it she will want to tear it down. She wrote me once that no matter where we "choose" to live, she will manage to come see us. But she will never bring her friends. Maggie and I thought about this and Maggie asked me, "Mama, when did Dee ever *have* any friends?"

She had a few. Furtive boys in pink shirts hanging about on washday after school. Nervous girls who never laughed. Impressed with her they worshiped the well-turned phrase, the cute shape, the scalding humor that erupted like bubbles in lye. She read to them.

When she was courting Jimmy T she didn't have much time to pay to us, but turned all her faultfinding power on him. He *flew* to marry a cheap city girl from a family of ignorant flashy people. She hardly had time to recompose herself.

WHEN SHE COMES I will meet—but there they are!

Maggie attempts to make a dash for the house, in her shuffling way, but I stay her with my hand. "Come back here," I say. And she stops and tries to dig a well in the sand with her toe.

It is hard to see them clearly through the strong sun. But even the first glimpse of leg out of the car tells me it is Dee. Her feet were always neat-looking, as if God himself had shaped them a certain style. From the other side of the car comes a short, stocky man. Hair is all over his head a foot long and hanging from his chin like a kinky mule tail. I hear Maggie suck in her breath. "Uhnnnh," is what it sounds like. Like when you see the wriggling end of a snake just in front of your foot on the road. "Uhnnnh."

Dee next. A dress down to the ground, in this hot weather. A dress so loud it hurts my eyes. There are yellows and oranges enough to throw back the light of the sun. I feel my whole face warming from the heat waves it throws out. Earrings gold, too, and hanging down to her shoulders. Bracelets dangling and making noises when she moves her arm up to shake the folds of the dress out of her armpits. The dress is loose and flows, and as she walks closer, I like it. I hear Maggie go "Uhnnnh" again. It is her sister's hair. It stands straight up like the wool on a sheep. It is black as night and around the edges are two long pigtails that rope about like small lizards disappearing behind her ears.

"Wa-su-zo-Tean-o!" she says, coming on in that gliding way the dress makes her move. The short stocky fellow with the hair to his navel is all grinning and he follows up with "Asalamalakim, my mother and sister!" He moves to hug Maggie but she falls back, right up against the back of my chair. I feel her trembling there and when I look up I see the perspiration falling off her chin.

"Don't get up," says Dee. Since I am stout it takes something of a push. You can see me trying to move a second or two before I make it. She turns, showing white heels through her sandals, and goes back to the car. Out she peeks next with a Polaroid. She stoops down quickly and lines up picture after picture of me sitting there in front of the house with Maggie cowering behind me. She never takes a shot without making sure the house is included. When a cow comes nibbling around the edge of the yard she snaps it and me and Maggie *and* the house. Then she puts the Polaroid in the backseat of the car, and comes up and kisses me on the forehead.

Meanwhile Asalamalakim is going through motions with Maggie's hand. Maggie's hand is as limp as a fish, and probably as cold, despite the sweat, and she keeps trying to pull it back. It looks like Asalamalakim wants to shake hands but wants to do it fancy. Or maybe he don't know how people shake hands. Anyhow, he soon gives up on Maggie.

"Well," I say. "Dee."

"No, Mama," she says. "Not 'Dee,' Wangero Leewanika Kemanjo!"

"What happened to 'Dee'?" I wanted to know.

"She's dead," Wangero said. "I couldn't bear it any longer, being named after the people who oppress me."

"You know as well as me you was named after your aunt Dicie," I said. Dicie is my sister. She named Dee. We called her "Big Dee" after Dee was born.

"But who was *she* named after?" asked Wangero.

"I guess after Grandma Dee," I said.

"And who was she named after?" asked Wangero.

"Her mother," I said, and saw Wangero was getting tired. "That's about as far back as I can trace it," I said. Though, in fact, I probably could have carried it back beyond the Civil War through the branches.

"Well" said Asalamalakim, "there you are."

"Uhnnnh," I heard Maggie say.

"There I was not," I said, "before 'Dicie' cropped up in our family, so why should I try to trace it that far back?"

He just stood there grinning, looking down on me like somebody inspecting a Model A car. Every once in a while he and Wangero sent eye signals over my head.

"How do you pronounce this name?" I asked.

"You don't have to call me by it if you don't want to," said Wangero.

"Why shouldn't I?" I asked. "If that's what you want us to call you, we'll call you."

"I know it might sound awkward at first," said Wangero.

"I'll get used to it," I said. "Ream it out again."

Well, soon we got the name out of the way. Asalamalakim had a name twice as long and three times as hard. After I tripped over it two or three times he told me just to call him Hakim-a-barber. I wanted to ask him was he a barber, but I didn't really think he was, so I didn't ask.

"You must belong to those beef-cattle peoples down the road," I said. They said "Asalamalakim" when they met you, too, but they didn't shake hands. Always too busy: feeding the cattle, fixing the fences, putting up salt-lick shelters, throwing down hay. When the white folks poisoned some of the herd the men stayed up all night with rifles in their hands. I walked a mile and a half just to see the sight.

Hakim-a-barber said, "I accept some of their doctrines, but farming and raising cattle is not my style." (They didn't tell me, and I didn't ask, whether Wangero (Dee) had really gone and married him.)

We sat down to eat and right away he said he didn't eat collards and pork was unclean. Wangero, though, went on through the chitlins and corn bread, the greens and everything else. She talked a blue streak over the sweet potatoes. Everything delighted her. Even the fact that we still used the benches her daddy made for the table when we couldn't afford to buy chairs.

"Oh, Mama!" she cried. Then turned to Hakim-a-barber. "I never knew how lovely these benches are. You can feel the rump prints," she said, running her hands underneath her and along the bench. Then she gave a sigh and her hand closed over Grandma Dee's butter dish. "That's it!" she said. "I knew there was something I wanted to ask you if I could have." She jumped up from the table and went over in the corner where the churn stood, the milk in it clabber by now. She looked at the churn and looked at it.

"This churn top is what I need," she said. "Didn't Uncle Buddy whittle it out of a tree you all used to have?"

"Yes," I said.

"Uh huh," she said happily. "And I want the dasher, too."

"Uncle Buddy whittle that, too?" asked the barber.

Dee (Wangero) looked up at me.

"Aunt Dee's first husband whittled the dash," said Maggie so low you almost couldn't hear her. "His name was Henry, but they called him Stash."

"Maggie's brain is like an elephant's," Wangero said, laughing. "I can use the churn top as a centerpiece for the alcove table," she said, sliding a plate over the churn, "and I'll think of something artistic to do with the dasher."

When she finished wrapping the dasher the handle stuck out. I took it for a moment in my hands. You didn't even have to look close to see where hands pushing the dasher up and down to make butter had left a kind of sink in the wood. In fact, there were a lot of small sinks; you could see where thumbs and fingers had sunk into the wood. It was beautiful light yellow wood, from a tree that grew in the yard where Big Dee and Stash had lived.

After dinner Dee (Wangero) went to the trunk at the foot of my bed and started rifling through it. Maggie hung back in the kitchen over the dishpan. Out came Wangero with two quilts. They had been pieced by Grandma Dee and then Big Dee and me had hung them on the quilt frames on the front porch and quilted them. One was in the Lone Star pattern. The other was Walk Around the Mountain. In both of them were scraps of dresses Grandma Dee had worn fifty and more years ago. Bits and pieces of Grandpa Jarrell's Paisley shirts. And one teeny faded blue piece, about the size of a penny matchbox, that was from Great Grandpa Ezra's uniform that he wore in the Civil War.

"Mama," Wangero said sweet as a bird. "Can I have these old quilts?"

I heard something fall in the kitchen, and a minute later the kitchen door slammed.

"Why don't you take one or two of the others?" I asked. "These old things was just done by me and Big Dee from some tops your grandma pieced before she died."

"No," said Wangero. "I don't want those. They are stitched around the borders by machine."

"That'll make them last better," I said.

"That's not the point," said Wangero. "These are all pieces of dresses Grandma used to wear. She did all this stitching by hand. Imagine!" She held the quilts securely in her arms, stroking them.

"Some of the pieces, like those lavender ones, come from old clothes her mother handed down to her," I said, moving up to touch the quilts. Dee (Wangero) moved back just enough so that I couldn't reach the quilts. They already belonged to her.

"Imagine!" she breathed again, clutching them closely to her bosom.

"The truth is," I said, "I promised to give them quilts to Maggie, for when she marries John Thomas."

She gasped like a bee had stung her.

"Maggie can't appreciate these quilts!" she said. "She'd probably be backward enough to put them to everyday use."

"I reckon she would," I said. "God knows I been saving 'em for long enough with nobody using 'em. I hope she will!" I didn't want to bring up how I had offered Dee (Wangero) a quilt when she went away to college. Then she had told me they were old-fashioned, out of style.

"But they're *priceless!*" she was saying now, furiously; for she has a temper. "Maggie would put them on the bed and in five years they'd be in rags. Less than that!"

"She can always make some more," I said. "Maggie knows how to quilt."

Dee (Wangero) looked at me with hatred. "You just will not understand. The point is these quilts, *these* quilts!"

"Well," I said, stumped. "What would *you* do with them?"

"Hang them," she said. As if that was the only thing you *could* do with quilts.

Maggie by now was standing in the door. I could almost hear the sound her feet made as they scraped over each other.

"She can have them, Mama," she said, like somebody used to never winning anything, or having anything reserved for her. "I can 'member Grandma Dee without the quilts."

I looked at her hard. She had filled her bottom lip with checkerberry snuff and it gave her face a kind of dopey, hangdog look. It was Grandma Dee and Big Dee who taught her how to quilt herself. She stood there with her scarred hands hidden in the folds of her skirt. She looked at her sister with something like fear but she wasn't mad at her. This was Maggie's portion. This was the way she knew God to work.

When I looked at her like that something hit me in the top of my head and ran down to the soles of my feet. Just like when I'm in church and the spirit of God touches me and I get happy and shout. I did something I never had done before: hugged Maggie to me, then dragged her on into the room, snatched the quilts out of Miss Wangero's hands and dumped them into Maggie's lap. Maggie just sat there on my bed with her mouth open.

"Take one or two of the others," I said to Dee.

But she turned without a word and went out to Hakim-a-barber.

"You just don't understand," she said, as Maggie and I came out to the car.

"What don't I understand?" I wanted to know.

"Your heritage," she said. And then she turned to Maggie, kissed her, and said, "You ought to try to make something of yourself, too, Maggie. It's really a new day for us. But from the way you and Mama still live you'd never know it."

She put on some sunglasses that hid everything above the tip of her nose and her chin.

Maggie smiled; maybe at the sunglasses. But a real smile, not scared. After we watched the car dust settle I asked Maggie to bring me a dip of snuff. And then the two of us sat there just enjoying, until it was time to go in the house and go to bed.

YELLOW RIBBONS

Susie Mee

HE HEARD THE ROAR of the helicopter even before the girl came running into the house. "They're here!" she screamed. "And they're flying low!"

"Not low enough to see through this haze, I betcha," he said, keeping his voice soft and calm. Lately he'd become an expert at this. It was as if he were willing himself not to fall apart. He pointed one of his crutches toward the wood cabinet that leaned against the kitchen sink. "Hand me my smokes, hon?"

But the girl was too distracted to do much more than peer out the dirty window pane. "If they spot it, we're goners. It's a Federal offense. The radio said so."

"That a fact?" Hammond's tone was somewhat sarcastic. But knowing how easy it was, all too easy, for a thirty-eight-year-old ex-roustabout to lay sarcasm on someone as young as Destry (who looked fourteen but *claimed* to be ten years older), he drew himself up short. "Relax, hon. They ain't gonna spot nothin. Not that close to the riverbank. They'll be blinded by all the reflection." He chuckled. "Anyway, I bet these small-town cops wouldn't recognize a marijuana plant if it rose up and hit 'em in the face."

She didn't bother answering. Instead she moved from the window to the door.

"Don't you be going out there, now," Hammond warned. "It'd be the same as waving a red flag." He hobbled over to get his cigarettes, then looked around for matches. "Hey."

"Hmmmmm?"

"Never mind." Pulling out the kitchen drawer, he rummaged through it. "Damn," he muttered.

"So what do we do?" she asked, gazing at him with fierce blue eyes. "Sit inside all day and roast to death? If we don't get locked up first. We should've been more careful."

"Aw, that ol' chopper'll be gone in a minute or two." Even as he spoke, the roar seemed to be growing fainter. "Sit down, hon. While we're waiting for the all-clear sign, I'll read you some Whitman." He picked up a copy of *Leaves of Grass* that he'd borrowed from the library.

"I'm tired of poetry," she said but sat anyway.

"Then I'll tell you a story. Ever read 'Jack and the Beanstalk'?" She shook her head. "Bet you did, and just don't remember. When I was a kid, I'd make my mama tell it to me over and over." Finding a kitchen match, he struck it on the sole of his shoe, lit the cigarette, and inhaled deeply. "Once upon a time, there was this here Georgia boy who was kind to *everybody*"—Hammond slapped his knee as though he were about to come up with a low joke—"including his mama, which was a good thing, too, since the two of 'em lived alone together with nothin' but an ol' spotted cow for comp'ny. Well, one Tuesday, Jack's mother told him to take that cow to Trade Day and sell her, because she'd just about quit givin milk. So he set off leading the cow down the highway. But just before he got there, a beggar man come along and offered to trade him a couple of beans for the cow. Jack just stood there. 'Now why would I be so stupid as to trade ol' Bossy here for a buncha dried-up pintos?' he asked. But the man swore up and down that if Jack planted these beans, 'the pleasures of earth would rise clear up to heaven and vice versie,' which Jack thought so much bullshit but still he couldn't help being impressed with the feller's gumption, and besides he looked like somebody who could use good luck as much as Jack could, so Jack let the man have the cow for the handful of beans. When he got home and told his mama what he'd done, she was fit to be tied! She grabbed up them beans and flung 'em ever which way. And what did Jack do? He went to bed, pulled the covers over his face and stopped up his ears to shut out her cussin'. Coupla' weeks later, he was taking a nap outside and spied this plant that had growed up. Being clean out of cigarettes, he had the notion to roll up a bunch of the leaves and smoke 'em then and there, which he did, and wellsir, that plant started shooting up to the sky barely pausing long enough for Jack to climb aboard. And *that*"—he put up a nicotine-stained finger—"is the story of the first marijuana."

There was a long pause. "What happened to Jack's daddy?" Destry asked, straining to fill in some missing gaps.

"*Daddy?*" He thought for a moment. "Disappeared. Shazam. Just like my ol' man. Leaving behind a trail of tears and heartache."

"That's a harsh judgment."

"Life is harsh, Miss Destry, which is the reason we need a beanstalk to latch on to once in a while." He cocked his head slightly. "Didn't I tell you that copter would be movin' on? I think it's probably safe to go out now."

Destry beat him to the door, and stepping off to the tiny, screened-in porch, breathed in deeply. "Still hot," she said, "but there's a breeze."

"Then catch it," Hammond grinned. "Don't let it get away."

She followed him through the thicket of pine saplings, weeds, and thorny shrubs that separated his house on Smoky Hill from the Nantooga River. Spying a blackberry bush halfway along the path, he reached in, picked off a few of the ripest, and handed them back. She must be starving, he thought, all they'd had that morning had been a cup of raisins and some stale Post Toasties that they'd eaten dry because the milk had run out. Destry had such a meager appetite that Hammond sometimes wondered if hunger wasn't the main reason for her testy moods. But he wasn't complaining. Having her around was like a gift. He suspected it wouldn't last much longer, though. He'd already heard her humming "California, Here I Come" over the kitchen sink.

SHE'D BEEN ON the same Greyhound Bus when he was returning from his latest go-round at Piedmont Hospital in Atlanta. This time he'd been outfitted with an artificial leg, though he preferred the crutches, as he kept telling the doctors over and over, finally giving up when nobody seemed to be paying attention, letting them measure his waist, his stump, bring in a physical therapist to show him how to fasten the thing on and move it forwards, backwards, praising him lavishly, like a difficult child, whenever he even halfheartedly followed instructions. He'd asked the therapist if the leg would enable him to live a normal life. The therapist nodded, then frowned. "Up to a point," he said. "Of course there will always be limitations." Limitations. Hammond repeated the word several times, wondering what to make of it. He thought of the one-legged man who'd spoken at an assembly program when he was in high school. This man, who'd been from New Jersey, had described, quite vividly, how his leg had been bitten off by a shark. Hammond couldn't remember the reason for his being invited to the school, or anything else about him. All he knew was that the man had been reappearing in his dreams recently. Always trying to chase Hammond down to tell him something, he didn't know what.

On the bus, he'd turned to the young girl who plopped down beside him. "Begging your pardon, miss, but I'm about to do something you might be too squeamish to witness."

"What's that?" She barely glanced up from the movie magazine she was rifling through.

"I'm about to remove this here artificial limb." He tapped on the polyethylene kneecap with his thumbnail.

But the girl was fascinated, especially when she found out that he'd been wounded in a mine explosion near the Cambodian border. "But I didn't lose my leg until fairly recently." He could have added that he'd lost his wife at the same time. "I mean, it was *here*, there just wasn't any feeling in it."

"Like Jon Voigt," she said, lending him her manicure scissors to snip away his pants leg. "Did you see *Coming Home?*"

"No'm, I don't get to too many movies, specially war movies."

"Oh, my lord, I couldn't live without movies!" the girl said.

"Where you headed?" Hammond asked, unfastening the leg and bending to stow it under the seat.

"California. That's where my mom is. She's a movie fan, too, just like me." The girl picked up the magazine, but threw it aside as if she preferred talking. "She went there a few months ago from West Virginia to scout out new locations, as she put it. She's a registered nurse so it's not hard to get work. Soon as she found an apartment, she called me. Said she'd help find me a job if I'd come out. She likes to brag that I was born in a movie theater, but that's not quite true." When she looked away, Hammond thought it was the end of the conversation, but then she turned back. "Mom was watching *Love with a Proper Stranger* starring Natalie Wood and Steve McQueen (both dead now, isn't that a shame?) and refused to leave until the happy ending. I was even named after a movie, but I bet you'll never guess which one."

Hammond shook his head. He was staring at her white skin.

"*Destry Rides Again.* I've never seen it, though I intend to one of these days."

"So what's your name?" Hammond asked, puzzled.

"Destry Mullins."

"Jackson Hammond." Hammond grabbed hold of her hand before she flicked it away. Part of the dark nail polish had worn off, giving her fingertips an unfinished look. "Everybody calls me Hammond. Isn't north Georgia a little out of your way?"

"Yeah, but I couldn't resist the temptation to see *Gone with the Wind* country. *Gone with the Wind*'s my all-time favorite. I've seen it sixteen times so far. Where do you live?"

"Gilead. It's our next stop."

After that, they were silent. Hammond was thinking about how much he dreaded entering his empty house. But at the same time, he didn't wish his wife back. "Treading water" was her favorite expression about him. She'd had other gripes, too. "Reading is no occupation," she'd say, referring to the library books he was always bringing home. Then he'd have to remind her how, for a whole year, he'd worked in the spinning room in the mill until finally, he just couldn't hack it anymore. "I'd soon be dead," he'd said, which was true. Most of all, she couldn't understand his anger. When one of the Church of Christ ladies had approached him holding out a bookmark with Jesus' picture on it, whining, "God loves you, son, in spite of your affliction," he'd knocked it out of her hand. "Now, there's no excuse for that," his wife had said. "No," he'd agreed, except it'd made him feel better.

Soon the bus began to approach brick warehouses, tall smokestacks, clumps of trailers with tiny dirt yards. "Doesn't look like much," Destry murmured.

"It ain't much," Hammond said, using the redneck speech that was now his stock and trade, even though he knew better, "and that's the challenge. How does a human being live here without going stark ravin' mad?" He smiled at her, feeling suddenly and unaccountably friendly. "Maybe you'd like to help me figure that out, Miss Destry." The "miss" gave a certain platonic tone to their relationship that he felt appropriate under the circumstances. He stood up to lift his small bag out of the overhead rack.

She looked at him.

"I mean, it seems only polite—after your assistance with my leg and all—to invite you to experience what a small southern town is actually like. No strings attached. Purely educational.''

Hammond could see her thinking hard. "What would your family say?"

"Nothin'. On accounta I ain't got one."

"Well, it *is* tempting. . . ."

"Chance of a lifetime," Hammond said, gathering his crutches and pulling her up. "Let's go."

They moved toward the front of the bus where the driver helped them off in spite of Hammond resisting his outstretched hand.

"Hey, wait!" Destry called out just as the bus was pulling off. "You forgot your leg!"

Hammond waved the driver on. "Reckon somebody else can get more use out of it than I can." He began hobbling away so fast that she had to run to catch up.

AT FIRST IT'D been fun camping out in the house together. It contained enough pieces of broken-down furniture, including a bedstead and cot—two items his wife had left behind—to keep them in relative comfort. But after a few weeks, Hammond began to notice Destry's restlessness, her pacing back and forth between the small rooms, so he started driving her around town on the custom-made moped that he'd bought with some of his disability money. He explained how the town used to be when he was a boy, before the river had become polluted and the woods had been cut down to build the small shotgun houses that lined the highway. He showed her the old inn that was now deserted, the town cemetery, the company store that was in the process of being torn down, the bronze doughboy in the plaza, festooned with yellow ribbons, now frayed and tattered. "The Mideast crisis has been over a long time," he'd said to the cop who'd stopped him from tearing them off. "It's not over till it's over," the cop said. "Know what I mean?" He only knew that the sight of them made him flinch.

Then he led her up to the dam, and beyond, to the path that ran along back of his house. It was when the two of them were standing on the riverbank, throwing stones across, that Hammond got the idea about growing marijuana.

"Lookit. We'll clear out a little patch right here. Don't nobody come down this way no more, so they'll never find it."

"Who's 'they'?"

"Ohhhh, the GBI agents, the state patrol, the local police . . . nobody to be serious about. One of the patients at the hospital give me some seeds as a farewell present and told me just how to make 'em sprout."

So that very day, Hammond borrowed a neighbor's small tractor and began "bush hogging" a little slope rising about seven feet from the water's edge. Urging the tractor through ground knotted with grasses and vines, Hammond felt better than he had in months, years even. Especially when he felt Destry's eyes on him. "You're a hard worker, aren't you?"

"When I set my mind to it."

"Is that what you did in Vietnam? Set your mind?"

But he didn't answer. There were lots of things he couldn't tell her. At least not just yet.

Finished with the work, he took a tiny roach out of his pants pocket and lit it. "My last one," he said, handing it over. She held it gingerly, inhaled, and immediately broke into a racking cough. "Ain't you never smoked pot before, Miss Destry?" And she had to admit that she hadn't. Soon the two of them were laughing and foraging through the weeds together, Hammond beating them down with one of his crutches. Afterward they lay facing the sun, Destry's head on his chest, him smoothing out her silky brown hair with his long fingers.

But back inside the house, he could feel the pent-up tension and knew he had to do something to relieve it. So after supper—pork 'n beans and corn bread cooked in his mama's old iron skillet—he threw a pillow at her, and she retaliated until they were both breathless and ready to call it quits. Then she retired, as usual, to the back room, and he to the cot, where he lay listening to her breathing until finally drifting off himself. He wondered about her. He wondered why she never wrote her mother or got a letter back. When he asked about this, she replied that she *had* telephoned once from a pay phone, while he was at the library. "Mom understands my need for independence," she said, and added, "just as I understand yours."

Next day, she announced over instant coffee that maybe she should be on her way, but he begged her to stay at least until the marijuana got ripe enough to sample. "The song of songs, dream of dreams, Miss Destry. You can't miss that." He tried to keep the desperation out of his voice, though whether he succeeded or not, he couldn't tell, especially when she said okay with such a lack of enthusiasm.

He usually spent mornings reading, while Destry slept or puttered about the house. He'd been working his way through the entire Harvard Classics, including Emerson, whom he particularly liked. Hammond had read "The Poet," and had been struck by Emerson's description of genius as "the activity that repairs the decays of things." "Gilead could sure use some genius," he thought. "Hell, the whole nation could use it." He felt this especially when hearing national leaders mouth off on television, their shallow opportunism barely concealed. "OPPORTUN-ISM = SHIT," he wrote in his notebook, wishing that he had Emerson's way with words.

Then he'd discovered Whitman, who'd hit him, he told Destry, "like a thunderbolt." When she asked why, he explained that he'd never known anybody who had such a knowledge of death. "Except myself," he added softly. He'd read "When Lilacs Last in the Dooryard Bloom'd" so many times that he knew parts of it by heart.

In the afternoons they rode around the country looking at old houses. He tried to explain to Destry that most antebellum plantations were not made of red brick and didn't have white columns in front. "The only columns in Gilead," he said, "are no more than ten years old. They belong to a dentist, a supervisor in the dye plant, and a former mayor."

But she wanted to see them anyway. As part of her education, he took her to the industrial waste-fill out near Trash Hollow. For several minutes, they stood in front of the barbed-wire fence surrounding the area. "This is the real cemetery," she murmured.

At night, they generally watched television, or he rented a video for the VCR, also purchased with disability money. "What the hell," he'd told his wife who'd considered it an extravagance, "if I'm immobile, I might as well have something to look at."

Destry would watch anything, but he was more picky. If he got bored, he would simply go into the kitchen and read. He tried to interest her in books, but after a few pages, she would lose patience, and start roaming around the room (though he did catch her once with his volume of Whitman, which she handed back as though it was tainted). He wondered if she might not be dyslexic—he'd read about the problem from a book that happened to be lying on the librarian's desk when he was checking out. Her verbal connections often surprised him—the comparison of cricket sounds to men "rubbing their whiskers" or description of sunflowers as "pinwheels."

ONE MORNING, DESTRY shook him violently awake. "Are you trying to tell me," she said, her voice shrill, "with all this talk of pollution, that the world's not a fit place to live in anymore? Because that's what I had a dream about last night! Excuse me, I mean a nightmare."

He raised up on his elbows, rubbing his eyes with one hand. "That's not what I meant exactly. Sure we got pollution. But in other ways, things is better . . . I guess. Mill kids go to college, become big executives, fly all over the world. Used to be everybody remained in their own little pigeonholes. Whatever you's born as was what you stayed."

"Why have you?"

"Why have I what?"

"Stayed?"

He thought for a minute. "Cause I hate all that upward mobility. If it was mere ambition, I wouldn't care. But most of it's greed."

She looked down on him. "Maybe you're just lazy."

"That could be," he said, closing his eyes. "Yeah, that's a definite possibility."

"And another thing. I haven't seen one house that even vaguely resembles Tara."

"The marijuana'll take care of that, hon. After you smoke a few roaches, you'll have Rhett Butlers coming out of the kazoo."

She smiled, then made a face at him. "Jackson Hammond, sometimes you talk so ugly you make me sick. I think you do it on purpose."

"You think so?"

"I do. . . ."

THAT WAS SEVERAL months ago, and now they were heading toward the river to harvest the first of the tiny crop. They had almost reached the spot when they heard a stirring from the pine thicket, together with a loud yelping. Hammond stopped in his tracks and waited while a young man dressed in camouflaged fatigues and holding a large dog on a tight leash stepped forward. "You Jackson Hammond?" the man asked, his gaze darting back and forth between Hammond and Destry. Under the man's left arm was a long package that Hammond surmised to be either a bazooka or some kind of blowtorch. If it hadn't been for Destry, he might have put up his hands then and there; instead, he decided to brazen it out.

"Yessir. I am. And I swear to tell the truth, the whole truth, and nothing but the truth, so help me God."

The young man frowned and glanced at Destry.

"He's making a joke," she said, and moved toward him as if trying to bridge the gap between them. "I'm Destry Mullins, Mr. Hammond's . . . boarder. Did anyone ever tell you that you look exactly like Charlie Sheen? Especially in that uniform." Her voice was so frankly admiring that the young man ducked his head in embarrassment.

"Sorry. I don't know any Sheens. Does he live around here?"

Destry couldn't help laughing. "You're cute." She turned to Hammond. "Isn't he cute?"

Ignoring her, Hammond held his ground. "What can I do for you?"

"Does this belong to you?" The boy held out the long package.

Hammond took it, and as he began tearing the paper away, saw immediately what it was. "Aw, shit," he groaned. "My leg. Where'd you get it?"

"The Greyhound people dropped it off at the police station. Somebody said it might be yours." Hammond struck the ground with it. "Hush! Stop it now!" the young man shouted, trying to calm the dog that took the gesture as a cue to start barking and pulling on his leash.

"What's the matter with him?" Destry asked.

"He must sniff pot around here. Didn't you hear the helicopter? There're two divisions combing this area." He pointed to his armband. "I'm with the purple division. Sorry about your leg, Mr. Hammond."

"It's okay, son. Amazing what people can do without." Hammond looked at the boy more closely. "What's your name?"

"Jim Bethune."

"You Gene Bethune's brother?"

"Yessir. He was killed at Bien Hoa."

Hammond looked away. "Good boy, Gene."

"Yessir."

"What are you doing with that uniform on, Bethune?"

He drew himself up as if about to salute. "I'm in the reserves, sir. Hoping to see some action one of these days." Taking off his cap, he showed them the yellow ribbon attached to the side.

Hammond stared at him. "Bethune, you're a goddamn fool. . . ."

The boy shifted. "You oughta watch your language, especially around . . ."

"She's heard worse. This is serious, Bethune."

"I'm a Christian, sir, and I don't appreciate God's name being taken in vain."

"Nothing is in vain, Bethune." He held up his crutches. "Don't people learn *anything?*"

"The Lord giveth, the Lord taketh away," Bethune said.

Hammond was so angry, he spat into the weeds. "What kind of horseshit is that?"

Bethune let the dog spring forward a few feet. "Sir, I don't want to remind you again that you are in the presence of a lady. . . ."

"That's right, Hammond," Destry said. "Curb your tongue."

"My tongue is definitely *not* what needs curbing here, Miss Destry, so if you don't mind, just butt out." He turned to the boy. "You, too, Bethune, you stupid asshole. And take that hound with you."

Bethune stood there for a moment, as if unsure about what to do. The dog was pulling toward the river and Hammond was pointing toward the road. At that moment, Destry stepped forward.

"Come on, Bethune, I'll walk back with you."

"Well, ma'am . . ."

"Let's go."

Hammond watched her link an arm through Bethune's and lead him away. Scowling, he continued on toward the river. For a while, he simply sat there in the shade of several pines, sniffing resin and listening to the sound of bobwhites. He expected her to reappear any moment, but she didn't. He considered throwing the leg into the river. But he didn't want it coming back to haunt him for the second time. How, in Christ's name, could he get rid of it? It wouldn't burn, it was too big for the garbage, maybe he could take it down to Trade Day and swap it, like the cow, for something useful. Then he got the idea of burying it. In a way, it would be like burying his old two-legged self. But he should wait until Destry returned. He shouldn't do anything that significant by himself. Hammond began ripping off leaves, wrapping them in newspaper that he'd stuck in his back pocket. When he was finished, he decided to crumple a few and smoke them, even if they weren't quite dry enough. When he got back to the house, he would lay the rest out on aluminum foil and stick them in the oven. He lay there inhaling and watching the sun's reflection on the opposite bank. But this time he didn't climb onto any beanstalk. This time he found himself thinking about Destry and wondering what she and Bethune were doing together, or at least what *she* was doing to him, since Bethune seemed incapable of much advanced thinking. Finally he shut his eyes.

By the time he heard the voice, it was almost dark. Or was it voices? Opening one eye, he looked straight into Destry's face bending over him. "Alone?" he asked, glancing around suspiciously.

"Of course. You intend sleeping here?"

"Might. Got everything I need."

She stood up and towered over him. "Everything?"

Was she vexing him on purpose? "I need your help, Miss Destry."

"With what? And stop calling me 'miss.'"

"I got to bury this here leg."

"Why?"

"To rid myself of it once and for all."

"But aren't you going to try and wear it?"

"Naw."

Crossing her arms, she looked down at him defiantly. "I'm not going to help you do that. You called Bethune a fool. Well, you're a fool too, Hammond. Maybe an even bigger one." Turning, she marched back toward the house.

BY THE TIME Hammond swung the screened door open and eased himself inside, she had almost finished packing the second of her two suitcases.

"Going somewhere?"

"Yep. California. Where I started out for in the first place."

"What about Tara?"

"As far as I can tell, Tara doesn't exist. Maybe it never did. Neither does the beanstalk. You taught me that and I thank you for it." Closing the suitcase, she snapped both locks. "Well, Hammond," she put out a hand. "Take care of yourself."

His first urge was to beg her not to leave. But what gave a one-legged man the right? The second was to say, I'll miss you. But the closest he could come was, "Things won't be the same around here without you, Miss Destry." He knew how stupid and worn-out the words sounded, though it hardly mattered because she seemed not to have heard.

"Don't call me 'miss' I told you."

Just then an ugly thought streaked through Hammond's mind, and he couldn't suppress it. "You're not running away with that Bethune, are you?"

She looked at him and shook her head. "Are you crazy? I took him off so we wouldn't end up in jail."

"That doesn't answer my question."

She shrugged. "I'd just soon run away with Rambo."

"I thought you liked him. You said he looked like Charlie Sheen."

"For your information, Charlie Sheen's a wimp." Picking up both suitcases, she headed for the door. When she turned back, Hammond had to admire her timing. "And Sylvester Stallone makes me puke."

HE KNEW SHE must hear the put-put-puttering noise behind her, in spite of the fact that she kept walking.

"Destry!" He slowed down. There was a long silence. "I don't want you to go."

Finally she stopped. "I have to, Hammond."

Another pause. "Yeah."

"But you could come with me." He searched her face to see if she was serious. "Maybe by the time we get there, you'll have figured out what you want to do. Because you have to do something. The Vietnam War's been over a long time. And you have to learn to wear that leg . . ." He started to protest. ". . . unless you want to stay a cripple."

"But I told you . . ."

"I know, I know . . . the greed . . . the pollution . . ."

"You think I'm just making excuses?"

"A little . . ."

"Well . . ." He tried to smile.

She looked at her watch. "You have time to get your things if you hurry. I'll wait for you at the bus station." Picking her suitcases back up, she started walking even faster.

He pulled up alongside. "Destry?" Again she halted and stood waiting. "What would your mother think if you suddenly showed up with me in tow?"

"Nothing."

"Come on, what would she say?"

Her chin went up. "Nothing."

"*Nothin'?*"

"That's right." She put her hands on her hips. "On accounta, I ain't got no mama," she drawled in imitation of Hammond. "You've heard of orphans? Well, you're looking at one."

Hammond's mouth went slack. "Why did you lie?"

She shrugged. "Everybody's entitled to a family. Even if it's made-up."

"Was everything else made-up, too?"

"No . . . I don't know. My real name's June Mullens." The swaggering tone dropped away. "Tell you one thing, though. I do like Jon Voigt. I may even *love* Jon Voigt. Will you come?"

For a second he stared at her, then lowered his eyes. "I got a confession, too," he said, making her wait another minute before he could get it out. "I was never in Vietnam in my whole goddam life."

"But your leg . . ."

"That happened earlier. A car accident." He paused to let her digest this.

"Why did *you* lie?"

"Because . . . it was a few notches down from anything heroic. Reckon we're both liars," he said finally.

"Storytellers," she said, amending the obvious.

Susie Mee • 352

"Tell me something." He drew back to look at her full-face. "Do two storytellers complement each other? Or cancel each other out?"

"It depends."

"On what?"

"Their stories." Putting a curled fist up to her lips, she blew a rat-a-tat-tat imitation-bugle call and began to recite—to Hammond's astonishment—the words of Whitman:

> I saw battle-corpses, myriads of them,
> And the white skeletons of young men, I saw them,
> I saw the debris and debris of all the slain soldiers of the war,
> But I saw they were not as was thought. . . .

Washed in the Blood

WASHED IN THE BLOOD

HEAVEN AND HELLFIRE may have faded and dimmed for some postmodern Yankees, but not for southerners. Words such as guilt, retribution, vexation, the smite of God, iniquities—all found in the Book of Job—have been part of the southern vocabulary since Civil War days, and even before. Along with the language comes a strong belief in a miraculous cause-and-effect. In a Biblical universe, everything is possible, and everything, even a gesture, can have repercussions.

Baptist, Methodist, Presbyterian, Church of Christ, Church of God, Holiness, Episcopal, and maybe Catholic is the religious lineup that exists in virtually every hamlet or town below the Mason-Dixon line. In these communities—and in spite of the powerful TV ministries that are piped into living rooms—many southerners still manage to make their way to Sunday church no matter what they might have been up to the night before. Religion not only lightens vast tunnels of loneliness, but orders one's life in a way that opposes the horrible chaos of sudden illness and death.

Lee Smith's "Tongues of Fire" provides an overview of southern religion—running the gamut from subdued respectable Protestantism to the slightly suspect, and certainly more noisy, charismatic. The protagonist starts as the typical southern child, who early on becomes indoctrinated into the faith: beginning with Sunday school, and then continuing with Bible School (where she colors in the twelve disciples), and church (where she sits beside her grandparents in the family pew, kept quiet by the promise of her favorite lemon meringue pie afterward). Later, however, she veers off the "straight and narrow" by indulging in an interest—like the southern interest in anything grotesque or outlawed—in the more aberrant forms of testifying and speaking in tongues.

Now people were jumping up all over the church, singing out and yelling, including Tammy's mother, who opened her mouth and screamed out in a language like none I had ever heard, yet a language which I felt I knew intimately, somehow, better than I knew English. It was *my language,* I was sure of it, and I think I might have passed out right then from the shock of sheer recognition except that Tammy grabbed my arm and yanked like crazy.

"Get ready!" she said.

"What?"

"She's fixing to fall," Tammy said just as her mother pitched backwards in a dead faint. We caught her and laid her out on the pew. She came to later, when church was over, and then we all had dinner on the ground out back of the church. Later I sneaked back into the fellowship hall on the pretext of going to the bathroom, so I could examine the pool in greater detail. It was in a little anteroom off the fellowship hall, right up against the double doors that led from the sanctuary, now closed. It was a plain old wading pool, just as I'd thought, covered now by a blue tarpaulin. I pulled back the tarp. The water was pretty cold. A red plastic barrette floated jauntily in the middle of the pool. I looked at it for a long time. I knew I would have to get in that water sooner or later. I would have to get saved.

When the child begins to grow up and leave the exotic aspects of religion behind, these still haunt her on occasion—as if amid all the angelic, the pure, the white, the bleached, the cloroxed, the albinoed, a little color is now and then desirable, even necessary.

THE APPROPRIATELY NAMED Shannon Pearl of "Gospel Song"— who seems to have been struck with all of God's terrible whiteness in one fierce blow—could have used some color. An albino by birth, Shannon is ferocious in spirit and ferociously ugly in body, an outcast, a holy monster who might have sprung directly from the pages of Flannery O'Connor rather than those of Dorothy Allison: "No amount of Jesus' grace would make her even marginally acceptable, and people had been known to suddenly lose their lunch from the sight of the clammy sheen of her skin, her skull showing blue-white through the thin, colorless hair and those watery pink eyes flicking back and forth, drifting in and out of focus"; she is also one mean little girl.

Shannon Pearl's main attraction for the narrator is that her father books gospel singers while her mother sews for them—embroiders "gilt-rendered scenes" on their costumes, knots tassels on their silk blouses. The narrator craves gospel the way some people crave grease or red clay: she prays—nay, pleads—to croon and mournfully howl like the Carter Family or Little Pammie Gleason or the Tuckerton Family do, or failing this, to simply be swept away by the music:

> How could I live with myself? How could God stand me? Was this why Jesus wouldn't speak to my heart? The music washed over me . . . *SOFTLY AND TENDERLY.* The music was a river trying to wash me clean. I sobbed and dug my heels into the dirt, drunk on grief and that pure, pure voice. It didn't matter then if it was whiskey backstage or tongue kissing in the dressing room.

Washed in the Blood · 359

Whatever it took to make that juice was necessary, was fine. I wiped by eyes and swore out loud. Get those boys another bottle, I said. Find that girl a hardheaded husband. But goddamn, get them to make that music. Make that music! Lord, make me drunk on that music.

The next Sunday I went off with Shannon and the Pearls for another gospel drive.

The epiphany at the end is one that James Joyce might have envied—although it is pure Dixie, containing the ingredients of melodrama and tragic release that we have seen before in writers like Glasgow and O'Connor.

ALL MELODRAMA HAS been gently expunged from "A New Life," a story that seems chillingly up-to-date in its religious implications. In the New South, splinter groups have increasingly split from larger congregations (there've even been splinter groups within splinter groups). Much of this splintering seems to hinge on the Fundamentalist issue, on the flinty, relentless, and unrelenting idea of what religion should be, which sometimes veers terrifyingly close to religious fascism.

With enormous subtlety and only a few brushstrokes of detail, Mary Ward Brown is able to suggest this religious obstinacy, as well as the small, sleepy Bible Belt town, the house with its lovely garden, and most of all, the widow, Elizabeth North, who cannot grieve for her deceased husband. She is courted by members of a newly organized religious group who call themselves the Keepers of the Vineyard—which sounds, it is noted wryly, like the name of a rock band.

Agreeing to attend one of their meetings, she is horrified to find herself drawn into a prayer circle in which everyone prays aloud.

Too soon, she hears Paul's voice beside her, charged with emotion. He's praying about the sin of pride in his life, but she can't pay attention because she will be next. Heavy galloping hoofbeats seem to have taken the place of her heart.

When Paul is through, she says nothing. *I pass* flashes through her mind, but she doesn't say it. She is unable to decide on, much less utter, a word. Her hands are wet with cold perspiration. She tries to withdraw them, but Paul on one side and the young woman on the other hold on tight. Fans hum back and forth as her silence stretches out.

At last someone starts to pray out of turn, and the circle is mended. As the prayers move back toward Steve, she gives a sigh of relief and tries, without being obvious, to change her position on the floor.

Steve gives a new directive. "We'll now lift up to God those with special needs tonight."

He allows them to think for a moment, then leads off. "I lift up Jane, in the medical center for diagnosis," he says. "Her tests begin in the morning."

They pray in silence for Jane, for someone in the midst of divorce, for a man who's lost his job. An unnamed friend with an unidentified problem is lifted up.

Louise clears her throat for attention, then hesitates before speaking out. When she does, her voice is girlish and sweet as usual.

"I lift up Elizabeth," she says.

Certain of their own relationship with God, the Vineyard members display little sensitivity towards Elizabeth's feelings. Like hard light on sun-baked southern soil, the denouement points up the cracks in such certainty.

Tongues of Fire

Lee Smith

THE YEAR I WAS thirteen—1957—my father had a nervous break-down, my brother had a wreck, and I started speaking in tongues. The nervous breakdown had been going on for a long time before I knew anything about it. Then one day that fall, Mama took me downtown in the car to get some Baskin-Robbins ice cream, something she never did, and while we were sitting on the curly chairs facing each other across the little white table, Mama took a deep breath, licked her red lipstick, leaned forward in a very significant way, and said, "Karen, you may have noticed that your father is *not himself* lately."

Not himself! Who was he, then? What did she mean? But I had that feeling you get in your stomach when something really important happens. I knew this was a big deal.

Mama looked all around, as if for spies. She waited until the ice cream man went through the swinging pink doors, into the back of his shop.

"Karen," she said, so low I could hardly hear her, "your father is having a nervous breakdown."

"He is?" I said stupidly.

The ice cream man came back.

"Sssh," Mama said. She caught my eye and nodded gravely, once. "Don't eat that ice cream so fast, honey," she said a minute later. "It'll give you a headache."

And this was the only time she ever mentioned my father's nervous breakdown out loud, in her whole life. The older kids already knew, it turned out. Everybody had wanted to keep it from me, the baby. But then the family doctor said Mama *ought* to tell me, so she did. But she did not elaborate, then or ever, and in retrospect I am really surprised that she ever told me at all. Mama grew up in Birmingham, so she talked in a very southern voice and wore spectator heels and linen dresses that buttoned up the front and required a great deal of ironing by Missie, the maid. Mama's name was Dee Rose. She said that when she married Daddy and came up here to the wilds of north Alabama to live, it was like moving to Siberia. It was like moving to Outer Mongolia, she said. Mama's two specialties were Rising to the Occasion and Rising Above It All, whatever "it" happened to be. Mama believed that if you can't say something nice, say nothing at all. If you don't discuss something, it doesn't exist. This is the way our family handled all of its problems, such as my father's quarrel with my Uncle Dick or my sister's promiscuity or my brother's drinking.

Mama had long red fingernails and shiny yellow hair which she wore in a bubble cut. She looked like a movie star. Mama drank a lot of gin and tonics and sometimes she would start on them early, before five o'clock. She'd wink at Daddy and say, "Pour me one, honey, it's already dark underneath the house." Still, Mama had very rigid ideas, as I was to learn, about many things. Her ideas about nervous breakdowns were:

1. The husband *should not* have a nervous breakdown.
2. Nobody can mention the nervous breakdown. It is shameful.

3. The children must *behave* at all times during the nervous breakdown.

4. The family must keep up appearances at all costs. *Nobody should know.*

Mama and I finished our ice cream and she drove us home in the white Cadillac, and as soon as we got there I went up in my treehouse to think about Daddy's breakdown. I knew it was true. *So this is it,* I thought. This had been it all along. This explained the way my father's eye twitched and watered now, behind his gold-rimmed glasses. My father's eyes were deep-set and sort of mournful at best, even before the twitch. They were an odd, arresting shade of very pale blue which I have never seen since, except in my sister Ashley. Ashley was beautiful, and my father was considered to be very good-looking, I knew that, yet he had always been too slow-moving and thoughtful for me. I would have preferred a more military model, a snappy go-getter of a dad. My dad looked like a professor at the college, which he was not. Instead he ran a printing company with my Uncle Dick, until their quarrel. Now he ran it by himself—or rather his secretary, Mrs. Eunice Merriman, ran it mostly by herself during the time he had his nervous breakdown. Mrs. Eunice Merriman was a large, imposing woman with her pale blond hair swept up in a beehive hairdo as smooth and hard as a helmet. She wore glasses with harlequin frames. Mrs. Merriman reminded me of some warlike figure from Norse mythology. She was not truly fierce, however, except in her devotion to my father, who spent more and more time lying on the daybed upstairs in his study, holding books or magazines in his hands but not reading them, looking out the bay window, at the mountains across the river. What was he thinking about?

"Oh *honestly,* Karen!" my mother exploded when I asked her this question. My mother was much more interested, on the day I asked her, in the more immediate question of whether or not I had been invited to join the Sub-Deb Club. The answer was yes.

But there was no answer to the question of what my father might be thinking about. I knew that he had wanted to be a writer in his youth. I knew that he had been the protégé of some old poet or other down at the university in Tuscaloosa, that he had written a novel which was never published, that he had gone to the Pacific Theater in the War. I had always imagined the Pacific Theater as a literal theater, somewhat like the ornate Rialto in Birmingham with its organ that rose up and down mechanically from the orchestra pit, its gold-leaf balconies, its chandelier as big as a Chevrolet. In this theater, my father might have watched such movies as *Sands of Iwo Jima* or *To Hell and Back*. Now it occurred to me, for the first time, that he might have witnessed horrors. Horrors! Sara Nell Buie, at school, swore that *her* father had five Japanese ears in a cigar box from the Philippines. Perhaps my father had seen horrors too great to be borne. Perhaps he too had ears.

But this did not seem likely, to look at him. It seemed more like mononucleosis to me. He was just *lying on the daybed.* Now he'd gotten his days and nights turned around so that he had to take sleeping tablets; he went to the printing company for only an hour or two each day. He rallied briefly at gin-and-tonic time, but his conversation tended to lapse in the middle of itself during dinner, and frequently he left the table early. My mother rose above these occasions in the way she had been trained to do as a girl in Birmingham, in the way she was training Ashley and me to do: she talked incessantly, about anything that entered her head, to fill the void. This was another of Mama's rules:

A lady never lets a silence fall.

Perhaps the most exact analysis of my father's nervous breakdown was provided by Missie, one day when I was up in the treehouse and she was hanging out laundry on the line almost directly below me, talking to the Gardeners' maid from next door. "You mean Missa Graffenreid?" Missie said. "He have *lost his starch,* is all. He be getting it back directly."

In the meantime, Mama seemed to grow in her vivacity, in her busyness, taking up the slack. Luckily my sister Ashley was a senior at Lorton Hall that year, so this necessitated a lot of conferences and visits to colleges. The guidance counselor at Lorton Hall wanted Ashley to go to Bryn Mawr, up North, but after the visit to Bryn Mawr my mother returned with her lips pressed tight together in a little red bow. "Those girls were *not ladies*," she reported to us all, and Bryn Mawr was never mentioned again except by Ashley, later, in fits of anger at the way her life turned out. The choices narrowed to Converse College in Spartanburg, South Carolina; Meredith College in Raleigh, North Carolina; Sophie Newcomb in New Orleans; and Sweet Briar, in Virginia. My mama was dead set on Sweet Briar.

So Mama and Ashley were very busy with college visits and with all the other activities of Ashley's senior year at Lorton Hall. There were countless dresses to buy, parties to give and go to. I remember one Saturday that fall when Ashley had a Coke party in the back garden, for the senior girls and their mothers. Cokes and finger sandwiches were served. Missie had made the finger sandwiches the day before and put them on big silver trays, covered by damp tea towels. I watched the party from the window of my room upstairs, which gave me a terrific view of the back garden and the red and yellow fall leaves and flowers, and the girls and their mothers like chrysanthemums themselves. I watched them from my window—just as my father watched them, I suppose, from his.

My mother loved to shop, serve on committees, go to club meetings, and entertain. (Probably she should have been running Graffenreid Printing Co. all along—I see this now—but of course such an idea would not have entered anyone's head at the time.) Mama ran the Flower Guild of the Methodist church, which we attended every Sunday morning, minus my father. She was the recording secretary of the Ladies' Auxiliary, which literally *ran the town* as far as I could see; she was a staunch member of the Garden Club and the Bluebird Book Club.

Her bridge club met every Thursday at noon for lunch and bridge, rotating houses. This bridge club went on for years and years beyond my childhood, until its members began to die or move to Florida. It fascinated me. I loved those summer Thursdays when I was out of school and the bridge club came to our house—the fresh flowers, the silver, the pink cloths on the bridge tables, which were set up for the occasion in the Florida room, the way Mama's dressing room smelled as she dressed, that wonderful mixture of loose powder (she used a big lavender puff) and cigarette smoke (Salems) and Chanel No. 5. The whole bridge club dressed to the hilt. They wore hats, patent-leather shoes, and dresses of silk shantung. The food my mama and Missie gave them was wonderful—is still, to this day, my very idea of elegance, even though it is not a menu I'd ever duplicate; and it was clear to me, even then, that the way these ladies were was a way I'd never be.

But on those Thursdays, I'd sit at the top of the stairs, peering through the banisters into the Florida room, where they lunched in impossible elegance, and I got to eat everything they did, from my own plate which Missie had fixed specially for me: a pink molded salad that melted on the tongue, asparagus-cheese soufflé, and something called Chicken Crunch that involved mushroom soup, chicken, Chinese noodles, pecans, and Lord knows what else. All of Mama's bridge-lunch recipes required gelatin or mushroom soup or pecans. This was Lady Food.

So—it was the year that Mama was lunching, Daddy was lying on the daybed, and Ashley was Being a Senior. My brother Paul had already gone away to college, to Washington and Lee up in Virginia. At that time in my life, I knew Paul only by sight. He was incredibly old. Nice, but very old and very busy, riding around in cars full of other boys, dashing off here and there when he was home, which was seldom. He used to tell me knock-knock jokes, and come up behind me and buckle my knees. I thought Paul's degree of bustle and zip was *promising*, though. I certainly hoped he would be more active than Daddy. But who could tell? I rarely saw him.

I rarely saw *anybody* in my family, or so I felt. I floated through it all like a dandelion puff on the air, like a wisp of smoke, a ghost. During the year of my father's nervous breakdown, I became invisible in my family. But I should admit that even before my invisibility I was scarcely noticeable, a thin girl, slight, brown-haired and brown-eyed, *undeveloped* (as Mrs. Black put it delicately in health class). There was no sign of a breast anyplace on my chest even though some other girls my age wore B and even C cups, I saw them in gym. I had gone down to Sears on the bus by myself the previous summer and bought myself two training bras, just so I'd have them, but my mother had never mentioned this subject to me at all, of course. And even after I got the training bras, I remained—I felt—still ugly, and still invisible in the midst of my gorgeous family.

Perhaps it is not surprising that I turned to God.

I had always been *interested* in religion, anyway. When I was a little girl, my favorite part of the summer was Vacation Bible School, with the red Kool-Aid in the little Dixie cups and the Lorna Doone cookies at break. I loved to color in the twelve disciples. I loved to make lanyards. I loved to sing "You Are My Sunshine" and "Red and Yellow, Black and White, They Are Precious in His Sight." I loved to hold hands with Alice Field, who was my best friend for years and years until her family moved to Little Rock, Arkansas. I loved Mrs. Treble Roach, the teacher of Vacation Bible School, a plump soft woman like a beanbag chair, who hugged us all the time. Mrs. Treble Roach gave us gold stars when we were good, and I was *very* good. I got hundreds of gold stars over the years and I believe I still have them upstairs someplace in a jewelry box, like ears.

I had always liked church too, although it was less fun. I associated church with my grandparents, since we sat with them every Sunday, third pew from the back on the left-hand side of the little stone Methodist church which my grandfather had attended all his life, which my grandmother had attended since their marriage fifty years before. Usually my mother went to church too; sometimes Ashley went to church, under duress ever since she became an atheist in tenth grade, influenced by an English teacher who was clearly *not a lady;* my father attended only on

Easter. Frankly, I liked those Sundays when none of them made it, when Mama just dropped me off in front of the church and I went in all alone, clutching my quarter for the collection plate, to sit with my grandparents. Even though I was invisible in my own family, my grandparents noticed me plenty. I was their good, good little girl . . . certainly, I felt, their favorite. I did everything I could to ensure that this was true.

My grandmother had wispy blue hair and a whole lot of earrings and brooches that matched. She was the author of four books of poems which Daddy had printed up for her at the printing company. She suffered from colitis, and was ill a lot. One thing you never wanted to do with Grandmother was ask her how she felt—she'd *tell* you, gross details you didn't want to know. My mama, of course, was entirely above this kind of thing, never referring to her own or anybody else's body in any way. My grandfather wore navy blue suits to church with red suspenders underneath. He was a boxy little man who ran the bus station and had a watch that could tell you the time in Paris, London, and Tokyo. I coveted this watch and had already asked Grandaddy to leave it to me when he died, a request that seemed to startle him.

After church, I'd walk up the street with my grandparents to their house on the corner across from the Baptist church and eat lunch, which frequently ended with lemon meringue pie, my favorite. I kept a close eye out the window for Baptists, whose service was dismissed half an hour later than ours. There were so many Baptists that it took them longer to do everything. In pretty weather, I sat out on the front porch so that I could see the Baptists more clearly. They wore loud suits, and made more noise in general than the quiet Methodists.

Our church had only forty-two members and about twenty of them, like my grandparents, were so old as to be almost dead already. I was not even looking forward to joining the MYF, which I'd be eligible for next year, because it had only eight members, two of them definite nerds. All they did was collect food for the poor at Thanksgiving, and stuff like that. The BTU, on the other hand, did great stuff such as have progressive dinners, Sweetheart Banquets, and go on trips to Gulf Shores. The BTU was a much snappier outfit than the MYF, but I knew better than to ask to join it. My mother had already explained to me the social ranking of the churches: Methodist at the top, attended by doctors and lawyers and other "nice" families; Presbyterian slightly down the scale, attended by store owners; then the vigorous Baptists; then the Church of Christ, who thought they were the only real church in town and said so. They said everybody else in town was going to hell except for them. They had hundreds of members. And then, of course, at the *very bottom* of the church scale were those little churches out in the surrounding county, some of them recognizable denominations (Primitive Baptist) and some of them not (Church of the Nazarene, Tar River Holiness) where people were reputed to yell out, fall down in fits, and throw their babies. I didn't know what this *meant,* exactly, but I knew I'd love to see it, for it promised drama far beyond the dull responsive readings of the Methodists and their rote mumbling of the Nicene Creed.

Anyway, I had been sitting on my grandparents' front porch for years eating pie and envying the Baptists, waiting without much hope to be seized by God for His heavenly purpose, bent to His will, as in *God's Girl,* my favorite book—a biography of Joan of Arc.

So far, nothing doing.

But then, that fall of Daddy's nervous breakdown, the Methodist church was visited by an unusually charismatic young preacher named Johnny Rock Malone while Mr. Treble Roach, our own preacher, was down at Duke having a hernia operation. I was late to church that day and arrived all by myself, after the service had already started. The congregation was on its feet singing "I Come to the Garden Alone," one of my favorite hymns. One unfamiliar voice led all the rest. I slipped in next to Grandaddy, found the right page in the hymnal, and craned my neck around Miss Eulalie Butters's big black hat to see who was up there singing so nice. It looked like an angel to me—probably the angel Gabriel, because of his curly blond hair. And he was so *young*—just out of seminary, somebody said after the service. It was a warm fall Sunday, and rays of colored light shot through the stained-glass windows at the side of the church, to glance off Johnny Rock Malone's pale face. "He *walks* with me, and He *talks* with me," we sang. My heart started beating double time. Johnny Rock Malone stretched out his long thin arms and spread his long white fingers. "Beloved," he said, curling his fingers, "let us pray." But I never closed my eyes that day, staring instead at the play of light on Johnny Rock Malone's fair face. It was almost like a kaleidoscope. Then the round rosy window behind him, behind the altar, began to *pulse* with light, to glow with light, now brighter now not, like a neon sign. I got the message. I was no dummy. In a way, I had been waiting all my life for this to happen.

The most notable thing about me as a child—before I got religious, I mean—was my obsessive reading. I had always been an inveterate reader of the sort who hides underneath the covers with a flashlight and reads *all night long*. But I did not read casually, or for mere entertainment, or for information. What I wanted was to feel all wild and trembly inside, an effect first produced by *The Secret Garden*, which I'd read maybe twenty times. And the Rev. Johnny Rock Malone looked exactly the way I had always pictured Colin! In fact, listening to him preach, I felt exactly the way I felt when I read *The Secret Garden*, just exactly.

Other books which had affected me strongly were *Little Women*, especially the part where Beth dies, and *Gone with the Wind*, especially the part where Melanie dies. I had long hoped for a wasting disease, such as leukemia, to test my mettle. I also loved *Marjorie Morningstar, A Tree Grows in Brooklyn, Heidi*, and books like *Dear and Glorious Physician, The Shoes of the Fisherman, Christy*, and anything at all about horses and saints. I had read all the Black Stallion books, of course, as well as all the Marguerite Henry books. But my all-time favorite was *God's Girl*, especially the frontispiece illustration picturing Joan as she knelt and "prayed without ceasing for guidance from God," whose face was depicted overhead, in a thunderstorm. Not only did I love Joan of Arc, I wanted to *be* her.

The only man I had ever loved more than Colin of *The Secret Garden*, to date, was Johnny Tremaine, from Esther Forbes's book of that title. I used to wish that it was *me*—not Johnny Tremaine—who'd had the hot silver spilled on my hand. I would have suffered anything (everything) for Johnny Tremaine.

But on that fateful Sunday morning, Johnny Rock Malone eclipsed both Colin and Johnny Tremaine in my affections. It was a wipeout. I felt as fluttery and wild as could be. In fact I felt too crazy to pay attention to the sermon which Johnny Rock Malone was, by then, almost finished with. I tried to concentrate, but my mind was whirling. The colors from the windows seemed to deepen and swirl. And then, suddenly, I heard him loud and clear, reading from *Revelations:* "And I saw a great white throne, and Him that sat on it, from whose face the earth and heaven fled away; and there was found no place for them. And I saw the dead, small and great, stand before God, and the books were opened . . . and whosoever was not found written in the book of life was cast into the lake of fire."

I can't remember much about what happened after that. I got to shake hands with him as we left the church, and I was surprised to find that his hand was cool, not burning hot—and, though bony, somehow as soft as a girl's. I looked hard at Johnny Rock Malone as he stood in front of our pretty little church, shaking hands. He was on his way to someplace else, over in Mississippi. We would never see him again. *I* would never see him again. And yet somehow I felt exhilarated and *satisfied,* in a way. I can't explain it. Back at my grandparents' house, I couldn't even eat any lemon meringue pie. I felt shaky and hot, like I might be getting a virus. I went home early.

My father was upstairs in his study, door closed. Nobody else was home. I wandered the house. Then I sat in the Florida room for a while, staring out at the day. After a while, I picked up my mother's sewing basket from the coffee table, got a needle and threaded it with blue thread, and sewed all the fingers of my left hand together, through the cuticle. Then I held out my hand and admired it, wishing desperately for my best friend Alice Field, of Little Rock. I had no best friend now, nobody to show my amazing hand to. Weird little Edwin Lee lived right across the street, but it was inconceivable that I would show *him,* the nerd, such a hand as this. So I showed it to nobody. I left it sewed up until Mama's white Cadillac pulled in the driveway, and then I cut the thread between my fingers and pulled it all out.

It was about this time too that I began to pray a lot (*without ceasing* was my intention) and set little fires all around the neighborhood. These fires were nothing much. I'd usually take some shredded newspapers or some Kleenex, find a few sticks, and they'd burn themselves out in a matter of minutes. I made a fire in my treehouse, in our garage, in the sink, in the basement, on Mrs. Butters's back patio, on Mr. and Mrs. Harold Castle's front porch, and in little Charlotte Lee's playhouse. Here I went too far, singeing off the hair of her Barbie doll. She never could figure out how it happened.

I entertained visions of being a girl evangelist, of appearing with Billy Graham on television, of traveling throughout Mississippi with Johnny Rock Malone. I'd be followed everywhere I went by a little band of my faithful. I made a small fire in the bed of Ashley's new boyfriend's pickup truck while he and my sister were in the den petting and watching the *Hit Parade*. They didn't have any idea that I was outside in the night, watching them through the window, making a fire in the truck. They all thought I was in bed!

Although I was praying a lot, my prayers were usually specific, as opposed to *without ceasing*. For instance I'd tell one friend I'd go shopping with her, and then something I really wanted to do would come up, and I'd call back and say I couldn't come after all, that my grandmother had died, and then I would go to my room and fling myself to the floor and pray without ceasing that my lie would not be found out, and that my grandmother would not really die. I made big deals with God—*if* He would make sure I got away with it this time, I would talk to Edwin Lee for five minutes on the bus, three days in a row, or I would clean out my closet. He did His part; I did mine. I grew in power every day.

I remember so well that important Friday when I was supposed to spend the night with Margaret Applewhite. Now Margaret Applewhite was totally boring, in my opinion—my only rival in the annual spelling bee (she won in third, I won in fourth and fifth, she beat me out in sixth with *catarrh,* which still rankled). Margaret Applewhite wore a training bra too. Our mothers, who played bridge together, encouraged our friendship. I'd rather do just about *anything,* even watch Kate Smith on TV, than spend time with boring Margaret Applewhite. Still, earlier that week when she'd called and invited me, I couldn't for the life of me think of any good reason to say no, so I'd said yes. Then that Friday right before sixth period, Tammy Lester came up to my locker popping her gum (against the rules: we were not allowed to chew gum in school) and—wonder of wonders—asked me to come home with her after school that very day and spend the night.

Tammy Lester! Shunned by Sub-Debs, sent to Detention, noticed by older boys. I couldn't believe it. I admired Tammy Lester more than any other girl in my entire class, I'd watched her from afar the way I had watched the Baptists. Tammy Lester lived out in the county someplace (in a trailer, it was rumored), she was driven in to school each morning by one or the other of her wild older brothers in a red pickup truck (these brothers slicked back their hair with grease, they wore their cigarette packs rolled up in the sleeves of their T-shirts), and best of all, she was missing a tooth right in front, and nobody had taken her to the dentist yet to get it fixed. The missing tooth gave Tammy a devilish, jaunty look. Also, as I would learn later, she could whistle through this hole, and spit twenty feet.

Her invitation was offhand. "You wanna come home with me today?" she asked, in a manner that implied she didn't give a hoot whether I did nor not. "Buddy's got to come into town tomorrow morning anyway, so he could bring you back."

"All right," I said, trying to sound casual.

"I'll meet you out front when the bell rings." Tammy flashed me her quick dark grin. She popped her gum, and was gone.

I didn't hesitate for a minute. I stopped Margaret Applewhite on her way to health class. "Listen," I said in a rush, "I'm so sorry I can't come spend the night with you, but my mother is having an emergency hysterectomy today, so I have to go straight home and help out." I had just learned about hysterectomies, from a medical book in the library.

Margaret's boring brown eyes widened. "Is she going to be all right?"

I sucked in my breath dramatically and looked brave. "We hope so," I said. "They think they can get it all."

Margaret walked into health. I sank back against the mustard yellow tile walls as, suddenly, it hit me: Margaret's mother knew my mother! What if Margaret's mother called my mother, and Mama found out? She'd be furious, not only because of the lie but because of the nature of the lie—Mama would *die* before she'd ever mention something like a hysterectomy. Mama referred to everything below the belt as "down there," an area she dealt with darkly, indirectly, and only when necessary. "Trixie Vopel is in the hospital for tests," she might say. "She's been having trouble *down there.*" *Down there* was a foreign country, like Africa or Nicaragua.

What to do? I wrote myself an excuse from gym, signed my mother's name, turned it in, and then went to the infirmary, where I lay down on a hard white cot and prayed without ceasing for upwards of an hour. I promised a lot: If Mama did not find out, I would sit with Lurice May at lunch on Monday (a dirty fat girl who kept her head wrapped up in a scarf and was rumored to have lice), I would be nice to Edwin Lee three times for fifteen minutes each, I would clean out under my bed, I would give back the perfume and the ankle bracelet I had stolen from Ashley, and I would put two dollars of my saved-up baby-sitting money in the collection plate at church on Sunday. It was the best I could do. Then I called my mother from the infirmary phone, and to my surprise, she said, "Oh, of course," in a distracted way when I asked if I could spend the night with Tammy Lester. She did not even ask what Tammy's father did.

Then *"Karen,"* she said in a pointed way that meant this was what she was *really* interested in, "do you have any idea where your sister is right now?"

"What?" I couldn't even remember *who* my sister was, right now.

"*Ashley,*" Mama said. "The school called and asked if she was sick. Apparently she just never showed up at school today."

"I'll bet they had some secret senior thing," I said.

"Oh." Mama sounded relieved. "Well, maybe so. Now who is it you're spending the night with?" she asked again, and I told her. "And what did you say her father does?"

"Lawyer," I said.

SPENDING THE NIGHT with Tammy Lester was the high point of my whole life up to that time. She did *not* live in a trailer, as rumored, but in an old unpainted farmhouse with two boarded-up windows, settled unevenly onto cinder-block footings. A mangy dog lay up under the house. Chickens roamed the property. The porch sagged. Wispy ancient curtains blew out eerily at the upstairs windows. The whole yard was strewn with parts of things—cars, stoves, bedsprings, unimaginable machine parts rusting among the weeds. I loved it. Tammy led me everywhere and showed me everything: her secret place, a tent of willows, down by the creek; the grave of her favorite dog, Buster, and the collar he had worn; on old chicken house that her brothers had helped her make into a playhouse; a haunted shack down the road; the old Packard out back that you could get in and pretend you were taking a trip. "Now we're in Nevada," Tammy said, shifting gears. "Now we're in the Grand Canyon. Now we're in the middle of the desert. It's hot as hell out here, ain't it?"

I agreed.

At suppertime, Tammy and I sat on folding chairs pulled up to the slick oilcloth-covered table, beneath a bare hanging lightbulb. Her brothers had disappeared. Tammy seemed to be cooking our supper; she was heating up Dinty Moore stew straight out of the can.

"Where's your daddy?" I asked.

"Oh, he's out West on a pipeline," she said, vastly unconcerned.

"Where's your mama?" I said. I had seen her come in from work earlier that afternoon, a pudgy, pale redheaded woman who drove a light blue car that looked like it would soon join the others in the backyard.

"I reckon she's reading her Bible," Tammy said as if this were a perfectly ordinary thing to be doing on a Friday night at gin-and-tonic time. "She'll eat after while."

Tammy put half of the Dinty Moore stew into a chipped red bowl and gave it to me. It was delicious, lots better than Lady Food. She ate hers right out of the saucepan. "Want to split a beer?" she said, and I said sure, and she got us one—a Pabst Blue Ribbon—out of the icebox. Of course I had never tasted beer before. But I thought it was great.

That night, I told Tammy about my father's nervous breakdown, and she told me that her oldest brother had gone to jail for stealing an outboard motor. She also told me about the lady down the road who had chopped off her husband's hands with an ax while he was "laying up drunk." I told her that I was pretty sure God had singled me out for a purpose which he had not yet revealed, and Tammy nodded and said her mother had been singled out too. I sat right up in bed. "What do you mean?" I asked.

"Well, she's real religious," Tammy said, "which is why she don't get along with Daddy too good." I nodded. I had already figured out that Daddy must be the dark handsome one that all the children took after. "And she was a preacher's daughter too, see, so she's been doing it all her life."

"Doing what?" I asked into the dark.

"Oh, talking in tongues of fire," Tammy said matter-of-factly, and a total thrill crept over me, the way I had always wanted to feel. I had hit pay dirt at last.

"I used to get embarrassed, but now I don't pay her much mind," Tammy said.

"Listen," I said sincerely. "I would give *anything* to have a mother like that."

Tammy whistled derisively through the hole in her teeth.

But eventually, because I was already so good at collective bargaining, we struck a deal: I would get to go to church with Tammy and her mother, the very next Sunday if possible, and in return, I would take

Tammy to the country club. (I could take her when Mama wasn't there; I was allowed to sign for things.) Tammy and I stayed up talking nearly all night long. She was even more fascinating than I'd thought. She had breasts, she knew how to drive a car, and she was part Cherokee. Toward morning, we cut our fingers with a kitchen knife and swore to be best friends forever.

The next day, her brother Mike drove me into town at about one o'clock. He had to see a man about a car. He smoked cigarettes all the way, and scowled at everything. He didn't say a word to me. I thought he was wonderful.

I arrived home just in time to intercept the delivery boy from the florist's. "I'll take those in," I said, and pinched the card which said, "For Dee Rose. Get well soon. Best wishes from Lydia and Lou Apple-white." I left the flowers on the doorstep, where they would create a little mystery later on, when Mama found them, and went upstairs to my room and prayed without ceasing, a prayer of thanksgiving for the special favors I felt He had granted me lately. Then before long I fell asleep, even as a huge argument raged all over the house, upstairs, and down, between Mama and my sister Ashley who had *just come in,* having stayed out all day and all night long.

"If a girl loses her reputation, she has lost *everything,*" Mama said. "She has lost her Most Precious Possession."

"So what? So what?" Ashley screamed. "All you care about is appearances. Who cares what I do, in this screwed-up family? Who really cares?"

It went on and on, while I melted down and down into my pink piqué comforter, hearing them but not really hearing them, dreaming instead of the lumpy sour bed out at Tammy's farm, of the moonlight on the wispy graying curtains at her window, of a life so hard and flinty that it might erupt at any moment into tongues of fire.

NOT ONLY WAS the fight over with by Sunday morning, but it was so far over with as not to have happened at all. I came in the kitchen late, to find Mama and Ashley still in their bathrobes, eating sticky buns and reading the funnies. It looked like nobody would be available to drive me to church. Clearly, both Ashley and Mama had Risen Above It All— Mama, to the extent that she was virtually levitating as the day wore on, hovering a few feet off the floor in her Sunday seersucker suit as she exhorted us all to hurry, hurry, hurry. Our reservations were for one o'clock. The whole family was going out for brunch at the country club.

Daddy was going too.

I still wonder what she said to him to get him up and dressed and out of there. I know it was the kind of thing that meant a lot to her—a public act, an event that meant *See, here is our whole happy family out together at the country club; see, we are a perfectly normal family; see, there is nothing wrong with us at all.* And I know that Daddy loved her.

Our table overlooked the first tee of the golf course. Our waiter, Louis, had known Daddy ever since he was a child. Daddy ordered a martini. Mama ordered a gin and tonic. Ashley ordered a lemon Coke. I ordered lemonade. Mama was so vivacious that she almost gave off light. Her eyes sparkled, her hair shone, her red lipstick glistened. She and Ashley were discussing which schools her fellow seniors hoped to attend, and why. Ashley was very animated too. Watching them, I suddenly realized how much Ashley was like Mama. Ashley laughed and gestured with her pretty hands. I watched her carefully. I knew Mama thought Ashley had lost her most precious possession (things were different *down there),* yet she didn't look any different to me. She wore a hot pink sheath dress and pearls. She looked terrific.

I turned my attention to Daddy, curiously, because I felt all of a sudden that I had not really seen him for years and years. He might as well have been off on a pipeline, as far as I was concerned. Our drinks arrived, and Daddy sipped at his martini. He perked up. He looked weird, though. His eyes were sunken in his head, like the limestone caves above the Tombigbee River. His skin was as white and dry as a piece of Mama's stationery. My father bought all his clothes in New York so they were always quite elegant, but now they hung on him like on a coat rack.

How much weight had he lost? Twenty pounds? Thirty? We ordered lunch. Daddy ordered another martini.

Now he was getting entirely too perky, he moved his hands too much as he explained to Ashley the theory behind some battle in some war. He stopped talking only long enough to stand up and shake hands with the friends who came by our table to speak to him, friends who had not seen him for months and months. He didn't touch his food. Underneath my navy blue dress with the sailor collar, I was sweating, in spite of my mother's pronouncement:

Horses sweat, men perspire, and women glow.

I could feel it trickling down my sides. I wondered if, as I grew up, this would become an uncontrollable problem, whether I would have to wear dress shields. We all ordered baked Alaska, the chef's specialty, for dessert. My mother smiled and smiled. I was invisible. When the baked Alaska arrived, borne proudly to our table by Louis, nobody could put out the flames. Louis blew and blew. Other waiters ran over, beating at it with linen napkins. My mother laughed merrily. "For goodness' sakes!" she said. My daddy looked stricken. Finally they got it out and we all ate some, except for Daddy.

Gazing past my family to the golfers out on the grass beyond us, I had a sudden inspiration. I knew what to do. I emerged from invisibility long enough to say, "Hey, Daddy, let's go out and putt," and he put his napkin promptly on the table and stood right up. "Sure thing, honey," he said, sounding for all the world like my own daddy. He smiled at me. I took his hand, remembering then who I had been before the nervous breakdown: Daddy's little girl. We went down the stairs, past the snack bar, and out to the putting green at the side of the building.

My dad was a good golfer. I was not bad myself. We shared a putter from the Pro Shop. We started off and soon it was clear that we were having a great time, that this was a good idea. The country club loomed massively behind us. The emerald grass, clipped and even, stretched out on three sides in front of us, as far as we could see, ending finally in a stand of trees here, a rolling hill there. This expanse of grass, dotted with pastel golfers, was both comforting and exhilarating. It was a nine-hole putting green. On the seventh hole, we were tied, if you figured in the handicap that my father had given himself. I went first, overshooting on my second stroke, sinking it with a really long shot on my third. I looked back over at Daddy to make sure he had seen my putt, but clearly he had not. He was staring out over the grass toward the horizon, beyond the hill.

"Your turn!" I called out briskly, tossing him the putter.

What happened next was awful.

In one terrible second, my father turned to me, face slack, mouth agape, then fell to his knees on the putting green, cowering, hands over his face. The putter landed on the grass beside him. He was crying. I didn't know what to do. I just stood there, and then suddenly the putting green was full of people—the pro, Bob White, in his jacket with his name on it, helping Daddy to his feet; our dentist, Dr. Reap, holding him by the other elbow as they walked him to our white Cadillac which Mama had driven around to pick us up in. Ashley cried all the way home. So did Daddy.

It was not until that day that I realized that the nervous breakdown was real, that Daddy was really sick.

I ran upstairs and prayed without ceasing for a solid hour, by the clock, that Daddy would get well and that we would all be *all right,* for I had come to realize somehow, during the course of that afternoon, that we might *not* be. We might never be all right again.

AT LEAST I had a New Best Friend. I banished all memory of Alice Field, without remorse. Tammy Lester and I became, for the rest of that spring, inseparable. The first time I brought her to my house, I did it without asking: I didn't want to give Mama a chance to say no. And although we had not discussed it, Tammy showed up dressed more like a town girl than I had ever seen her—a plaid skirt, a white blouse, loafers, her dark hair pulled back and up into a cheerful ponytail. She could have been a cheerleader. She could have been a member of the Sub-Deb Club. No one could have ever guessed what she had in her pocket—a pack of Kents and a stolen kidney stone once removed from her neighbor, Mrs. Gillespie, who had kept it in a jar on her mantel. But even though Tammy looked so nice, Mama was giving her the third degree, "How many brothers and sisters did you say you had?" and "Where was your Mama *from?*"

This interrogation took place upstairs in Mama's dressing room. Suddenly, to everyone's surprise, Daddy lurched in to fill the doorway and say, "Leave those little girls alone, Dee Rose, you've got your hands full already," and oddly enough, Mama *did* leave us alone then. She didn't say another word about it at the time, turning back to her nails, or even later, as spring progressed and Ashley's increasing absences and moodiness became more of a problem. Before long, Daddy refused to join us even for dinner. Mama *did* have her hands full. If I could occupy myself, so much the better.

I WILL NEVER forget the first time I was allowed to go to church with Tammy and her mother. I had spent the night out at the farm, and in the morning I was awake long before it was time to leave. I dressed carefully, in the yellow dress and jacket Mama had ordered for me only a couple of months before from Rich's in Atlanta. It was already getting too small. Tammy and her mother both looked at my outfit with some astonishment. They didn't have any particular church clothes, it turned out. At least, they didn't have any church clothes as fancy as these. Tammy wore a black dress which was much too old for her, clearly a hand-me-down from someplace, and her mother wore the same formless slacks and untucked shirt she always wore. I could never tell any of her clothes apart. For breakfast that morning, we had Hi-Ho cakes, which we ate directly from their cellophane wrappers, and Dr. Peppers. Then we went out and got into their old blue car, which threatened not to start. *Oh no!* I found myself suddenly, terribly upset. I realized then how very much I was dying to hear Tammy's mother speak in tongues of fire, a notion that intrigued me more and more the better I got to know her, because usually she *didn't speak at all*. Never! Her pale gray eyes were fixed on distance, the way my daddy's had been that day at the golf course. The engine coughed and spluttered, died. Then finally Tammy's mother suggested that Tammy and I should push her down the muddy rutted driveway and she'd pop the clutch. I had never heard of such a thing. In my family, a man in a uniform, from a garage, came to start cars that wouldn't start. Still, we pushed. It started. I got mud all over the bottom of my yellow dress.

Which didn't matter at all, I saw as soon as we got to the church. There were old men in overalls, younger men in coveralls with their names stitched on their pockets, girls in jeans, boys in jeans. The men stood around by their trucks in the parking lot, smoking cigarettes. The women went on in, carrying food. Tammy's mother had a big bag of Fritos. The church itself was a square cinder-block building painted white. It looked like a convenience store. Its windows were made of the kind of frosted glass you find in rest rooms. The only way you could tell it was a church was from the hand-lettered sign on the door, MARANATHA APOSTOLIC CHURCH ALL COME IN. I asked Tammy what "Maranatha" meant and she said she didn't know. Tammy would rather be at *my* house on Sundays, so she could look through Mama's jewelry, eat lemon me-ringue pie at my grandmother's, and stare at Baptists. She had made this plain. I'd rather be at her house, in general; she'd rather be at mine. We walked into her church.

"This way." Tammy was pulling my arm. Men sat on the right-hand side of the church. Women sat on the left. There was no music, no Miss Eugenia Little at the organ. Men and women sat still, staring straight ahead, the children sprinkled among them like tiny grave adults. The pews were handmade, hard, like benches, with high, straight backs. There was no altar, only the huge wooden cross at the front of the church, dwarfing everything, and a curtain, like a shower curtain, pulled closed behind it. A huge Bible stood open on a lectern with a big jug (of what? water?) beside it. More people came in. My heart was beating a mile a

minute. The light that came in through the frosted-glass windows produced a soft, diffuse glow throughout the church. Tammy popped her gum. Tammy's mother's eyes were already closed. Her pale eyelashes fluttered. Her mouth was moving and she swayed slightly, back and forth from the waist up. Nothing else was happening.

Then four women, all of them big and tough-looking, went forward and simply started singing "Rock of Ages," without any warning or any introduction at all. I almost jumped right out of my seat. Some of the congregation joined in, some did not. It seemed to be optional. Tammy's mother did not sing. She did not open her eyes either. The women's voices were high, mournful, seeming to linger in the air long after they were done. "Praise God!" "Yes, Jesus!" At the conclusion of the song, people throughout the church started shouting. I craned my neck around to see who was doing this, but the back of the pew was too high, blocking a lot of my view. They sang again. I had never heard any music like this music, music without any words at all, or maybe it was music without any music, it seemed to pierce my brain. I was sweating under my arms again.

The preacher, Mr. Looney, entered unobtrusively from the side during the singing. Initially, Mr. Looney was a disappointment. He was small and nondescript. He looked like George Gobel. Tammy had told me he was a security guard at the paper mill during the week. He spoke in a monotone with a hick accent. As he led us all in prayer—a prayer that seemed to go on forever, including everybody in the church by name— my mind wandered back to a time when I was little and our whole family had gone to Gulf Shores for a vacation, and Ashley and Paul were there too, and all of us worked and worked, covering Daddy up with sand, and Mama wore a sailor hat. By the end of the prayer, I was crying, and Mr. Looney had changed his delivery, his voice getting stronger and more rhythmical as he went into his message for the day. This message was pretty simple, one I had heard before. God's wrath is awful. Hell is real and lasts forever. It is not enough to have good intentions. The road to Hell is paved with those. It is not enough to do good works, such as taking care of the sick and giving to the poor. God will see right through you. The only way you can get to Heaven is by turning over your whole will and your whole mind to Jesus Christ, being baptized in the name of the Father, Son, and Holy Ghost, and born again in Glory.

"Does sprinkling count?" I whispered to Tammy. I had been sprinkled in the Methodist church.

"No," she whispered back.

Mr. Looney went on and on, falling into chant now, catching up his sentences with an "Ah!" at the end of each line. People were yelling out. And then came, finally, the invitational, "Just as I am, without one plea, but that Thy blood was shed for me, O Lamb of God, I come, I come!"

The stolid-looking young woman sitting two seats over from us surprised me by starting to mumble suddenly, then she screamed out, then she rushed forward, right into Mr. Looney's arms.

I twisted my head around to see what would happen next. Mr. Looney blessed her and said that she would "pass through to Jesus" by and by.

"What does he mean, 'pass through to Jesus'?" I was still whispering, but I might as well have been speaking aloud; there was so much commotion now that nobody else could have heard me.

Tammy jerked her head toward the front of the church. "Through them curtains, I reckon," she said.

"What's back there?" I asked, and Tammy said it was a swimming pool that people got baptized in.

And sure enough, it was not long before Mr. Looney pulled back the curtains to reveal a kind of big sliding glass door cut in the wall, with a large wading pool right beyond it, the kind I had seen in the Sears catalog. Mr. Looney pulled the heavy young woman through the curtains and hauled her over the edge of the pool. The water reached up to about midthigh on both of them. I couldn't believe they would just walk into the water like that, wearing all their clothes, wearing their *shoes!* Mr. Looney pulled back the woman's long hair and grasped it firmly. Her face was as blank and solid as a potato. "In the name of the Father and the Son and the Holy Ghost!" Mr. Looney yelled, and dunked her all the way under, backwards. Although she held her nose, she came up sputtering.

Now people were jumping up all over the church, singing out and yelling, including Tammy's mother, who opened her mouth and screamed out in a language like none I had ever heard, yet a language which I felt I knew intimately, somehow, better than I knew English. It was *my language,* I was sure of it, and I think I might have passed out right then from the shock of sheer recognition except that Tammy grabbed my arm and yanked like crazy.

"Get ready!" she said.

"What?"

"She's fixing to fall," Tammy said just as her mother pitched backwards in a dead faint. We caught her and laid her out on the pew. She came to later, when church was over, and then we all had dinner on the ground out back of the church. Later I sneaked back into the fellowship hall on the pretext of going to the bathroom, so I could examine the pool in greater detail. It was in a little anteroom off the fellowship hall, right up against the double doors that led from the sanctuary, now closed. It was a plain old wading pool, just as I'd thought, covered now by a blue tarpaulin. I pulled back the tarp. The water was pretty cold. A red plastic barrette floated jauntily in the middle of the pool. I looked at it for a long time. I knew I would have to get in that water sooner or later. I would have to get saved.

I was so moved by the whole experience that I might have actually broken through my invisible shield to tell Daddy about it, or even Ashley, but Mama met me at the door that afternoon with an ashen face and, for once, no makeup.

"Where in the world have you all *been?*" she shrilled. "I've been trying to call you all afternoon."

"We ate lunch out at the church," I said. "They do that." Out of the corner of my eye, I watched Tammy and her mother pull away in the battered blue car and wished I were with them, anywhere but here. I didn't want to know whatever Mama had to say next. In that split second, several possibilities raced through my mind:

1. Grandmother really *has* died.
2. Ashley is pregnant.
3. Ashley has eloped.
4. Daddy has killed himself.

But I was completely surprised by what came next.

"Your brother has been in the most terrible wreck," Mama said, "up in Virginia. He's in a coma, and they don't know if he'll make it or not."

PAUL HAD BEEN drunk, of course. Drunk, or he might not have lived at all, somebody said later, but I don't know whether that was true or not. I think it is something people say after wrecks, whenever there's been drinking. He had been driving back to W&L from Randolph-Macon, where he was dating a girl. This girl wrote Mama a long, emotional letter on pink stationery with a burgundy monogram. Paul was taken by ambulance from the small hospital in Lexington, Virginia, to the University of Virginia hospital in Charlottesville, one of the best hospitals in the world. This is what everybody told me. Mama went up there immediately. Her younger sister, my Aunt Liddie, came to stay with us while she was gone.

Aunt Liddie had always been referred to in our family as "flighty." Aunt Liddie "went off on tangents," it was said. I wasn't sure what this meant. Still, I was glad to see her when she arrived, with five matching suitcases full of beautiful clothes and her Pekingese named Chow Mein. Back in Birmingham she was a Kelly girl, so it was easy for her to leave her job and come to us. The very first night she arrived, Liddie got me to come out on the back steps with her. She sat very close to me in the warm spring night and squeezed both my hands. "I look on this as a wonderful opportunity for you and me to get to know each other better," Aunt Liddie said. "I want you to tell me *everything*."

But I would tell her nothing, as things turned out. This was to be our closest moment. The very next week, Liddie started dating Mr. Hudson Bell, a young lawyer she met by chance in the bank. Immediately, Liddie and Hudson Bell were *in love,* and Ashley and I were free—within the bounds of reason—to come and go as we pleased. Aunt Liddie asked no questions. Missie cooked the meals.

This was just as well with me, for I had serious business to tend to.

I knew it was up to me to bring Paul out of that coma. I would pray without ceasing, and Tammy would help me. The first week, we prayed without ceasing only after school and on the weekend. Paul was no better, Mama reported from Charlottesville. The second week, I gave up sitting on soft chairs and eating chocolate. I paid so much attention to the unfortunate Lurice May that she began avoiding me. Paul had moved his foot, Mama said. I doubled my efforts, giving up also Cokes and sleeping in bed. (I had to sleep flat on the floor.) Also, I prayed without ceasing all during math class. I wouldn't even answer the teacher, Mrs. Lemon, when she called on me. She sent me to Guidance because of it. During this week, I began to suspect that perhaps Tammy was not praying as much as she was supposed to, not keeping up her end of the deal. Still, I was too busy to care. I gave up hot water; I had to take cold showers now.

The third weekend of Mama's absence and Paul's coma, I spent Saturday night with Tammy, and that Sunday morning, at Tammy's church, I got saved.

When Mr. Looney issued his plea, I felt that he was talking right to me. "With every head bowed and every eye closed," he said, "I want you to look into your hearts and minds this morning. Have you got problems, brother? Have you got problems, sister? Well, give them up!

Give them over to the Lord Jesus Christ. If his shoulders are big enough to *bear the cross,* they are big enough to take on your little problems, beloved. Turn them over to him. He will help you now in this life, here in this vale of tears. And He will give you Heaven Everlasting as a door prize. Think about it, beloved. Do you want to burn in Hell forever, at the Devil's barbecue? Or do you want to lie in banks of flowers, listening to that heavenly choir?''

I felt a burning, stabbing sensation in my chest and stomach—something like heartburn, something like the hand of God. The idea of turning it all over to Him was certainly appealing at this point. Another week of prayer, and I'd flunk math for sure. The choir sang, "Softly and tenderly, Jesus is calling, calling for you and for me." Beside me, Tammy's mama was starting to mumble and moan.

Mr. Looney said, "Perhaps there is one among you who feels that his sin is too great to bear, but no sin is too black for the heavenly laundry of Jesus Christ, He will turn you as white as snow, as white as the driven snow, hallelujah!'' Mr. Looney reached back and pulled the curtains open, so we could all see the pool. Tammy's mama leaped up and called out in her strangely familiar language. Mr. Looney went on, "Perhaps there is a child among you who hears our message this morning, who is ready now for Salvation. Why, a little child can go to Hell, the same as you and me! A little child can burn to a crisp. But it is also true that a little child can come to God—right now, right this minute, this very morning. God don't check your ID, children. God will check your souls." "Come home, come home," they sang.

Before I even knew it, I was up there, and we had passed through those curtains, and I was standing in the water with my full blue skirt floating out around me like a lily pad. Then he was saying the words, shouting them out, and whispering to me, "Hold your nose," which I did, and he pushed me under backwards, holding me tightly with his other hand so that I felt supported, secure, even at the very moment of immersion. It was like being dipped by the big boys at ballroom dancing, only not as scary. I came up wet and saved, and stood at the side of the pool while Mr. Looney baptized Eric Blankenship, a big gawky nineteen-year-old who came running and sobbing up the aisle just as Mr. Looney got finished with me. Eric Blankenship was confessing to all his sins, nonstop, throughout his baptism. His sins were a whole lot more interesting than mine, involving things he'd done with his girlfriend, and I strained to hear them as I stood there, but I could not, because of all the noise in the church.

And then it was over and everyone crowded forward to hug us, including Tammy. But even in that moment of hugging Tammy, who of course had been baptized for years and years, I saw something new in her eyes. Somehow, now, there was a difference between us, where before there had been none. But I was wet and freezing, busy accepting the congratulations of the faithful, so I didn't have time to think any more about it then. Tammy gave me her sweater and they drove me home, where Aunt Liddie looked at me in a very fishy way when I walked in the door.

"I just got baptized," I said, and she said, "Oh," and then she went out to lunch with Hudson Bell, who came up the front walk not a minute behind me, sparing me further explanations.

Aunt Liddie came back from that lunch engaged, with a huge square-cut diamond. Nobody mentioned my baptism.

But the very next night, right after supper, Mama called to say that Paul was fine. All of a sudden, he had turned to the night nurse and asked for a cheeseburger. There seemed to be no brain damage at all except that he had some trouble remembering things, which was to be expected. He would have to stay in the hospital for several more weeks, but he would recover completely. He would be just fine.

I burst into tears of joy. I knew I had done it all. And for the first time, I realized what an effort it had been. The first thing I did was go into the kitchen and fix myself a milk shake, with Hershey's syrup. And my bed felt so good that night, after the weeks on the floor. I intended to pray without ceasing that very night, a prayer of thanksgiving for Paul's delivery, but I fell asleep instantly.

When Mama came back, I hoped she would be so busy that my baptism would be overlooked completely, but this was not the case. Aunt Liddie told her, after all.

"Karen," was Mama's reaction, "I am *shocked!* We are not the kind of family that goes out in the county and immerses ourselves in water. I can't imagine what you were thinking of," Mama said.

I looked out the window at Mama's blooming roses. It was two weeks before the end of school, before Ashley's graduation.

"Well, *what?*" Mama asked. She was peering at me closely, more closely than she had looked at me in years.

"Why did you do it?" Mama asked. She lit a cigarette.

I didn't say a thing.

"Karen," Mama said. "I asked you a question." She blew a smoke ring.

I looked at the roses. "I wanted to be saved," I said.

Mama's lips went into that little red bow. "I see," she said.

So later, that next weekend when she refused to let me spend the night out at Tammy's, I did the only thing I could: I lied and said I was going to spend the night with Sara Ruth Johnson, and then prayed without ceasing that I would not be found out. Since it was senior prom weekend and Mama was to be in charge of the decorations and also a chaperone, I felt fairly certain I'd get away with it. But when the time came for the invitational that Sunday morning in the Maranatha Church, I simply could not resist. I pushed back Tammy's restraining hand, rushed forward, and rededicated my life.

"I don't think you're supposed to rededicate your life right after you just dedicated it," Tammy whispered to me later, but I didn't care. I was wet and holy. If I had committed some breach of heavenly etiquette, surely Mr. Looney would tell me. But he did not. We didn't stay for dinner on the ground that day either. As soon as Tammy's mother came to, they drove me straight home, and neither of them said much.

Mama's Cadillac was parked in the drive.

So I went around to the back of the house and tiptoed in through the laundry room door, carrying my shoes. But Mama was waiting for me. She stood by the ironing board, smoking a cigarette. She looked at me, narrowing her eyes.

"Don't drip on the kitchen floor, Missie just mopped it yesterday," she said.

I climbed up the back stairs to my room.

The next weekend, I had to go to Ashley's graduation and to the baccalaureate sermon on Sunday morning in the Confederate Chapel at Lorton Hall. I sat between my grandparents. My Aunt Liddie was there too, with her fiancé. My daddy did not come. I wore a dressy white dress with a little bolero jacket and patent leather shoes with Cuban heels— my first high heels. I felt precarious and old, grown-up and somehow sinful, and longed for the high hard pews of the Maranatha Church and the piercing, keening voices of the women singers.

But I never attended the Maranatha Church again. As soon as my school was over, I was sent away to Camp Allegheny in West Virginia for two months—the maximum stay. I didn't want to go, even though this meant that I would finally have a chance to learn horseback riding, but I had no choice in the matter. Mama made this clear. It was to separate me from Tammy, whom Mama had labeled a Terrible Influence.

"And by the way," Mama said brightly, "Margaret Applewhite will be going to Camp Allegheny too!" Oh, I could see right through Mama. But I couldn't do anything about it. Camp started June 6, so I didn't have time to pray for a change in my fate. She sprang it on me. Instead, I cried without ceasing all that long day before they put me and my trunk, along with Margaret Applewhite and her trunk, on the train. I tried and tried to call Tammy to tell her good-bye, but a recorded message said that her line had been disconnected. (This had happened several times before, whenever her mama couldn't pay the bill.) My father would be going away too, to Shepherd Pratt Hospital in Baltimore, Maryland, and Ashley was going to Europe.

Sitting glumly by Mama at the train station, I tried to pray but could not. Instead, I remembered a game we used to play when I was real little, Statues. In Statues, one person grabs you by the hand and swings you around and around and then lets you go, and whatever position you land in, you have to freeze like that until everybody else is thrown. The person who lands in the best position wins. But what I remembered was that scary moment of being flung wildly out into the world screaming, to land however I hit, and I felt like this was happening to us all.

TO MY SURPRISE, I loved camp. Camp Allegheny was an old camp, with rough-hewn wooden buildings that seemed to grow right out of the deep woods surrounding them. Girls had been carving their initials in the railings outside the dining hall for years and years. It was a tradition. I loved to run my fingers over these initials, imagining these girls—M.H., 1948; J.B., 1953; N.M., 1935. Some of the initials were very old. These girls were grown up by now. Some of them were probably dead. This gave me an enormous thrill, as did all the other traditions at Camp Allegheny. I loved the weekend campfire, as big as a tepee, ceremoniously lit by the Camp Spirit, whoever she happened to be that week. The Camp Spirit got to light the campfire with an enormous match, invoking the spirits with an ancient verse that only she was permitted to repeat. At the end of each weekly campfire, a new Camp Spirit was named, with lots of screaming, crying, and hugging. I was dying to be the Camp Spirit. In fact, after the very first campfire, I set this as my goal, cooperating like crazy with all the counselors so I would be picked. But it wasn't hard for me to cooperate.

I loved wearing a uniform, being a part of the group—I still have the photograph from that first session of camp, all of us wearing our navy shorts, white socks, and white camp shirts, our hair squeaky-clean, grinning into the sun. I loved all my activities—arts and crafts, where we made huge ashtrays for our parents out of little colored tiles; swimming, where I already excelled and soon became the acknowledged champion of the breaststroke in all competitions; and drama, where we were readying a presentation of *Spoon River*. My canoeing group took a long sunrise trip upstream to an island where we cooked our breakfast out over a fire: grits, sausage, eggs. Everything had a smoky, exotic taste, and the smoke from our breakfast campfire rose to mingle with the patchy mist still clinging to the trees, still rising from the river. I remember lying on my back and gazing up at how the sunshine looked, like light through a stained-glass window, emerald green and iridescent in the leafy tops of the tallest trees. The river was as smooth and shiny as a mirror. In fact it reminded me of a mirror, of Ashley's mirror-topped dressing table back home.

And the long trail rides—when we finally got to take them—were even better than the canoe trips. But first we had to go around and around the riding ring, learning to post, learning to canter. The truth was, I didn't like the horses nearly as much as I'd expected to. For one thing, they were a lot *bigger* than I had been led to believe by the illustrations in my horse books. They were as big as cars. For another thing they were not lovable either. They were smelly, and some of them were downright mean. One big old black horse named Martini was pointed out to us early on as a biter. Others kicked. On a trail ride, you didn't want to get behind one of these. Still, the trail rides were great. We lurched along through the forest, following the leader. I felt like I was in a western movie, striking out into the territory. On the longest trail ride, we took an overnight trip up to Pancake Mountain, where we ate s'mores (Hershey bars and melted marshmallows smashed into a sandwich between two graham crackers), told ghost stories, and went to sleep finally with the wheezing and stamping of the horses in our ears.

Actually, I liked the riding counselors better than I liked the horses. The regular counselors were sweet, pretty girls who went to school at places like Hollins and Sweet Briar, or else maternal, jolly older women who taught junior high school during the regular year, but the riding counselors were tough, tan, muscular young women who squinted into the sun and could post all day long if they had to. The riding counselors said "Shit" a lot, and smoked cigarettes in the barn. They did not speak of college.

My only male counselor was a frail, nervous young man named Jeffrey Long, reputed to be the nephew of the owner. He taught nature study, which I loved. I loved identifying the various trees (hickory, five leaves; ironwood, the satiny metallic trunk; maple, the little wings; blue-berried juniper; droopy willow). We made sassafras toothbrushes, and brushed our teeth in the river.

On Sundays, we had church in the big rustic assembly hall. It was an Episcopal service, which seemed pretty boring to me in comparison with the Maranatha Church. Yet I liked the Prayer Book, and I particularly liked one of the Episcopal hymns, which I had never heard before, "I Sing a Song of the Saints of God," with its martial, military tune. I imagined Joan of Arc striding briskly along in a satin uniform, to just that tune. I also liked the hymn "Jerusalem," especially the weird lines that went, "Bring me my staff of burnished gold, bring me my arrows of desire." I loved the "arrows of desire" part.

We all wore white shirts and white shorts to church. After church we had a special Sunday lunch, with fried chicken and ice cream, "I scream, you scream, we all scream for ice cream!" we'd shout, banging on the tables before they brought it out. (In order to have any, you had to turn in an Ice Cream Letter—to your parents—as you came in the door.)

On Sunday nights, we all climbed the hill behind the dining hall for vespers. We sat on our ponchos looking down on the camp as the sun set, and sang "Day Is Done." We bowed our heads in silent prayer. Then, after about ten minutes of this, one of the junior counselors played "Taps" on the bugle. She played it every night at lights out too. I much admired the bugler's jaunty, boyish stance. I had already resolved to take up the bugle, first thing, when I got back home.

And speaking of home, I'd barely thought of it since arriving at Camp Allegheny. I was entirely too busy. I guess that was the idea. Still, every now and then in a quiet moment—during silent prayer at vespers, for instance; or rest hour right after lunch, when we usually played Go Fish or some other card game, but sometimes, *sometimes* I just lay on my cot and thought about things; or at night, after "Taps," when I'd lie looking up at the rafters before I fell asleep—in those quiet moments, I did think of home, and of my salvation. I didn't have as much time as I needed, there at camp, to pray without ceasing. Besides, I was often too tired to do it. Other times, I was having too much fun to do it. Sometimes I just forgot. To pray without ceasing requires either a solitary life or a life of invisibility such as I had led within my family for the past year.

What about my family, anyway? Did I miss them? Not a bit. I could scarcely recall what they looked like. Mama wrote that Paul was back home already and had a job at the snack bar at the country club. Ashley was in France. Daddy was still in Baltimore, where he would probably stay for six more months. Mama was very busy helping Aunt Liddie plan her wedding, which I would be in. I would wear an aqua dress and dyed-to-match heels. I read Mama's letter curiously, several times. I felt like I had to translate it, like it was written in a foreign language. I folded this letter up and placed it in the top tray of my trunk, where I would find it years later. Right then, I didn't have time to think about my family. I was too busy doing everything I was supposed to, so that I might be picked as Camp Spirit. (Everybody agreed that the current Camp Spirit, Jeannie Darling from Florida, was a stuck-up bitch who didn't deserve it at all.) At the last campfire of First Session, I had high hopes that I might replace her. We started out by singing all the camp songs, first the funny ones such as "I came on the train and arrived in the rain, my trunk came a week later on." Each "old" counselor had a song composed in her honor, and we sang them all. It took forever. As we finally sang the Camp Spirit song, my heart started beating like crazy.

But it was not to be. No, it was Jeanette Peterson, a skinny boring redhead from Margaret Applewhite's cabin. I started crying but nobody knew why, because by then everybody else was crying too, and we all continued to cry as we sang all the sad camp songs about loyalty and friendships and candle flames. This last campfire was also Friendship Night. We had made little birch-bark boats that afternoon, and traded them with our best friends. At the end of the campfire, the counselors passed out short white candles which we lit and carried down to the river in a solemn procession. Then we placed the candles in our little boats and set them in the water, singing our hearts out as the flotilla of candles entered the current and moved slowly down the dark river and out of sight around the bend. I clung to my New Best Friend and cried. This was Shelley Long from Leesburg, Virginia, with a freckled, heart-shaped face and a pixie haircut, who talked a mile a minute all the time. It was even possible that Shelley Long had read more books than I had, unlike my Old Best Friend Tammy back at home in Alabama, who had not read any books at all, and did not intend to. Plus, Shelley Long owned a pony and a pony cart. She had shown me a picture of herself at home in Leesburg, driving her pony cart. Her house, in the background, looked like Mount Vernon. I was heartbroken when she left, the morning after Friendship Night.

IT RAINED THAT morning, a cold drizzle that continued without letup for the next two days. About three-quarters of the campers left after First Session, including everybody I liked. Margaret Applewhite stayed. My last vision of the departing campers was a rainy blur of waving hands as the big yellow buses pulled out, headed for the train station and the airport. All the girls were singing at the top of their lungs, and their voices seemed to linger in the air long after they were gone. Then came a day and half of waiting around for the Second Session campers to arrive, a day and a half in which nobody talked to me much, and the counselors were busy doing things like counting the rifle shells. So I became invisible again, free to wander about in the rain, free to pray without ceasing.

Finally the new campers arrived, and I brightened somewhat at the chance to be an Old Girl, to show the others the ropes and teach them the words to the songs. My New Best Friend was Anne Roper, from Lexington, Kentucky. She wasn't as good as Shelley, but she was the best I could do, I felt, considering what I had to pick from. Anne Roper was okay.

But my new counselor was very weird. She read aloud to us each day at rest hour from a big book named *The Fountainhead,* by Ayn Rand. Without asking our parents, she pierced all our ears. Even this ear piercing did not bring my spirits up to the level of First Session, however. For one thing, it never stopped raining. It rained and rained and rained. First, we couldn't go swimming—the river was too high, too cold, too fast. We couldn't go canoeing either. The tennis courts looked like lakes. The horses, along with the riding counselors, stayed in their barn. About all we could do was arts and crafts and Skits, which got old fast. Lots of girls got homesick. They cried during "Taps."

I cried then and at other odd times too, such as when I walked up to breakfast through the constant mist that came up now from the river, or at church. I was widely thought to be homesick. To cheer me up, my weird counselor gave me a special pair of her own earrings, little silver hoops with turquoise chips in them, made by Navajos.

Then I got bronchitis. I developed a deep, thousand-year-old Little Match Girl cough that started way down in my knees. Because of this cough, I was allowed to call my mother, and to my surprise, I found myself asking to come home. But Mama said no. She said,

We always finish what we start, Karen.

So that was that. I was taken into town for a penicillin shot, and started getting better. The sun came out too.

But because I still had such a bad cough, I did not have to participate in the all-camp Game Day held during the third week of Second Session. I was free to lounge in my upper bunk and read the rest of *The Fountainhead,* which I did. By then I had read way ahead of my counselor. I could hear the screams and yells of the girls out on the playing fields, but vaguely, far away. Then I heard them all singing, from farther up the hill, and I knew they had gone into Assembly to give out the awards. I knew I was probably expected to show up at Assembly too, but somehow I just couldn't summon up the energy. I didn't care who got the awards. I didn't care which team won—the Green or the Gold, it was all the same to me—or which cabin won the ongoing competition among cabins. I didn't even care who was Camp Spirit. Instead I lolled on my upper bunk and looked at the turning dust in a ray of light that came in through a chink in the cabin. I coughed. I felt that I would die soon.

This is when it happened.

This is when it always happens, I imagine—when you least expect it, when you are least prepared.

Suddenly, as I stared at the ray of sunshine, it intensified, growing brighter and brighter until the whole cabin was a blaze of light. I sat right up, as straight as I could. I crossed my legs. I knew I was waiting for something. I knew something was going to happen. I could barely breathe. My heart pounded so hard I feared it might jump right out of my chest and land on the cabin floor. I don't know how long I sat there like that, waiting.

"Karen," He said.

His voice filled the cabin.

I knew immediately who it was. No question. For one thing, there were no men at Camp Allegheny except for Mr. Grizzard, who cleaned out the barn, and Jeffrey Long, who had a high, reedy voice.

This voice was deep, resonant, full of power.

"Yes, Lord?" I said.

He did not speak again. But as I sat there on my upper bunk I was filled with His presence, and I knew what I must do.

I jumped down from my bunk, washed my face and brushed my teeth at the sink in the corner, tucked in my shirt, and ran up the hill to the assembly hall. I did not cough. I burst right in through the big double doors at the front and elbowed old Mrs. Beemer aside as she read out the results of the archery meet to the rows of girls in their folding chairs.

Mrs. Beemer took one look at me and shut her mouth.

I opened my mouth, closed my eyes, and started speaking in Tongues of Fire.

I CAME TO in the infirmary, surrounded by the camp nurse, the doctor from town, the old lady who owned the camp, the Episcopal chaplain, my own counselor, and several other people I didn't even know. I smiled at them all. I felt great, but they made me stay in the infirmary for two more days to make sure I had gotten over it. During this time I was given red Jell-O and Cokes, and the nurse took my temperature every four hours. The chaplain talked to me for a long time. He was a tall, quiet man with wispy white hair that stood out around his head. I got to talk to my mother on the telephone again, and this time she promised me a kitten if I would stay until the end of camp. I had always, always wanted a kitten, but I had never been allowed to have one because it would get hair on the upholstery and also because Ashley was allergic to cats.

"What about Ashley?" I asked.

"Never you mind," Mama said.

So it was decided. I would stay until the end of camp, and Mama would buy me a kitten.

I got out of the infirmary the next day and went back to my cabin, where everybody treated me with a lot of deference and respect for the rest of Second Session, choosing me first for softball, letting me star in Skits. And at the next-to-last campfire, I was named Camp Spirit. I got to run forward, scream and cry, but it was not as good as it would have been if it had happened First Session. It was an anticlimax. Still, I did get to light the very last campfire, the Friendship Night campfire, with my special giant match and say ceremoniously:

> Kneel always when you light a fire,
> Kneel reverently,
> And thankful be
> For God's unfailing majesty.

Then everybody sang the Camp Spirit song. By now, I was getting *really tired of singing.* Then Anne Roper and I sailed each other's little birch-bark boats off into the night, our candles guttering wildly as they rounded the bend.

All the way home on the train the next day, I pretended to be asleep while I prayed without ceasing that nobody back home would find out I had spoken in tongues of fire. For now it seemed to me an exalted and private and scary thing, and somehow I knew it was not over yet. I felt quite sure that I had been singled out for some terrible, holy mission. Perhaps I would even have to *die,* like Joan of Arc. As the train rolled south through Virginia on the beautiful August day, I felt myself moving inexorably toward my Destiny, toward some last act of my own Skit which was yet to be played out.

THE MINUTE I walked onto the concrete at the country club pool, I knew that Margaret Applewhite (who had flown home) had told everybody. Dennis Jones took one look at me, threw back his head, and began to gurgle wildly, clutching at his stomach. Tommy Martin ran out on the low board, screamed in gibberish, and then flung himself into the water. Even I had to laugh at him. But Paul and his friends teased me in a more sophisticated manner. "Hey, Karen," one of them might say, clutching his arm, "I've got a real bad tennis elbow here, do you think you can heal it for me?"

I was famous all over town. I sort of enjoyed it. I began to feel popular and cute, like the girls on *American Bandstand.*

But the kitten was a disaster. Mama drove me out in the county one afternoon in her white Cadillac to pick it out of a litter that the laundry lady's cat had had. The kittens were all so tiny that it was hard to pick— little mewling, squirming things, still blind. Drying sheets billowed all about them, on rows of clotheslines. "I want *that* one," I said, picking the smallest, a teeny little orange ball. I named him Sandy. I got to keep Sandy in a shoe box in my room, then in a basket in my room. But as time passed (Ashley came home from Europe, Paul went back to W&L) it became clear to me that there was something terribly wrong with

Sandy. Sandy *mewed too much,* not a sweet mewing, but a little howl like a lost soul. He never purred. He wouldn't grow right either, even though I fed him half-and-half. He stayed little and jerky. He didn't act like a cat. One time I asked my mother, "Are you *sure* Sandy is a regular cat?" and she frowned at me and said, "Well, of *course* he is, what's the matter with you, Karen?" but I was not so sure. Sandy startled too easily. Sometimes he would leap straight up in the air, land on all four feet, and just stand there quivering, for no good reason at all. While I was watching him do this one day, it came to me

Sandy was a Holy Cat. He was possessed by the spirit, as I had been. I put his basket in the laundry room. I was fitted for my aqua semiformal dress, and wore it in Aunt Liddie's wedding. Everybody said I looked grown-up and beautiful. I got to wear a corsage. I got to drink champagne. We had a preschool meeting of the Sub-Deb Club, and I was elected secretary. I kept trying to call Tammy, from pay phones downtown and the phone out at the country club, so Mama wouldn't know, but her number was still out of order. Tammy never called me.

Then Ashley invited me to go to the drive-in movie with her and her friends, just before she left for Sweet Briar. The movie was *All That Heaven Allows,* which I found incredibly moving, but Ashley and her friends smoked cigarettes and giggled through the whole thing. They couldn't be serious for five minutes. But they were being real nice to me, so I volunteered to go to the snack bar for them the second or third time they wanted more popcorn. On the way back from the snack bar, in the window of a red Thunderbird with yellow flames painted on its hood, I saw Tammy's face.

I didn't hesitate for a minute. I was *so* glad to see her! "Tammy!" I screamed. The position of My Best Friend was, of course, vacant. I ran right over to the Thunderbird, shifted all the popcorn boxes over to my left hand, and flung open the door. And sure enough, there was Tammy, *with the whole top of her sundress down.* It all happened in an instant. I saw a boy's dark hair, but not his face—his head was in her lap.

Tammy's breasts loomed up out of the darkness at me. They were perfectly round and white, like tennis balls. But it seemed to me that they were too high up to look good. They were too close to her chin.

Clearly, Tammy was Petting. And in a flash I remembered what Mama had told me about Petting, that

> a nice girl does not Pet. It is cruel to the boy to allow him to Pet, because he has no control over himself. He is just a boy. It is all up to the girl. If she allows the boy to Pet her, then he will become excited, and if he cannot find relief, then the poison will all back up into his organs, causing pain and sometimes death.

I slammed the car door. I fled back to Ashley and her friends, spilling popcorn everyplace as I went.

On the screen, Rock Hudson had been Petting too. Now we got a close-up of his rugged cleft chin. "Give me one of those cigarettes," I said to Ashley, and without batting an eye, she did. After three tries, I got it lit. It tasted great.

The next day, Ashley left for Sweet Briar, and soon after that, my school started too. Whenever I passed Tammy in the hall, we said hello, but did not linger in conversation. I was put in the Gifted and Talented group for English and French. I decided to go out for JV cheerleader. I practiced and practiced and practiced. Then, one day in early September, my cat Sandy—after screaming out and leaping straight up in the air— ran out into the street in front of our house and was immediately hit by a Merita bread truck.

I knew it was suicide.

I buried him in the backyard, in a box from Rich's department store, along with Ashley's scarab bracelet which I had stolen sometime earlier. She wondered for years whatever happened to the bracelet. It was her favorite.

I remember how relieved I felt when I had smoothed the final shovelful of dirt over Sandy's grave. Somehow, I knew, the last of my holiness, of my chosenness, went with him. Now I wouldn't have to die. Now my daddy would get well, and I would make cheerleader, and go to college.

Now I could grow up, get breasts, and have babies. Since then, all these things have happened. But there are moments yet, moments when in the midst of life a silence falls, and in these moments I catch myself still listening for that voice. *"Karen,"* He will say, and I'll say, "Yes, Lord. Yes."

Gospel Song

Dorothy Allison

AT NINE, I KNEW exactly who and what I wanted to be. Early every Sunday morning I got up to watch the *Sunrise Gospel Hour* and practice my secret ambition. More than anything in the world I wanted to be a gospel singer—a little girl in a white fringed vest with silver and gold crosses embroidered on the back. I wanted gray-headed ladies to cry as they saw my pink cheeks. I wanted people to moan when they heard the throb in my voice as I sang of the miracle in my life. I wanted a miracle in my life. I wanted to be a gospel singer and be loved by the whole wide world.

All that summer, while Mama was off at work, I haunted the White Horse Cafe over on the highway. They had three Teresa Brewer songs on the jukebox, and the truckers loved Teresa as much as I did. I'd sit out under the jalousie windows and hum along with her, imagining myself crooning with a raw and desperate voice. Half asleep in the sun, reassured by the familiar smell of frying fat, I'd make promises to God. If only He'd let it happen! I knew I'd probably turn to whiskey and rock-and-roll like they all did, but not for years, I promised. Not for years, Lord. Not till I had glorified His Name and bought my mama a yellow Cadillac and a house on Old Henderson Road.

Jesus, make me a gospel singer, I prayed, while Teresa sang of what might have been God and, then again, might have been some black-eyed man. Make me, oh make me! But Jesus must have been busy with Teresa 'cause my voice went high and shrill every time I got excited, and cracked and went hoarse if I tried to croon. The preacher at Bushy Creek Baptist wouldn't even let me stand near the choir to turn the pages of a hymnal. Without a voice like Teresa's or June Carter's, I couldn't sing gospel. I could just listen to it and watch the gray-headed ladies cry. It was an injustice I could not understand or forgive. It left me with a wild aching hunger in my heart and a deep resentment I hid from everyone but God.

MY FRIEND SHANNON Pearl had the same glint of hunger in her watery pink eyes. An albino, perennially six inches shorter than me, Shannon had white skin, white hair, pale eyes, and fine blue blood vessels showing against the ivory of her scalp. Blue threads under the linen, her mama was always saying. Sometimes Shannon seemed strangely beautiful to me, as she surely was to her mother. Sometimes, but not often. Not often at all. But every chance she could get, Mrs. Pearl would sit her daughter between her knees and purr over that gossamer hair and puffy pale skin.

"My little angel," Mrs. Pearl would croon, and my stomach would push up against my heart.

It was a lesson in the power of love. Looking back at me from between her mother's legs, Shannon was wholly monstrous, a lurching hunched creature shining with sweat and smug satisfaction. There had to be something wrong with me, I was sure, the way I went from awe to disgust where Shannon was concerned. When Shannon sat between her mama's legs or chewed licorice strings her daddy held out for her, I purely hated her. But when other people would look at her hatefully or the boys up at Lee Highway would call her "Lard Eyes," I felt a fierce and protective love for her, as if she were more my sister than Reese. I felt as if I belonged to her in a funny kind of way, as if her "affliction" put me deeply in her debt. It was a mystery, I guessed, a sign of grace like my Catholic Aunt Maybelle was always talking about.

I met Shannon Pearl on the first Monday of school the year I entered the third grade. She got on the bus two stops after Reese and me, walking stolidly past a dozen hooting boys and another dozen flushed and whispering girls. As she made her way up the aisle, I watched each boy slide to the end of his seat to block her sitting with him and every girl flinch away as if whatever Shannon had might be catching. In the seat ahead of us Danny Powell leaned far over into the aisle and began to make retching noises.

"Cootie Train! Cootie Train!" somebody yelled, as the bus lurched into motion and Shannon still hadn't found a seat.

I watched her face—impassive, contemptuous, and stubborn. Sweat was showing on her dress but nothing showed in her face except for the eyes. There was fire in those pink eyes, a deep fire I recognized, banked and raging. Before I knew it I was on my feet and leaning forward to catch her arm. I pulled her into our row without a word. Reese stared at me like I was crazy, but Shannon settled herself and started cleaning her bottleglass lenses as if nothing at all was happening.

I glared at Danny Powell's open mouth until he turned away from us. Reese pulled a strand of her lank blond hair into her mouth and pretended she was sitting alone. Slowly, the boys sitting near us turned their heads and began to mutter to each other. There was one soft "Cootie Bitch" hissed in my direction, but no yelling. Nobody knew exactly why I had taken a shine to Shannon, but everyone at Greenville Elementary knew me and my family—particularly my matched set of cousins, big unruly boys who would just as soon toss a boy as a penny against the school walls if they heard of an insult against any of us.

Shannon Pearl spent a good five minutes cleaning her glasses and then sat silent for the rest of the ride to school. I understood intuitively that she would not say anything, would in fact generously pretend to have fallen into our seat. I sat there beside her watching the pinched faces of my classmates as they kept looking back toward us. Just the way they stared made me want to start a conversation with Shannon. I imagined us discussing all the enemies we had in common while half the bus craned their necks to try to hear. But I couldn't bring myself to actually do that, couldn't even imagine what to say to her. Not till the bus crossed the railroad tracks at the south corner of Greenville Elementary did I manage to force my mouth open enough to say my name and then Reese's.

She nodded impartially and whispered "Shannon Pearl" before taking off her glasses to begin cleaning them all over again. With her glasses off she half shut her eyes and hunched her shoulders. Much later, I would realize that she cleaned her glasses whenever she needed a quiet moment to regain her composure, or more often, just to put everything around her at a distance. Without glasses, the world became a soft blur, but she also behaved as if the glasses were all that made it possible for her to hear. Commotion or insults made while she was cleaning her glasses never seemed to register at all. It was a valuable trick when you were the object of as much ridicule as Shannon Pearl.

Christian charity, I knew, would have had me smile at Shannon but avoid her like everyone else. It wasn't Christian charity that made me give her my seat on the bus, trade my third-grade picture for hers, sit at her kitchen table while her mama tried another trick on her wispy hair—*Egg and cornmeal, that'll do the trick. We gonna put curls in this hair, darling, or my name an't Roseanne Pearl*—or follow her to the Bushy Creek Highway Store and share the blue popsicle she bought us. Not Christian charity; my fascination with her felt more like the restlessness that made me worry the scabs on my ankles. As disgusting as it all seemed, I couldn't put away the need to scratch my ankles, or hang around what Granny called "that strange and ugly child."

Other people had no such problem. Other than her mother and I, no one could stand Shannon. No amount of Jesus' grace would make her even marginally acceptable, and people had been known to suddenly lose their lunch from the sight of the clammy sheen of her skin, her skull showing blue-white through the thin, colorless hair and those watery pink eyes flicking back and forth, drifting in and out of focus.

Lord! But that child is ugly.

It's a trial, Jesus knows, a trial for her poor parents.

They should keep her home.

Now, honey. That's not like you. Remember, the Lord loves a charitable heart.

I don't care. The Lord didn't intend me to get nauseous in the middle of Sunday services. That child is a shock to the digestion.

I had the idea that because she was so ugly on the outside, it was only reasonable that Shannon would turn out to be saintlike when you got to know her. That was the way it would have been in any storybook the local ladies' society would have let me borrow. I thought of *Little Women, The Bobbsey Twins,* and all those novels about poor British families at Christmas. Tiny Tim, for Christ's sake! Shannon, I was sure, would be like that. A patient and gentle soul had to be hidden behind those pale and sweaty features. She would be generous, insightful, understanding, and wise beyond her years. She would be the friend I had always needed.

That she was none of these was something I could never quite accept. Once she relaxed with me, Shannon invariably told horrible stories, most of which were about the gruesome deaths of innocent children. . . . *And then the tractor backed up over him, cutting his body in three pieces, but nobody seen it or heard it, you see, 'cause of the noise the thresher made. So then his mama come out with iced tea for everybody. And she put her foot down right in his little torn open stomach. And oh Lord! don't you know . . .*

I couldn't help myself. I'd sit and listen, openmouthed and fascinated, while this shining creature went on and on about decapitations. She loved best little children who had fallen in the way of large machines. It was something none of the grown-ups knew a thing about, though once in a while I'd hear a much shorter, much tamer version of one of Shannon's stories from her mama. At those moments, Shannon would give me a grin of smug pride. Can't I tell it better? she seemed to be saying. Gradually I admitted to myself what hid behind Shannon's impassive pink and white features. Shannon Pearl simply and completely hated everyone who had ever hurt her, and spent most of her time brooding on punishments either she or God would visit on them. The fire that burned in her eyes was the fire of outrage. Had she been stronger or smarter, Shannon Pearl would have been dangerous. But half-blind, sickly, and ostracized, she was not much of a threat to anyone.

Shannon's parents were as short as she was, and almost as pale. Mr. and Mrs. Pearl ran a religious supply store downtown south of Main Street, a place where you could get embossed Bibles, bookmarks with the 23rd Psalm in blue relief, hot plates featuring the Sermon on the Mount, and Jesus and that damned lamb on everything imaginable— slipcovers, tablecloths, even plastic pants to go over baby diapers. It seemed a hell of a way for grown people to make a living, and it didn't quite cover Shannon's medical expenses. Mrs. Pearl had to run a sewing service on the side, and Mr. Pearl did bookings for country and gospel singers.

The latter made all the difference in how I felt about the Pearls. Shannon got to meet them: the Blue Ridge Mountain Boys, the Tuckerton Family, the Carter Family, Little Pammie Gleason (blessed by God), the Smoky Mountain Boys, and now and then—every time he'd get saved— Johnny Cash. Sunday morning, Sunday evening, Wednesday prayer service, revival weeks; Mr. Pearl would book a hall, a church, or a local TV program. Because Shannon got to go, after a while so did I. I tried to stop worrying about my fascination with the Pearls, crediting it to the more acceptable lust for gospel music.

DRIVING FROM Greenville to Greer on Highway 85 past the Sears Roebuck warehouse, the air base, the rolling green and red mud hills— a trip we made almost every other day—my stepfather never failed to get us all to sing like some traveling gospel family. *WHILE I WAS SLEEPING*

SOMEBODY TOUCHED ME, WHILE I WAS SLEEPING, OH! SOMEBODY TOUCHED ME . . . MUST'HA BEEN THE HAND OF THE LORD. . . .

Full voice, all out, late evening gospel music filled the car and shocked the passing traffic. My stepfather never drove fast, and not a one of us could sing worth a damn. My sisters howled and screeched, my mama's voice broke like she, too, dreamed of Teresa Brewer, and my stepfather made sounds that would have scared cows. None of them cared, and I tried not to let it bother me. I'd put my head out the window and howl for all I was worth. The wind filled my mouth and the roar obscured the fact that I sang as badly as any of them. Sometimes at the house I'd even go sing into the electric fan. It made my voice buzz and waver like a slide guitar, an effect I particularly liked, though Mama complained it gave her a headache and would give me an earache if I didn't cut it out.

I took the fan out on the back porch and sang to myself. Maybe I wouldn't get to be the star on the stage, maybe I'd wind up singing background in a "family"—all of us dressed alike in electric blue fringed blouses with silver embroidery. All I needed was a chance to turn my soulful brown eyes on a tent full of believers, sing out the little break in my mournful voice. I knew I could make them love me. There was a secret to it, but I would find it out. If Shannon Pearl could do it to me, I would find a way to do it to the world.

SHANNON'S MAMA, Mrs. Pearl, thought I was a precious child.

"Those eyes of yours could break the heart of God," she'd tell me, and pat my black hair fiercely. I'd blink my eyes and try to tear up for her. "Lashes, Bob, look at the lashes on this child. You grow up you can do Maybelline commercials on the television, honey. 'Course not that you're going to want to. You don't ever let anybody talk you into putting any of that junk on you. Your eyes are a gift from GOD!''

Mrs. Pearl had more ways of saying *God* and *Jesus* than any preacher I'd ever heard. She could put it out real soft and low—*gawd*—so that you imagined Him as an uncle in the family, quiet and well-mannered; or drag it out long and loud—*GOOOODDDD*—a shocking hollow-voiced moan that rocked me like thunder.

Jesus was even better. Everybody said *Jesus* so much, you could forget who and what he was supposed to be, but Mrs. Pearl rationed her *Jesuses*, never failing to give you the sense that Jesus was a real person: a little boy used to bringing doves back to life, a quiet young man never known to curse or fornicate, a man aged by the sin of the world, a life sacrificed for you personally.

It was a bit much to bear at nine, but I expected you got used to it as you got older.

MRS. PEARL'S SPECIALTY sewing was the backbone of the Pearl family income. Not surprisingly, she was famous for gilt-rendered scenes on the costumed sleeves and jackets of gospel performers. I got to where I could spot a Mrs. Pearl creation on the Sunrise Gospel Hour without even trying too hard. She had a way of putting little curlicues at the base of the cross that was supposed to suggest grass, but for everyone who knew her, it was an artist's signature.

Mrs. Pearl loved her work. "I feel like my whole life is a joy to the Lord," she'd say, knotting tassels on a red silk blouse for one of the younger Carter girls. "My sewing, Mr. Pearl's work, the store, my precious daughter." She'd glance over at Shannon with a look that mirrored the close-up of Mary and the Baby in the center of the *Illustrated Christian Bible* that was always on special down at the store. "Everything that comes to us is a blessing or a test. That's all you need to know in this life . . . just the certainty that God's got His eye on you, that He knows what you are made of, what you need to grow on. Why questioning's a sin, it's pointless. He will show you in His own good time. And long as I remember that, I'm fine. It's like that song Mr. Pearl likes so much . . . 'Jesus is the engineer, trust his hand on the throttle . . . !'"

Shannon giggled and waved me out on the porch. "Sometimes Mama needs a little hand on her throttle. You know what I mean?" She laughed and rolled her eyes like a broken kewpie doll. "Daddy has to throttle her back down to a human level or she'd take off like a helium angel."

I couldn't help myself. I laughed back, remembering what my Aunt Grace had said about Mrs. Pearl. *If she'd been fucked right just once, she'd have never birthed that weird child.* I poked Shannon on one swollen arm, just in case she could read behind my eyes.

"Your mama's an an-gel," I whispered hoarsely, mocking the way Mrs. Pearl would say that, "just an an-gel of Ga-ahd."

"Gaa-ad da-am right," Shannon whispered back, and I saw her hatred burning pink and hot in those eyes. It scared and fascinated me. Was it possible she could see the same thing in my eyes? Did I have that much hate in me? I looked back at Mrs. Pearl, humming around the pins in her mouth. A kind of chill went through me. Did I hate Mrs. Pearl? I looked 'round at their porch, the baby's breath hanging in baskets and the two rocking chairs with hand-sewn cushions. Shannon's teeth flashed sunlight into my eyes.

"You look like the devil's walking on your grave."

I shivered, and then spit like my granny would. "The grave that I'll lie in an't been dug yet." It was something I'd heard Granny say. Shannon grabbed my arm and gave it a jerk.

"Don't say that. It's bad luck to mention your own grave. They say my Grandmother McCray joked about her burying place on Easter morning and fell down dead at evening service." She jerked my arm again hard. "Think about something else quick." I looked down at her hand on my arm, puffy white fingers gripping my thin brown wrist.

"That child will rot fast when she goes," Granny had said once. I felt nauseous.

"I got to go home." Openmouthed, I pulled air in fast as I could. "Mama wants me to help her hang out the laundry this afternoon."

"Your mama's always making you work."

And yours never does, I thought. I took a deep breath, trying to get my stomach under control. Sometimes I really couldn't stand Shannon

Pearl. "We're gonna go to the diner for super tonight. They have peach cobbler this time of year."

"My daddy's gonna make fresh ice cream tonight." Shannon smiled a smile full of the pride of family position. "We got black walnuts to put on it."

I didn't say anything. She would. She would rot very fast.

THERE WAS A circuit that ran from North Carolina to South Carolina, Tennessee, Georgia, Alabama. The gospel singers moved back and forth on it, a tide of gilt and fringed jackets that intersected and paralleled the country western circuit. Sometimes you couldn't tell the difference, and as times got harder certainly Mr. Pearl stopped making distinctions, booking any act that would get him a little cash up front. More and more, I got to go off with the Pearls in their old yellow DeSoto, the trunk stuffed with boxes of religious supplies and Mrs. Pearl's sewing machine, the backseat crowded with Shannon and me and piles of sewing. Pulling into small towns in the afternoon so Mr. Pearl could do the setup and Mrs. Pearl could repair tears and frayed edges of embroidery, Shannon and I would go off to picnic alone on cold chicken and chow-chow. Mr. Pearl always brought tea in a mason jar, but Shannon would rub her eyes and complain of a headache until her mama gave in and bought us RC Colas.

Most of the singers arrived late.

It was a wonder to me that the truth never seemed to register with Mr. and Mrs. Pearl. No matter who fell over the boxes backstage, they never caught on that the whole Tuckerton family had to be pointed in the direction of the stage, nor that Little Pammie Gleason—*Lord, just thirteen!*—had to wear her frilly blouse long-sleeved 'cause she had bruises all up and down her arms from that redheaded boy her daddy wouldn't let her marry. They never seemed to see all the "boys" passing bourbon in paper cups backstage or their angel daughter, Shannon, begging for "just a sip." Maybe Jesus shielded their eyes the way he kept old Shadrach, Meshach, and Abednego safe in the fiery furnace. Certainly sin didn't touch them the way it did Shannon and me. Both of us had learned to walk carefully backstage, with all those hands reaching out to stroke our thighs and pinch the nipples we barely had yet.

"Playful boys," Mrs. Pearl would laugh, stitching the sleeves back on their jackets, the rips in their pants. It was a wonder to me that she couldn't smell the whiskey breath set deep in her fine embroidery. But she didn't, and I wasn't gonna commit the sin of telling her what God surely didn't intend her to know.

"Sometimes you'd think Mama's simple," Shannon told me. It was one of those times I was keeping my head down, not wanting to say anything. It was her *mama*. I wouldn't talk about my mama that way even if she was crazy. I wished Shannon would shut up and the music would start. I was still hungry. Mrs. Pearl had packed less food than usual, and Mama had told me I was always to leave something on my plate when I ate with Shannon. I wasn't supposed to make them think they had to feed me. Not that that particular tactic worked. I'd left half a biscuit, and damned if Shannon hadn't popped it in her mouth.

"Maybe it's all that tugging at her throttle." Shannon started giggling funny, and I knew somebody had finally given her a pull at a paper cup. Now, I thought, now her mama will have to see. But when Shannon fell over her sewing machine, Mrs. Pearl just laid her down with a wet rag on her forehead.

"It's the weather," she whispered to me, over Shannon's sodden head. It was so hot, the heat was wilting the pictures off the paper fans provided by the local funeral home. But if there had been snow up to the hubcaps, Mrs. Pearl would have said it was the chill in the air. An hour later, one of the Tuckerton cousins spilled a paper cup on Mrs. Pearl's sleeve, and I saw her take a deep, painful breath. Catching my eye, she just said, "Can't expect that frail soul to cope without a little help."

I didn't tell her that it seemed to me that all those "boys" and "girls" were getting a hell of a lot of "help." I just muttered an almost inaudible *yeah* and cut my sinful eyes at them all.

"We could go sit under the stage," Shannon suggested. "It's real nice under there."

It was nice, close and dark and full of the sound of people stomping on the stage. I put my head back and let the dust drift down on my face, enjoying the feeling of being safe and hidden, away from all the people. The music seemed to be vibrating in my bones. *TAKING YOUR MEASURE, TAKING YOUR MEASURE, JESUS AND THE HOLY GHOST ARE TAKING YOUR MEASURE. . . .*

I didn't like the new music they were singing. It was a little too gimmicky. *TWO CUPS, THREE CUPS, A TEASPOON OF RIGHTEOUS. HOW WILL YOU MEASURE WHEN THEY CALL OUT YOUR NAME?* Shannon started laughing. She put her hands around me and rocked her head back and forth. The music was too loud, and I could smell whiskey all around us. My head hurt terribly; the smell of Shannon's hair was making me sick.

"Uh huh uh," I started to gag. Desperately I pushed Shannon away and crawled for the side of the stage as fast as I could. Air, I had to have air.

"Uh huh uh," I rolled out from under the stage and hit the side of the tent. Retching now, I jerked up the side of the tarp and wiggled through. Out in the damp evening air, I just let my head hang down and vomited between my wide, spread hands. Behind me Shannon was gasping and giggling.

"You're sick, you poor baby." I felt her hand on the small of my back pushing down comfortingly.

"Lord God!"

I looked up. A very tall man in a purple shirt was standing in front of me. I dropped my head and puked again. He had silver boots with cracked heels. I watched him step back out of range.

"Lord God!"

"It's all right," Shannon got to her feet beside me, keeping her hand on my back. "She's just a little sick." She paused. "If you got her a Co-Cola, it might settle her stomach."

I wiped my mouth, then wiped my hand on the grass. I looked up. Shannon was standing still, sweat running down into her eyes and making her blink. I could see she was hoping for two cokes. The man was still standing there with his mouth hanging open, a look of horror and shock on his face.

"Lord God," he said again, and I knew before he spoke what he was gonna say. It wasn't me who'd surprised him.

"Child, you are the ugliest thing I have ever seen."

Shannon froze. Her mouth fell open and as I watched, her whole face seemed to cave in. Her eyes shrank to little dots and her mouth became a cup of sorrow. I pushed myself up.

"You bastard!" I staggered forward and he backed up, rocking on his little silver heels. "You goddamned gutless son of a bitch!" His eyes kept moving from my face to Shannon's wilting figure. "You think you so pretty? You ugly sack of shit! You shit-faced turd-eating . . ."

"SHANNON PEARL!"

Mrs. Pearl was coming 'round the tent.

"You girls . . ." She gathered Shannon up in her arms. "Where have you been?" The man backed further away. I breathed through my mouth, though I no longer felt so sick. I felt angry and helpless and I was trying hard not to start crying. Mrs. Pearl clucked between her teeth and stroked Shannon's limp hair. "What have you been doing?"

Shannon moaned and buried her face in her mama's dress. Mrs. Pearl turned to me. "What were you saying?" Her eyes glittered in the arc lights from the front of the tent. I wiped my mouth again and said nothing. Mrs. Pearl looked to the man in the purple shirt. The confusion on her face seemed to melt and quickly became a blur of excitement and interest.

"I hope they weren't bothering you," she told him. "Don't you go on next?"

"Uh, yeah." He looked like he wasn't sure. He couldn't take his eyes off Shannon. He shook himself. "You Mrs. Pearl?"

"Why that's right." Mrs. Pearl's face was glowing.

Gospel Song · *417*

"I'd heard about you. I just never met your daughter before."

Mrs. Pearl seemed to shiver all over but then catch herself. Pressed to her mama's stomach, Shannon began to wail.

"Shannon, what *are* you going on for?" She pushed her daughter away from her side and pulled out a blue embroidered handkerchief to wipe her face.

"I think we all kind of surprised each other." The man stepped forward and gave Mrs. Pearl a slow smile, but his eyes kept wandering back to Shannon. I wiped my mouth again and stopped myself from spitting. Mrs. Pearl went on stroking her daughter's face but looking up into the man's eyes.

"I love it when you sing," she said, and half giggled. Shannon pulled away from her and stared up at them both. The hate in her face was terrible. For a moment I loved her with all my heart.

"Well," the man said. He rocked from one boot to the other. "Well . . ."

I reached for Shannon's hand. She slapped mine away. Her face was blazing. I felt as if a great fire was burning close to me, using up all the oxygen, making me pant to catch my breath. I laced the fingers of my hands together and tilted my head back to look up at the stars. If there was a God, then there would be justice. If there was justice, then Shannon and I would someday make them all burn. We walked away from the tent toward Mr. Pearl's battered DeSoto.

"Some day," Shannon whispered.

"Yeah," I whispered back. We knew exactly what we meant.

"BULLSHIT AND APPLEBUTTER," Granny Mattie laughed later when I told her about it. "Some of these Christian women will believe anything for the sake of a gospel singer."

"Anything." I loved the way she said that. Granny's *Christian women* came out like new spit on a dusty morning, pure and precious and deeply satisfying.

"Anything," I echoed her, and she grinned at me with her toothless,

Dorothy Allison • 4 1 8

twisted mouth. We were sitting in the backyard close together in Mama's lawn chairs. Granny always complained about Mama not living in houses with porches and rocking chairs, but she liked Mama's reclining lawn chair. Now she reached out, put her hand on the back of my neck, squeezed, and laughed.

"You got a look like your granddaddy sometimes." She pinched me and laughed again. "Bastard was meaner than a snake, but he had his ways. And didn't I love his ways? Lord Christ!" She pulled back and rolled the snuff around in her mouth.

"Man had only two faults I couldn't abide. Wouldn't work to save his life and couldn't stay away from gospel singers. Used to stand out back of revival tents offering 'em the best whiskey made in Greenville County. Then he'd bring me that slush they cleaned out of the taps. Bastard!" She stiffened and looked back over her shoulder, afraid my mama might be behind her. Mama didn't allow anybody to use that word in her house.

"Well, shit," she spit to the side. "You got a little of that too, don't you? A little of that silliness, that revival crap?"

"Aunt Grace says you a heathen."

"Oh Aunt Grace, huh. Aunt Grace fucked her oldest boy."

My mouth fell open. Granny wiped her chin.

"Don't you go telling your mama everything you hear."

"No ma'am."

"And don't go taking that gospel stuff seriously. It's nice to clean you out now and then, but it an't for real. It's like bad whiskey. Run through you fast and leave you with a pain'll lay you down." She wiped her chin again and sighed. I hated that sigh. I liked her better when she was being mean. When she started sighing, she was likely to start crying. Then her face would squeeze down on itself in a way that scared me.

"I an't no fool." I rocked my chair back and forth, pushing off hard with my bare feet. Granny's face twitched, and I saw the light come back into her eyes.

"You know how your mama feels about that word." It was true.

Mama had given me one of her rare spankings for calling Reese a fool. She hated it almost as much as *bastard*.

"An't no fool and an't no bastard." I rocked steadily, watching Granny's face.

Granny laughed and looked back over her shoulder nervously. "Oh, you gonna be the death of your mama, and won't I be sorry then?"

She didn't look sorry. She looked better with the lights back in her eyes. I said it again.

"An't no fool and an't no bastard."

Granny started laughing so hard she choked on her snuff.

"You're both, and you just silly 'bout that music just like your grand-daddy." She sounded like she was gonna strangle from laughing. "And goddamn, he was both too."

IT WAS A family thing, after all. My Uncle Jack got work building a carport and took some of the money to get Mama a little electric record player and four records. "That's all I'm giving for free," he told her, scooping up gravy with one of her biscuits. "Get you some of those June Carter songs you like. What's that funny one? 'Nickelodeon,' right?"

He scooped and sopped, and drank sweet tea down like it was whiskey. Mama said he'd eaten so many of her biscuits by now, he was like a child of her own.

"A man belongs to the woman that feeds him."

"Bullshit," Aunt Grace insisted. "It's the other way around and you know it. It's the woman belongs to the ones she's got to feed."

"Maybe. Maybe."

Out of those four records, there was only one Mama liked, and she damn near wore it out. "The Sign on the Highway," it was called, and after a while I could sing it from memory.

The sign on the highway the scene of the crash . . . the people pulled over to let the hearse pass . . . their bodies were found 'neath the signboard that read . . . Beer, Wine, and Whiskey for sale just ahead. . . .

Mama couldn't help herself. She cried every time she heard it and she wanted to hear it all the time. It was a gospel song, of course, a kind of a gospel song. Mama would play it over and over, and half the time I'd come in to sit with her while she played it. We'd sit, her with a glass of tea in one hand and the other over her eyes, and me as close to her as she'd let me, both of us crying quietly so no one would notice. Uncle Jack would come in and laugh at us.

"Look at you two. You just as crazy as you can be. Look at you. Crying over some people didn't never really die. 'At's only a slide guitar and some stupid people can't make a living no other way 'cept acting the fool in front of people like you." He took some biscuits out of the towel-wrapped bowl on the table and stomped off out the screen door, while Mama went on crying and I sat still. He kicked each step as he went down.

"I swear this family's got shit for brains."

"I LIKE YOUR family," Shannon sometimes said, though we both knew that was a polite lie. "Your mama's a fine woman," Roseanne Pearl would agree, while she eyed my too-tight raggedy dresses. She reminded me of my stepfather's sisters looking at us out of smug, superior faces, laughing at my mama's loose teeth and my sister's curls done up in paper scraps. Whenever the Pearls talked about my people, I'd take off and not go back for weeks. I didn't want the two parts of my life to come together.

WE WERE LIVING out past Henderson Road, on the other side of White Horse Highway. Up near the highway a revival tent had been erected. Some evenings I would walk up there on my own to sit outside and listen. The preacher was a shouter, something I had never liked. He'd rave and threaten, and it didn't seem as if he was ever gonna get to the invocation. I sat in the dark, trying not to think about anything, especially not about the whipping I was going to get if I stayed too long. I kept seeing my Uncle Jack in the men who stood near the highway sharing a bottle in a paper sack, black-headed men with blasted, rough-hewn faces.

Was it hatred or sorrow that made them look like that, their necks so stiff and their eyes so cold?

Did I look like that?

Would I look like that when I grew up? I remembered Aunt Grace putting her big hands over my ears and turning my face to catch the light, saying, "Just as well you smart; you an't never gonna be a beauty."

At least I wasn't as ugly as Shannon Pearl, I told myself, and was immediately ashamed. Shannon hadn't made herself ugly, but if I kept thinking that way I just might. Mama always said people could see your soul in your face, could see your hatefulness and lack of charity. With all the hatefulness I was trying to hide, it was a wonder I wasn't uglier than a toad in mud season.

The singing started. I sat forward on my heels and hugged my knees, humming. Revivals are funny. People get pretty enthusiastic, but they sometimes forget just which hymn it is they're singing. I grinned to myself and watched the men near the road punch each other lightly and curse in a friendly fashion.

You bastard.

You son of a bitch.

The preacher said something I didn't understand. There was a moment of silence, and then a pure tenor voice rose up into the night sky. The spit soured in my mouth. They had a real singer in there, a real gospel choir.

SWING LOW SWEET CHARIOT . . . COMING FOR TO CARRY ME HOME . . . AS I WALKED OUT IN THE STREETS OF LAREDO . . . SWEET JESUS . . . LIFT ME UP, LIFT ME UP IN THE AIR. . . .

The night seemed to wrap all around me like a blanket. My insides felt as if they had melted, and I could just feel the wind in my mouth. The sweet gospel music poured through me and made all my nastiness, all my jealousy and hatred, swell in my heart. I knew, I knew I was the most disgusting person in the world. I didn't deserve to live another day. I started hiccupping and crying.

"I'm sorry. Jesus, I'm sorry."

How could I live with myself? How could God stand me? Was this why Jesus wouldn't speak to my heart? The music washed over me . . . SOFTLY AND TENDERLY. The music was a river trying to wash me clean. I sobbed and dug my heels into the dirt, drunk on grief and that pure, pure voice. It didn't matter then if it was whiskey backstage or tongue kissing in the dressing room. Whatever it took to make that juice was necessary, was fine. I wiped my eyes and swore out loud. Get those boys another bottle, I said. Find that girl a hardheaded husband. But goddamn, get them to make that music. Make that music! Lord, make me drunk on that music.

The next Sunday I went off with Shannon and the Pearls for another gospel drive.

DRIVING BACKCOUNTRY WITH the Pearls meant stopping in at little country churches listening to gospel choirs. Mostly all those choirs had was a little echo of the real stuff. "Pitful, an't it?" Shannon sounded like her father's daughter. "Organ music just can't stand against a slide guitar." I nodded, but I wasn't sure she was right.

Sometimes one pure voice would stand out, one little girl, one set of brothers whose eyes would lift when they sang. Those were the ones who could make you want to scream low against all the darkness in the world. "That one," Shannon would whisper smugly, but I didn't need her to tell me. I could always tell which one Mr. Pearl would take aside and invite over to Gaston for revival week.

"Child!" he'd say, "you got a gift from God."

Uh huh, yeah.

Sometimes I couldn't stand it. I couldn't go in one more church, hear one more choir. Never mind loving the music, why couldn't God give me a voice? I hadn't asked for thick eyelashes. I had asked for, begged for, gospel. Didn't God give a good goddamn what *I* wanted? If He'd take bastards into heaven, how come He couldn't put me in front of those hot lights and all that dispensation? Gospel singers always had money in their pockets, another bottle under their seats. Gospel singers had love and safety and the whole wide world to fall back on—women and church and red clay solid under their feet. All I wanted, I whispered, all I wanted was a piece, a piece, a little piece of it.

Shannon looked at me sympathetically.

She knows, I thought, she knows what it is to want what you are never going to have.

THAT JULY WE went over to the other side of Greer, a part of the county I knew from visiting one of the cousins who worked at the air base. Off the highway we stopped at a service station to give Mrs. Pearl a little relief from the heat.

"You ever think God maybe didn't intend us to travel on Sunday afternoon? I swear he makes it hotter than Saturday or Friday."

Mrs. Pearl sat out in the shade while Mr. Pearl went off to speak to the man that rented out the Rhythm Ranch. Shannon and I cut off across a field to check out the headstones near a stand of cottonwood. We loved to read the mottoes and take back the good ones to Mrs. Pearl to stitch up on samplers and sell in the store. My favorites were the weird ones, like "Now He Knows" or "Too Pure." Shannon loved the ones they put up for babies, little curly headed dolls with angel wings and heartbreaking lines like "Gone To Mama, or "Gone Home."

"Silly stuff." I kicked at the pieces of clay pot that were lying everywhere. Shannon turned to me, and I saw tears on her cheeks.

"No, no, it just tears me up. Think about it, losing your own little baby girl, your own little angel. Oh, I can't stand it. I just can't stand it." She gave big satisfied sobs and wiped her hands on her blue gingham pockets.

"I wish I could take me one of these home. Wouldn't you like to have one you could keep up? You could tell stories to the babies."

"You crazy."

Shannon sniffed. "You just don't understand. Mama says I've got a very tender heart."

"Uh huh." I walked away. It was too hot to fight. It was certainly too hot to cry. I kicked over some plastic flowers and a tattered green cardboard cross. This was one of the most boring trips I'd ever taken with the Pearls. I tried to remember why I'd even wanted to come. At home Mama would be making fresh iced tea, boiling up sugar water to mix in it. Reese would be slicing peaches. My stepfather would be working on the lawn mower. I swatted at mosquitoes and hoped my face wasn't sunburning. I stopped.

The music coming through the cottonwoods was gospel.

Gut-shaking, deep-bellied, powerful voices rolled through the dried leaves and hot air. Not some piddlyshit thin-voiced choir, this was the real stuff. I could feel the whiskey edge, the grief and holding on, the dark night terror and determination of real gospel.

"My God," I whispered, and it was the best *My God* I'd ever put out, a stretched-out, scared whisper that meant I just might start to believe He hid in cottonwoods.

There was a church there, clapboard walls standing on cement blocks and no pretense of stained-glass windows. Just yellow glass reflecting back sunlight, all the windows open to let in the breeze and let out that music.

AMAZING GRACE . . . HOW GREAT THOU ART . . . TO SAVE A WRETCH LIKE ME. . . . A woman's voice rose and rolled over the deeper men's voices, rolled out so strong it seemed to rustle the leaves on the cottonwood trees.

AMEN.

LORD.

"Sweet Jesus, she can sing."

Shannon ignored me and kept pulling up wildflowers.

"You hear that? We got to tell your daddy."

Shannon turned her head to the side and stared at me with a peculiar angry expression. "He don't handle colored. An't no money in handling colored."

At that I froze, realizing that such a church off such a dirt road had to be just that—a colored church. And I knew what that meant. Of course I did. Still I heard myself whisper, "That an't one good voice. That's a church full."

"It's colored. It's niggers." Shannon's voice was as loud as I'd ever heard it and shrill with indignation. "My daddy don't handle niggers." She threw down her wildflowers and stomped her foot. "And you made me say that. Mama always said a good Christian don't use the word *nigger*. Jesus be my witness, I wouldn't have said it if you hadn't made me."

"You crazy. You just plain crazy." My voice was shaking. The way Shannon said *nigger* tore at me, the tone pitched exactly like the echoing sound of my stepfather's sister mouthing *trash* when she thought I wasn't close enough to hear. Later, much later, I would even wonder what it was that she heard in my voice that made her as angry as I was. Maybe it was the heat, maybe it was the shame we both were feeling, or maybe it was simply that Shannon Pearl and I were righteously tired of each other.

Shannon threw another handful of flowers at me. "I'm crazy. Me? What do you think you are? You and your mama and your whole family. Everybody knows you're all a bunch of drunks and thieves and whores. Everybody knows you just come round so you can eat off my mama's table and beg scraps of stuff we don't want no more. Everybody knows who your are . . ."

I was moving before I could stop myself, my hands flying up to slap together right in front of her face—a last-minute attempt not to hit her. "You bitch, you white-assed bitch." I wrung my hands, trying to hold on, to keep myself from slapping her pasty, ugly face. *Don't you never hit anybody in the face,* Mama always said.

"You little shit, you fuck-off." I put the words out as slick and fast as any of my uncles. Shannon's mouth fell open. "You just fuck off." I kicked red dirt up onto her pink-and-white skirt.

Shannon's face twisted. "You an't never gonna go to another gospel show with us again! I'm gonna tell my mama what you said, what you called me, and she an't ever gonna let you come near me again."

"Your mama, your mama. You'd piss in a Pepsi bottle if your mama told you to."

"Listen to you. You . . . you trash. You nothing but trash. Your mama's trash, and your grandmama, and your whole dirty family . . ."

I hit her then. With my hand wide open, I swung at her face, but I was too angry. I was crazy angry and I tripped, falling with my hands spread onto the red dirt. My right hand slapped into a broken clay pot, hurting me so bad I could barely see Shannon's dripping flushed cheeks.

"Oh . . . shit. You . . . shit." If I could have jumped up and caught her, I would have ripped out handfuls of that cotton candy hair.

Shannon stopped moving back and watched as I pushed myself up and grabbed my right hand with my left. I was crying, I realized, the tears running down my face while behind us the choir had never stopped singing. That woman's voice still rolled over the cottonwoods. *WAS BLIND BUT NOW I SEE. . . .*

"You're ugly." I swallowed my tears and spoke very quietly. "You're God's own ugly child and you're gonna be an ugly woman. A lonely, ugly old woman."

Shannon's lips started to tremble, poking out of her face so that she was uglier than I'd ever seen her, a doll carved out of cold grease melting in the heat.

"You ugly thing," I went on. "You monster, you greasy cross-eyed stinking sweaty-faced ugly thing!" I pointed all my fingers at her and spit at her patent leather shoes. "You so ugly, your own mama don't even love you." Shannon backed off, turned around, and started running.

"Mamaaaaa . . . ," she wailed as she ran. I kept yelling "ugly, ugly" after her, more to keep myself from crying than to hurt her anymore.

"Ugly . . . ugly . . . ugly."

MAMA DIDN'T WANT to know why Shannon and I had quarreled. The only thing she got angry about was Mrs. Pearl telling her that I'd hit Shannon in the face. "You can put somebody's eye out, hitting them in the face. No reason to be hitting people anyway."

"No ma'am."

"Well . . ." She looked at me closely. I knew she was waiting for me to tell her something, but I just kept my eyes on the table. "They should have brought you home right away, 'stead of making you sit in the car while they went all over everywhere."

"Yes ma'am." I didn't have a thing to say about Shannon Pearl.

Mama sighed tiredly, "Well, you just stay out of trouble the rest of the summer. I don't want to be explaining your behavior to other people all the time."

"No ma'am."

For most of August my stepfather was out of work, so Mama let me stay over at Aunt Alma's house. I spent my time organizing the cousins in acting out complicated stories, half of which were drawn from television programs. As long as everybody did what I told them, I was the best baby-sitter Aunt Alma had ever seen.

"You can be Francis Marion," I told Butch. "Reese and I will be Cherokee warriors, Patsy can be the British commander, David will be the cowardly colonist, and Dan can be a colonist on our side."

"Swamp fox, swamp fox, where have you been?" Butch began singing but Patsy cut him off. "Why do I have to be the British commander? Why can't you be the bad guy and let me be a Cherokee?"

"'Cause you don't climb trees worth a pig's ass. Everybody knows Indians can climb trees."

"Then I get to ride the horse, and I want to ride Dan's bike, not Butch's old one."

"If she gets to ride my bike, then I want to wear your cap."

"We don't use my cap in this one. We only use my cap when we play Johnny Yuma." I was losing patience and I certainly didn't want to give up my rebel cap. Uncle Jack had brought it back from the Fort Sumter general store just before he got sent to the county farm for busting a man's jaw and breaking a window at the Cracker Blue Cafe. The cap he gave me was beautiful—gray, soft, with a slouched-forward brim, and the stars and bars stitched in yellow thread.

"Johnny Yuma," Butch started singing again, trying hard to imitate

Johnny Cash's deep voice. "He roamed through the west . . . JOHNNY YUMA THE REBEL . . . He wandered alone . . ."

"You always wear it." Dan swatted Butch's rear end and turned back to me with a look of sweet reasonableness. "Don't matter if we're playing Frankenstein's monster, and you know didn't nobody wear no cap like that in the Frankenstein movie."

"Oh, for crying out loud." I let Dan wear my cap, but I lost interest in the swamp fox. Who'd ever heard of him before he showed up on Walt Disney?

Blue and Garvey would only play with us about half the time. They had recently taken up smoking and were busy practicing pitching pennies. When school started again, they planned to wipe out the lunch money of half the sixth grade. Meanwhile, they would only play when I proposed a plot they really liked.

"Let's play 'The Dalton Boys' again," Blue kept suggesting. He'd perfected the trick of diving off his bicycle after pretending to be shot and he loved to show it off.

"It's the Dalton *Girls*," I insisted. Reese and I had seen the movie twice and would have seen it a third time if the theater hadn't closed down.

"Well maybe, but everybody remembers the Dalton *Boys*." Blue and Garvey had seen the movie too, and hadn't gotten over how the Dalton brothers had been killed off in the first scene so the women could learn to shoot guns and rob banks. "I don't think that movie was real anyway. I bet you their sisters never robbed no banks."

"What you want to bet?" Reese challenged. She'd loved the movie as much as I had. "You think a girl can't beat your ass? You think I can't beat your ass?"

"Oh, you couldn't scare a chicken off a nest of water moccasins!"

"You're the one scared of water moccasins. Aunt Alma said you pissed your pants when she took you blackberrying, all 'count of you stepped near a little green snake. Thinking it was some old water moccasin . . ."

"You shut your chicken piss mouth."

"You shut yours!"

"Girls!"

"Boys!"

Aunt Alma made us break it up. She sent the boys to play in the backyard and told us girls we'd have to stay in the front.

"If you can't play together, I'll keep you apart."

"I don't want to be 'round no stupid boys anyway." Sometimes I agreed with every word out of my little sister's mouth.

"But what we gonna play now?" Patsy whined. "We can't ride the bikes in the front yard. We can't do much of nothing in the front yard."

I spun my rebel cap on my fist and had a sudden inspiration.

"We're gonna play mean sister."

"What?" Patsy kept wiping the snot off her lip. Mama swore Patsy had had a runny nose since she was born. "She'll be wiping snot the day she's married, wiping snot the day she dies." I gave Patsy the handkerchief I'd sneaked out of my stepfather's drawer for a bandana.

"We're gonna play mean sisters," I told them all again, and I could see in my mind's eye Shannon Pearl's twisted mean face. "First we're gonna play Johnny Yuma's mean sisters, then Francis Marion's mean sisters, the Bat Masterson's. Then we'll think of somebody else."

Reese looked confused. "What do mean sisters do?"

"They do everything their brothers do. Only they do it first and fastest and meanest."

Reese still looked confused, but Patsy whooped.

"Yeah! I want to be the Rifleman's mean sister"

Patsy ran off to get Dan's old broken plastic rifle. All afternoon she pretended it was a sawed-off shotgun like the one on *Wanted: Dead or Alive*. Reese finally got into it and started playing at being shot off the porch. I took Aunt Alma's butcher knife and announced that I was gonna be Jim Bowie's mean sister, and no one was to bother me.

I practiced sticking Aunt Alma's knife into the porch and listened to the boys cursing in the backyard. I was mean, I decided. I was mean and vicious, and all I really wanted to be doing was sticking that knife in Roseanne Pearl's fancy sewing. She'd called me an evil child when Shannon told her what I'd said. She hadn't wanted to hear what her darling daughter had said to me.

That evening, Patsy entertained the whole family by running up and down the porch steps yelling, "Ten-four, Ten-four" until she knocked over Aunt Grace's glass of tea.

"What in God's name are you playing at, child?"

"I was being Broderick Crawford's mean sister," Patsy wailed, wiping her nose.

"His what?" Uncle Bo started laughing into his glass. "His what!" He rocked back on his cane-bottom chair and ground his cigarette out on the porch floor. Aunt Alma shook her head and looked at Patsy like she had gone crazy.

"Broderick Crawford's mean sister! My Lord, what they don't think up."

Patsy was humiliated and angry. She pointed at me. "She told me about it. She told me I could."

Bo reached out and slapped my fanny. "Girl, you got a mind that scares me." He swatted me again, but lightly, and he kept grinning. "Broderick Crawford's mean sister."

I didn't care. I played mean sister all summer long.

ONE SUNDAY LATE in August, Shannon Pearl called our house. "I'm not gonna apologize," she said right away, as if no time at all had passed. Her voice sounded strange after not hearing it for so long.

"I don't care what you do," I told her. I held the phone with my shoulder and picked my cuticles with my fingernails.

"Stop that," Mama said, as she went by me on her way to the kitchen.

"Yes ma'am," I said automatically.

"What's that?" Shannon sounded hopeful.

"I was talking to my mama. Why'd you call me?"

There was a sigh, and then Shannon's voice cleared a couple of times. "Well, I thought I should. No sense us fighting over something so silly, anyway. I bet you can't even remember what it was about."

"I remember," I told her, though I really couldn't have said what had started us fighting and my voice sounded cold even to me. For a moment I was ashamed, then angry. Why should I care if I hurt her feelings? Who was she to me?

"My mama said I could call you," Shannon whispered. "She said I could ask you over this Sunday. We're gonna have a barbecue for some of Daddy's people from Mississippi. They're bringing us some Georgia peaches and some eggshell pecans." I bit at my thumbnail and said nothing.

"You could ask your mama if you could come," Shannon's voice sounded breathless and desperate, almost squeaky. "If you wanted to," she added. I wondered what she had told her mama in order to get her to agree I could come over. Out on the porch Reese had started shouting at Patsy.

"You don't even know how to play this game!"

Why should I go to the Pearls' house and watch her fat relatives eat themselves sick?

"Mama gave me a record player," Shannon said suddenly. "I got a bunch of records for it."

"Yeah?"

"Lots of 'em." I heard her mother saying something in the background. "I got to go. Are you gonna come?"

"Maybe. I don't know. I'll think about it." I hung up the phone and saw Mama was watching me from the kitchen. "Shannon wants me to come over to her house this Sunday. They're having a barbecue."

"You want to go?"

"Maybe. I don't know." Mama nodded and handed me a towel.

"Well, you tell me before Sunday. I an't gonna want no surprises on Sunday morning. I might want to spend the whole day in bed, you never can tell." Mama laughed, and I ran over and hugged her. I loved it when she laughed like that. It made the whole house feel warm and safe.

"I might want to go on a trip myself." Mama laughed again and slapped my behind lightly. "But I an't going nowhere till we get these dishes done girl, and it's your turn to dry."

"Yes ma'am."

I DIDN'T PLAN to go. I really didn't. I certainly didn't call Shannon back and I didn't say anything to Mama either. But Sunday afternoon I started walking toward Shannon's house, carrying Reese's tin bucket as if I was gonna go hunting for muscadines. Along the way I shook the vines and tried to imagine swinging from them. Every time Reese or I tried, we wound up falling on our behinds. Maybe they had a different kind in Africa. Probably didn't grow muscadines either.

I hummed as I walked, snatches of Mama's favorite hymns and mine, alternating between "Somebody Touched Me" and "Oh Sinner Man." Reese always sang it as "Whoa Sinner Man," which invariably made Uncle Jack bark out his donkey's bray laugh. Actually it looked like we weren't going to see Uncle Jack until next summer. He'd got into another fight down at the county farm, and Aunt Grace said a bunch of men had held him down and shaved all his black hair off. I tried to imagine him bald-headed.

"That'll slow down his womanizing." Aunt Grace had been almost pleased.

"What's *womanizing?*" Reese hadn't learned yet that asking questions about most things the aunts said to each other just got you pushed outside. I'd tried to tell her that if she ever wanted to learn anything, she should just shut up and listen and try to figure it out later.

"What are you doing listening to other people's business?" Mama had been really angry. "You get out of here, all of you."

"See what you did." I'd been righteously indignant. I wasn't used to being put out with the little kids. "Now we'll never know why they shaved his head."

"Oh, I know that already." Reese gave me a smirk and put her arm around Patsy. "Granny said he tried to cut some fellow's dick off."

I'D NEVER COME up to the Pearl's house from the back before. I usually came down the road from the Sears Tire Center, but that Sunday I cut through the backyards of the big houses on Tyson Circle and through the parking lot of the Roberts Dairy Drive-In. Mrs. Pearl had planted magnolia and mums all along the back of their property so no one could see that parking lot, and I had to wiggle past some of the mums that were planted close up to their fence.

There were a lot of people there, and they all looked like Pearls. Big puffy men stood around holding massive glasses of iced tea and grinning at skinny pale women with thin flyaway hair. Some kids were running around over near the driveway where some big boys were taking turns cranking an ice-cream maker. Two card tables had been set up in addition to the big redwood picnic table Mrs. Pearl was so proud of getting last year. It looked like people had already been eating but the charcoal grill was still smoldering, and Shannon Pearl was standing beside it looking as miserable as any human being could.

I stood still and watched her. She was playing with a long-handled fork and looking over every now and then at the other children playing. Her face was flushed pink and sweaty, and she looked swollen in her orange-and-white organdy dress. I remembered how Mama said Mrs. Pearl just didn't know how to dress her daughter.

"She shouldn't put her in all that embroidery as fat as that child is, it just makes her look bigger."

I agreed. Shannon looked like a sausage stuffed in a too-small casing. She also looked like she had been crying. Past the tables, Mrs. Pearl was sitting with half a dozen wispy, thin women, two of whom were holding babies.

"Precious. Precious," I heard someone exclaim in a reedy voice.

"You fat old thing." One of Shannon's cousins ran part her and play-whispered loud in her ear. "You must'a eat nothing but pork since you was born. Turned you into the hog you are." He laughed and ran on. Shannon pulled off her glasses and started cleaning them on her skirt.

"Jesus shit," I whispered to myself.

I had always suspected that I was the only friend Shannon Pearl had in the world. That was part of what made me feel so mean and evil around her, knowing that I didn't really care enough about her to be her friend. But hearing her cousin talk to her that way brought back to me the first time I'd met her, the way I'd loved her stubborn pride, the righteous rage she turned on her tormentors. She didn't look righteous at that moment. She looked tired and hurt and ashamed. Her face made me feel sick and angry, and guilty about her all over again.

I kicked at the short wooden fence for a moment and then swung one leg up to climb over. All right, she was a little monster, but she was my friend and the kind of monster I could understand. Twenty feet away from me, Shannon sniffed and reached for the can of lighter fluid by the grill. She hadn't even seen me watching her.

AFTERWARD, PEOPLE KEPT asking me what happened.

"Where were you?" Mr. Carson, the County Sheriff, kept asking me, "and what exactly did you see?" He never gave me a chance to tell him. Maybe because it was hard to hear over Mrs. Pearl screaming. With all the confusion and shouting, his questions sounded both formal and meaningless.

"Uh huh, and where were you?" He kept looking over his shoulder toward the grill and the sputtering fat fire.

I knew then he hadn't heard a word I said. But Mrs. Pearl did. She heard me clear, and I thought she was gonna come right over the people holding her. She was trying to get her hands on me. She kept screaming "YOU!" like I had done something myself, but all I had done was watch. I was sure of that. I had never gotten two steps past the fence.

Shannon had put her glasses back on. She had the lighter fluid can in one hand, and she took up that long-handled fork in the other. She poked the coals with the fork and sprayed them with the fluid from the can.

The can made a popping noise as she squeezed it. She was trying to get more of the coals burning, it seemed. Or maybe she just liked the way the flames leaped up. She sprayed and sprayed, and pulled back and sprayed again.

Shannon shook her hand. I heard the lighter fluid can sputter and suck air, and then I saw the flame run up right to the can. It looked like the flame went out. Then it came back with a boom. The can exploded, and fire ballooned out in a great rolling ball.

Shannon didn't even scream. She had her mouth wide open, and it seemed as if she just breathed the flames in. Her glasses went opaque, her eyes disappeared, and all around her skull her fine hair stood up in a crown of burning glory. Her dress whooshed and disappeared in orange-yellow smoky flames. I saw the fork fall, the wooden handle burning. I saw Mrs. Pearl come to her feet and start to run toward her daughter. I saw all the men dropping their iced tea glasses. I saw Shannon stagger and stumble from side to side, and then fall in a heap. Her dress was gone. I saw the smoke turn black and oily. I saw Shannon Pearl disappear from this world.

THEY HELD THE funeral at Bushy Creek Baptist. Mrs. Pearl insisted on laying an intricately embroidered baby blanket over the coffin. I gave it one glance and then kept my head down. Mrs. Pearl had put a baby cherub with pink cheeks and yellow hair on the spot that was probably covering Shannon's blackened features. I kept my hand in Mama's and my mouth shut tight.

"Did you ever see her?" Mrs. Pearl was saying to the preacher they'd brought in from their family church in Mississippi. "She was just an angel of the Lord."

The preacher nodded and laid his hands on top of Mrs. Pearl's where she was hugging close a great bunch of yellow mums. Beyond them, the choir director had one hand on Mr. Pearl's elbow. Mr. Pearl was as gray as a dead man. I watched from under my lowered lashes while the choir director pushed a paper cup into Mr. Pearl's hand and whispered in his ear. Mr. Pearl nodded and sipped steadily. He kept looking over at his wife and the flowers she was gripping so tightly.

"She loved babies, you know. She was always a friend to the less fortunate . . . all her little friends are here today . . . and she could sing. Oh! You should have heard her sing."

I remembered Shannon's hoarse wavering voice humming in the backseat of her daddy's car after she had told me a particularly horrible story. Was it possible Mrs. Pearl had never heard her daughter sing? I looked over to Mr. Pearl and saw his head go down again. If it had been me in that ball of flame, would they have come to my funeral?

Mrs. Pearl lifted her face from the closely held flowers. Her watery eyes flickered back and forth across the pews. She doesn't understand anything, I thought. Mrs. Pearl's eyes moved over me sightlessly while her hands gripped and crushed the flowers pressed against her neck. She started to moan suddenly like a bird caught in a blackberry bush, moaning softly, tonelessly, while the preacher carefully pushed her down into the front pew. The choir director's wife ran over and put her arm around Mrs. Pearl while the preacher desperately signaled the choir to start a hymn. Their voices rose smoothly while Mrs. Pearl's moan went on and on, rising into the close sweaty air, a song with no meter, no rhythm— but gospel, the purest gospel, a song of absolute hopeless grief.

I turned and pushed my face into my mama's dress. Nothing could cover the persistent smell of barbecue.

A NEW LIFE

Mary Ward Brown

THEY MEET BY CHANCE in front of the bank. Elizabeth is a recent widow, pale and dry-eyed, unable to cry. Paul, an old friend, old boyfriend, starts smiling the moment he sees her. He looks so happy, she thinks. She's never seen him look so happy. Under one arm he carries a wide farm checkbook, a rubber band around it so things won't fall out.

"Well. This is providential." He grips her hand and holds on, beaming, ignoring the distance he's long kept between them. Everything about him seems animated. Even his hair, thick, dark, shot with early gray, stands up slightly from his head instead of lying down flat. In the sunlight the gray looks electric. "We've been thinking about you," he says, still beaming. "Should have been to see you."

"But you *did* come." Something about him is different, she thinks, something major. It's not just the weight he's put on.

"We came when everyone else was there and you didn't need us. We should have been back long ago. How are you?"

"Fine," she says, to end it. "Thank you."

He studies her face, frowns. "You don't look fine," he says. "You're still grieving, when John is with God now. He's well again. Happy! Don't you know that?"

She turns toward the bank with no reply. She can't stand such remarks.

But it does explain Paul. She's heard that he and his wife, Louise, are in a new religious group in town, something that has sprung up outside the church. They call themselves Keepers of the Vineyard. Like a rock band, someone said.

Behind them, small-town traffic moves up and down the street, a variety of midsize cars and pickup trucks, plus an occasional big car or van. In front, the newly remodeled bank updates a street of old red-brick buildings. Some are painted white, green, gray. Around the corner the beauty shop is pink with white trim.

This is the southern Bible Belt, where people talk about God the way they talk about the weather, about His will and His blessings, about why He lets things happen. The Vineyard people claim that God also talks to them. Their meeting place is a small house on Green Street, where they meet, the neighbors say, night and day.

Their leader is the new young pastor of the Presbyterian church, called by his first name, Steve. Regular church members look on the group with suspicion. They're crazy, the church people say. They go too far.

When told, Steve had simply shrugged. "Some thought Jesus was a little crazy, too," he'd said, with a smile.

He is a spellbinding preacher and no one moves or dozes while he speaks, but his church is split in two. Some are for him and some against him, but none are neutral. He is defined by extremes.

Paul opens the door to the bank for Elizabeth. "What are you doing tonight?" he asks, over her shoulder.

When she looks back, surprised, he winks.

"Louise and I could come over after supper," he says. "How about it?"

She understands his winks and jokes. They're cover-up devices, she'd discovered years ago, for all he meant to hide. New hurts, old wounds, the real Paul Dudley. Only once had she ever seen him show pain. When his favorite dog, always with him, had been hit by a truck, he'd covered his face with his hands when he told her. But the minute she'd touched him, ready to cry too, he'd stiffened. "I'll have to get another one," he'd said. And right away, he had. Another liver-spotted pointer.

"You're turning down a good way of life, though," her mother had said, a little sadly, when she didn't take the ring. It had been his mother's diamond. He'd also inherited a large tract of land and a home in the country.

She'd never confessed one of her reservations about Paul, for fear that it might sound trivial. He had simply made her nervous. Wherever they'd gone, to concerts, plays, movies, he hadn't been able to sit still and listen, but had had to look around and whisper, start conversations, pick up dropped programs. Go for more popcorn. He had rummaged through his hair, fiddled with his tie, jiggled keys in his pocket, until it had been all she could do not to say, "Stop that, or I'll scream!"

He hadn't seemed surprised when she told him. Subdued at first, he had rallied and joked as he went out the door. But he'd cut her out of his life from then on, and ignored all her efforts to be friendly. Not until both were married to other people had he even stopped on the street to say hello.

Back home now in her clean, orderly kitchen, Elizabeth has put away groceries and stored the empty bags. Without putting it off, she has subtracted the checks she'd just written downtown. Attention to detail has become compulsive with her. It is all that holds her together, she thinks.

JUST BEFORE DAYLIGHT-savings dark, Paul and Louise drive up in a white station wagon. Paul is wearing a fresh short-sleeved shirt, the top of its sleeves still pressed together like uncut pages in a book. In one hand he carries a Bible as worn as a wallet.

Louise, in her late forties like Elizabeth, is small and blond. Abandoned first by a father who had simply left home, then by a mother his leaving had destroyed, she'd been brought up by sad, tired grandparents. Her eyes are like those of an unspoiled pet, waiting for a sign to be friendly.

When Elizabeth asks if they'd like something to drink now or later, they laugh. It's a long-standing joke around Wakefield. "Mr. Paul don't drink nothing but sweet milk," a worker on his place had said years ago.

"Now would be nice," he says, with his happy new smile.

Elizabeth leads the way to a table in her kitchen, a large light room with one end for dining. The table, of white wood with an airy glass top, overlooks her back lawn. While she fills goblets with tea and ice, Paul gazes out the window, humming to himself, drumming on the glass top. Louise admires the marigolds, snapdragons, and petunias in bloom. Her own flowers have been neglected this year, she says. Elizabeth brings out a pound cake still warm from the oven.

"Let's bless it," Paul says, when they're seated.

He holds out one hand to her and the other to Louise. His hand is trembling and so warm it feels feverish. Because of her? Elizabeth can't help thinking. No. Everyone knows he's been happy with his wife. Louise's hand is cool and steady.

He bows his head. "Lord, we thank you for this opportunity to witness in your name. We know that You alone can comfort our friend in her sorrow. Bring her, we pray, to the knowledge of your saving grace and give her your peace, which passes understanding. We ask it for your sake and in your name."

He smiles a benediction, and Elizabeth cuts the cake.

"The reason we're here, Elizabeth"—He ignores the tea and cake before him—"is that my heart went out to you this morning at the bank. You can't give John up, and it's tearing you apart."

A New Life · 441

What can she say? He's right. She can't give John up and she *is* torn apart, after more than a year.

"We have the cure for broken hearts," he says, as if stating a fact.

Louise takes a bite of cake, but when he doesn't she puts down her fork. On her left hand, guarded by her wedding band, is the ring that Elizabeth remembers.

"I have something to ask you, Elizabeth." Paul looks her boldly in the eye. "Are you saved?"

She turns her tea glass slowly clockwise, wipes up the circle beneath it with her napkin. "I don't know how to answer that, Paul," she says. "What happened to John did something to my faith. John didn't deserve all that suffering, or to die in his prime. I can't seem to accept it."

"Well, that's natural. Understandable. In my heart I was rebellious myself, at one time."

She frowns, trying to follow. He hadn't been religious at all when she'd known him. On the contrary, he'd worked on a tractor all day Sunday while everyone else went to church, had joked about people who were overly religious.

"But I had an encounter with Jesus Christ that changed my life," he says. His eyes redden. "I kept praying, with all my heart, and He finally came to me. His presence was as real as yours is now." He shakes his head. "You have to really want Him, though. Most people have to hit rock bottom, the way I did, before they do. You have to be down so low you say, 'Lord, I can't make it on my own. You'll have to help me. *You* take over!'"

Now he's lost her. Things had gone so well for him, she'd thought. He'd had everything he said he wanted out of life when they were dating—a big family, and to live on his land. He'd been an only child whose parents had died young. Louise had been orphaned too, in a way. So they'd had a child every year or two before they quit, a station wagon full of healthy, suntanned children. Some of them driving themselves by now, Elizabeth had noticed.

As for her, rock bottom had been back in that hospital room with John, sitting in a chair by his bed. Six months maybe, a year at the most, they'd just told her in the hall. She'd held his hand until the Demerol took effect and his hand had gone limp in hers. Then she'd leaned her head on the bed beside him and prayed, with all her heart. From hospital room to hospital room she had prayed, and at home in between.

"I've said that too, Paul, many times," she says. "I prayed, and nothing happened. Why would He come to you and not me?"

"Because you were letting something stand in your way, my dear." His smile is back, full force. "For Him to come in, you have to get rid of self—first of all your self-*will!* 'Not my will but Thine be done,' He said on the cross."

He breaks off, takes a drink of tea as if famished. With the first bite of cake, he shuts his eyes tight. A blissful smile melts over his face.

"Umh, umh!" He winks at Louise. "How about this pound cake, Mama!"

LATE THE NEXT afternoon, Elizabeth is watering flowers in her backyard. Before, she grew flowers to bring in the house, zinnias for pottery pitchers, bulbs for clear glass vases. Now she grows them for themselves, and seldom cuts them. She has a new irrational notion that scissors hurt the stems. After what she's seen of pain, she wants to hurt nothing that lives.

From where she stands with the hose, she sees a small red car turn into her driveway. In front of the house, two young girls in sundresses get out.

"Mrs. North?" the first girl says, when Elizabeth comes up to meet them. "You probably don't remember me, but I'm Beth Woodall and this is Cindy Lewis. We're from the Vineyard."

Beth is blond and pretty. A young Louise, Elizabeth thinks. But Cindy has a limp and something is wrong with one arm. Elizabeth doesn't look at it directly.

"What can I do for you girls?"

"Oh, we just came to see you," Beth says. "Paul and Louise thought we might cheer you up."

In the living room, Beth is the speaker. "We all knew your husband from the paper, Mrs. North. He was wonderful! My dad read every line he ever wrote, and says this town is lost without him." She pushes back her hair, anchors it behind one ear. Her nails, overlong, pale as seashells, seem to lag behind her fingers. "We've all been praying for you."

Elizabeth rubs a wet spot the hose has made on her skirt. "Thank you," she says, embarrassed.

"I know how you feel," Beth says quickly. "My boyfriend, Billy Moseley, was killed in a wreck last year. He'd been my boyfriend since grammar school, and we'd have gotten married someday, if he'd lived." Her eyes fill up with tears. "We were just always . . . together."

Elizabeth remembers Billy. Handsome, polite. A star athlete killed by a drunk driver. She feels a quick stir of sympathy but, like everything painful since John died, it freezes before it can surface. Now all of it seems packed in her chest, as in the top of a refrigerator so full the door will hardly shut. She looks back at Beth with dry guilty eyes.

"Well, I'm all right now," Beth says. "But I thought it would kill me for a while. I didn't want to live without Billy, until I met the people at the Vineyard. They made me see it was God's will for him to die and me to live and serve the Lord. Now I know he's in heaven waiting for me, and it's not as bad as it was." She shrugs. "I try to help Billy's mother, but she won't turn it over to the Lord."

The room is growing dark. Elizabeth gets up to turn on more lights, which cast a roseate glow on their faces, pale hands, narrow feet in sandals.

"Would you girls like a Coke?" she asks.

Beth blinks and sniffs to dry her eyes. "Yes, ma'am," she says. "Thank you. A Coke would be nice."

They follow Elizabeth to the kitchen, where she pours Coca-Cola into glasses filled with ice cubes.

"You must get lonesome here by yourself," Cindy says, looking around. "Are your children away from home or something?"

Elizabeth hands her a glass and paper napkin. "I don't have children, Cindy," she says. "My husband and I wanted a family, but couldn't have one. All we had was each other."

"Ah!" Beth says quickly. "*We'll* be your children, then. Won't we, Cindy?"

IT IS SEVEN o'clock in the morning and Elizabeth is drinking instant coffee from an old, stained mug, staring dejectedly out the kitchen window. During the night, she'd had a dream about John. He'd been alive, not dead.

John had been editor-publisher of the Wakefield *Sun,* the town's weekly paper, had written most of the copy himself. In the dream, they'd been in bed for the night.

John had liked to work in bed, and she had liked to read beside him, so they'd gone to bed early as a rule. Propped up on pillows, he had worked on editorials, for which he'd been known throughout the state. At times, though, he had put aside his clipboard and taken off his glasses. When he turned her way, his eyes—blue gray and rugged like the tweed jacket he'd worn so many winters—could take on a look that made the book fall from her hand. Later, sometimes, onto the floor.

In the dream, as he looked at her, the phone by their bed had rung. He'd forgotten a meeting, he said, throwing off covers. He had to get down there. It had already started, a meeting he couldn't afford to miss. Putting on a jacket, he had stopped at the bedroom door.

"I'll be right back," he'd promised.

But he wasn't back and never would be, she'd been reminded, wide awake. In the dark, she had checked the space beside her with her hand to be sure, and her loss had seemed new again, more cruel than ever, made worse by time. If only she could cry, she'd thought, like other widows! Cry, everyone told her. Let the grief out! But she couldn't. It was frozen and locked up inside her, a mass that wouldn't move.

She had waked from the dream at two in the morning and hasn't been back to sleep since. Now she's glad to be up with something to do, even if it's only an appointment with her lawyer. She has sold John's business but kept the building, and the legalities are not yet over. She wants to be on time, is always on time. It is part of her fixation on detail, as if each thing attended to were somehow on a list that if completed could bring back meaning to her life.

In the fall she will go back to teaching school, but her heart is not in it as before. For twenty years she had been, first of all, John's wife—from deadline to deadline, through praise, blame, long stretches of indifference. He couldn't have done it without her, he'd said, with each award and honor he'd been given.

Now no other role seems right for her, which is her problem, she's thinking, when the front doorbell rings.

Louise is there in a pink summer dress, her clean hair shining in the sun. She smells of something fresh and floral.

"May I come in?"

Still in a rumpled nightgown and robe, aware of the glazed-over look in her eyes, Elizabeth opens the door wider, steps back. "I have an appointment," she says, smiling as best she can. "But come in. There's time for a cup of coffee."

At the white table, Louise takes the place she'd had before. "I won't stay long," she says.

Elizabeth puts on a pot of real coffee, gets out cups and saucers, sits down across from Louise. Outside, all is quiet. Stores and offices won't open until nine. So why is Louise in town at this hour?

"I was praying for you," she says, as if in answer. "But the Lord told me to come and see you instead."

Elizabeth looks at her, stares. "God told you?" she asks, in a moment.

Their eyes meet. Louise nods. "He wanted you to know that He loves you," she says. "He wanted to send you His love by me." Her face turns a sudden bright pink that deepens and spreads.

Elizabeth says nothing. A car starts up and drives off next door. A dog barks. When the coffee is ready, she pours it. She's learned to drink hers black, but Louise adds milk and sugar.

"Come to the Vineyard with us next time, Elizabeth," Louise says suddenly.

This is what she came for, Elizabeth thinks, and it's more than an invitation. It's a plea, as from someone on the bank to a swimmer having trouble in the water.

"It could save your life!" Louise says.

THE VINEYARD IS a narrow, shotgun-style house of the 1890s, last used as a dentist's office. It has one large front room, with two small rooms and a makeshift kitchen behind it. Elizabeth, having been welcomed and shown around, stands against the wall of the front room with Paul and Louise. The group is smaller than she'd expected, and not all Presbyterian. Some are from other churches as well, all smiling and excited.

Everything revolves around Steve, a young man in jeans who looks like a slight blond Jesus. When Elizabeth is introduced, he looks her deep in the eyes.

"Elizabeth!" he says, as if he knows her already. "We were hoping you'd come. Welcome to the Vineyard."

He says no more and moves on, but she has felt his power like the heat from a stove. She finds herself following him around the room with her eyes, wishing she could hear what he says to other people.

The night is hot and windows are open, but no breeze comes through. Rotary fans sweep away the heat in front of them monotonously, in vain. Someone brings in a pitcher of Kool-Aid, which is passed around in paper cups.

"Okay, people." Steve holds up his cup and raises his voice for attention. "Let's have a song."

Everyone takes a seat on the floor, in a ring shaped by the long narrow room. A masculine girl with short dark hair stands up. She tests one key then another low in her throat, and leads off. "We are one in the Spirit, we are one in the Lord . . ."

Most of the singers are young, in shorts or jeans, but some are middle-aged or older. Of the latter, the majority are single women and widows like Elizabeth. The young people sit with folded legs, leaning comfortably forward, and the men draw up one leg or the other. But the women, in pastel pants suits or sleeveless dresses, sit up like paper dolls bent in the middle.

The song gains momentum for the chorus, which ends, "Yes, they'll know-oh we are Christians by our love!"

"All *right*," Steve says. "Time to come to our Lord in prayer."

Someone clambers up to turn off the light switch and someone else lights a candle on the Kool-Aid table. In the dim light Steve reaches out to his neighbor on each side, and a chain of hands is quickly formed.

Without a hand to hold in her new single life, Elizabeth is glad to link in. She could be joining the human race again, she thinks, smiling at the young woman on her left and Paul on her right. Paul's hand no longer trembles but feels as it had in high school—not thrilling but dependable, something to count on.

The room is suddenly hushed. "For the benefit of our visitor," Steve says, "we begin with sentence prayers around the circle, opening our hearts and minds to God."

Elizabeth feels a rush of misgiving. *Oh, no!* she thinks. *I can't do this!* She's never prayed out loud in her life except in unison, much less ad-libbed before a group.

But Steve has already started. "We thank you, Heavenly Father, for the privilege of being here. Guide us, we pray, in all we say and do, that it may be for the extension of your kingdom. We thank you again for each other, but above all for your blessed son Jesus, who is with us tonight, here in this circle."

On Steve's right, a young man with shoulder-length hair takes up at once. "I thank you, Lord, for turning me around. Until I found You, all

I cared about was that bottle. But You have living water, better than any drink on earth!''

Eagerly, one after the other, they testify, confess, ask help in bringing others to Jesus as Lord and Savior. They speak of the devil as if he's someone in town, someone they meet every day.

In her turn, a checkout girl from the supermarket starts to cry and can't stop. From around the circle come murmurs of "God bless you" and "We love you" until her weeping begins to subside.

"My heart's too full tonight," the girl says at last. "I have to pass."

On each side, Elizabeth's hands are gripped tighter. The back of her blouse is wet with sweat. The room begins to feel crowded and close.

"Praise God!" a man cries out in the middle of someone's prayer.

"Help me, Lord," a woman whimpers.

A teenage boy starts to pray, his words eerily unintelligible. Tongues? Elizabeth wonders, electrified. They do it here, she's heard. But something nasal in his voice gives the clue, and she has a wild impulse to laugh. He's not speaking in tongues but is tongue-tied from a cleft palate.

Too soon, she hears Paul's voice beside her, charged with emotion. He's praying about the sin of pride in his life, but she can't pay attention because she will be next. Heavy galloping hoofbeats seem to have taken the place of her heart.

When Paul is through, she says nothing. *I pass* flashes through her mind, but she doesn't say it. She is unable to decide on, much less utter, a word. Her hands are wet with cold perspiration. She tries to withdraw them, but Paul on one side and the young woman on the other hold on tight. Fans hum back and forth as her silence stretches out.

At last someone starts to pray out of turn, and the circle is mended. As the prayers move back toward Steve, she gives a sigh of relief and tries, without being obvious, to change her position on the floor.

Steve gives a new directive. "We'll now lift up to God those with special needs tonight."

He allows them to think for a moment, then leads off. "I lift up Jane, in the medical center for diagnosis," he says. "Her tests begin in the morning."

They pray in silence for Jane, for someone in the midst of divorce, for a man who's lost his job. An unnamed friend with an unidentified problem is lifted up.

Louise clears her throat for attention, then hesitates before speaking out. When she does, her voice is girlish and sweet as usual.

"I lift up Elizabeth," she says.

ELIZABETH HAS AVOIDED the telephone all day, though she's heard it ring many times. The weather is cloudy and cool, so she's spent the morning outside, weeding, hoeing, raking, and has come to one decision. She will not see the soul savers today.

Tomorrow, it may be, she can face them. Today, she will do anything not to. They were holding her up, she thinks, not for her sake but their own. They refuse to look on the dark side of things, and they want her to blink it away too. If she can smile in the face of loss, grief, and death, so can they. They're like children in a fairy tale, singing songs, holding hands. Never mind the dark wood, the wolves and witches. Or birds that eat up the bread crumbs.

During lunch she takes the phone off the hook, eats in a hurry, and goes back out with magazines and a book. For supper she will go to Breck's for a barbecue and visit with whoever's there. When she comes back, the day will be over. "One day at a time" is the new widow's motto.

She is drying off from a shower when the front doorbell rings. She doesn't hurry, even when it rings again and someone's finger stays on the buzzer. The third time, she closes the bathroom door, little by little, so as not to be heard. Gingerly, as if it might shock her, she flips off the light switch.

Soon there is knocking on her back door, repeated several times. She can hear voices but not words. When she continues to keep quiet, hardly breathing for fear they will somehow know or divine that she's there, the knocking stops and the voices, jarred by retreating footsteps, fade away. At last, through a sneaked-back window curtain, she can see the small red car moving off.

And suddenly, in her mind's eye, she can also see herself as from a distance, towel clutched like a fig leaf, hiding from a band of Christians out to save her soul!

For the first time in her widowhood, she laughs when she's alone. It happens before she knows it, like a hiccough or a sneeze. With an ease she'd thought lost forever, she laughs again, more.

Still smiling, she dresses in a hurry and is about to walk out the back door when the front doorbell rings.

This time she goes at once to face them. Beth and Cindy, plus Steve and two policemen, stare back at her. The policemen are in uniform, dark blue pants and lighter blue shirts, with badges, insignia, and guns on their belts. Obviously, they've been deciding how to get in the house without a key.

For a moment no one speaks. Then Beth, wide-eyed, bursts out, "You scared us to death, Mrs. North! We thought you had passed out or something. We knew you were in there because of your car."

"I didn't feel like seeing anyone today." Elizabeth's voice is calm and level. Where did it come from, that unruffled voice? Something has come over her, she thinks. She should be mad or upset, and she's not.

"Sorry we bothered you, Mrs. North," the older policeman says. "Your friends here were worried."

Out of the blue, Elizabeth is suffused with what seems pure benevolence. For a split second, and for no reason, she is sure that everything is overall right in the world, no matter what. And not just for her but for everyone, including the dead. The air seems rarified, the light incandescent.

"It was no bother," she says, half-dazed. "I thank you."

Steve has said nothing. His eyes are as calm as ever, the eyes of a true believer, blessed or cursed with certainty. His focus has been steadily on her, but now it breaks away.

"Let's go, people," he says lightly. "God bless you, Elizabeth. Glad you're okay."

ELIZABETH HAS SLEPT all night, for once. As she sits down to cereal and coffee, she is sure of one thing. She has to start what everyone tells her must be "a whole new life" without John, and she has to do it now. Though frozen and numb inside still, she can laugh. And she has experienced, however fleetingly, what must have been grace.

When a car door slams out front, not once but twice, she gets up without waiting for anyone to ring or knock. It is Paul and Louise, for the first time not smiling. Paul has on khaki work clothes. Louise has brushed her hair on top, but underneath sleep tangles show.

On the living-room sofa, they sit leaning forward. Paul rocks one knee nervously from side to side, making his whole body shake from the tension locked inside him.

"They should have come to us instead of going to the police," he says at once. "They just weren't thinking."

"No. It was my fault," Elizabeth says. "I should have gone to the door."

"Why *didn't* you?" Louise asks.

"Well . . ." She falls silent.

"Our meeting upset you?" Paul asks, in a moment.

Elizabeth's housecoat is old and too short. They catch her like this every time, she thinks. Why can't they call before they come, like everyone else? She begins to check the snaps down her front.

"Level with us, honey," Paul says. "We're your friends. What upset you so much?"

Except for the faint click of a snap being snapped, the room is utterly quiet.

"We need to pray about this," Paul says. "Let's pray . . ."

"No!" Elizabeth is on her feet without thinking. "No, Paul. I can't!" She's out of breath as from running. "This has got to stop! I can't be in your Vineyard. You'll have to find somebody else!"

Mary Ward Brown · 452

He's silent for so long a countdown seems to start. Then he stands up slowly, Louise beside him as if joined. At the door, with his hand on the knob, he turns.

"Well, Elizabeth," he says. "I guess it's time to say good-bye."

Her heart slows down as if brakes had been applied. The beats become heavy, far apart. She can feel them in her ears, close to her brain.

"I'm sorry, Paul!" she says quickly. Before his accusing eyes, she says it again, like holding out a gift she knows to be inadequate. "I'm *sorry!*"

But this time he has no joke or smile. Without a word, he takes Louise by the arm and guides her out the door.

Elizabeth watches them walk to the car, side by side but not touching. Paul opens the door for Louise, shuts her quickly in, and gets behind the wheel himself. The station wagon moves out of sight down the driveway.

Elizabeth's cereal is soggy, her coffee cold. She pushes it all away, props her elbows on the table, and buries her face in her hands. Suddenly, as from a thaw long overdue, she's crying. Sobs shake her shoulders. Tears seep through her fingers and run down her wrists. One drop falls on the glass top, where it sparkles like a jewel in the morning sunlight.

Passing On

PASSING ON

THE WORD "DEATH" is rarely mentioned in the South, although it's on the tip of everybody's tongue, especially in regions where the local funeral home is likely to be the liveliest place in town. To speak of death as a conclusion is to polarize it, to oppose it against life instead of thinking of it as "another place," not the place we are used to, but a place that Jesus has prepared for us. "In my Father's house are many mansions . . . ," the Bible states. "In my Father's house," "passed on," "gone ahead," "departed," "asleep in Jesus" are all synonyms for what one southern woman termed with a shudder "the D word."

But no matter what death is called, it still remains the Great Secret. Many of the complex feelings and mysteries surrounding it may be found in the three stories in this section.

The first, "The Grave" by Katherine Anne Porter, is a beautifully controlled, low-keyed fable about the timelessness of death, and the manner in which it constantly hovers over life, no matter how diligently we might try to ignore it, and also the part that memory plays in rendering death both potent and meaningless:

> They peered into the pits all shaped alike with such purposeful accuracy, and looking at each other with pleased adventurous eyes, they said in solemn tones: "These were graves!" trying by words to shape a special, suitable emotion in their minds, but they felt nothing except an agreeable thrill of wonder: they were seeing a new sight, doing something they had not done before. In them both there was also a small disappointment at the entire commonplaceness of the actual spectacle. Even if it had once contained a coffin for years upon years, when the coffin was gone a grave was just a hole in the ground. Miranda leaped into the pit that had held her grandfather's bones. Scratching around aimlessly and pleasurably as any young animal, she scooped up a lump of earth and weighed it in her palm. It had a pleasantly sweet, corrupt smell, being mixed with cedar needles and small leaves, and as the crumbs fell apart, she saw a silver dove no larger than a hazel nut, with spread wings and a neat fan-shaped tail. The breast had a deep round hollow in it.

Twenty years later, in a kind of Proustian sense memory, the narrator recalls the "sweet corrupt smell," and with it a realization of both the fleeting quality of time and the impermeability of flesh—both of which are involved in the idea of death.

KATHERINE ANNE PORTER confronts death slantwise, but in "And with a Vengeance," Margaret Gibson confronts it head on, or rather her character, Miss Telia Hand, does. "Miss T." is known to her family and the community-at-large as an old maid, a virgin, but what goes on inside her mind would doubtless stun them.

The ancient Greeks understood the association of Eros (love) with Thanatos (death), and it is this connection that looms so heavily and soars so high in the story: a measure of death from childhood to old age, from earth to sky.

> There's a quality of freedom about dying, not the lightness of removing a rain-soggy woolen great-coat and moving to the fire, feeling yourself float with the flame and the smoke up into the air, becoming air incandescent and pure. More like the gracious release after constipation. There is lightness surely, but the eye, the focus of observation and absorbed attention never pulls away from a sensation of body. So there's this marvelous freedom, not the freedom that churchmen and books discuss, the spirit relinquishing flesh, but a freedom of self. Participation in something which no one else will ask to share in. A phenomenon of self isolated and alone, essentially alone.

It is the author's brilliance that she is able to involve us in this lone passage, so that we, too, wrestle with the angel of death, achieving, as Miss T. does, neither victory nor defeat, but something beyond the banality of such opposites.

THE LAST STORY, "The Third of July" by Elizabeth Cox, reminds us of the way in which death puts things in perspective, causing petty grievances and querulous irresolutions and even celebrations to pale beside the vision of an untimely end. In this case the vision is an automobile accident that disrupts a family and kills a young boy. The randomness and unalterability of the event is both shattering and hopeless. How does one talk about it? What does one learn from it? The protagonist, Nadine, tries to describe it to her friend Miss Penny, an old woman, who's been watching a television game show:

> "There was a wreck," she began and leaned across the table so Miss Penny could hear. "Over near Hardison's Poultry. A truck ran into a station wagon. The whole family got hurt." Miss Penny reached for more slices of tomato. Her face had not yet lost its

flush. "It was pretty bad," Nadine said. "A man and his wife, a boy about sixteen."

"What?"

"Their *son* about six*teen*." Nadine spoke louder. "He was killed right off, but the man might live, and the woman." She stopped leaning and slumped back. "I don't know about the woman though." Nadine's gaze shifted to something outside the window.

"*Ten thousand dollars,*" Miss Penny said. Her voice emphasized each word equally.

From the kitchen window Nadine could see bags of web in the crab-apple trees. "Tomorrow's the Fourth of July," she told Miss Penny. Neither of them turned away from the window.

The story implies that a modicum of hope can be found in our constant struggle to make life better for ourselves and for those we love by paying closer attention to one another and to our shared moments before the final separation—that is, if death is final, and if it is, indeed, a separation. Opinions are endless—and like all good fiction, these stories raise questions rather than offering solutions.

THE GRAVE

Katherine Anne Porter

THE GRANDFATHER, dead for more than thirty years, had been twice disturbed in his long repose by the constancy and possessiveness of his widow. She removed his bones first to Louisiana and then to Texas as if she had set out to find her own burial place, knowing well she would never return to the places she had left. In Texas she set up a small cemetery in a corner of her first farm, and as the family connection grew, and oddments of relations came over from Kentucky to settle, it contained at last about twenty graves. After the grandmother's death, part of her land was to be sold for the benefit of certain of her children, and the cemetery happened to lie in the part set aside for sale. It was necessary to take up the bodies and bury them again in the family plot in the big new public cemetery, where the grandmother had been buried. At last her husband was to lie beside her for eternity, as she had planned.

The family cemetery had been a pleasant small neglected garden of tangled rose bushes and ragged cedar trees and cypress, the simple flat stones rising out of uncropped sweet-smelling wild grass. The graves were lying open and empty one burning day when Miranda and her brother Paul, who often went together to hunt rabbits and doves, propped their twenty-two Winchester rifles carefully against the rail fence, climbed over, and explored among the graves. She was nine years old and he was twelve.

They peered into the pits all shaped alike with such purposeful accuracy, and looking at each other with pleased adventurous eyes, they said in solemn tones: "These were graves!" trying by words to shape a special, suitable emotion in their minds, but they felt nothing except an agreeable thrill of wonder: they were seeing a new sight, doing something they had not done before. In them both there was also a small disappointment at the entire commonplaceness of the actual spectacle. Even if it had once contained a coffin for years upon years, when the coffin was gone a grave was just a hole in the ground. Miranda leaped into the pit that had held her grandfather's bones. Scratching around aimlessly and pleasurably as any young animal, she scooped up a lump of earth and weighed it in her palm. It had a pleasantly sweet, corrupt smell, being mixed with cedar needles and small leaves, and as the crumbs fell apart, she saw a silver dove no larger than a hazel nut, with spread wings and a neat fan-shaped tail. The breast had a deep round hollow in it. Turning it up to the fierce sunlight, she saw that the inside of the hollow was cut in little whorls. She scrambled out, over the pile of loose earth that had fallen back into one end of the grave, calling to Paul that she had found something, he must guess what . . . His head appeared smiling over the rim of another grave. He waved a closed hand at her. "I've got something too!" They ran to compare treasures, making a game of it, so many guesses each, all wrong, and a final showdown with opened palms. Paul had found a thin wide gold ring carved with intricate flowers and leaves. Miranda was smitten at sight of the ring and wished to have it. Paul seemed more impressed by the dove. They made a trade, with some little bickering. After he had got the dove in his hand, Paul said, "Don't you know what this is? This is a screw head for a *coffin!* . . . I'll bet nobody else in the world has one like this!''

Miranda glanced at it without covetousness. She had the gold ring on her thumb; it fitted perfectly. "Maybe we ought to go now," she said, "maybe one of the niggers'll see us and tell somebody." They knew the land had been sold, the cemetery was no longer theirs, and they felt like trespassers. They climbed back over the fence, slung their rifles loosely under their arms—they had been shooting at targets with various kinds of firearms since they were seven years old—and set out to look for the rabbits and doves or whatever small game might happen along. On these expeditions Miranda always followed at Paul's heels along the path, obeying instructions about handling her gun when going through fences; learning how to stand it up properly so it would not slip and fire unexpectedly; how to wait her time for a shot and not just bang away in the air without looking, spoiling shots for Paul, who really could hit things if given a chance. Now and then, in her excitement at seeing birds whizz up suddenly before her face, or a rabbit leap across her very toes, she lost her head, and almost without sighting she flung her rifle up and pulled the trigger. She hardly ever hit any sort of mark. She had no proper sense of hunting at all. Her brother would be often completely disgusted with her. "You don't care whether you get your bird or not," he said. "That's no way to hunt." Miranda could not understand his indignation. She had seen him smash his hat and yell with fury when he had missed his aim. "What I like about shooting," said Miranda, with exasperating inconsequence, "is pulling the trigger and hearing the noise."

"Then, by golly," said Paul, "whyn't you go back to the range and shoot at bull's-eyes?"

"I'd just as soon," said Miranda, "only like this, we walk around more."

"Well, you just stay behind and stop spoiling my shots," said Paul, who, when he made a kill, wanted to be certain he had made it. Miranda, who alone brought down a bird once in twenty rounds, always claimed as her own any game they got when they fired at the same moment. It was tiresome and unfair and her brother was sick of it.

The Grave · 463

"Now, the first dove we see, or the first rabbit, is mine," he told her. "And the next will be yours. Remember that and don't get smarty."

"What about snakes?" asked Miranda idly. "Can I have the first snake?"

Waving her thumb gently and watching her gold ring glitter, Miranda lost interest in shooting. She was wearing her summer roughing outfit: dark blue overalls, a light blue shirt, a hired-man's straw hat, and thick brown sandals. Her brother had the same outfit except his was a sober hickory-nut color. Ordinarily Miranda preferred her overalls to any other dress, though it was making rather a scandal in the countryside, for the year was 1903, and in the back country the law of female decorum had teeth in it. Her father had been criticized for letting his girls dress like boys and go careering around astride barebacked horses. Big sister Maria, the really independent and fearless one, in spite of her rather affected ways, rode at a dead run with only a rope knotted around her horse's nose. It was said the motherless family was running down, with the Grandmother no longer there to hold it together. It was known that she had discriminated against her son Harry in her will, and that he was in straits about money. Some of his old neighbors reflected with vicious satisfaction that now he would probably not be so stiff-necked, nor have any more high-stepping horses either. Miranda knew this, though she could not say how. She had met along the road old women of the kind who smoked corn-cob pipes, who had treated her grandmother with most sincere respect. They slanted their gummy old eyes side-ways at the granddaughter and said, "Ain't you ashamed of yoself, Missy? It's against the Scriptures to dress like that. Whut yo Pappy thinkin about?" Miranda, with her powerful social sense, which was like a fine set of antennae radiating from every pore of her skin, would feel ashamed because she knew well it was rude and ill-bred to shock anybody, even bad-tempered old crones, though she had faith in her father's judgment and was perfectly comfortable in the clothes. Her father had said, "They're just what you need, and they'll save your dresses for school . . ." This sounded quite simple and natural to her. She had been brought up in rigorous economy. Wastefulness was vulgar. It was also a sin.

These were truths; she had heard them repeated many times and never once disputed.

Now the ring, shining with the serene purity of fine gold on her rather grubby thumb, turned her feelings against her overalls and sockless feet, toes sticking through the thick brown leather straps. She wanted to go back to the farmhouse, take a good cold bath, dust herself with plenty of Maria's violet talcum powder—provided Maria was not present to object, of course—put on the thinnest, most becoming dress she owned, with a big sash, and sit in a wicker chair under the trees . . . These things were not all she wanted, of course; she had vague stirrings of desire for luxury and a grand way of living which could not take precise form in her imagination but were founded on family legend of past wealth and leisure. These immediate comforts were what she could have, and she wanted them at once. She lagged rather far behind Paul, and once she thought of just turning back without a word and going home. She stopped, thinking that Paul would never do that to her, and so she would have to tell him. When a rabbit leaped, she let Paul have it without dispute. He killed it with one shot.

When she came up with him, he was already kneeling, examining the wound, the rabbit trailing from his hands. "Right through the head," he said complacently, as if he had aimed for it. He took out his sharp, competent bowie knife and started to skin the body. He did it very cleanly and quickly. Uncle Jimbilly knew how to prepare the skins so that Miranda always had fur coats for her dolls, for though she never cared much for her dolls she liked seeing them in fur coats. The children knelt facing each other over the dead animal. Miranda watched admiringly while her brother stripped the skin away as if he were taking off a glove. The flayed flesh emerged dark scarlet, sleek, firm; Miranda with thumb and finger felt the long fine muscles with the silvery flap strips binding them to the joints. Brother lifted the oddly bloated belly. "Look," he said, in a low amazed voice. "It was going to have young ones."

Very carefully he slit the thin flesh from the center ribs to the flanks, and a scarlet bag appeared. He slit again and pulled the bag open, and there lay a bundle of tiny rabbits, each wrapped in a thin scarlet veil. The brother pulled these off and there they were, dark gray, their sleek wet down lying in minute even ripples, like a baby's head just washed, their unbelievably small delicate ears folded close, their little blind faces almost featureless.

Miranda said, "Oh, I want to *see*," under her breath. She looked and looked—excited but not frightened, for she was accustomed to the sight of animals killed in hunting—filled with pity and astonishment and a kind of shocked delight in the wonderful little creatures for their own sakes, they were so pretty. She touched one of them ever so carefully, "Ah, there's blood running over them," she said and began to tremble without knowing why. Yet she wanted most deeply to see and to know. Having seen, she felt at once as if she had known all along. The very memory of her former ignorance faded, she had always known just this. No one had ever told her anything outright, she had been rather unobservant of the animal life around her because she was so accustomed to animals. They seemed simply disorderly and unaccountably rude in their habits, but altogether natural and not very interesting. Her brother had spoken as if he had known about everything all along. He may have seen all this before. He had never said a word to her, but she knew now a part at least of what he knew. She understood a little of the secret, formless intuitions in her own mind and body, which had been clearing up, taking form, so gradually and so steadily she had not realized that she was learning what she had to know. Paul said cautiously, as if he were talking about something forbidden: "They were just about ready to be born." His voice dropped on the last word. "I know," said Miranda, "like kittens. I know, like babies." She was quietly and terribly agitated, standing again with her rifle under her arm, looking down at the bloody heap. "I don't want the skin," she said, "I won't have it." Paul buried the young rabbits again in their mother's body, wrapped the skin around her, carried her to a clump of sage bushes, and hid her away. He came out again at once and said to Miranda, with an eager friendliness, a confidential tone quite unusual in him, as if he were taking her into an important secret on equal terms: "Listen now. Now you listen to me, and don't ever forget. Don't you ever tell a living soul that you saw this. Don't tell a soul. Don't tell Dad because I'll get into trouble. He'll say I'm leading you into things you ought not to do. He's always saying that. So now don't you go and forget and blab out sometime the way you're always doing . . . Now, that's a secret. Don't you tell."

Miranda never told, she did not even wish to tell anybody. She thought about the whole worrisome affair with confused unhappiness for a few days. Then it sank quietly into her mind and was heaped over by accumulated thousands of impressions, for nearly twenty years. One day she was picking her path among the puddles and crushed refuse of a market street in a strange city of a strange country, when without warning, plain and clear in its true colors as if she looked through a frame upon a scene that had not stirred nor changed since the moment it happened, the episode of that far-off day leaped from its burial place before her mind's eye. She was so reasonlessly horrified she halted suddenly staring, the scene before her eyes dimmed by the vision back of them. An Indian vendor had held up before her a tray of dyed sugar sweets, in the shapes of all kinds of small creatures: birds, baby chicks, baby rabbits, lambs, baby pigs. They were in gay colors and smelled of vanilla, maybe. . . . It was a very hot day and the smell in the market, with its piles of raw flesh and wilting flowers, was like the mingled sweetness and corruption she had smelled that other day in the empty cemetery at home: the day she had remembered always until now vaguely as the time she and her brother had found treasure in the opened graves. Instantly upon this thought the dreadful vision faded, and she saw clearly her brother, whose childhood face she had forgotten, standing again in the blazing sunshine, again twelve years old, a pleased sober smile in his eyes, turning the silver dove over and over in his hands.

AND WITH A VENGEANCE

Margaret Gibson

''TELL THAT BUZZARD to get and you stay out too. Can't a woman have any peace? You tell him to get.''

Marie closes the door. Downstairs a screen door slams. A car door shuts and the car goes off out of the humming. Gnats and cicadas.

High hot sun behind the browned shade pulled down to the window musks the room jonquil gold. This room smells like a female dog in her season. She is glad it is summer, July, hot as every July she has known in all her fifty-seven years. At least when she dies they will have to put her in the ground quickly, almost at once.

So Armistead had come, mule-faced, braying out commands, orders; used to authority and obedience. He has come as they all have, begging, cajoling, pleading, humoring, commanding, impatient in patience and all moving dreamlike in a line that has no end, still and intractable moving in a bas-relief processional into her room, by the foot of her bed, pausing momentarily and eternally to be defined in full relief against the window shade light, then speaking, betraying, uttering what she had always imagined they would say at this time, then fading off, first the voice then the figure as it moved to join the ranks of those on the frieze who had come and gone, making room for the processioned numbers waiting as they do, patient in impatience, to float by, soliciting, beseeching, stone and mist shapes carved on her eyes. All but one had come. He will not and she can hope that this is because he is dead, dead a long time.

The pain comes across her belly again, deep inside. As if railroad tracks were being set down, a deep spike hammered in at intervals on the line of cold iron to hold it together. It is no worse really than the menstrual pain she had suffered from the angry womb every month for all her life since she was twelve. The pain will be harder, Dr. Rucker had said. It would seem to be in the cards that she would have her labor, without husband, lover, or curled and yet unbreathing fetus. As if it were due her, born a woman and having to pay for it.

Her hand gropes beside her on the rumpled sheet and finds the book. *Arma virumque cano,* that is all of the Latin she recalls. The translation falls open easily to chapter four, and she rests the book on her stomach and tries to read. It is too dark in the room but she knows the words. *But the queen finds no rest,* and her head falls back on the pillow. She stops.

There is the whispering sound again. As if she is in a field of wheat whose every brittle gossipy tongue clatters windily, demanding voice. But there is no wind. The amber shade is as solid as a wall. The book falls to the floor as she takes the straw fan and waves it across her face. She will have Marie burn or bury the books, the bookcase, too. She will watch to see that it is done.

The long braid of her hair, which she pulls up over her head across the middle where it is parted, hangs down the center of her face. For every gold hair something exciting would happen, her father told her when she was little. She cannot count much gold now in the gray and yellowed white old woman hair.

He changed the fable later, as everything changes with a slow rotation on the axis and you are never in the same place twice, never. He said to her looking through the bottle at her, said to her, every hair on your head is a month you live, every month you live a hair falls; when you fall dead you are bald as the day you come. This her father had said Adelaide had said I leave you heathens together Jefferson said nothing said her father why don't you get married to don't matter who somebody Mattie had screamed and the door slammed I've got to find somebody you can't kill off in me you kill me you funny old maid French said leave me alone don't touch me alone. The pendulum swings tick and tock and tick.

"Miss T. What's overcome you? Sitting there swinging your hair in your face like an I don't know what."

The pendulum stops. There are two eyes. All the voices are gone out into the world again, out of her head. The two eyes before her widen. They are Marie.

"Come on now. Pull yourself up. Mr. Sweeny is downstairs with the papers. Come on now."

Everything is fine. The procession starts up again. Here is her voice. "Well, send him on up then. Why do you stand there gawking? Go on."

"Yessem."

"Marie, why don't you bring Miss Lady Feathers up here now too. Bring her on up."

"Up here? Now?" The eyes stretch like balloons.

"Here. Now."

Into the room comes the bald head with the three hairs streaked like an incision across the top, the head of Mr. Sweeny glistening with damp shiny perspiration. His pate looks like a fish bowl or space helmet cracked and leaking. He wears the fragile gold spectacles she has always despised on man or woman. He fidgets with them unconsciously and perpetually. This figure on the urn has a sheaf of white crackling paper and he sits nervously on the chair and nearly tips it over. She laughs at him, for in addition to his innate and inimitable nervous femininity, he does not know that he is being framed by the window and amber shade for all her eternity.

He says that he is prepared and authorized by law to prepare her bequests in a suitable and proper manner. He says it is his most grievous duty. He blinks three times behind the spectacles.

"You snuffing your nose for some reason? Smell something, do you?"

"What, why no, Miss Handy; ah, why no."

"Yes you do, and I do too. It's the earth steaming up and cracking open to receive the body."

"Body." He glances quickly as if he may have failed to observe a presence in the room.

"Body. My body. Heavens, Mr. Sweeny, if you can't call a spade what it is, what are you doing here now? People don't usually make their plans to give away all they own unless they know they won't be needing it once the body's covered up, do they?" She waves a lilac handkerchief at him in somber flirtation.

He blinks.

The air is thick and hot enough to fold like cloth. When Marie opens the door a breeze stammers on her forehead. Marie bends over to shove Miss Lady Feathers into the room.

"No, Marie. Put her here on the bed covers, on the top sheet. Do as I say now and run along."

Mr. Sweeny's eyeballs nearly pop through his spectacles. Marie puts the fluffed white hen on the bed covers and leaves the room without looking in the man's direction.

Miss Lady Feathers serenely surveys the white lawn before her. She adapts more readily than Mr. Sweeny.

"Miss Lady Feathers is the connoisseur's chicken, Mr. Sweeny."

He agrees. Fervently.

Miss Lady Feathers watches Mr. Sweeny suspiciously. Perhaps she sees herself in the glass of the gold spectacles, perhaps she admires the perfect egg-shaped dome above her reflection. She arches her neck out hen-fashion toward Mr. Sweeny who pulls his face back. The movements are repeated, stage-rehearsed, a ballet. When she laughs at their recognition scene, the track of pain declares itself in her stomach. She must get on with it.

"Acknowledge the fact, Mr. Sweeny, that our Miss Lady Feathers considers you some sort of lovely rooster and pray let's begin. Won't take long; I haven't much to give away. Now. Just some money in the bank which they'll use up putting me in the ground most likely. If there's any left, give that to Marie. You got that?"

Mr. Sweeny's pen squeaks and sets Miss Lady Feathers to stalking up and down the bed. It is an inhuman disrespectful noise.

"Then there's this farm and this house. Set it down that the whole kit and kaboodle—whatever is legal for that—goes to either my brother Gordon or to Bill Handy. Except my books and I will take care of that. So just the house." Mr. Sweeny looks over at the small bookcase, the rows of brown covers, tattered, vague gold titles.

"But on the condition that whichever of them wants it has to live here. That's a condition. And they can't sell it for ten years. Unless they die too. You got that?"

He has questions squirming on his tongue like snakes. Suppose neither wants it. And suppose both do and both will live here.

"Won't both of them want it. And one will. I know what I'm doing and up against. There've been stranger leave-takings in these parts."

Mr. Sweeny looks at the chicken, then to her, and back to the chicken. "Yes, Ma'am."

"And one more thing and then you can get on downstairs and have Marie give you some lemon cake she did up this morning. I haven't completely forgot all my manners. But one more thing first. I mean to be buried right here on this land. In no churchyard, hear me. Raise up the shade, Mr. Sweeny."

Mr. Sweeny dabs at the little O on the cord of the window shade as if it is a mouth with teeth. The glare coming in the window is the lightning on the way to Damascus, the searing halo of saints and martyrs. She cannot face it and shuts her eyes. She hears her voice coming quickly and the words one after the other like dogs on the scent at a fox hunt.

"I can't look, Mr. Sweeny, but you can see the copse of holly bushes with the tall pines growing in the center. Yes? That's it, that's where you can put the body in." He jumps, or she hears him stumble into the chair when she says *you* as if she meant that he personally has to wield the shovel. "Now put down the shade."

When she hears the shade pulled to the sill finally—after Mr. Sweeny first lets it fly up and wrap around the cylinder, cord and all—she opens her eyes in the honeyed heavy room. "Now I'll tell you why. Just so you can explain if you have to. Not that what I tell you will be much of an explanation. You remember Tom T. who used to have all those goats on his front lawn? He is cracked as a porcelain pitcher but I respect his mind. He told me that one night as he put water out for the goats he saw a tall magnificent buck deer come to a stream where there hadn't been deer or stream for one hundred years. This just proved to him, as he told me, that nobody and no thing that dies is ever drawn off this land to any abstract heaven or hell. When I'm dead, Mr. Sweeny, I will stay where I have lived and where whoever comes after, if it's only the progeny of Miss Lady Feathers there, will be able to find me, right here in the hidden character of the land. You got to die here to stay here. That's why I'll have no hordes of relations convincing me to leave my home even now in pain, especially now."

Mr. Sweeny opens his mouth to say something, mouths syllables, looks brokenly around. The fine incision on the shell of his head throbs, widens.

"Go long now and have you some lemon cake. Oh and tell Marie to bring Miss Lady Feathers some cake too. That's a lad."

He is gone, insubstantial. The air which had clothed him and fixed and held him in place closes on the gap he leaves in the room. One more in the procession.

The wheat field whisperings surround her, inaudible gossips. There is a strange rustling of something stirring in the wheat. The heavy bristled fruit heads of the tall wheat scratch her face, make her forehead prickle, it is so hot. Yet not unbearable.

And with a Vengeance · 473

There's a quality of freedom about dying, not the lightness of removing a rain-soggy woolen great-coat and moving to the fire, feeling yourself
float with the flame and the smoke up into the air, becoming air incandescent and pure. More like the gracious release after constipation. There
is lightness surely, but the eye, the focus of observation and absorbed
attention never pulls away from a sensation of body. So there's this marvelous freedom, not the freedom that churchmen and books discuss, the
spirit relinquishing flesh, but a freedom of self. Participation in something
which no one else will ask to share in. A phenomenon of self isolated and
alone, essentially alone. If not entirely, for this is the time that the unend-
ing procession of lived and living lives begins. But essentially. And with
the freedom of being inviolate in your own body, free of any intrusion.
Yet there is a dim resentment, a haze of precognitive emotion stirring
behind the conscious freedom. She knows in the firefly firelight summer
haze of her mind that she would like to talk about, discuss, tell this new
freedom to someone, anyone really.

Others would not understand, and even if they could, would not let
you speak to them of these things. Other people are so fidgety about
someone else's dying. You are kept from telling anything, anything more
than where it hurts. They are shy, embarrassed. Curious, no doubt. Yes
the hypocrites are curious for they are, and they know it, in the presence
of an event both holy and obscene. To them she is an event, no more a
person, but an event to be charted and chronicled down in local history
perhaps, but not likely in personal memory. An event. Not even a biolog-
ical experiment, nothing so concrete. While she, for the first time feels
herself more totally and fully and fruitfully herself. Pity those who die
unconscious in their sleep. Pity those who die screaming against the pain,
finally opiate and senseless. Pity the nervous and prying outsiders who
come to look and talk of themselves, hardly looking her in the eye out of
a primitive fear that the event is contagious. They are tactful in their fear.
And although they would not admit obscenity, they know it is this, for
why else would all religions, all peoples, everyone she had known here
in Amelia stress the holiness, the sanctity, the blessed participation of

unity with the All Being if there were not an element of obscene contraband to exorcize? There is a union if you will admit unity to be total absorption of self in body beyond human violation.

This hand inside her belly, the hand with the spikes and the mallet, the hand that lays the railroad tracks deep across, this is no foreign hand to be fought. If there is resentment against the final labor pains, the irrevocable bequest of her birth and sex, there is at least the consolation that the hand is essentially her own; her labor is self-induced. There is something the living do not know. Death is not the Satanic or Godly, handsome or pock-faced stranger who enters the room, the black hand reaching for the victim's throat. Personify it if you will, and doubtless she will before the day, her day, is ended. Not the outsider, not the stranger, but familiar, known, born inside oneself; a presence as personal as one's own, her own, past; organic, implanted outgrowth welling up and spreading throughout the inroads of self and body.

She has never been afraid of death the way most people are when they think about it at all. When she was young and innocent with the belief in the connection between desire and the attainment of the desired object, she had heard her mother cry out to the cook, oh I wish I were dead, and weeks later she was dead. No one saw her die, no one suspected she would; she herself possibly had no knowledge. They woke one morning and she had died. Nothing fearful there. The lady in the coffin who they said was her mother was not. Adelaide, pressing her hand as a proper and protective older sister should in front of other people, had said, look Telia, isn't she beautiful and beautifully asleep, our mother. It was no one she knew. Her mother had vanished, leaving no part of herself behind to be handled and sighed over, the memory of her life bartered and bargained for. She was simply gone.

When her father had died, again she was not allowed to participate in or focus on it. The focus of everyone's commiseration was on the *way* he had died, crushed by the tractor late at night in the field. What was he doing there, how did it happen—these were the questions. Not what did it mean, this death. To her it meant having to care for Gordie, who had found the body she was never permitted to see. To her, then, death was not something that happened directly to you. It was still an outsider, an abstraction, and the only consequence was Gordie's great hurt. Hurt was palpable and alive. Death means there will be lonely people left. In her pain now she is feeling their unfelt deaths, but without fear.

No one will miss her now.

Gordon might if she could get him back to the farm, away from whatever it was that held him in Richmond now, away from her.

Mattie would not, although she would grieve and think herself sincerely hurt. There was no more self there to hurt. She was her children now. She sees Mattie nursing the first girl in this room, in this bed looking serenely like an obscene Madonna off into the eyes of the devout imaginary Renaissance painter.

This same baby girl would not miss her, she whose hand she had slapped more than once. And Mattie, consoling her once, thinking herself unheard, saying how Aunt T. had changed, was no longer herself.

She was herself. Had she changed? People do not change but grow more like themselves the older they are.

Miss Lady Feathers here will have no regrets. See the cock of her head as she struts. She will not be touched or tampered with. The pure white feathers. The amber eye-rock.

Armistead, if he could abrogate the conditions she had set with Mr. Sweeny, if he could get his square man's hands on her house, her farm, her land, he would remember her. He would remember to raze house, stable, coop and well house; pine tree and holly copse, her own headstone. He would remember to plant her with corn or wheat. She would become kernel and cob, shucks and silks, and he would eat her or shell her and feed her to the hens and kill and fry their plump, her henplump flesh or slop her to the hogs and smoke and cure her. He would remember when his belly growled or when the hush in his pocket and purse grew ominous.

A figure is moving across the urn, the front of viewless stone before her: moving deliberate and slow and shadowless as noon across the field, the wheat field blurred and impressed across the surface, not dainty Adamsesque boughs of wheat fruit garlanded and gathered and flower-trimmed, contained in shocks or baskets of suspended rhythm eye-dripping across the breded rim; but fields, years and years of them, full-blown as ocean and seaweed or tall cedar forests clapping music out. The urn is a bell and the figure moves, glides more than moves, dances more than glides full in the wind of the wheat receding and advancing like memory dispelling time. Little Boy Blue come blow, luting Pan, satyr, brief centaur, merman enchanted imbibing the conch shell, fantastical and brave he comes. He comes at last. He may be dead, he may not be; yet he comes in the sway of wheat on the still and soundless sway-stopped full stone earth of the urn.

Sweat at the armpits of the blue denim workshirt. As she has dreamed it, not daring to dream, fearing the words she would, will utter in their endless variation and fishtailed slippery musical score notes across the bars of her mind; fearing what was and was not and was feared to be, to become memory. The face, viewless and stolid as sky-fields stands there, suspends there, cloud-cropped, vacant. And it listens.

And when he comes, she is on the beach near Norfolk far from home, walking on peach-colored sand. She is barefoot and the sand is still noon-warm. Her hair, freed from the braids, luffs like a sail behind her; before her the wind teases into her body. His eyes shape her as the sculptor carving the woman for the prow of an antique ship. Her eyes are the old color of the arbor grapes before the fire took them and the house. He comes as Odysseus to Nausicaa, naked and battered by the sea. He holds a sea-bush before him. They stand there in the wet scruff of water face to face, sun crazy as a skittle going down behind the dune. Saying: there is no place else for us to meet. You know the old place burned. But of course you know for you might have held the match with the woman who set it, her hair burning swift as paper kindling. Adelaide married Jefferson and Gordon left and Father died out in that same field. But you know all this. Admit a hand in all that has happened to me, admit, admit. I have seen you—it will be no good to deny it—lurking. The back of your head in a car racing ahead of me. Once I saw you in the Courthouse store but you slipped out the back when I came in. More than once, many times, I have fancied seeing you in the edge of woods along the yard at New Handy, eyes like fox eyes at my windows. Do not deny it. You have had a hand, confess, in all that has passed since that summer night. All of you, your puppy-faced kind, your sex baring your sex before the world, winking cocksure that no one will call the bluff; all of you are alike, all the same, all the same. You all bring ruin into the cup of a moment. You think the same things, pursue and do the same, the same. Oh, I have watched too and warned and some have listened. Put down your proud head, lower the flag of your manhood, confess. Confess.

He lowers his head; he stammers.

Or maybe she is in Richmond and has done nothing more complex than to go to the drug pharmacy to buy a box of Band-Aids from the counter clerk and there, remarkably and suddenly, she looks over to the man next to her waiting with his cheap purchase and it is he. And right there in the pharmacy in the section where lipstick and Evening in Paris perfume meet the magical blue and green medicine bottles and gay low-powered pills and ace bandages, she speaks to him low and hurried and secret. Tell me, tell me, was I all right that night. Do you remember it, tell me. She does not tell him how she has learned to find that place in her that jumps and whistles tight as a tuning fork. She watches the face turn colors under the dirty straw hat in the drug store.

The door of the old Ford car is open and the motor is still running. He has pulled her outside the car into the grass not two miles from her house. The house that will burn. No. No.

Or she is driving the highway that goes from Amelia to Chula and she sees a road gang in the coffee brown work clothes and loose chains on the ankles. They march in file, they dig in file. The policeman has a rifle. She stops the car and if the guard permits, she speaks to him. I knew all along you would end this way. It's no use my saying how's it been with you because I've known. What is it, rape or arson, murder or pig stealing? It does not matter. How were the flop houses, the sunless basements with the roaches; how often did you fever on a strange mattress diseased and broken, with the woman you had broken, dreamed to break? It does not matter. I have seen it all. What matters is this meeting. I have met you, other places in my mind, to laugh with you at this old joke. Only you will laugh as I do when I tell you how the gossip raged for a time and then settled or blew away like pot-ash. And then how the voices were always lowered when it came time to discuss these things in others' lives, for I was an old maid. To everyone I am old and virgin. You will laugh with me at this joke.

Someone must laugh with me at this joke.

There was a time I would have cut off my hair and begged. Now you are in chains and that is good. The convict wipes the sweat off his face and stares at her.

Now he comes walking through the wheat which is rustling like a woman's hair combed into electricity. Birds, black birds, rise and billow in clouds behind him as he passes. His face is blank; it has always been blank as a vacant car lot, an unplowed field, a wall of cinder block.

The hand in her belly tightens on the mallet and drives in the spike, making connection now. As the hand tightens, there is corresponding contraction behind her eyes. She thinks he has come to let her secret out, to let it be kited across the wheat field skies. They would all know. They would all know.

Miss Lady Feathers hen-steps back from the stranger. A hideous vocabulary pecks into the air. Beaked and feathered. Not to be touched or taken. The amber eyes.

He is standing there now at the foot of the bed, the heavy honey light in the room sticking about them. Behind him in the wheat field, the procession from the urn has broken up. Children run through the fields, balloons and steamers stammer crazily; everyone she has ever known, ever touched, runs in circles through the field. There is a low chant under the laughter and they run to it. Backs to her, they run away. Wait. He has something to tell you. They run on and on forever.

The man at the foot of her bed, the man who has the blank stone face and scars for eyes, has his hands at the heavy belt between the denim and denim of shirt and trousers, unbuckling. She closes her eyes and there is a man there. White globes of the most pristine white lob into the cave of her eyes. She presses tighter and tighter and the circles increase their size. She will be martyred.

He is still there. Frozen, statue-like. He has not moved, his hands are at his buckle. All is still. He will not speak the awful secret and the others have gone away, all merrily away.

Behind him breaking from the wheat field and breaking into the veneer of light in this room, there is the bird. It is gold, huge, jade-eyed, taloned. The heavy wings lift it up above the smoke of the wheat which is burning now, burning. The man at the bedpost stands, around him the smoke wheels, the bird beats, fanning the flames. It speaks and the voice is gold-tubed like an organ in a vast cathedral as it moves and the words come into her saying Virgin Virgin and the man at the bedpost smiles now and the bird, the freak gold-feathered and constantly wheeling in a whirligig windmill above her, repeats his call closer and closer. He is over her now, the sheets ripple in the wind-beat, he cries Virgin and a word obscene and one-syllabled rises from her throat, it is out in the air and she waits to hear it as the bird, apocalyptic, takes her eyes into the dark.

The Third of July

Elizabeth Cox

THE NIGHT KEPT UP one of those almost-silent rains until dawn, and now the mist rose and leaves showed their waxy shine. Nadine combed her hair, but decided not to wash it. She pulled on her skirt and the blouse with cornflowers, and put away the pile of sewing she had promised to finish before tomorrow. Nadine was a seamstress. People brought their clothes for her to hem and make alterations.

Today was the third of July. Harold had left early for the field and would work late so he could take off all day on the Fourth. Nadine prepared a lunch for herself and another one for Miss Penny. Two days a week she took lunch to Miss Penny, and she would take it today. The old woman was like a mother to Nadine, ever since the year her own mother died when she was nineteen. The year Bill was born too early. She put chicken salad and sliced tomatoes in a small basket made by Bill when he was six years old. She placed two pears inside and thought of the day he handed it to her.

Nadine Colby had been married for thirty years, but on this morning she wrote a note to Harold after he left. *Dear Harold, I have rented an apartment in Mebane and if you want to see me you can call and ask to come by. Things cannot go on as they have.* She signed it, *Love.*

A shaft of sunlight moved into the bedroom as Nadine packed her bags and put them into the car. She had already paid a month's rent for an apartment ten miles away in Mebane. Her sister lived nearby, but Nadine did not like her husband, so the apartment was a perfect alternative.

She left the note in a conspicuous place on the counter. Harold would see it when he came in. She fixed some dinner that could be heated up—a plate of meat loaf, potatoes and creamed corn. Nadine wondered now if he would still take the whole next day off.

Her reason for leaving was based on one small happening: Harold came in one night, and though she knew who it was when he got out of his truck and started toward the house, Nadine thought he was someone different. His hair stuck up on one side and he carried his cap which he usually wore into the house and threw down on the hall table. But on this particular evening she thought he was a stranger, someone coming with bad news—telling her Harold was dead, or hurt. She imagined herself falling into the arms of this stranger and letting him hold her. All of these thoughts came in a few moments while Harold opened the door and said, "Whoa! It's hot!" Then she recognized his voice.

That night Nadine couldn't sleep. She lay next to Harold beneath the sheet and wondered how her life would be like without him. If she left, it would have to be quickly and quietly, as though there had been a murder she could do nothing about.

He was foreign to her now, as was Bill. Her son was thirty, and had been the reason they got married. Harold and Nadine planned to have four children, though Bill was the only one.

The last time he came home Nadine said, "You don't look a thing like your daddy anymore, you know that?" She picked him up at the airport on Easter weekend. "Not a thing like him. And you used to favor him so strong."

"Lotta changes," was all Bill said.

"No one but me would know you were even kin."

Bill rode next to his mother with his long legs cramped in front of him. He had offered to drive, but Nadine insisted on doing so herself. She wore a navy blue dress with a large white pin at her bosom, bought especially for Bill's visit. She felt pretty as she drove him home.

Bill was a salesman for MetroLife Insurance Company and he had purchased this car for his parents—a Chrysler New Yorker. He had driven it into the driveway one Saturday and said it was theirs. Everyone in town knew Bill was wealthy and that he had bought them the car.

Their son came home on the Fourth. He also made regular visits for Christmas and Easter, but this year he would not come in July. Nadine told him he was getting stingy, though she meant self-centered. She had loved telling people how Bill always spent certain days with them, and how she could count on him. But now Bill lived with a woman executive in his insurance company, and they were going off somewhere for the Fourth.

"I don't know what's going to happen if that woman gets pregnant," Nadine told Harold.

"They'll probably get married like we did." Harold didn't think things had changed all that much, but he remembered when Nadine had seemed soft. Her softness had unraveled with the years, and he felt left with just a thin wire of who she was. But he never mentioned it. He loved his wife, even her sharp tongue. And he loved the way she sometimes exploded with laughter at something funny he said.

Yesterday at breakfast, Harold read the paper and Nadine stared at the page that blocked his face. She imagined how he might speak to her, if he knew she was going to leave. *Nadine,* he spoke in her mind, *Don't leave. Please don't.* He would beg. He would kiss her, then kiss her again, hard.

The Third of July · 483

Yesterday when he put down the paper, he asked, "What're we gonna do on the Fourth?"

Nadine didn't know until that moment how much she wanted out. She did not want to spend the Fourth of July with him. She would write the note on the Third, and let him go. As she thought of it, she felt like the ghost of someone more than a real person.

"Anything," she said.

Harold kissed her cheek and left for the field.

NADINE WASHED THE breakfast dishes and poured the rest of her coffee into the azalea bushes. She wanted to pick up the dry cleaning in town before going to Miss Penny's house. She placed the note where Harold would be sure to see it.

She had not gone five miles before coming upon an accident. A Ford station wagon had speeded past her only a few minutes before, and Nadine marveled at how this grief might have been her own. When she arrived at the wreck there was still a vibrancy lingering, as after a bell.

The car collided with a truck carrying chickens. It was the kind of crash that occurs in the movies where an audience roars with laughter as some fat farmer gets out stomping the ground and flapping his arms and elbows about—moving as the chickens themselves might move.

She hoped to see that now, even looked for someone to climb out of that screaming chicken truck, but as she drew closer she saw the driver tucked over the wheel. The station wagon's front end looked crumpled and the man driving had been thrown clear. He lay sprawled in the road. Nadine heard him groan for help and felt glad the car had not been her own.

She looked both ways for help, but no one was coming in either direction. She could not hurry toward the accident—her arms and legs felt like rubber bands. The man in the road was barely conscious. She stood over him, then squatted and placed her fingers on the pulse of his neck. She had seen this done on TV.

"My family," the man said. It was a question. He pointed toward the car as though he thought maybe Nadine hadn't noticed it yet. His head lay turned at a peculiar angle.

"Quiet now. You lie quiet." She patted the man's shoulder as if he had a contagious disease, then she moved back. He pointed again to the car. There was no sign of blood and Nadine hoped he was all right. "I'll check them for you," she said. The man seemed grateful to her, and closed his eyes.

The man in the truck was still slumped at the wheel. Four crates of chickens had fallen onto the hood. One of the chickens still flapped around, but less now. There were more crates in the ditch, where others squawked and fought to get free.

She heard another sound that came from the backseat of the car. Gurgling. A woman weighing almost three hundred pounds lay across the backseat. She had been sleeping when the accident occurred. Her head was on a pillow and she lay covered with a lightweight blanket that was soaked with blood. Nadine, who always turned away from such sights on TV or in a movie, opened the door of the car.

The woman was drowning, the gurgling noise came from her own throat, which lay exposed by a low-neck dress, her skin white, supple. Nadine ducked into the backseat to help, and she thought how this woman must be about her own age. The effort for breath came closer now. But the woman's hands jerked as a child's does in deep sleep, and the top of her head was pushed askew, so that it hung precariously like a lady's small hat about to fall off.

Without even thinking, Nadine reached two fingers into the woman's throat and began to dig out debris. She dug again and again as though she were clearing out the hole of a sink. The woman began to cough and as she did her eyes opened—unseeing.

Nadine could see the place where the forehead split. She reached to place it straight, and the man from the road called out again the question about his family. Nadine said, "They're fine. You be quiet now," and it was the calmest voice she had ever heard. She continued to clean the woman's throat, making her cough a few more times before the breathing came back. "You'll be all right," she told the woman, in case she could hear.

A young boy in the front seat curled slightly forward. About sixteen, Nadine thought. She got out to open the other car door, wiping her hands on her skirt. Some of the chickens wrestled free of their crates and walked around in the road. Another one had flown to a low branch. She glanced again to the man at the wheel of the truck. He hadn't moved. She wished he would.

She searched the highway again, but there was no sign of help. As she opened the front car door, she expected to find the boy as she had found the woman, but only a small amount of blood trickled onto his shirt and pants. The dashboard had struck his chest and he leaned forward onto it like a mannequin. He wore shorts and his strong legs had planted themselves to the floor as he braced for the impact. His arms caught the dashboard, but had fallen to his sides as the dashboard caught him. The windshield shattered and coated him with a shower of glass that spread fine as Christmas glitter. Nadine wondered if he had ever played football.

When she looked up, she could see Emmett Walker coming across the field. She felt happy to see him though she did not usually wish to see Emmett. In fact, she went out of her way to avoid him. Emmett wore coveralls and his red hair was almost completely gray. His arms and face, though, still exposed his freckles from boyhood. Once, for three weeks, Nadine and Emmett had been sweethearts. Nadine could not imagine that now.

"I heard the crash from the field," he said. "Are they all dead?" He stared at the boy's shimmering back.

"Seems so," was what Nadine said, forgetting about the man in the road. She held her mouth as though it were full of food, then pointed to the backseat where the woman lay. Emmett peered through the window without commenting.

He turned to the chicken truck. "What about him?"

"I don't know." They walked toward the truck. Nadine wondered if she would be left here all day with Emmett and what she would do. They

Elizabeth Cox · 486

had seen each other in town, and at gatherings they spoke pleasantly. Now they were suddenly talking in concerned tones and moving together as parents through a room full of sick children.

Emmett pried upon the door of the truck. The man's face was hidden by the horn, but his eyes lay open and his lips moved in an effort to speak.

"Listen," said Emmett, and he put his head closer to the steering wheel. "He's not moving. Something's wrong with his neck."

They went to each of the bodies, Nadine speaking low, explaining. But as she started to open the door of the car where the woman lay, they heard a siren approaching. Emmett put his hand on Nadine's shoulder and pointed to the ambulance coming over a far hill, arriving more slowly than the siren made it seem.

"I called the hospital," Emmett said.

Nadine went to stand beside the man in the road. He began to scream the name of his wife, *"Mamie, Mamie."*

"Shhh," she told him. The ambulance driver and his attendant secured the stretcher beneath him, then called for Emmett's help. The man asked again about his family, and Nadine said not to worry. "Everything will be taken care of now."

"Somebody's still in the truck," Emmett said and pointed to the tucked figure. "He's not moving." The attendant nodded and motioned toward the car, as if asking a question. Emmett shook his head and the driver reached into the backseat to check the woman's pulse. He stared boldly at the odd hairline.

"She's still alive," he said to Emmett.

Emmett peered through the window, expecting—he didn't know what—maybe for the woman to sit up, say something.

"Wouldn't be though." The driver directed his eyes toward Emmett. "Who did this? *You?*" The floor was full of Nadine's work.

Emmett looked at Nadine. She had her back to them as though the whole scene were something she had not yet witnessed—her back rigid, cocked for protection.

The Third of July · 487

"Hey, lady. You do this?"

She retreated the way a child does who has been reprimanded, her tongue in her cheek, worried. She nodded and held their admiration, then walked toward them as fragile and blue as smoke.

"Well, you saved her life, lady." He spoke softly and to the side, so that only Nadine could hear him, then he amended his statement. "Might have saved her life."

It took all three of them to lift the woman from the car, then Nadine stood back as they tore the front seat apart, trying to pull the boy from the dashboard. She wished she knew his name, and hoped she had saved Mamie's life. They placed the son in the back of the ambulance, and Mamie next to him. The man from the chicken truck was strapped near the front. Everyone looked dead.

As the ambulance disappeared, Nadine and Emmett stood beside each other. What followed was a silence as pure as that between lovers. Then Emmett faced Nadine and she turned to Emmett, and they resembled people who see their reflections in a mirror, slouched in a way they never imagined themselves.

Nadine opened her mouth and said, "I hope that woman lives. You think she will?" She wondered if she should take Emmett's hand or touch him, but didn't.

"Yes." He went to the truck where chickens were scattered in the road. They had stopped their squawking. One was still in the tree. "I'll drive these over to Hardison's Poultry." He pulled the crates together. "What's left of them." He picked up the crates from the road and climbed into the truck. He turned the key several times before hearing it catch. As he drove off, he waved good-bye and Nadine waved back. She walked to the car and checked the salad. It was still cool.

Miss Penny was watching TV when Nadine arrived. She didn't hear the knock on the door, so Nadine walked in and called to her. Miss Penny was folding towels and placing each one beside the chair, fixing them like small bales of hay about to be stored in a barn. She was watching a game show.

When she lifted her head to respond to Nadine's voice, the pupils of her eyes were large and gave an expression of spectral intensity—hollow, not sad. A cataract operation had made them sensitive to light, so the blinds and drapes were pulled. The room, after the full sunlight of the road, seemed to Nadine unusually dark.

"I'll put this in the kitchen." Nadine patted Miss Penny's chair as she walked by. She wanted to scrub her hands and wipe her skirt clean.

"There's a man on here who'll win ten thousand dollars if he can answer this last question," Miss Penny said. Nadine took it as a silencing. The TV blared the question and the announcer declared him winner. Bells rang, people clapped and cried, and Miss Penny told her, "I could've won me ten thousand dollars." She pushed herself from the chair to go to the kitchen.

"Don't know what you'd do with it," said Nadine. She watched the old woman hobble to the kitchen and fall into a chair.

"I'd buy me something."

"Don't know what you need." Nadine spooned salad onto plates and set two places at the table. Her tongue felt dry and she asked Miss Penny if there was some iced tea. Miss Penny pointed to a pitcher. She always made tea and took out the ice trays before Nadine arrived, but today Nadine was two hours late and the ice was mostly water. They put slivers that remained into the tea and sipped it.

"I had the right answer," Miss Penny persisted. She tasted the salad and Nadine gave her a napkin.

"You can't spend the money you have now, let alone ten thousand dollars." They helped themselves to the tomatoes. "What would you spend it on?"

"I'd pay somebody to look after my dogs."

"You don't have any dogs," said Nadine, "and don't need any."

"I would if I had all that money." Miss Penny's words, though simple, were true. "I'd need a lot of things." She thought for a moment, chewing her food with meticulous care. "I'd get some dogs. Not the regular kind, but show dogs. The ones you can train and take to shows."

The Third of July · 489

"You'd like that?" Nadine asked, surprised to find a new interest in a woman she had known as long as she could remember. She thought there were no more surprises left between them.

"Show dogs." Miss Penny's face flushed at the thought of it. "I always have wanted to do something like that."

Nadine wished to say something about the accident, to tell someone what she had done and how she wasn't afraid to see Emmett anymore. "There was a wreck," she began and leaned across the table so Miss Penny could hear. "Over near Hardison's Poultry. A truck ran into a station wagon. The whole family got hurt." Miss Penny reached for more slices of tomato. Her face had not yet lost its flush. "It was pretty bad," Nadine said. "A man and his wife, a boy about sixteen."

"What?"

"Their *son* about six*teen*." Nadine spoke louder. "He was killed right off, but the man might live, and the woman." She stopped leaning and slumped back. "I don't know about the woman though." Nadine's gaze shifted to something outside the window.

"*Ten thousand dollars,*" Miss Penny said. Her voice emphasized each word equally.

From the kitchen window Nadine could see bags of web in the crab-apple trees. "Tomorrow's the Fourth of July," she told Miss Penny. Neither of them turned away from the window.

Nadine washed the few dishes and put away the bales of towels into the hall cabinet. She decided not to go to Mebane, but to go back home. "I'll put these pears in the refrigerator." She held up the pears. Miss Penny's eyes unclouded and hardened clear as stones.

On her way home, she picked up the dry cleaning and stopped at the pet shop to look at dogs not yet full-grown. On Tuesday she would buy one and take it to Miss Penny. He would outlive her by six years.

THE NOTE TO Harold had not been touched, but she left it propped against the sugar jar. The house looked older now. Each object seemed to have a separate life of its own. When Nadine saw herself in the mirror over the fireplace, she became aware of the frame around her face.

She called the hospital, but the line was busy. She had already unpacked her bag and put the clothes into drawers where they had been—her blouses, her good blue dress, two nightgowns, a sweater, four pairs of shoes. She put her umbrella in the hall closet and went to sit across from the large picture window.

Twilight made the room silver, drapes shimmering like creek water. The late sun dropped halfway from sight, going down behind the trees like some wild head, and Nadine wondered if everyone wished for life to be different.

When the phone rang, it was Emmett. She heard his voice and her mouth worked itself into a smile. He called to tell her about Mamie and Robert Harkins. "The man will live," he said. "And the woman, she'll live too." For one moment Nadine could not even straighten her legs. "But that boy, he didn't make it. He was dead when we saw him."

"What about the man in the truck?"

"His back was broke and some ribs. But he's all right, or will be." Emmett coughed as though he didn't have much to say, but wanted to think of something. "The truck driver was Buck Hardison's nephew."

"Why, I think I know him," Nadine said. "I think I met him once when he was a little boy." She wanted the conversation to go on, and she thanked Emmett, so he said she was welcome. "You were fine help," she told him through the silence in the cord. "I mean, really," and she spoke as if trying to convince him of something important.

"Well," said Emmett.

Nadine watched the sun go all the way down and wondered if Emmett had turned to see out his own window. "It's getting dark," she said.

When they hung up, Nadine sat until she could see nothing but her own dark reflection in the window and the reflection of the lamp beside her. Harold would be in soon. She decided to wash her hair. She was bending her head over the sink and rinsing for the second time, when she heard Harold come in.

"Nadine?"

She wrapped her hair in a towel and went to the kitchen. Harold held the note that Nadine had not thrown out. He held it, but didn't say anything.

"You want something to eat?" she asked him.

Harold said he did.

Nadine did not get the covered plate of meat loaf and creamed corn. Instead, she took out some flounder and began to prepare it for baking with lemon and butter. She cut up new potatoes to go with it and told Harold about the wreck.

She told about the man, the boy, the woman she saved, the truck driver who was Buck Hardison's nephew. She told him she had seen Emmett, and how they had worked together. Her telling went from the time she took out the fish, cooked it, and then sat down with Harold to eat.

The note lay on the counter as they talked. Harold had carefully placed it next to the sugar, facedown. He listened attentively and ate everything Nadine put before him. When she was through washing the dishes, he walked up behind her to turn her around. He slowly unwrapped the towel from her head. Her hair was damp and frizzy, and he rubbed it dry with his hands.

ABOUT THE AUTHORS

DOROTHY ALLISON was born in Greenville, South Carolina. Her first published fiction was a collection of stories, *Trash,* which included "Gospel Song," the story in this anthology. Her novel *Bastard out of Carolina* was a National Book Award finalist in 1992. Her most recent publication is *Skin,* a book of essays. Ms. Allison lives in California.

Before publishing her first novel, *Baby of the Family,* TINA McELROY ANSA worked as a copy editor and news reporter for the *Atlanta Constitution* and *Charlotte Observer.* Her second novel, *Ugly Ways,* appeared in 1993. Ms. Ansa lives in St. Simons, Georgia.

DORIS BETTS has been hailed by a large number of critics as one of America's finest fiction writers. Her short story collections—*The Astronomer and Other Stories* and *Beasts of the Southern Wild and Other Stories*—have received numerous awards. Her long-awaited novel, *Souls Raised from the Dead,* was published in 1994. She lives and teaches in North Carolina.

MARY WARD BROWN has lived in the same house—on a three-hundred-acre plantation in Alabama—for most of her life. During the 1950s she studied creative writing at the University of Alabama and the University of North Carolina. Her short story collection, *Tongues of Flame,* won the Ernest Hemingway Foundation Award for best first fiction.

ELIZABETH COX has published two novels, *Familiar Ground* and *The Ragged People Fall out of Love.* The story included in this anthology appeared in the 1994 O. Henry Award short story collection. She lives in Massachusetts and North Carolina.

MARGARET GIBSON grew up in Richmond, Virginia, and received her B.A. from Hollins College. She has published four books of poetry; her latest, *The Vigil,* was a finalist in the 1993 National Book Award in Poetry. Ms. Gibson has also published fiction in numerous quarterlies and journals. Her story "And with a Vengeance" appeared in *Stories of the Modern South.*

ELLEN GILCHRIST's second collection of short stories, *Victory over Japan,* won the National Book Award for fiction in 1984. Ms. Gilchrist's poetry has also won numerous prizes and has been widely published. Her most recent novels include *I Can't Get You Close Enough* and *Net of Jewels.* Born in Vicksburg, Mississippi, she now lives in Fayetteville, Arkansas.

ELLEN GLASGOW was born in Richmond, Virginia, in 1873 and grew up in the shadow of what she termed "the dark furies of Reconstruction." After a lonely childhood, she slowly began to make her way as a writer, but not until *Barren Ground* in 1925 did she achieve any real recognition. This book was followed by *A Sheltered Life,* which greatly enhanced her growing reputation. In 1942, she won the Pulitzer Prize for *In This Our Life.*

MARY HOOD's first collection of stories, *How Far She Went* simultaneously won the Flannery O'Connor Award for short fiction and the Southern Review/LSU Short Fiction Award, both in 1984. She subsequently published *And Venus Is Blue*, a novella and short stories. Ms. Hood lives in Woodstock, Georgia, a small town near Atlanta.

ZORA NEALE HURSTON was born in 1891 in Eatonville, Florida, the first incorporated all-black town in America (where her mother advised her to "jump at the sun"). She later studied anthropology at Columbia with the noted Franz Boas, who profoundly influenced her work. Her job as a writer and folklorist took her all over the United States and to Jamaica, Haiti, and Bermuda. Her books include a novel, *Their Eyes Were Watching God*, and *Spunk: The Selected Stories of Zora Neale Hurston*. After decades of neglect (following her death in 1960), she is now recognized as one of the seminal writers of this century.

Born in Lexington, Kentucky (where she currently resides), GAYL JONES attended Connecticut College and Brown University. She has published two novels; a book of short fiction, *White Rat;* three books of poetry; and several plays.

Born in Mayfield, Kentucky, BOBBIE ANN MASON gained national attention in 1982 with the publication of *Shiloh and Other Stories*, which was nominated for a number of literary prizes and won the Ernest Hemingway Foundation Award. Her subsequent books include another collection of stories, *Love Life*, and the novels *In Country, Spence + Lila*, and *Feather Crowns*.

SUSIE MEE grew up in Trion, Georgia, a mill town near the Georgia-Tennessee border, and studied at Yale Drama School and (much later) at Hollins College. She has published a book of poetry, a novel—*The Girl Who Loved Elvis*—and a number of short stories. Although she currently lives in New York, she returns to the South often.

ELIZABETH SEYDEL MORGAN's "Economics" was published in the *Best Stories from the South*, 1992. As a screenplay, it won a first prize in the

1993 Virginia Film Festival. Born in Atlanta, Ms. Seydel graduated from Hollins College, and now lives in Richmond, Virginia. In addition to her fiction, she has published two books of poetry.

MARY NOAILLES MURFREE, who was born in 1850 and died in 1922, was the first writer to bring both the state of Tennessee and the region of southern Appalachia to widespread public attention through fiction. She lived in Murphreesboro, near Nashville, Tennessee, where her family owned a plantation called Grantland. During her lifetime, she wrote twenty-eight books, of which only *In the Tennessee Mountains* has been reprinted.

During her relatively brief lifetime (she was born in 1925 and died in 1964), FLANNERY O'CONNOR published only one collection of short stories, *A Good Man Is Hard to Find,* and two short novels, *Wise Blood* and *The Violent Bear It Away.* (Another book of short stories was published posthumously, as was a collection of letters entitled *The Habit of Being.*) Yet her voice was so original, her influence so pervasive, that she is known as a rare master of the short story form. In her early twenties, Ms. O'Connor contracted lupus and was forced to move back to the family farm near Milledgeville, Georgia, which she later called a "blessing" in terms of her writing.

KATHERINE ANNE PORTER has long been considered one of this century's most distinguished writers. Her novel *Ship of Fools* was an enormous popular success, but it is chiefly for her short stories that she is known and admired. Her *Collected Stories* was awarded both the Pulitzer Prize in Fiction and the National Book Award in 1965. Born in Indian Creek, Texas, in 1890, she died in 1980.

One of the best-beloved of southern authors, LEE SMITH graduated from Hollins College in Roanoke, Virginia, and later attended the Sorbonne. In addition to novels such as the acclaimed *Oral History,* she has published several collections of short stories, including *Me and My Baby View the Eclipse* from which the story "Tongues of Fire" is taken. Her most recent books are *The Devil's Dream,* published in 1992, and *Saving Grace,* published in 1995. She lives in Chapel Hill, North Carolina.

Born in Carrolton, Mississippi, ELIZABETH SPENCER was educated at Vanderbilt University. Among other awards, she has received the Award of Merit Medal for the Short Story from the American Academy and Institute of Arts and Letters. Her books include *The Stories of Elizabeth Spencer, The Light in the Piazza, The Salt Line,* and *Jack of Diamonds and Other Stories.* She is a professor of creative writing at the University of North Carolina at Chapel Hill.

ALICE WALKER attended Spelman College in her native state of Georgia, later graduating from Sarah Lawrence. A poet, essayist, and fiction writer, Ms. Walker's novel *The Color Purple* won the Pulitzer Prize in 1981. Her two short story collections are *In Love & Trouble: Stories of Black Women* and *You Can't Keep a Good Woman Down.* She lives in California.

EUDORA WELTY, among the most honored of American writers, has been awarded the Pulitzer Prize, the National Medal for Literature, the American Academy of Arts and Letters Howells Medal, and numerous honorary doctorates and fellowships. Ms. Welty published her first collection of short stories, *A Curtain of Green and Other Stories,* in 1941 and is the author of five novels and three short story collections. She resides in Jackson, Mississippi, in the house built by her family.